Constant

The Confidence Game

Book One

Rachel Higginson

Constant

The Confidence Game
Book One

Rachel Higginson

Copy Editing by Amy Donnelly of Alchemy and Words
Cover Design by Caedus Design Co.

Other Romances by Rachel Higginson

The Five Stages of Falling in Love (Adult Second Chance Romance)

Every Wrong Reason (Adult Second Chance Romance)

Bet on Us (Bet on Love Series)
Bet on Me (Bet on Love Series)

The Opposite of You (Opposites Attract)
The Difference Between Us (Opposites Attract)
The Problem with Him (Opposites Attract) coming June, 2018

Tiffany,
Without you I would definitely be less put together.
And not nearly as fun.
You're one of my favorite people ever.
Here's to this constant friendship of ours, manicure
hopping, extra-long lunches and
online shopping for life.

Constant

Scheme.

Scam.

Con.

Long or short, we're talking about the same thing—the confidence game.

A petty criminal doesn't understand the nuances that go into creating the flawless con. Conning isn't a last-minute misdemeanor or the consequence of a faulty moral compass. No. A true confidence game takes skill, finesse, hours of planning and plotting and finally, when your team has been assembled and the stars align and the wind blows just right, it takes perfect execution.

The morally upright, law-abiding citizens of the world look down their noses. They assume the worst, believing that con artists are nothing more than depraved and corrupt. Social outcasts that can't keep real jobs. But by assuming the worst, they're ignoring the most important trait this type of person possesses—they are artists.

A true confidence game isn't haphazard or carried out thanks to a penchant for laziness. A real con is carefully pieced together over months. Tireless preparation and cautious consideration form the bedrock of every game. But even the most prudent con can't plan everything. The fates throw their hand in too. Kindly or maliciously, the artist depends on them for grace.

And in the end, the game must be played perfectly. Everything must go according to plan. Everything must fall into place and happen exactly right. The stakes are high. The risks are great.

Yet the consequences are not enough to turn us away.

We've heard the siren's song and responded to her deathly lure. We're not criminals. We're artists.

Con artists.

At least I was once upon a time. Before different realities surfaced, forcing me to reprioritize. Maybe that's the difference between criminals and good people—what they have to lose and how desperately they're willing to gamble with it.

I had been willing to gamble before. I had chanced everything often and won every single time. Until one day, the reward wasn't worth the risk. Until I knew I had to leave the darkness behind, even if it meant giving up the game.

Not that the game had been all that great. It was a tangled web that left me empty and shallow, wrapped up in the chains of my own making. The game was greedy, all-consuming, demanding blood for payment and my soul for insurance.

There had been moments during that time I thought I wouldn't survive. I stood at the precipice of death and peered over the edge. One misstep or ill-timed gust of wind and I would have tipped over, fallen down the black abyss and never resurfaced.

Sometimes when I looked back at those moments, those infinitely dark and twisted times, I couldn't breathe. I would feel my heart shatter all over. I would experience the tearing, crushing, ripping apart of my limbs and muscles, my tendons and veins, my heart and my mind. I would forget how to breathe.

I would forget how to be.

Until I remembered him.

He was the one constant in my life that had pushed me through the darkness. He was the one constant in my life that loved me beyond everything else, beyond what I was or had been or could ever be. He wanted me to be better. He wanted to be better for me.

The problem was he was as tangled in the madness as I was.

I didn't live that life anymore. I had broken free and found something safe to build a new foundation for myself. But I couldn't remember the past without imagining his smile or his eyes, his touch. I couldn't think about where I had been without thinking of where we were supposed to go.

Where he was supposed to take me.

Sometimes life doesn't work out the way you plan. Sometimes circumstances change and sometimes they're for the better.

But he was my constant then and he is the constant ghost that haunts me now.

I might not be with him, but he will always be with me.

Chapter One

Fifteen Years Ago

*A*wesome. Another back alley.

There were only a handful of activities that regularly occurred in the darkened backstreets of downtown DC and none of them were appropriate for a ten-year-old girl.

I knew that well, since I had witnessed my fair share of seedy behavior from this city. But that had never stopped my pops from dragging me along with him to all of his work dealings.

"Keep up, Caro," he snapped when his crew came into sight.

The morning sun didn't reach this alley, and the cool air pulled the hair to standing on my bare arms. "I should be in school, Dad. I have a science test today."

He glanced quickly over his shoulder at me, his expression only marginally apologetic. "I called them this morning. Told them you had strep."

Anger burned beneath my skin, turning my face red with frustrated emotion. I ducked my head and let my short bob fall over my cheeks.

"Relax. It's a free day off school. You should be thanking me. When I was a kid I would have killed for my old man to call in for me. The test'll be there tomorrow."

"That's not the point. I don't care that I'm not there. I don't want to be *here*."

He grunted. "Yeah? Then you shouldn't be so good at what you do."

I stopped walking and ground to a halt. He was blaming this on me? *Me?* I didn't even know what to say. The words and arguments and furious thoughts I wanted to throw at him tangled on my dry tongue, a retort-worthy traffic jam.

Sensing that I wasn't following him, he turned around and walked the few steps back to me. He shot a glance to the cluster of men hovering between a rusted metal door and an oozing dumpster.

"Come on, Caro, I'm just kidding," he insisted, even though we both knew he was not. "This is a favor to Roman, all right? There's this truck. The cargo is... worth our time, yeah?"

I lifted my chin defiantly. "I thought you didn't do this stuff anymore. I thought you got promoted."

His bulbous nose turned red. "I did get promoted. This is a one-time thing. They need me. And I need you."

My dad, Leon Valero, had recently been bumped up from high level lackey to bookie. He worked for brothers that ran an organized crime syndicate in the underbelly of Washington, DC. They weren't the biggest outfit or the most infamous, but over the years they'd developed a reputation that held weight.

My dad had worked for them way longer than I had been alive. Bookie was supposed to be a better job than whatever he was doing before. Bookmaker meant more respect in the organization, a bigger cut of the paycheck. He took bets on anything you could take bets on and paid out winners and beat the crap out of you if you couldn't settle your debt.

This promotion was supposed to mean more stability for me. He wouldn't be gone as much. He'd make more money. He wouldn't need me for jobs anymore.

Promises, promises.

"Look," Dad coaxed. "Frankie's here."

I glared over at the only other girl my age I was allowed to play with. Her long hair was somehow darker than mine, and I had always considered mine black. Hers was more like ink. Or oil. Today she hid it beneath a hat. "That's 'cause Frankie will do whatever it takes to prove she's not a princess."

My dad ignored my comment. He knew I was right. But the problem was she *was* a princess. At least as far as the two of us were concerned.

"We need you, Caro." His voice dropped when he continued. "Frankie and Gus ain't got half the set of balls you do. This can't happen without you."

I rolled my eyes and turned to glare at the ivy clustered brick wall that lined the alley but something else captured my attention instead. Not really something, but someone. Someone new.

I could recognize all the usual players. They were guys my dad and his bosses trusted. Most of them were grown-ups that I was supposed to call uncle. As if making them part of our already dysfunctional family somehow made them better humans. They were low-level goons at best—murderers, criminals and drug dealers at worst. But I went along with the lie. Uncle Brick. Uncle Vinny. Uncle Fat Jack. My life was a cautionary tale.

Then there were the kids. Frankie was the only other girl I really knew. There were girls at school, but none of them paid attention to me. I was the poor, tragic outcast that cut her hair short because she didn't have a mom around to teach her how to braid it or hell, put it in something as simple as a ponytail. Frankie and I were close for that reason. It wasn't easy being raised by this pack of animals. But she didn't go to my school. She went to some swanky private school that made her wear skirts and knee-high socks every day. As the orphan niece of the three brothers that ran the syndicate, she was basically royalty as far as I was concerned, and way higher up on the food chain.

Then there were Atticus and Augustus—known as Gus—brothers and sons of the *derzhatel obschaka,* the bookkeeper, Ozzie Usenko. He held one of the highest positions in the *bratva.* Even though the brothers weren't much older than me, they were already in training to be regular, paid members of the crew.

Especially Atticus, even though he'd just turned sixteen. He was born for the life. I saw the hunger in his eyes every time we were allowed to be part of a job. He wanted this. He wanted to be one of the soldiers.

Gus wasn't as serious about it. He wasn't really serious about anything. Atticus was scary and intense and so devoted to the brothers. Gus just didn't want the shit beat out of him by his dad should he choose not to participate.

It was a worthy pursuit. His dad was mean as hell.

15

The syndicate didn't enlist kids to help with big jobs often. It was usually just me or the brothers. There was less at stake if they lost one of us. It sounded harsh, but I knew it to be true. And I was the most expendable of them all. I was a minor and the daughter of a bookie, a position easily replaceable and not all that important. Which was why I made it a point to never get pinched. They might not care what happened to me, but I did.

The brothers that ran the syndicate would always protect Frankie—the only surviving child of their beloved dead sister. The only reason she was allowed to go along for the ride was because nobody wanted to tell her no. Although they were going to have to start soon. Frankie hated her uncles. She blamed them for the death of her parents. Her mom was killed by soldiers from the Italian family competing for the same foothold the *pakhan,* her brothers, also known as the bosses, were. And her dad, who happened to be Italian, died at their hands in retaliation. Frankie only did this shit to punish her uncles.

The kid against the wall was probably Gus's age. Although it was hard to tell. Despite his height, he was half-starved and too skinny. His gangly arms and legs looked like I could snap them in half if I put enough pressure on them. But then his face looked old. Older than Gus and Atticus, maybe even older than my dad. His eyes were tired and his mouth pulled into a tight frown that was both sad and scary at the same time.

"Who's that?" I lifted my chin in the direction of the kid.

Dad shook his head. "We need someone skinny for the back end."

"He's *bratva*?"

"Nah, he's a stray. Jack found him digging through a dumpster and offered him a meal for his help."

I looked at my Uncle Jack who happened to be the size of a dumpster and wouldn't know the first thing about living on the streets and starving. Not that I did either. For all of Dad's shortcomings, he had at least always made sure we had a place to stay and food to eat.

But this kid screamed street urchin. He had that cagey look about him that said way more about his current lifestyle than he wanted anyone to see. I would have bet anything that a hot meal had sounded like winning the lottery. I could imagine Uncle Jack's promises of low risk for a big reward.

Of course the kid would say yes.

The problem was, I knew my Uncle Jack and there was no way he was going to waste another second on this kid once the job was done.

Unless it was to tie up loose ends, which meant the kid would disappear.

Forever.

My stomach turned uneasily. "The Smithsonian," I looked my father in the eye. "If I help you, you take me to the Smithsonian."

"Again?" I stared him down. He rolled his eyes. "Is that it?"

"And I want to bring Frankie."

His frown turned into a grimace. "Yeah, well we'll see what Roman has to say about that."

Her oldest uncle would say yes. After I gave Frankie the opportunity to spend the day with me and my dad, she wouldn't care where we were going. And Roman wouldn't be able to tell her no. He never could.

"So you're in?"

It pained me to agree to today's activities, but I did. I didn't really have a choice anyway. "What's the job?"

"The Screaming Eagle," he explained. "The mark is that electronics store next to the 7-Eleven. They got a big truck of TVs coming in."

My lips parted and I breathed a slow, steady exhale of relief. As far as jobs went, the Screaming Eagle was low risk, little more than normal kid stuff. The most danger I would see was having my ass chewed by the electronics store manager.

But I couldn't let my dad know that. If he even got a whiff of my relief, he wouldn't hesitate to force me into more if this crap.

Instead I asked, "It takes all of us to pull off The Screaming Eagle?"

He made a sound in the back of his throat. "Lest I insult your ego, it will only be you, Gus and Frankie on the inside. Atticus is here to drive the truck."

"And the new kid?"

Dad glanced at him one more time. "Don't worry about the new kid."

I looked at Frankie so I could check out the new kid one more time without being noticed. If Dad didn't want me to worry about him, the kid must have a super bad part today. Or for after the robbery.

Leon was many things, but he always shot shit straight with me.

The kid in question stared down at his sneakers that were full of holes. His dark hair was long and shaggy over his ears, and his skin had that dull quality that happened when you didn't eat healthy food. He'd shoved his hands into his jeans pockets, but his thumbs stuck out revealing dirty fingernails and grimy fingers.

"What's the hold up, Valero?" Vinnie called from the back of the alley.

My dad didn't even spare him a glance, just shouted over his shoulder. "Just a minute." He turned to face me. "I'll let you know when we're ready to go. You good with everything else?"

I wasn't good with any of it, but I nodded anyway.

Dad left me to go talk to the guys. To be honest, what I did was a small part of the job. I created a distraction by causing a scene—classic misdirection. While everyone's eyes were on me, the rest of the guys slipped inside and took what they wanted.

It sounded simple. But it wasn't. There was finesse to it, skill. Frankie and Gus could make a lot of noise, but rarely could they capture an entire store's attention for the necessary amount of time. The real reason Dad kept me out of school today was because I was the best damn liar he'd ever met.

Frankie and Gus started walking over to me. Frankie looked pissed as usual and Gus looked like he could care less. Like usual. But my eyes were on the new kid.

My dad's words bounced around my head like a pinball in one of those trucker games at the arcade. He'd said not to worry about the new kid.

Yeah, right.

His eyes darted around the alley as I approached him, like he was trying to look at anything but me. He bounced up and down on his heels, his elbows locked at his side. He was getting ready to run.

Seeing his nerves made me slow my approach. I'd met plenty of street kids over the years. The syndicate always seemed to have low risk, odd jobs for them that paid in hot meals or a ride somewhere. The kids got something out of it and the syndicate got practically free labor from minors that didn't know anything about the organization. It was a win for everybody but the FBI who would rather arrest someone integral to the brotherhood, someone that they could prosecute. As long as they were low level jobs, I never worried about what happened to the kids. But this was different.

Pulling one into an actual con meant an extra witness, someone that hadn't pledged their loyalty to the crew.

I smelled him before I reached him and my heart kicked in my chest. He was like a stray puppy. With a broken leg. And someone had just cut off his tail, stolen his bone and then dragged him through the sewer.

Seriously, what was that smell?

"Hey," I called out softly, trying not to spook him. "I'm Caroline."

His Adam's apple bobbed up and down as he swallowed. "Uh, hey."

He looked away again, dismissing me. I recognized the look. I was dismissed a lot around my dad's associates. Nobody thought much of the little girl that was always tagging along with her part-time loser of a dad. Nobody noticed me when they talked business in hushed tones or passed money back and forth in dimly lit bars that smelled like piss and old men. I was just the sometimes useful child of a bookie.

But it irked me that this homeless kid treated me the same way.

At least I had showered this morning.

"I've never seen you around before," I pushed, my voice harder, my body stiffer.

He tipped his head back and looked at the narrow strip of sky visible between the two tall buildings surrounding us. "Huh."

He kept his mouth open and I got a good look at his teeth. He had all of them that I could see, which was surprising. And even more confusing was that they were mostly white. He smelled bad, but with teeth like that, he couldn't have been homeless for too long.

"Do you have a name?"

"No."

I resisted the urge to growl. "If we're going to work together, I should know your name."

His head dropped and he finally met my eyes. Bright, deep, impossibly blue. I wasn't prepared for eyes like that. Against his dirty face, they shined like lasers. "We're not working together. I'm doing something different."

My curiosity jumped inside me, like bubbles fizzing in a Coke. "What are you doing?"

His gaze shifted to Jack and Vinnie. "Something different."

I had decided to kick him in the shin when Frankie and Gus stepped up next to us. Irritation buzzed beneath my skin. I liked Frankie. I did. But she was so pretty. And now the new kid would only pay attention to her and I would never figure out what his role was.

Or what his name was.

"Who's your new friend, Caro?" Gus asked, all wide smiles and happy energy.

Frankie adjusted her worn baseball cap. "New recruit?"

The kid quickly shook his head. "Nah. This is a one-time thing."

The three of us exchanged a look. We'd heard that before. Not with kids our age, but men that got sucked into the life. Everyone said that.

The job, whatever the job was, was always a one-time thing. Nobody set out to live a life of crime. It was something you fell into ass-backward and then spent the rest of your life trying to figure out how to crawl your way out.

Or you just succumbed.

Either way, it always started out as a one-time-only promise.

"You hungry?" I guessed.

His too-bright gaze cut to mine. "Fucking starving."

I backed up another step at his harsh language. It wasn't the words that surprised me, it was how he said it. The tone that punched through the air and hit my cheek with a bruising blow.

This kid was desperate. And that made him something more than pathetic or worrisome. It made him feral. Predatory.

He wasn't here because he wanted to be, but because he had to do *something* to survive. And for some stupid reason, that made me want to help him.

I had a tiny, beat up little black kitten in the corner of my bedroom for the very same reason.

"Enough with the cats, Caro," my dad had groaned last week when I brought the battered thing home. "You can't save all the stray cats in DC. You know that, right?"

Maybe Dad was right about the cats, but I could save this kid.

"What's your name?" I asked him bluntly.

He glared at me until I wanted to look away, until I wanted to let him win this staring contest and pretend like I hadn't said anything. "Sayer," he finally admitted. "Sayer Wesley."

"Sayer Wesley," I repeated as if I couldn't help myself. The words whooshed out of me on a breath I hadn't realized I had been holding. It was probably a fake name, but it sounded so real. So right. Like the first real piece of truth I'd ever heard.

His expression turned into a sneer, "That's right, Caroline. Got a problem with my name?"

I felt Gus and Frankie look at me, their eyes curious and accusing. Nobody called me Caroline. Not even my dad. I was always Caro. But I had introduced myself to this kid as Caroline.

Why had I done that?

Feeling weird and off my game and completely unnerved by this street kid, I rolled my eyes like it wasn't a big deal. "Frankie, give Sayer your hat."

She tugged it down over her eyes. "No."

Shooting her a frustrated scowl, I jerked my chin at Sayer Wesley. "He's not doing what we're doing, and there are cameras all over those streets. Let him protect his face at least."

She sucked in her bottom lip and contemplated my suggestion. Turning to him, she asked, "What are they paying you?"

He lifted one shoulder, his jaw ticking near his ear. "Food. Maybe a place to stay tonight."

The three of us shared another look.

"Caro, Frankie, let's go!" my dad shouted from across the alley.

"Give him your hat, Frankie," I hissed. "At least give him a chance to get away from the cops."

Sayer's body had tensed at my words, keen awareness rocking through him and transforming his face from desperate to terrified.

Someone else shouted at us to hurry up. Frankie ripped off her hat, her black curls cascading down her back like a waterfall. I watched Sayer's expression, waiting for him to be momentarily mesmerized, but his expression stayed the same. He had a good poker face. I could give him that.

She tossed the hat at him. He caught it and slammed it on, pulling it low on his forehead.

"Let's go," Gus suggested. "It's not worth pissing them off."

Frankie and Gus turned toward my dad and the rest of the crew, stalking off down the alley already playing the part of obnoxious kids without supervision.

Sayer started to walk after them, but I grabbed his forearm, unwilling to let him enter into this unprepared. "Make them realize you're valuable," I told him quickly.

His eyes narrowed, but he didn't say anything.

Not knowing if he got it or not, I went on. "If you want food or a place to stay you have to earn it. And if you don't, they'll let you get caught." I glanced over my shoulder toward my dad and his associates. "Or worse."

When I turned back to Sayer, those freaky blue eyes were glued to me again. "Why are you telling me this?"

I shrugged. I didn't really have an answer. "You'd do the same for me."

His head tilted. "No, I wouldn't."

His honesty made me smirk. "Now you will." I leaned in, dropping my voice to a whisper. "You owe me a favor."

21

His eyes widened and his lips pressed into a straight line. I was too pleased with myself not to smile, so I quickly turned around and hurried to catch up with my friends.

"Let's go, kid!" Jack shouted after Sayer. He stepped forward, out of the alley and into the confidence game that would irrevocably change his life. The confidence game that would change us both forever.

I didn't know what happened to Sayer until later that night. Frankie, Gus and I did our thing. We walked into the electronic store and cased the joint for an hour. We never intended to steal anything, but we acted suspicious as hell until all of the store employees had their eyes on us. Just when the manager made a beeline over to kick us out, I pulled out pockets full of crumpled one dollar bills and with tears in my eyes, asked what I could buy my dad for his birthday.

He took me over to a display of watches and feeling sufficiently guilty, he gave me all his attention. Frankie and Gus crowded around when he bent over to pick one up for me and I pickpocketed his wallet just for fun.

I had a bad habit of taking something for myself whenever I was on a job. Frankie called them my trophies. But it wasn't like I wanted to remember the job or show off or anything. It was more like insurance or collateral. I needed to start saving for the day my dad stopped taking care of me or got himself killed.

I paid for a cheap watch with a black cuff and made sure to sniffle in gratitude at the counter. Frankie, Gus and I left the store. The alarm rang just as we stepped on the sidewalk.

A delivery truck driver came sprinting around the corner, shouting after his truck that was speeding off down the street, already lost in traffic.

After driving another block, the truck would pull into a parking garage that happened to have no working security cameras, where it would quickly be unloaded into another truck and abandoned for the feds to find.

Sirens blared through the afternoon bustle of downtown DC and two cop cars screeched to a halt in front of us. Frankie, Gus and I stared at the entire scene with wide-eyed fascination—like ten-year-old kids were supposed to do. We moved out of the way when asked, but hung around while the cops took statements and talked to witnesses and tried to figure out what had happened.

Turns out the security cameras had been turned off during the heist. And the delivery driver had been somehow locked in the dumpster behind the building. Nobody saw the thief or realized anything was wrong until the driver had been able to get free of his trash prison. Nobody could even identify the driver since it hadn't seemed that anything was amiss until after the truck was gone.

The manager of the store was dumbfounded. The driver understandably furious. And the cops totally befuddled.

They even asked us if we had seen anything. To which we replied, "No, officer, we were just buying a birthday present for my dad."

"Why don't you get on home then," they suggested. "You don't need to be hanging around a crime scene."

We nodded solemnly and headed off down the street. Our job was over so we had the rest of the day to kill. We decided to grab pizza at our favorite place.

Later that night, my dad would tell me what a great job I did and hand me fifty bucks for being such a good girl. I would ask him how much his cut was and he would smile slyly at me and say, "Don't you worry about it, baby girl. Just know that we don't need to worry about anything for a while."

That was always his answer. He was obsessed with this idea of not worrying about anything.

The irony was that because of his job, I worried about everything all the time.

But we didn't get caught today. So at least there was that.

And neither did Sayer Wesley.

I wouldn't know what happened to him for a couple of months, but I would think of him every day until then.

Chapter Two

Present Day

They say old habits die hard. Which was why I was currently biting my thumbnail and trying to talk myself out of grabbing the twenty-ounce bottle of Cherry Coke from behind the refrigerator glass.

Soda was bad for me.

I believed that.

I told myself that every day.

And yet here I was, in a Mexican standoff with the gas station cooler. "No, Caroline. You don't need it." Talking to myself was another bad habit I couldn't seem to break. At least mumbling under my breath didn't lead to cavities, cellulite or cancer.

"One Coke isn't going to give you cancer," I whispered argumentatively. I opened the cooler door and reached inside, my fingers brushed over the smooth plastic of the beverage I wanted so badly. It had been a rough day. I was tired and bone-deep exhausted. Two separate symptoms that should go hand in hand but had totally different origins.

One came from a fitful night's sleep. The other from a lifetime of waking hours that never seemed to go like they should.

Slamming the cooler door, I ripped open the next one and grabbed a Vitamin Water instead. Coke probably wasn't going to give me cancer, but it was for sure going to give me cellulite and my ass did not need any help in that department.

Making my way to the checkout counter, I glanced around the small space, noticing the cameras behind the clerk's head that showed squares of the store, the gas pumps and all the various people in both spots.

I got in line behind a middle-aged woman with a coffee in one hand and her cellphone in the other and a kid trying to pay for his gas in change and ripped dollar bills. Both of them were so self-absorbed with their purchases that neither of them noticed me step in line behind them.

Not that I wanted them to. But how people stood in line said a lot about what kind of people they were. For instance, the teenager at the counter needed to stop spending all his money on weed and take a shower. He was also $2.47 short if he wanted to put an even twenty dollars of gas in his tank.

And the woman in front of me had two kids, or at least two kids she was willing to brag about on Instagram, a cheating husband, and eczema. She also had a six hundred dollar fall collection Marc Jacobs purse hanging over her shoulder. She had no idea how easy it would be for someone to brush by her on their way out the door and snatch the wallet half hanging out of her flashy handbag.

Not that I would do that.

Not anymore at least.

But like I said, old habits die hard.

To be honest though, these days I'd rather have her purse than her identity.

But not the cheating husband. From the text messages I read over her shoulder to her friend Sherry, he was a real piece of work.

Weren't they all?

When it was my turn, I placed my Vitamin Water, the small bag of pistachios I'd grabbed last minute, the big pack of Swedish Fish and white cheddar popcorn on the counter. "Thirty dollars on pump six too," I told the clerk.

He started to ring me up while I kept my eyes glued to the security monitors. Lucky for me, they even clearly displayed myself and the people behind me.

26

Old instinct burned through me and I fought the urge to duck my head and hide my face. Innocent people didn't have a reason to hide. The normal, everyday American woman walked around with a smile on her face, totally oblivious to how many times she'd been caught on camera. She didn't snarl at Big Brother. She blissfully went about her day unaware of all the different ways her life was recorded.

That was me now. Blissfully unaware.

Or maybe willfully ignorant was a better way to describe it.

"Credit or debit?" the kid behind the cash register asked.

I swallowed down the constant anxiety that followed me everywhere. "Credit."

Pulling out the card from my less expensive but better-secured wallet than the lady before me, I read the raised words, Caroline Baker, with the same kind of accusatory disbelief I always did.

The machine processed the card and blinked that my purchase was approved in understated victory. A gentle breath of relief puffed out of me.

I had a good job and a steady paycheck, but I would never be able to stop the anxiety that came alongside every purchase.

Would this be the moment the card stopped working?

Would this be the moment I realized my account had been cleaned out?

Would this be the moment they found me? The moment they ripped my safe haven away and dragged me back to hell?

When I'd come face to face with the past I'd worked so hard to escape?

"Do you want a receipt?" the clerk asked.

I nodded. "Yes, please." Proof that my card worked. Proof that I was still free.

Outside, the cool evening wrapped around my body, cocooning me in fall and campfire scents and crisp mountain air. I smiled at the burnished sun dipping behind the peaks of bare mountain tops. It was Friday night. Finally.

I couldn't wait to get home, strip out of these work clothes and curl up on the couch for the rest of the night.

Did that make me old? Was twenty-five old?

No, I suppose not. But for me, Friday night movie nights were the highlight of my week. My days of clubbing and partying and living wild were so over. Welcome consistency and dependability and normalcy. I was having the time of my life getting to know them.

I reached my black Murano with the plastic sack of goodies swinging at my side. With my thumb on the keyless entry, I was just about to open my door when a white paper tucked into the window seam caught my eye. It was only a small square, but it had been purposely placed on the driver's side so I would see it.

My mouth dried out immediately and I resisted the urge to glance around. What would a normal person in America do? What was the protocol for a flyer tucked in your window?

"Read it," I whispered in answer.

Threading my hand through the plastic sack handles, I plucked the paper from the window and read it. It was an advertisement for the new hotel up the mountain. The Lodge at Blackburn advertised a hot tub on every patio and private condos with spectacular views, typical accommodations for this part of Colorado. I already knew all about the resort. My roommate was a manager over there.

My heartbeat picked up, thumping quickly in my chest, racing to outrun the adrenaline rushing in my blood. Clutching the paper in my icy fingers, I told myself not to panic. It was a coincidence—probably. That was all.

My wonky heart didn't listen.

I tucked the flyer into my purse and nonchalantly pumped my gas. Then I calmly climbed into the driver's seat and started the SUV. Letting it warm up for a minute, I finally let myself examine the black Mercedes across the street. Was the person in the car waiting for me to turn my car on? Was someone watching me?

I dropped my forehead on the steering wheel and tried to talk myself into a rational response to my questions. I just wanted to go home, throw on yoga pants and remind myself that black Mercedes didn't follow me anymore. Only I didn't drive directly home.

Instead, I wound around and around the small tourist town of Frisco, Colorado until I couldn't stall any longer, until I knew they would be worried if I didn't check in at home. It took everything in me to head that direction, to not just drive all night. Away from this city, and this state and the hateful flyer that sat inconspicuously in my purse.

The Lodge at Blackburn.

The Lodge held no meaning for me other than that was where Francesca worked. It was just another pricy resort to pull in tourists. But then there was the handwriting in the corner, the penciled chicken scratch that whispered something more sinister.

I didn't recognize the writing nor did I know what it meant. Or if it was even meant for me. But I did know that I didn't like it.

Where is he? was all the note said.

That could have been a message for anyone, meant for anyone. It wasn't necessarily targeted at me.

By the time I finally let myself go home, I had worked out most of the instinct to flee—although not all of it.

Panic was a healthy emotion for me. I could never let my guard drop. I could never get comfortable here no matter how much I loved this town nestled in a picturesque valley, surrounded by the towering Rocky Mountains on every side. I could never let myself feel safe enough or removed enough or complacent enough.

I had too much to worry about. Too much at stake.

And because of that, it meant I couldn't just drop everything and run. I was caught in the game of impossible balance between fleeing the life I used to have and carving out a new one. I didn't have the resources I used to. I didn't have the flexibility.

By the time I turned down my street, I had convinced myself the message wasn't meant for me. I thought back to that gas station parking lot and remembered white flyers on every car door. It was an accident.

It was a mistake.

And the reason I knew that was because if that message had truly been meant for me, I would already be dead.

Chapter Three

After parking in the underground garage of my apartment building, I took the elevator to the sixth floor, snacks in hand. I could smell the pizza as soon as I stepped into the hallway. We had a Friday night tradition in my house.

One that apparently started without me if I was late.

Before I could fully unlock the door, it swung open, revealing my smiling best friend and a giggling four-year-old girl with a mop of dark ringlets. "Popcorn!" the little girl squealed as she smashed into my thighs and threw her arms around me.

Francesca grabbed the door before it could hit Juliet in the back of the head.

"My name is Caroline," I told the top of the little girl's head. "Not popcorn."

She kept her arms around me, but looked up at me with another one of her contagious laughs bubbling out of her. "I like Popcorn better," she told me.

I cupped one side of her angelic face. "Me too."

Francesca waved her arm frantically. "All right, Princess Unicorn, let Popcorn in the door so we can eat."

31

Juliet stepped on my toes so I could walk her all the way into our apartment. "Princess Unicorn?" I asked with one eyebrow raised.

"Aunt Francesca wanted me to be Princess Poop!" she exclaimed with equal parts outrage and amusement.

That didn't surprise me at all.

I turned to my best—and to be honest, the argument could be made she was my only—friend in the entire world and glared at her. "Really, Francesca? Princess Poop?"

Leaning on the kitchen island, she grinned at me. "What?"

"I don't even know where to start with you."

Her smile stretched wider. "Hey now. If anyone knows anything about being a princess it's me."

"Why Aunt Francesca?" Juliet asked all innocent eyes and sheltered childhood.

Francesca held Juliet's earnest gaze and with all the gravity and truth in the world said, "Because I used to be a princess."

"No way!" Juliet squealed. She swiveled back to me. "Mommy, is that true? Did Aunt Francesca really used to be a princess?"

I hugged Juliet closer to me, hating that Francesca had brought up our past, hated that she'd invoked the ghosts that still haunted both of us. "She was a princess a very, very long time ago."

Juliet's energy was contagious though and it was hard not to smile when my daughter's head swiveled back and forth between us so quickly. "For real? The crown and the dress and the whole big castle?"

I shared a look with Francesca and mouthed for real. I was a single mom and the only help I had with raising Juliet was Francesca. We all lived together in our three-bedroom apartment that we'd had since before Juliet was born. The only outside influence Juliet had was from her daycare and preschool. And while she occasionally came home saying funny things she'd picked up at those places, the majority of her dialogue was copied from Francesca and me.

This sometimes made for interesting emails from teachers. They didn't encourage their kids to jump to their feet during naptime and shout, "Would the real Slim Shady please stand up?"

I blamed Francesca for that one.

The bad influence in question flicked open the pizza boxes, revealing our usual order of Thai Pie for us and another with cheese and olives for Juliet—which Francesca and I would inevitably finish later tonight around midnight. We'd tell Juliet that the pizza trolls ate it while she was sleeping.

I was a good mom like eighty-five percent of the time. Then there was that fifteen percent that was all lies so I could eat her snacks and not feel bad about the calories.

Everybody knew kid calories didn't count.

Said the woman that just talked herself off the Cherry Coke ledge.

"You got me there, kid. I didn't have a crown or dress," Francesca admitted.

Juliet left me to take a seat at the kitchen island, across from her aunt. "Those are the best part!"

Francesca tilted her head back and forth, not convinced. She refused to wear dresses when we were kids. Hell, she still refused to wear dresses. "I had something better."

Juliet's eyes widened. "What did you have?"

Some of the light dimmed in Francesca's eyes and her mouth twitched with the effort to keep smiling. "I had power."

"And?" Juliet pushed, not at all impressed with that word.

Francesca felt that too, so she upped the ante. "And I had servants."

Juliet threw her head back and giggled again. It was impossible to tell if she believed Francesca or not, but at least she was entertained. For my part, I half expected the Frisco Police Department to bang on our door any second and demand to know exactly what Francesca was princess of.

That would be an interesting conversation.

"What are we watching tonight?" I asked in an effort to change the subject.

Juliet didn't hesitate. She threw her hands up and shouted too loudly for our paper-thin apartment walls. "*Princess Bride!*"

I shot Francesca a helpless look. "Again?"

"It's the theme for tonight. Also, it's her favorite," Francesca defended. "Look at that face? How am I supposed to tell her no?"

I hadn't even set my purse and bag of goodies down or made it past the entryway. But when Juliet looked up at me, blinking her brilliant blue eyes, I knew she was going to get whatever she wanted no matter what. That was power. She might not have understood the meaning of the word, but she had it.

All joking aside, I did think of myself as a good mom that eighty-five percent of the time. I disciplined when necessary. I didn't spoil her. She had an unwavering bedtime and age-appropriate chores. But whenever she gave me that puppy dog look with those big, dewy eyes I just couldn't resist, she got her way.

So maybe I spoiled her more than I liked to admit.

She was still a good kid.

I dropped my purse next to my shoes and prepared myself to be dominated by the four-year-old I was supposed to be in charge of.

Folding her hands in front of her, she blinked rapidly and whispered, "Please, Mommy?"

Done. Dead. She slayed me.

Struggling to keep my stern expression I said, "As you wish, Princess Poop."

The three of us erupted in silly laughter, relaxing into the evening and forgetting about the rest of the outside world, then got busy with our Friday night o' fun. After pizza, we curled up together on the couch and shared popcorn and candy. Juliet fell asleep halfway through the movie, but Francesca and I kept watching. We always did.

This had been our routine for at least three years. Ever since Juliet had the attention span for TV. I didn't let her watch very much of it during the week, but Friday night was all about the movie.

I had always loved our ritual, this night that we made our own. In the beginning, Francesca didn't always stick around for the whole movie or eat pizza with us, preferring to be alone or with some random hookup. But now it was as much her night as it was ours.

We were a family. Not a conventional one or even one made by blood, but we looked out for each other, we supported each other and we protected each other. I knew from experience that blood could be bought and loyalty wasn't an inherited trait. Francesca was my family because she picked me and I picked her and there was nothing in this world that could make us let go.

It had always felt safe with just the three of us, disconnected from the rest of the world as we made a life for ourselves in this valley. That was how we wanted it. When Francesca and I settled here, we made the conscious choice to keep our lives small, but normal.

Something neither Francesca nor I had ever had before.

Except tonight felt strange. I pulled my sleeping daughter closer to my side and pondered the note I'd found on my car at the gas station. Was it worth bringing up to Francesca?

Or was I being paranoid?

Fine, I knew I was being paranoid. I was always paranoid. Being paranoid had kept me alive for twenty-five years. I wasn't going to quit on the one thing that was working for me.

But was this worth uprooting our lives and starting over for?

That was a conversation I wasn't ready to have yet.

"Something's on your mind," Francesca accused quietly.

I turned to my friend. "Something's always on my mind, Frankie."

She flinched at her old nickname, the one that I hardly ever called her anymore. Frankie Volkova was dead as far as the two of us were concerned.

Also as far as her uncles were concerned.

Her tone turned cutting, sharp with the edge of fear. To speak our old nicknames was to invite trouble, to conjure the ghosts both of us were desperate to keep buried. "Well, why don't you tell me what it is, *Caro*."

I ignored her defensiveness and tried to articulate my whirlwind thoughts. "I have a funny feeling."

She softened some, letting out her misplaced aggression in a long sigh. "Is it the pizza, Princess Poop?"

A laugh bubbled out of me. "Maybe."

We were silent for a long time. Francesca changed the input on the TV and turned it to late night reruns of *The Real Housewives*. I thought the conversation was over. After living together for so long and knowing each other our entire lives, sometimes we didn't need to hash everything out. I knew what she was thinking most of the time and she knew what was going on in my head.

And for some reason we still liked each other.

After a while, she voiced her thoughts. "We'd be dead already," she said. "You know it as well as I do, Caroline. If they knew where we were, we'd already be dead."

I had thought the same thing, but that didn't erase the panic fluttering in my chest.

I turned to face her again, knowing she was right. My fingers curled around Juliet's shoulder reflexively, protecting my daughter from those ominous ghosts hovering nearby. "So you feel safe here?"

A sad smile tilted the corners of her mouth. "There is not a place on this planet where I would feel safe. But I think we're well hidden. And for me, that's enough."

The flyer was still tucked into my purse.

Where is he?

Where is who?

"What if we're not hidden well enough, Frankie? What will we do?"

She turned back to the TV, her dark eyes clouded with memories of our past. "Run." She tightened her grip on the remote, her knuckles

35

turning white with the intensity of her grip. "And this time we won't stop."

My body remained still, calm, rested, but inside my chest my heart pounded with two fists and my blood rushed through my veins like it was being chased. The TV was alive with sound and noise and rich women screeching at each other, but my head felt like someone had thrust it under water. I heard nothing but the whooshing of my own frantic thoughts.

Frankie and I had escaped a world of nightmares by the skin of our teeth. We were lucky to be alive. And even luckier to have found a place to make our home. But not a day went by that I didn't think back on what our lives used to be and feel the chill of it creep over my skin, like a specter reaching out from the grave to pull me inside.

I sat there for another hour, struggling to tuck all the escaped demons of my past back into the carefully locked box that I usually kept them in. It took a while for my heartbeat to slow and my panic to subside and for everything that I used to be to fit once more inside that internal prison. But I managed.

I picked up Juliet, softly grunting at how big she'd gotten. Her long hair tumbled over my arm as I carried her to her bedroom and she curled her body into mine lovingly.

Laying her on her princess-themed bed, I tucked her in beneath the fluffy pink duvet and kissed her forehead. "I love you, sweet Juliet," I whispered to her like I did every night, repeating the lyrics of the Neil Diamond song she was named after.

She didn't respond, she was too asleep to care. Instead, she flipped over and found a more comfortable position.

My insides ached as I watched her sweet, sleeping figure for long moments. I had a terrifying past, but she was my beautiful future. She was the reason I ran and the reason I would always run. She was worth all of the other trouble.

I pressed a hand to my stomach as it flipped again. Instinct warned that something was coming. This time I listened. And prepared myself. And girded my resolve against whatever it was.

The first time I ran was so Juliet could live. And nothing had changed. If I had to run every day for the rest of my life to keep my daughter alive, I would.

Chapter Four

*M*onday morning came too soon. After a relaxing weekend of having breakfast at our favorite log cabin diner and catching up on laundry and afternoons at the park with my little girl, I wasn't ready for the reality of the work week.

I dropped Juliet off at the preschool that seconded as a daycare in the afternoon and hurried to work only fifteen minutes behind schedule. Unfortunately, there was zero traffic on Main Street so I had no excuse for my boss other than apologizing for the kind of human I was. Which was a late human. Always late.

I blamed Juliet. Before she was born, I acutely remembered being on time everywhere I needed to go.

Knowing I would be late, but that Maggie was full of grace and mercy as long as there was a hazelnut latte involved in my apology, I grabbed a couple at the local coffee shop and then headed seventeen minutes out of town and up the mountain to a secluded little cabin resort called Maggie's on the Mountain.

The resort was a collection of adorable one and two bedroom cottages that were dated but charming. We boasted a getaway that actually got you away. Away from the city and work and even cell service.

Everyone loved us on days one and two. Not so much by the end of the week. By then, the seclusion always settled in for our guests. Thankfully, we also offered free Wi-Fi to alleviate the separation anxiety from their useless smart phones.

Maggie had hired me when we first moved here. I'd pulled into town four months pregnant with a fresh social security card, zero credit history and a constant flow of tears. I had been a mess.

Maggie took me in, offered to pay me in cash and didn't ask questions. Later I'd figured out that she'd assumed I had fled an abusive boyfriend.

I never corrected her.

Hurrying into the office I found her at her usual spot, leaning over the front desk, glasses perched on the end of her nose, long gray hair pulled back in a low, loose bun. I plopped the latte in front of her and put on my best smile.

"Call off the searches," she deadpanned to no one. "She's not dead after all."

"Aw, Mags. Were you worried about me?"

She looked up at me with the best poker face I had ever seen. "Worried? No. Annoyed? Yes. Worst case scenario though, if you go missing out on the mountain it might drum me up some business."

We were booked almost solid through March. Like this woman needed more business.

She had too much business for her meager staff as it was.

Resisting the urge to smile, I nudged her latte toward her. "If it makes you feel any better, I really am sorry. I've been working on this excuse that involves a bear, an orphan and a basket of puppies. Do you want to hear it?"

She reached for her coffee and tentatively took a sip. We were headed in the right direction. A full gulp meant total forgiveness. "Let me guess," she drawled. "The orphan was selling the puppies on the side of the road when the bear came barreling out of the woods?"

"Wrong. The orphan was selling the bear when the puppies came barreling out of the woods. Don't worry, I saved the day. Crisis averted."

Her lips twitched but she restrained her smile. "You're here now, so you might as well get to work."

I sighed. "Might as well."

She shoved the daily list at me. Maggie was all about lists. To do lists. To buy lists. To see lists. If it existed in the physical world, Maggie had a list for it.

When I first started here, I'd been a kind of jack of all trades. Mostly I had worked in housekeeping. After I fixed a hot tub in one of the guest cottages, she added me to the maintenance staff. When I decided to go to college in Breckenridge and get my hospitality management degree, she moved me to the office. Now I was her second in command. She relied on me to run things during the week. In return for loyalty and good management, she let me have evenings and weekends off to spend with Juliet.

"The Gillett's decided to stay another week? I thought they hated it here."

Maggie took a long pull of her coffee. "It seems they've had a breakthrough. Their therapist suggested more time away from the city to fully explore the healing process."

I rolled my eyes. "Who goes on a romantic getaway with their therapist?"

Maggie snorted. "Someone who just got caught cheating with his secretary. But if you ask me the only one getting anything out of this weekend is the shrink."

"Good for him for suggesting they stay another week. Might as well take advantage of the perks."

She lifted her gaze to meet mine. "You don't think he's a crook? Taking advantage of poor Mrs. Gillett and her scumbag husband?"

"I think he agrees with us that her husband is a scumbag." I examined Maggie's question one more time. "But I don't know that he's a crook. He's just... taking advantage of an opportunity."

"I guess that's one way to put it," Maggie mumbled, clearly not agreeing with me.

The edges of the daily list crinkled in my hands as I held the paper too tightly. I wanted to backpedal. I wanted to change my opinion. Of course the therapist was robbing them. Of course that wasn't okay.

But I couldn't. The words had been spoken. And I was too paranoid about suspicious behavior to explain my sometimes wish-washy moral compass.

Instead, I stared hard at the list and tried to stop the words from blurring. Thankfully, Maggie changed the subject.

"Oh, you got a package on Saturday," she said. "It's in the office."

"That's strange. Do you know who it's from?"

She shook her head. "Didn't pay attention. The FedEx guy dropped it off with the rest. Just happened to notice your name on the label right before I opened it."

"Okay, I'll check it out. It's probably address labels or socks or something." She raised a curious eyebrow. "I can't think of anything else I would have ordered and then forgotten about."

"Maybe you didn't order anything. Maybe it's from someone else."

I snorted, brushing her off. "Not likely."

"From your parents?" she pressed. "A long-lost uncle? Old boyfriend?"

Plopping my chin into my hand, I leaned over the counter and grinned at her. "Fishing are we?" It wasn't like Maggie to pry into my personal life. We had a very strict you stay out of my business, I'll stay out of yours silent agreement. When it came to skeletons in the closet, I was an amateur compared to this woman.

Okay, maybe she wasn't wanted by one of the scariest Russian mob syndicates on the East Coast, but she had her fair share of secrets.

She waved her hand through the air. "Just curious. You never take vacation. I've only ever seen you with that roommate of yours. I know you and still like you. Surely there are other people out there that also know you and still like you."

I swallowed down the truth until it hit stomach acid and burned up in the churning of my nerves. "There are plenty of people out there that know me and still like me, but to be honest I've always been a loner. I don't have a lot of friends back home."

"Family?"

I rolled my eyes, but gave her some truth. "Just my dad. He's not really the package sending kind of guy."

"What happened to your mom?"

"Your guess is as good as mine," I told her, fully honest this time. "She took off after I was born. My dad met her at a strip club. She was his favorite dancer. Dad said she liked the idea of playing house, settling down. But after I was born, she realized real fast that the mom life was not for her."

Maggie's jaw turned to steel. "I will never understand women like that. Being a mom isn't a choice. You got a kid, you're a mom. End of story."

I smiled and it was genuine and a little sad and filled with memories of my choices. "I feel the exact same way. As soon as I found out I was pregnant with Jules, life changed for me. Every decision I made after that was for her. I was done thinking about me."

Maggie winked at me. "That's because you're one of the good ones. Despite your mom being a piece of shit."

My hand fluttered to my heart, full of faux indignation. "Magdalen Marie! How dare you talk about my mother that way!"

She grinned at me. "Oh, like you haven't thought that."

Once or twice, but I couldn't reward Maggie's bad behavior. "All right, sassy pants, go away now so I can get some work done."

She pushed to standing and headed toward the office with the morning newspaper in one hand and the coffee I brought for her in the other. "Don't forget about your package."

I had already forgotten about it. "Oh, right. I'll investigate it during my lunch break."

"You're not the least bit curious right now?"

"Not when I'm forty-five minutes behind on this list and the McGregors are having issues with their sink!"

"Atta girl."

We parted ways for the morning. I would see her around lunchtime when I took over her office to have a few minutes of peace and eat my ham sandwich. That's when I would deal with the mystery package.

I truly was curious. All morning as I hopped from job to job and checked in new guests and highlighted little maps of the property so they could find their cottage, I wracked my brain trying to remember what I ordered and forgot about.

But I couldn't come up with anything. I had decided halfway through my coffee that I would find time to sneak in the office and find out what it was, but then there wasn't time. Too many people needed my help or advice or credit card swiping skills.

By eleven, I was hungry and the insides of my fingers were stained yellow from the highlighter I had been using.

The office door jingled and I pasted on my professional smile, expecting the Garcias. Instead one of the most gorgeous men I'd ever seen in real life walked through the door. My shoulders slumped and my throat dried out as I watched him. The morning light followed him inside, highlighting his tall frame, casting him in a soft gold halo. He tossed his head to the side in an effort to make his golden-brown waves stay out of his eyes. And his smile was bright—megawatt. He was all classic good looks and genuine smiles and no criminal record.

And he was here for me.

41

"Morning, Caroline," he murmured as he approached the counter. "You're looking lovely as ever."

Glancing down at my simple outfit of skinny jeans and a boho black tunic, I could only smile at the compliment. My long dark hair was braided over my shoulder and I was wearing minimal makeup today. I had been going for nondescript.

Not lovely.

"You're sweet, Jesse," I told him. His confident smile faltered. I bit my bottom lip to hide that I noticed. Jesse Hasting had been born and bred in the Colorado Rockies and had the body to prove it. His family owned a ranch not far from Frisco and he'd spent his formative years roping cows and riding horses and whatever else it was they did on ranches. Now as an adult, he owned his own property adjacent to his parent's gigantic estate with the intention to someday take over the entire operation.

Town gossip had it that his old man didn't plan on handing over the reins until Jesse settled down. Jesse was in his late twenties, looked like he'd been carved from the mountain itself and had a small fortune of his own. It didn't take a genius to see that he wasn't planning on getting married anytime soon. But the man did love to date. And recently he'd decided that he should date me. "How are you this morning?"

"I'm good." He leaned on the counter, bringing us closer together than I was ready for. "How are you this morning?"

My lips twitched with a reluctant smile. "I'm good too."

"Busy morning on the mountain?"

This man was trouble. Not just because he looked like sin and a good time, but because he was genuinely nice. His big brown eyes were nothing but sincere and open, and right next to that fun-loving smile was a deep, adorable dimple.

Thankful for something neutral to talk about, I latched on to a conversation of facts. "We are busy this morning. The holiday rush started early this year."

"I've noticed. I think it has something to do with all the Halloween activities in Summit County. We're losing our off season."

I wrinkled my nose. I had felt the same thing. "It's good for the economy, right?"

He made a sound in the back of his throat. "Sure. Let's go with that."

We shared a conspiratorial look. His family made money by means of their own, but most of the natives in this part of Colorado relied on out-of-towners. November through March was considered the busy season, but summer wasn't much different anymore. We used to get a small break in April and May and September and October, but lately we seemed to be packed year-round.

I traced a trail on the map in front of me with the closed highlighter. "What's up? Do you need to speak to Maggie?"

He leaned in closer. "I actually came to see you."

"Oh, really?"

His smile turned irresistibly bashful. "Really."

"Are you wanting to rent a cottage for the weekend? Or the clubhouse? Perhaps an afternoon in a hot tub?"

I felt his low rumble of a laugh in my belly, sending unfamiliar tingles buzzing through me. "You rent out your hot tubs for just the afternoon? I'm not sure how I feel about that."

Keeping a straight face, I said, "I mean, we don't give everyone the afternoon special. Just, you know, those unique guests that are willing to pay by the hour."

His laughter died and the way his eyes widened was maybe one of my favorite things ever. "No way."

I loosed a smile and finally shook my head. "I'm totally kidding. Although let's put a pin in that. It's not a terrible idea."

He laughed again and flicked the highlighter in my hand. "It's most certainly a terrible idea. But please let me be there when you run it by Maggie."

"I'll see what I can do."

We shared another smile and the light in his eyes turned serious. Jesse Hasting was a catch. Every single girl that lived in Summit County and most of the tourists that passed through took one look at this guy and started ovulating. I wasn't any different.

Okay, I was a lot different.

And my ovaries didn't really ovulate on command anyway.

But I was still crazy for dreading the question I could see formulating in the depths of his rich, chocolate eyes.

Jesse cleared his throat and started rubbing the back of his neck that had very suddenly turned bright red. "There's this band that's going to be in town tomorrow night. I went to college with the lead singer and they're pretty good. They're playing down on Main Street at Foote's Rest. The weather is supposed to be really nice and it should be a fun time. And I'm wondering if you'd like to go with me?"

"Jesse Hasting are you nervous?" I tried to repress my smile, but I wasn't totally successful.

"*You're* making me nervous, Caroline Baker."

I flinched, barely, at the sound of my fake last name. "I've watched you walk up to complete strangers and ask them out," I accused. "One time I saw you pull a girl off her seat and start dancing with her at Foote's without even asking her. You just assumed she'd want to dance with you—it didn't help much that you were right!"

The high planes of his cheeks darkened with embarrassment. "Well, those women aren't you, Caroline. You're a hell of a lot more intimidating than random women at a bar halfway through a bottle of Grey Goose."

His comment made me laugh. "And why is that?"

Jesse cleared his throat. "Because you're going to say no."

"Well, if you knew I was going to say no, why did you ask me?"

Some of his confidence returned, kicking his lips up into a cocky smile. "Because I figure it's worth the shot. And maybe you said no the first couple times because of Juliet. But maybe if you keep getting to know me, eventually you won't say no. And if you keep getting to know me, and I keep asking you, then eventually you'll say yes."

I tried really hard not to be flattered. I mean, I really gave it my all. But it was impossible not to feel special after a man like Jesse Hasting put so much effort in trying to date me.

Over the years, Jesse had asked me out a couple times very nonchalantly, and when I'd turned him down he hadn't acted like he cared all that much. But last summer something changed in him. Instead of the casual, offhand invitations to dinner, he had started to actually pursue me. He stopped by my work, he bought me little things like coffee or an ice cream cone if he saw me in town, he went to events that he knew I was going to be at. And he knew Juliet.

Maybe he didn't know everything about her. But he knew I had a daughter. And he knew I was raising her on my own. And that didn't seem to deter him.

Also, the two of them were thick as thieves. Which I found particularly troubling. Because I didn't mind their friendship. Or the way he could make her laugh. Or the way he seemed to genuinely care about her.

It was hard to say no to him. He didn't realize how hard.

And not just because he was this standup guy that was also super-hot and responsible and nice. I mean, they just didn't make guys like Jesse anymore.

But to be honest, the hardest reason to say no to all his attention was basically because I was in desperate need of a good lay. Let's be real, the last time I had a night worth bragging about was the night Juliet was conceived. And while I was in no hurry to repeat that particular ordeal, it had been a long, very long, super long dry spell.

It was on the tip of my tongue to say yes to this man. A night out of the house surrounded by other grown-ups, good beer and decent music sounded awesome. A night hanging out with this particular grown-up sounded even better.

But I couldn't do it.

I had Juliet to think about.

And my fragile existence in this town was built like a house of cards.

I didn't have time to date. Especially not men like Jesse Hasting.

"Maybe someday, far down the road, in the very, very distant future, every one of my answers might not be no," I told him with a gentle expression. "But today it still has to be. I'm so sorry."

Undeterred by my negative answer, he tilted so that all his body rested on one forearm. "You're not into good music?"

"No, I am."

"Then it must be the venue?

"I love Foote's."

"Then it's the company."

"It's not!" My hand landed on his closed fist and I squeezed. I hated the disappointment in his voice. I hated even more that I was the one that put it there. "Jesse, I know this sounds cliché, but I'm just not in a position to date anyone. I wish that I was, because I would be so into it. Into you. But seriously, my life is all about Juliet right now. I just... not that this would necessarily happen with you or whatever... but I just don't want men going in and out of her life depending on who her mom's dating. I don't want to give her a crazy childhood. Or at least I don't want her to know how bad things are. And she likes you. I want her to keep liking you. Does that make sense?"

Instead of agreeing with me or fleeing in the opposite direction like he should have, he opened his fist and turned it so that we could press our hands together. "Are things bad, Caroline?"

My blurted confession hovered heavily in the air over our heads, like a thundercloud pregnant with rain, ready to burst. "Things are fine. I didn't mean it like that."

His gaze held mine captive. "Do you need help?"

I cleared my throat and simultaneously pushed away the pride that screamed *no*, and the girl inside me that wanted to crumble on the floor and start weeping while saying *YES. YES, PLEASE. YES*. It was hard being a single mother. I mean, whatever happened in my past was a whole different struggle.

Taking care of one tiny human was a lot of work. And even with Francesca's help, there was still so much to do for Juliet. "I just meant, like, in the sense that I'm a single mom and I can't seem to get to anything on time. In the sense that Juliet is growing up so fast in some ways and not fast enough in others, and I'm trying to balance her and work and health insurance and dentist appointments and trying not to drown. You're a good guy, Jesse. You deserve a girl that can give you her full attention. With me, you'd always be third."

His head tilted to the side. "Third?"

"Behind Francesca," I explained. "We're basically a Spice Girls song."

That didn't clear things up for him. "Spice Girls?"

I smiled and this time it was real and not forced, genuine and not covering other emotions that I was too chicken shit to share with him. "Friendship was super important to them."

His shoulders shook with laughter. "Obviously I invited you to the wrong concert."

I rolled my eyes at him. "Whatever you need to tell yourself."

"No, I need a lot more than that," he admitted. "My ego's taken a serious blow over the last couple months."

I patted his hand and then pulled back. There was no reason for us to keep holding hands. "Aw, poor baby. Like I said, the offer for by-the-hour hot tub services are open any time. We'll call it the friends and family discount."

His eyebrows shot up to his hairline. "You're offering your services?"

My face heated with embarrassment. "Oh, not, er, not mine. We'd call in a professional for that."

We realized what I'd said at the same time and both burst into more laughter.

"What's going on out here?" Maggie asked from the doorway. "It sounds like a party."

Finally! My rescue. What had she been doing back there? Eavesdropping probably.

"Oh, hi there, Jesse." Maggie pretended to be surprised. "What brings you up here?"

His cheeks reddened again. "Oh, nothing. I was just in the area. Thought I would say hi to Caroline."

"That was sweet of you." She turned to me, her eyes casting laser beams of accusation at me. "Wasn't that so nice of him, Caroline? He's such a thoughtful man." She turned back to Jesse, making all of this ridiculously awkward. "You're a thoughtful man, Jesse. We could use some more of you in this day and age."

"Well, uh, thank you, ma'am," he mumbled, taking a step to the side. Away from Maggie.

She continued to smile at him and bat her eyelashes. "You're welcome." She dropped a perfectly square brown cardboard cube in front of me. "Thought I'd bring this out to you, Caroline, since you're so determined to ignore it."

My polite expression strained as I wrestled my hands to the side to keep from snatching it out of sight. I wanted to knock it off the counter and kick it across the room. I had no idea where it came from or whose name was on the return address. I didn't want to know.

The funny feelings from last week returned with a biting edge, coiling in my stomach, a snake ready to strike.

My smile wobbled, but I managed to say, "Oh, thanks. I was just coming to grab it when Jesse stopped by."

"Mmm-hmmm."

I ignored Maggie and turned to Jesse. "I got a package." It was such a dumb thing to say, but the curious look on his face prompted me to explain.

Only now he didn't know how to respond. "Cool," he said.

I wanted to bang my head on the counter. Or grab the package, race out the front door and chuck it off the mountain.

It was in moments like these that I questioned Jesse's sanity. Had he really just asked me out? The most awkward human on the planet?

"Who's it from?" Maggie pressed.

Stealing courage from some deep, buried place inside me, I glanced at the label. There wasn't a name attached to it, just an address from somewhere in Ohio—a state that meant absolutely nothing to me.

No offense, Ohio.

"I don't know."

"Well, aren't you going to open it?" Maggie pressed, clearly obsessed with the whole ordeal.

Reaching for scissors from the pen canister, I sliced the seam with shaky fingers. This was one of the most surreal moments of my life. Who knew what was in this box?

Secrets from my past?

A bomb?

A severed head?

Okay, the severed head probability was a bit of a stretch. But a mysterious package showing up out of the blue just screamed trouble.

"Good Lord, darlin', the suspense is killing me," Maggie groaned.

I glanced at Jesse nervously, before committing to my future. Normal people weren't afraid of mysterious packages. Well-adjusted, nightmare-free people just opened them, excited to find out what was inside.

Reminding myself that I was a normal person or at least supposed to be pretending to be one, I peeled back the flaps and braved a look.

Was I relieved? It wasn't a head.

It was worse.

Dread curdled with terror followed by a painful shot of panic.

The box was nearly empty save for a single flower that had been beaten and battered in transportation. Petals and pollen littered the box, staining it their crimson color. I felt my own color leech from my face, my hands trembling as I picked up the note taped to the bottom.

"What is it?" Maggie asked, her voice laced with concern.

I cleared my throat and licked dry lips. "A Waterlily Dahlia. It's my favorite flower."

Maggie moved to stand next to me, sensing danger. "Who's it from?"

Turning the note over, I had to blink a couple times before the words written there made sense. I kept the note close so she couldn't see the quickly scrawled words.

Found this for **You**

"It doesn't say." I shoved the note into my pocket and tried to remember what the handwriting on the first flyer looked like. Was it the same?

Similar?

Jesse leaned forward and tipped the box toward him with his long pointer finger. The flower fell with the movement, thudding against the box. "Hmm. That was a goofy way to send it."

"They should have had it delivered," Maggie agreed. "It's ruined after shipping."

"It's pretty though. What did you say it's called?" Jesse asked.

My lips were numb when I said, "Waterlily Dahlia." The words conjured up all kinds of unbidden memories from my past.

A bouquet of Waterlily Dahlias on a mahogany table not meant for me.

A tall, lanky kid reaching for them, spilling a few droplets of water on the expensive finish. "For you."

"It doesn't count if you steal them," I told him, unable to resist a smile and the way butterflies assaulted my belly.

His low laugh chased me through the spacious room. "I beg to differ," he argued. "Danger, uncertainty, potential time in the slammer. These flowers were won at a price. Anybody can buy flowers from a store. They practically give them away. But how many guys have scaled two stories, rewired an alarm system and risked his life just to get you flowers?"

I rolled my eyes, hating the way my cheeks blushed. At the same time, I couldn't help but love the attention from Sayer. "It just happened to me last week. Twice actually."

He closed the distance between us, handing me a single stem he'd plucked from the crystal vase. "Liar."

"Thief."

His lips pressed against mine in the next second—hungry, greedy, possessive. I had to stretch up on my tiptoes to reach him. His arms wound around my waist and held me against him. My heart slammed into my rib cage, jumping with anticipation and excitement and too many feelings for this boy.

He pulled back to whisper in my ear, "Take the flower, Caro."

I nodded, letting him close my fist around it. Holding it out under the moonlight from the floor to ceiling windows, I wondered at its beauty. "What kind of flower is it?"

Sayer shook his head. "It's yours. That's what kind it is."

Tearing my gaze away from the blossom to Sayer's blazing blue eyes, I felt myself fall deeper in love with him. Was that even possible? He already had all of my heart. What was I giving him now? My soul? My life essence?

The next week a bouquet of those same flowers showed up on my doorstep. The note said, Waterlily Dahlias. It took me a week to track them down. But, Six, I would have searched for them for the rest of my life for you.

The box containing this flower wasn't from Sayer. I would have recognized his handwriting. And he wouldn't have sent me crimson.

He would have sent white.

And never like this.

Who else was looking for me?

"I don't know who it's from," I told Jesse and Maggie honestly. "The whole thing is weird."

"Are you okay?" Jesse asked, getting that I wasn't acting okay.

I sucked in a deep breath and willed my frantic nerves to still. Then I met his eyes. It was always important to meet someone's eye when you wanted to lie to them. Most people with a secret couldn't handle the shame. Most people wanted to duck their head or focus on something else when they had to stretch the truth. But if you could meet their eyes when you lied to them, they hardly ever suspected that what you were saying was anything but the fact.

"I'm fine," I told him confidently, not flinching, not turning away. "It just surprised me." Adding a smile, I closed the box and turned around to toss the entire thing in the trash can. The box was awkward for the small receptacle, but I didn't really want to throw it away. I wanted to save it for later so I could examine it in private. "Anyway, I should get back to work. Our next should be here any second."

Jesse took the hint graciously. Tipping his head to me, he continued to hold my gaze. "If you change your mind about tomorrow night, you'll let me know?"

I refused to let my smile crack. "You'll be the first." And then I winked at him. Because why the hell not.

"Bye, Mags."

"Bye, darlin'."

The bells on the door jingled on his way out. Maggie and I silently watched him climb into his King Kong of a truck and reverse down the driveway.

When nothing was left of him but the kicked-up dust from his double row of rear tires, Maggie turned her scowl on me. "You going to explain that flower to me now that he's gone?"

I pulled paperwork in front of me and focused on that. "Maggie, there's nothing to explain. You know just as much as I do."

"Mm-hmmm."

50

I dropped my pen and lifted my wide-eyed gaze. "In other, more exciting news, Jesse asked me out again!"

Her lips twitched with another repressed smile. This woman never smiled unless she absolutely had to. It was maddening. "I'm assuming you turned him down again."

A surprise laugh bubbled out of me. "Well... Juliet. Of course I turned him down."

"Atta girl. It's better to play hard to get with a catch like Jesse Hasting. That way when you finally say yes, he'll already be halfway in love with you."

"That's not what I'm doing!" I called to her back since she'd already headed out the door to do the devil only knew what.

"I believe you!" she called back, sounding not at all like she believed me.

I huffed at the paperwork in front of me. The threatening note still burned in my pocket. *Found You*. But who had found me?

And why?

Chapter Five

Fifteen Years Ago

I speed walked to Frankie's side as soon as we stepped into the warehouse. Men moved around stacks and stacks of cardboard boxes. A big shipment of something had come in. I didn't know what. They didn't give me those details.

But my dad had been called in. This was apparently an all hands on deck situation. It was almost midnight on a school night. I should have been home sleeping, but Dad said he couldn't risk leaving me behind tonight.

I didn't like the sound of that. I lived with the knowledge that Dad's job was typically dangerous. But this was something worse than usual.

Frankie was here too, which meant Roman, Dymetrus and Aleksander were somewhere presiding over the entire operation. I caught sight of a table filled with guns. Big guns. Small guns. Scary guns.

Frankie sat on the ground, with her back propped against the wall, her knees pulled to her chest. Her hair was at her nape wrapped in a bun, hidden beneath her usual baseball hat. She was wearing a sweat suit top and bottom that matched. I would bet a hundred bucks the pants had Juicy written across the butt.

"Your old man dragged you out of bed too?" she asked with sleepy eyes.

I took a seat next to her on the cold ground. "What's going on?"

"We're at war over this shipment," she explained listlessly.

"What do you mean, we're at war?"

"With the Irish. These are their guns."

She sounded so bored that it was hard to take her seriously. "Frankie, be real."

Stretching out her legs, she yawned first and then filled me in. "Roman wants more territory. The Irish were unwilling to negotiate. In fact, everyone has been unwilling to negotiate. Anyway, to prove a point, Roman intercepted this shipment of guns. The Irish understandably want them back, but my uncles refuse. So now we'll kill them with their own weapons, my uncles will expand their territory and the other families will cooperate moving forward."

"Holy shit."

Frankie looked at me for the first time, pain amplified in her big black eyes. She hated her uncles. She hated that her mom had died and left her to their care. She hated that she didn't have a dad because of them. She hated what they stood for and the lives they took in the name of power and expansion and just plain arrogance.

I didn't blame her. I couldn't understand this life. It didn't matter that I had been raised in this world or that it was all I knew. It was obvious to anyone with a soul that what our families did was wrong. I knew that killing people for greed and influence was not right.

Sometimes when Frankie and I were alone, we talked about what it would be like to run away. We dreamed of distant places untouched by mafia and career criminals. We whispered about the Bahamas or somewhere in remote Africa. Or just anywhere that wasn't here.

But those were daydreams that meant nothing in real life. Neither of us could escape this life. At least not now. And Frankie had it worse than me. She was stuck here forever. There was nothing her uncles wouldn't do to find her, to keep her with them. She was the Volkov princess. I at least had a chance at a better life once I graduated high school.

There were things I didn't say to Frankie because I knew the words would hurt her feelings. But I planned on college somewhere far away. I wouldn't even need Leon's permission. I had money I'd been saving since the first time he ever paid me for a job. All I had to do was keep making money. And then I'd find a college on the other side of the country and just never come home.

Dad could come visit me if he wanted to or not. But either way, I was never coming back to DC again.

And maybe someday, Frankie could come join me. Maybe her uncles would let her make her own life away from the carnage of their world.

Eight more years.

I could last eight more years.

We fell silent as the Volkov army moved efficiently around us to unpack boxes and catalog the guns—so many guns. Despite the huge score, the men were tense tonight, keenly aware there would be consequences for their actions.

War was inevitable. And surely the Irish still had plenty of weapons. These hadn't been meant simply to outfit their operation. They were going to sell them.

The syndicate hadn't just stolen arms, they'd taken away a massive paycheck.

The Irish were going to be pissed.

Atticus walked into the building, followed by Gus, who spotted us immediately. A second later Gus's dad, Ozzie, walked in. He was followed closely by the kid from the alley, who was still wearing Frankie's hat. A couple guys close by, stopped what they were doing to pat the kid on the head or give him a playful punch. He seemed to be getting congratulations. It appeared he was accepted by this crazy group.

My mouth dried out and a bad feeling crawled through my chest—like a spider scurrying across a counter in search of a hiding spot. "How did Roman find out about the shipment?"

Frankie's eyebrows rose curiously. "Do you really not know?"

I tore my eyes off the new kid and looked at my friend. "Tell me."

Her big eyes narrowed in an accusatory glare. "It's all thanks to you, Caro."

"What do you mean? Frankie, explain it."

Gus started walking toward us, so she dropped her voice. "You told him to prove his worth, remember?"

My head swiveled back to face the guns. I did this?

This was my fault?

I felt sick.

Worse than sick.

What's worse than sick?

Dead.

I felt dead.

"What's up, m'ladies?"

Frankie and I made a simultaneously disgusted sound. Gus was two years older than us, but way dumber.

His smile wobbled, but he still slid down the wall and took a seat next to me. He bumped his shoulder against mine. "Surprise slumber party?"

"Apparently."

He started picking at his shoelaces. "They should have let you guys come over to my house or something. This sucks that we have to hang out here."

Gus's house was a lot like Frankie's in that they had live-in guards. His dad was the bookkeeper for the Vor, basically third level from the top in command over the entire organization. Oz was insanely smart. I didn't understand everything about what he did, but from what Frankie said, her uncles couldn't do anything without him.

He was also straight up evil.

It was his second-best life skill. First came the math, then came the sadism. And he'd passed his evil genius onto his children. Atticus got the evil and Gus was the genius.

Like actual genius. He also got the brunt of his dad's insanity.

I dropped my head on Gus's boney shoulder. "That's not a bad idea. You should go tell your dad."

He blew a heavy breath out, making his lips flap together. "Yeah, right. I'll just punch myself in the face while I'm at it."

We all looked at where Oz stood in a huddle with the three *pakhan* and one of their second in command, Rocco. My lip curled and my hands clenched into fists at my side. I decided to add Gus to my list of refugees. One day, I would get them both out.

One day we'd be free of this place.

Gus laughed and it startled me. I looked at him and he nudged his chin in the direction of the new kid. "What's he doing?"

The three of us watched as he wandered aimlessly around the room, watching the men unpacking boxes until they told him to scram. Then he'd walk over to another group and hover until they moved him along.

It was obvious what he was doing—learning. The question was why.

"Is it true he's living with you?" I asked Gus.

"Yeah, he didn't have a home I guess, and Roman didn't want him living on the streets anymore. Especially after tonight."

56

Fat Jack turned and raised a backhand to him and Sayer scurried off to a darkened corner of the warehouse. It was obvious Sayer was pushing his luck with these guys, but didn't realize it. They'd been happy to pat him on the head earlier, but now he was in their way and they were trying to work.

"He's going to get the shit beat out of him," I mumbled.

"Nah," Gus argued. "He's one of them now. Roman made it official after the shipment was secured."

My heart jumped to my throat. "What do you mean?"

"Caro, he's a Six. They made him earlier today."

I couldn't hear my question over the rushing of my blood. "Why?"

Gus jutted his chin toward the crates of guns and guns and more guns. "Why do you think? Either he's *shestyorka* or he's dead. They did him a kindness."

I scrambled to my feet before I could talk myself out of it and hurried along the walls of the warehouse, careful to stay out of the way. I found him hovering in darkness, watching the operation like he was going to be given a test on it tomorrow. His arms were crossed over his chest, his head tilted forward, his eyes hungry for every terrible and illegal thing before him.

He didn't even acknowledge me when I prowled over to him. I slapped his shoulder finally getting his attention. "I want to see it."

When he still didn't reply, I slapped his arm again. "I want to see it, Sayer. Show it to me."

"Show you what?" he growled, finally granting me a quick, annoyed glance.

"Gus said they made you. I want to see proof."

He rubbed his hand over his mouth and continued to stare at the men. His brothers. His thieves in law.

"Show it to me," I demanded. And then I broke. I felt awful and guilty and to blame. I hadn't meant this. I hadn't meant for him to become this. I had just wanted... I just hadn't wanted him to die. "Please, Sayer."

He finally turned to me. His eyes hard and tough and ready for the life ahead of him—as if he had any idea what he'd just gotten himself into.

"You have to earn it."

"Excuse me?"

He held my gaze. He was serious. "I'll show it to you, but you have to earn it first."

I rolled my eyes and stepped back. "You're gross."

He followed after me, grabbing my wrist before I could flee. "Wait, no. God… no. That's not what I meant. I didn't mean… I mean, come on how old are you? Eight?"

"You're truly an asshole."

His lips twitched. "Fine, I know you're ten. Still, I'm not asking you to make out with me or anything."

I canted my head, expecting something so much grosser than kissing. I was only ten, yeah, but I'd grown up around dirty old men and the women willing to sleep with them. I wasn't exactly naïve when it came to sex. It made me think that maybe Sayer was though if the worst thing he could think of was making out.

"How old are you?"

His chin lifted defiantly. "Thirteen."

I kept my snide comment about him being a real man to myself. I was too irritated with him and this situation and myself to trust the words I wanted to say. "And now you're theirs. For life."

An irritated look flashed over his face before he wiped it away and gentled his hold on my wrist. "Do something for me and I'll let you see what you want to see."

"I don't need to see it. You just confirmed that it's there. That's all I wanted."

His lips broke into a wide smile. "Damn, you're good. I didn't even see that coming."

I shrugged one shoulder. "You're not going to make it very long if I can trip you up, Wesley. Better figure your crap out fast."

He was irritated again, but he hid it well. He leaned forward, those blue eyes glowing in the dingy warehouse lighting. "I know you want to see it. You're practically vibrating with curiosity. It's one tiny favor. Not even a big deal to someone like you." He rocked back on his heels. "If you can back up your reputation."

I snorted. "What reputation?"

"Best pickpocket on the East Coast. That's what Gus says, but he's probably lying."

"Gus doesn't lie," I confirmed. If he'd spent any time with Gus he would know that. It was like Gus was totally incapable of saying something untrue. That's why he had to keep going on jobs with me. Trial by fire. His dad wanted him to figure it out or pay the consequences.

I suspected Gus preferred the consequences, which was why he continued to tell the truth.

Juvie would be a vacation compared to that house.

"What's the job?" I was disappointed with myself for jumping at Sayer's challenge. But I couldn't help it. Plus, I didn't want Gus to be wrong. Okay, maybe I wasn't the best pickpocket on the East Coast. It was a big coast after all. But I could hold my own.

He smiled again and it was alarming. I felt the air rush out of my lungs and my tongue dry out. This kid had a secret weapon and all he had to do was smile.

"Atticus has something of mine," he explained. "I want it back."

His words were a bucket of ice water on my head. He had to be out of his freaking mind. "No way. Are you crazy? Because Atticus is. He'll murder me if I take something from him."

"Then don't get caught."

I snarled something my dad would have said. "If it's yours, why don't you just ask Atticus for it? I'm sure he'll realize the mistake and hand it over."

"I'm sure you're out of your damn mind. He didn't accidentally pick it up. He took it off my body and put it on his. He said if I tried to get it back he would murder me. I'm inclined to believe him."

My lips pressed into a frown in an attempt to hold back my information. I couldn't do it though. Whatever it was about this kid, he got all my secrets out of me. "He can't kill you. Your one of his brothers now. He's sworn to protect you and you him."

"Okay, fine, maybe not kill me, but beat me until like right before I die. He's a psycho."

That was true. Atticus was a psycho. "What is this thing?"

"A necklace," he said. "Well, a chain. With a key hanging on it."

"Aw, that's sweet. You know, when I first walked over here, I thought you were missing something. Turns out it was jewelry. Aren't you pretty?"

"Shut up. It's not like that. It's just... it's like this... it's the last thing I have of my parents. They're dead and all I have is that key." He wiped a hand over his face and I suddenly felt very bad. Again. "I just want it back, okay?"

"Fine," I huffed. "Fine, I'll get it. But I want the record to show that if I manage to pull this off, we're even. And I don't just mean because you're going to show me the tattoo, but like for everything. For me getting you into this whole stupid mess. We're even, okay?"

"Uh, okay? I... I mean, I never thought you owed me for that. You saved my life."

Tears welled in my eyes, but I refused to let them fall. "No, I did the opposite."

Before he could argue with me, I spun around and headed into the crowd. I realized I forgot to ask Sayer where Atticus had put this key on a chain, which was a stupid mistake. But I couldn't turn around now.

I ducked behind boxes and blended into the walls until I was closer to Atticus. He was standing with some of his *boyeviks*—his soldiers. They were talking in low tones with the occasional low rumble of laughter between them.

As I approached I realized they were talking about a girl. A young girl and what a beauty she was going to be when she got older.

Oh God, I hoped it wasn't me.

I didn't want to be on any of these guys' radars. "She's already too good for us, yeah? A real fucking princess. Just imagine her in another six or seven years," Atticus snarled. I breathed a sigh of relief. They were talking about Frankie.

Loyalty to my friend overrode my temporary relief and I had the strongest urge to knee him in the balls. And then knee all of them in the balls.

No, better yet I would turn them in to Roman, let the boss know they were talking about his niece. He would murder them all for me.

But first I had to get this chain.

Three seconds before I opened my mouth I had the awareness to get really freaking nervous, but I couldn't let the panic stop me. I pushed it down, way, way down and launched into the con.

"Hey, Atticus?" I continued to approach the table they were standing at, although I was cautious. He lifted his head, barely acknowledging me. Some of the guys around him backed up so I could approach him, but nobody really looked at me. Deciding I couldn't wait for an invitation, I launched the first layer. "Gus is wondering if we can go back to your house and wait this out there?"

Atticus lifted his head, furious and annoyed. "How the fuck should I know? Go ask Ozzie, little girl."

"He's with the *pakhan*," I said quickly, meaning the bosses. "I can't disturb him."

"Yeah, well you can't disturb me either. That's a rule now." A couple of his friends laughed at his assholery, but most of them continued to pretend I didn't exist.

I set my hand on the table, implementing stage two, and leaned on it, knocking off several rounds of ammunition to the floor. While Atticus threw his hands up in the air and started cursing me, I scanned his body for signs of the chain.

When he started to bend over to pick up my mess, I caught sight of it poking out the back of his t-shirt. With zero time to waste, I bent over too. "Oh, my gosh! I'm so sorry. Let me get those." Thrusting my head forward, I managed to clip the side of his head, our temples colliding.

"Son of a bitch," he growled at the sharp pain.

"Ow!" I hissed, bringing my hand to my face—but not before my fingers brushed the back of his neck as he hunched over, unclasping the chain. If it had been a more complicated locking mechanism, I wouldn't have pulled it off, but luckily it was just a simple insert. I cupped my hand over my head and winced. "I'm so sorry, Atticus. It was an accident."

He stood up and the necklace slipped through his T-shirt and landed on the floor. I slid my foot over it before he noticed. Sure, my stance was a little wider than what was comfortable, but the key was to act cool.

"I don't care that it was an accident," he barked. "You're in the way, Caro. And now you're pissing me off. Just go wait over there with the other kids and leave me the hell alone."

"Are you sur—"

"Seriously. Go away before I hit you."

Well, on that note… The sad thing was that I actually believed him. He didn't care that I was a girl or a child compared to him. He would lay me out. No doubt.

"Just let me help—" I bent over again to pick up the rolling shells and managed to discreetly pick up the chain. Sure enough, there was a key at the end of it. Closing my fist around it, I stood up and slipped it into my pocket unseen.

Thankfully, Atticus had had enough. "Just go, already. You're not helping."

I took three quick steps back. "Well… okay… but only if you're sure."

He stilled and met my gaze. Nothing but black, black anger glared back at me. "Caro, for fuck's sake."

Holding up my hands in surrender, I turned toward Gus and Frankie. Going to Sayer would be way too suspicious. But I had his necklace now and he had the tattoo I was anxious to see. When the men got busy later, we would exchange goods. For now, the necklace burned a hole in my pocket and I waited on pins and needles for Atticus to figure out what I'd taken.

I had only made it halfway across the floor when Atticus bellowed my name. "Caro! Are you fucking kidding me?"

The entire warehouse ground to a stop, weapons and boxes paused in every direction. My steps faltered and I turned bright red from the unwanted attention.

"Caro!" Atticus growled. "You goddamn little thief."

"What's the problem?" Rocco snarled from his post by Roman.

"She stole from me," Atticus hollered. I could feel his livid gaze burning a hole in my back. I could feel it searing into me, ripping me apart inside his head. "She fucking pickpocketed me."

I expected judgment. Punishment. I had stolen something from one of the brothers. And who was I? Nobody. The sometimes useful child of their sometimes useful bookie. They were going to freaking kill me. Or at least cut off my hand— the thief's reprimand.

But instead of cries for blood, the brothers started laughing. Slowly at first, just snickers or snorts of surprise. Then full on laughter. It cut through the tension in the room, making the air breathable again.

Except for me.

They were laughing at me. And it wasn't like I was super sensitive or anything. I could handle being poked fun at.

But this was an army of killers handling stolen guns. It was strange. And I was super uncomfortable.

The presence of the necklace, more than ever, burned in my pocket, practically lighting my pants on fire. Which would be fitting for the liar I was.

One of the guys by Atticus pushed his shoulder. "Aw, shit, man, the little girl stole from you."

More laughter.

"Bested by a baby!" someone else shouted from across the room.

More laughter.

"Enough!" Roman stepped forward, his accented voice slicing through the warehouse, ending the chaos and the good mood. "Get to work unless you'd rather the Irish have their guns back. Your throats'll be slit by morning and you'll have copper pennies where your eyes should be, but at least you've had a good laugh, *da*?"

The room was silent again as faces turned to stone once more and the unpacking began again. I didn't know what to do. Did that mean I was okay? Or that Roman was three seconds away from giving Atticus permission to murder me?

"Atticus, bring the child here so that my men can focus."

I caught Frankie's eye from across the room. Her face had turned white as a ghost. Her eyes bugged and her mouth had dropped open. No part of her expression gave me courage.

If I needed confirmation that I was about to be executed, it was written all over Frankie's stupid face.

Ugh.

Atticus grabbed the back of my neck and jerked me toward him. My squeak of surprise quickly turned to a wince of pain as he shoved me toward the *pakhan*.

He pressed his face against the back of my bowed head. "Now you've done it, bitch."

I focused on my feet. And not tripping. Not on my inability to breathe or think or run away.

Out of the corner of my eye, I saw my dad moving toward his bosses, his hands twisting the hat in his hands until it was bent out of shape. It would seem he had as much faith in me surviving this as Frankie did.

Holy cow. What had I done?

Chapter Six

Fifteen Years Ago

The three brothers were speaking in low tones to Ozzie and the two men that were called the two spies—they were the second in command of the organization. Ruthless. Brutal. Terrifying. And also brothers. Twins actually. Rocco and his identical brother, Boris. The six men towered over me, all dominating strength and choking power.

I had never been this close to any of the brothers before, or the two spies. I wasn't even sure if any of Frankie's uncles realized I was her only friend. Or that I was the daughter of their recently promoted bookie. Occasionally, my father and Ozzie would work together, but I was still terrified of the man.

And equally as terrified of his son that was currently squeezing my neck so tightly I knew he was going to leave a bruise. He pushed me toward the *pakhan* and I stumbled over my feet before I righted myself.

"This girl stole from you?" Boris demanded of Atticus.

"She's a nuisance," Atticus growled. "I was focused on working. She was in the way. I wasn't paying attention like I should have been."

"And that's her fault?" Dymetrus asked in a low, menacing voice.

Atticus's expression flattened. "She's a pickpocket. She steals for her dad. She's good at what she does." All of his accusations were true. None of them felt like a compliment.

They were crimes to be punished.

Sins to be judged.

"Your father is the bookie?" Aleksander asked, his eyes on my dad who stood a few yards away, not speaking.

Not defending me.

My chest squeezed, but I managed to answer. "Y-yes. Leon Valero."

Roman's eyes narrowed. "And you are?"

"Caro Valero."

The three brothers shared a meaningful look I couldn't hope to decipher. "You helped recently with a shipment of TVs?" Rocco asked.

I nodded. "And the shipping container two months ago." I closed my eyes and willed my nerves to get out of the way of my memory. "And the, the… the thing at the bank."

"How old are you?" Roman demanded.

My heart dropped to my stomach and started swimming around, doing laps, permanently refusing to go back where it belonged. "T-ten."

Roman nudged his chin at Atticus. "He's right that you're good at what you do, *da*?"

I shrugged. His question felt like a trap.

Roman didn't need a better answer than that. "What did you steal from him?"

My hands trembled from fear and I started to sweat. I couldn't show him. I certainly couldn't tell him—and not only because I was nervous. This was going to end so badly for me.

"Show him, Caro," my dad demanded from the distance.

The six men towering over me, glared at my father for speaking without permission. Now I was terrified for his sake.

Just to get their attention back on me, I lifted my hands that were covered by the sleeves of my hoodie. The men turned back to me. Atticus's grip on my neck tightened. With trembling fingers, I pulled out his wallet.

Atticus snatched it away from me, quickly checking it for money. "There was a hundred-dollar bill in here, Caro."

His fury made it difficult to swallow. I was playing a risky game. And I was losing.

But before I could retrieve the money, Aleksander spoke up. "Are you telling me that she took your wallet straight from your person. And now, standing before us, she continues to rob you?"

Atticus didn't respond verbally. His furious glare said everything for him.

"Little girl," Aleksander laughed, "what courage you have."

I shook my head quickly. "It-it's not courage."

Aleksander continued to stare at me. They all did. With expressions I could not read. I felt like an exotic animal at the zoo, locked away, put on display, expected to perform.

"What were you going to do with the money?" Roman asked in a careful tone.

"Candy," I lied. "And I want a new doll." I didn't, but that's what all men assumed girls my age wanted.

Atticus made an outraged sound. "Hand it over. The game's done, Caro. You've had your fun, but now you're caught."

Except Roman lifted a hand to stop me. "The girl has earned the money."

Atticus and I were both stunned silent. *What?*

"No," Atticus argued after he'd recovered. "That money is mine."

"And you lost it to a child. That's your fault, not hers. Let this be a lesson, Atticus. You want to be a *vor*, but you're not even aware of common pickpockets."

I felt Atticus's defeat rock through his body. If he didn't hate me before, he would certainly hate me now. And he would definitely murder me.

"Now back to work you go," Dymetrus ordered. "You'll need your wages even more after tonight."

Atticus swallowed thickly, probably the pride that refused to wash itself down, and turned around. But before he'd made it two steps, Roman called after him. "And you're not to lay a hand on this girl. We are not in the business of hurting children, Atticus. Is that understood?"

I turned just enough to watch Atticus nod stiffly. "I understand," he said. And then stalked back to his table.

For some idiotic reason, I felt more vulnerable now that Atticus wasn't here with me. Sure, he wanted to gut me. But he was also the buffer between me and the *pakhan*. Now it was just me standing before them and I had no idea why they hadn't dismissed me yet.

"Th-thank y-you," I told them, deciding that was what they were waiting for.

"What did you really take?" Roman asked. My heart picked up speed, racing in my chest. He stared at me with crystal clear clarity, like he could see right through me, like he could see every thought in my head and unspoken word hiding on my tongue.

The truth sat there, waiting to be confessed. Of course, I would tell him the truth. Lying to Roman Volkov was the stupidest thing I could do.

It was suicide.

He would probably pull out his gun and shoot me right here in front of his men. In front of my dad.

And yet, I couldn't make myself tell him what he wanted to hear. I'd gotten away with it. Atticus's wallet had been a distraction and it had worked.

I wasn't going to give up Sayer's chain.

I'd earned it.

"His money," I said, the words wrapped with confidence I didn't feel.

Roman took a menacing step forward, threatening me with his body. He rippled with power. Cruel intent vibrated off him like a palpable thing in the air. This man wasn't just dangerous, he was evil. He had the authority to end me. And Sayer. And my dad. He was everything bad guys were made of and he knew I wasn't telling the truth. "Don't lie to me."

My chin lifted in defiance and the lie hiding in my inner being became a feral creature protecting the truth. It prowled back and forth inside me, baring razor-sharp teeth dripping with venom. "You're my dad's boss," I told him. "I would never lie to you." I turned to my dad, shooting him a terrified look. My eyes begged him to help me.

When I looked back at Roman, his perceptive gaze had narrowed. "Your dad works for me, but do you really know who I am?"

I dropped my eyes, a play of respect, and tucked my hands into my pockets. My fingertips brushed the chain, but I kept my expression the same. "Y-you're the *pakhan*."

"That's right," he confirmed gently, softer than I'd ever heard him speak before. He wanted me to trust him, to let down my guard. "I'm the *pakhan*. Which means I am the ultimate authority. I own all of the men in this warehouse. I own your father. And most of all, I own you. I'll give you one more chance to tell me the truth, child. Tell me what you took from Atticus and you'll be free, without consequences. Lie to me again and I will break both of your dad's hands. Is that what you want? Do you want me to break your father's hands?"

I hiccupped a sob and it was real. Shaking my head back and forth, I sniffled, "No, please don't. Please don't hurt my daddy."

His voice remained cold, completely devoid of emotion. "Then tell me what you really took from Atticus."

My lungs shuddered as I tried to steady my breathing. The truth pushed forward in my mouth, demanding that I spill it.

I had no doubt that Roman would follow through with his threat. Boris moved toward my dad, putting a heavy hand on his shoulder.

My dad wasn't a small man, but Boris towered over him. All bulk and Russian grit, the spy was made of only muscle and hatred. Dad didn't say anything, but his eyes pleaded with me to give Roman whatever he wanted.

The truth.

The necklace.

Whatever this scary man demanded.

But I knew something my dad didn't. If I told Roman the truth, my dad would be saved but I wouldn't be. Boris might break both of my dad's hand, but he would cut off one of mine. Broken bones healed, but medical science had yet to make a hand regrow. My fate would rest with the man I lied to.

I would risk Dad to save myself. The hardest con game I had played yet.

Letting the tears fall unchecked, I turned back to Roman with a trembling chin. "Please don't hurt him," I begged softly. "I didn't take anything but the wallet." I sniffled and pulled the money from my pocket. "You can have it. You can have all of it. It's all I took, I swear." Roman only stared at me, so I pushed forward, hiccupping more lies until they sounded like truth, until I believed them myself. "It was just a dare. I was bored and I just wanted to do something. It was just a dare to see if I could get his wallet. It was stupid. I'm sorry. Here, take the money. I don't even want it. I'm so sorry."

Nobody reached for the money. They didn't need Atticus's hundred bucks.

"Who dared you?" Dymetrus asked quietly, his voice hard rock against my soft, mushy tears.

"F-Frankie," I wailed louder than I needed to. "I'm so sorry."

The three bosses looked across the warehouse to where their niece still sat against the wall, and back to me.

"Please," I begged. "I'm so sorry. I'll never do it again. I swear. I'm so sorry. Please don't hurt my dad. Please believe me."

Roman's expression wrinkled in disgust. "Enough, girl. No more of the useless crying."

I wiped at my nose with the back of my hand, and took a trembling breath desperate to follow that order. It was difficult, but I managed to stop the flow of tears by keeping my eyes downcast, focused on the floor and not the scary men getting ready to do something awful.

"What do you think, Roman?" Aleksander asked, amusement ringing in his jovial voice. "Is the girl lying? Should we have her father's hands broken?"

Dymetrus laughed next, the tension miraculously breaking. "It looks as though Boris is dying to break some bones, brother. Maybe we should give him this kindness, *da*?"

Roman chuckled, low and sinister. "No, brothers, the girl has promised she isn't lying. I'm inclined to believe her."

All the men in the half circle let out surprised chuckles. "Is that so?" Ozzie asked.

"She has promised that the money was all she took. Atticus hasn't claimed that she's taken anything else. There's no reason to continue torturing the girl."

I kept my eyes trained on my shoes, so they wouldn't see the victory I knew was there. "Th-thank you," I told them with another sniffle. "Thank you so much."

"All right, girl, get out of here," Rocco ordered.

I spun around, my tears already dried and my fear disappearing quickly. There was a smile trying to break free on my face so I determined not to turn around or look at them again. Instead, I threw myself into my dad's arms and hugged him tightly, burying my face in his flannel jacket that smelled like cigarettes and cheap whiskey.

He wrapped his arms around me and kissed the top of my head affectionately. More scheming. More conning.

From both of us.

He started scolding me softly, but I couldn't hear him. My ears were whooshing with the disbelief that I'd gotten away with it. I'd conned the *pakhan*.

I'd stolen from Atticus.

"Caroline," Roman called from behind me.

Shit.

Shit, shit, shit.

I half turned my head, keeping my cheek pressed against my dad's chest. "Yes?"

"You have a gift. I have not seen anyone so young lie so proficiently before," Roman told me. It was a compliment. And at the same time, it was not at all a compliment. "You are very convincing."

I immediately started to protest. "I didn't—"

He held up a hand, cutting me off. "When you get older you will work for me."

My dad moved me around his body, stepping in front of me. "Roman, that is too generous. Your offer is very kind, but she's—"

"She will come work for me, Leon," Roman insisted. "When she is thirteen. That is how many years?" I opened my mouth, but Roman quickly added, "The truth this time, *krasivaya devushka.*"

"Th-three," I whispered. "I'm ten."

"Three years then," Roman agreed. Then he turned away from me and resumed his discussion with his brothers.

I sucked in a deep breath that felt like life and death all at once.

"Are you an idiot?" My dad hissed against the top of my head as he pressed another kiss there. "Goddamn, Caro, how could you be so careless?"

I stepped back from him, hating him in this moment. This was his fault. Didn't he see that? He brought me into this world. He kept me here. He regularly made me go on jobs for him. Did he really think I was somehow safe from this life?

I was in a warehouse filled with stolen guns. At midnight. Because he was afraid the Irish would find me if he left me at home.

And this was my fault?

"You're surprised? And here I thought this was a family business. Just trying to make me dear, old dad proud." Turning around, I skirted along the edges of the warehouse until I was safe with my friends again—the people as equally forced into this ugly world as I was.

I sat down next to Frankie and laid my head on her shoulder. She didn't say anything. Gus didn't either. There was nothing to say.

Out of the three of us, I had been the most likely to escape this world. To get out. And now I was as tied to it as they were. My fate was sealed. I had three years to run away or sell my soul to the devil himself.

We eventually fell asleep, huddled together against the wall. We kept each other warm, and hid each other's secrets and didn't speak of the future or what had happened tonight or the sorrow that filled us all.

I didn't see Sayer again until the guns were all unpacked and loaded into trucks headed in separate directions. I had awoken to find most of the warehouse cleared out. Frankie had left a few hours earlier with her uncles and Gus was nowhere to be seen.

Deciding I should find my dad before he left me, I stretched my stiff legs and set out to search for him. The warehouse was eerily quiet now, littered with trash and the peace these men were leaving behind. War. War with the Irish. We'd be lucky to survive.

Sayer was hiding behind stacks of now empty boxes when I reached the far corner of the warehouse. He reached out when I walked by and grabbed my hand, yanking me behind the cardboard with him.

"Hey," he hissed. "Are you crazy?"

Too tired to defend myself, I blinked at him and said, "Maybe." Guess, we were jumping right into it then.

"He could have killed you! Or broken your dad's hands!"

"I know," I agreed through a yawn. "But if I had told him the truth he would have done those things no matter what."

"You shouldn't have done that," Sayer snarled. "That was stupid."

Irritated with him for blaming me, I slammed my hands on my hips. "No, I saved myself. That was smart. You're the one that lost something important. That makes you the stupid one."

He made an ugly face. "Yeah, well maybe I should learn to lie like you."

My eyes bugged. "Uh, yeah! How else do you expect to stay alive? You're already in the life, so you better figure it out fast. Don't be stupid anymore. And never, ever get caught."

His expression softened at the same time his eyes lightened, like a switch had been turned on in them. "You got it?"

Glancing around to make sure nobody was looking at us, I retrieved the necklace from my pocket. It was a simple silver chain with a key looped through. Plain. Simple. Insignificant. But Sayer's entire body relaxed at the sight of it. "Thank you," he whispered.

I dropped it into his hand and he closed his fist around it at the same time he closed his eyes. I felt funny looking at him, seeing the relief on his face and the affection he had for this one tiny thing. Sayer felt more for this one necklace than I had ever felt for anything, even my dad. This weird key, necklace thing was something he loved, something he would have found a way to get back by himself had I not offered.

Clearing my throat, I hoped to pull him out of whatever it was that he was doing. I felt uncomfortable. And he had a deal to settle.

"Okay, let's see it," I said to him.

His eyes opened, looking truly confused. "See what?"

"The tattoo," I growled. "It's your turn. Pay up."

He rolled his eyes. "You really want to see it?"

"Show it to me already."

Fastening the necklace around his neck first, he took his sweet time tucking it beneath his T-shirt and then putting his hands on the hem of his shirt.

I felt weird again.

Where was this tattoo?

"All right, you asked for it," he mumbled.

He began lifting his shirt slowly, revealing a tanned, flat stomach. I quickly glanced around again, embarrassed by everything. Every single thing.

And yet too fascinated to tell him to stop.

He was so different looking than when I first met him. He was clean this time and he didn't smell bad. Actually, he kind of smelled good. His hair had been trimmed and he'd started to put on weight so he didn't look like a skeleton anymore.

There was a long scar over the plane of his stomach, reaching from his ribs, across his middle, straight through his belly button. I was fixated on that long, puckered line of white flesh. How had he gotten that? Had it been bad?

Whatever had caused it had to have been bad for it to be that long and pronounced.

I was about to ask him about it, when his shirt lifted all the way over his chest to reveal an orthodox cross just over his heart. I forgot all about his scar in an effort to take in all the details of that tattoo.

The lines were still red and raised and it was shiny from the salve he'd put over it. But it was breathtaking all the same. Darkly beautiful. The old style of cross looked so big on his thin frame, and too mature for his thirteen-year-old body.

It was the mark of the syndicate.

It was his mark as a thief.

He was theirs now, for life.

With one tattoo, he'd sealed his fate.

I had leaned forward without realizing it. Raising a trembling hand, I softly traced the lines of the cross, finding the number six in the center. He sucked in a sharp breath at my touch, his chest jerking, bringing me fully awake to realize I was only a couple inches away from him and my hands were on him.

73

Blinking up at him, I took a small step back. "Sorry," I whispered. "It's pretty."

He leaned forward, erasing the space I'd just put between us. His blue eyes darkened with laughter. "Pretty?"

"Er, not pretty. I mean, cool. It looks cool."

"I thought you hated it?" he asked. "I thought you hated this life."

"I do." I tucked my hair behind my ear and willed my feet to stay still. "I, uh, I'm just glad you're not dead."

His head dropped toward mine. I lifted my face thinking he was going to tell me a secret. "Me too," he whispered. "I have you to thank for that."

Then he kissed me.

Kissed me!

My mouth was half open and my eyes were all the way open and I wasn't expecting it at all. But he didn't seem to care. His lips brushed mine, and then again, and then for longer. They were so much softer than I expected. And wetter. And my stomach did this weird flipping thing and I thought about kneeing him in the balls, and at the same time asking him to kiss me again.

But before I could do any of that or get my thoughts together or just run away, he murmured, "See you round, Six," in my ear and walked away.

I stayed there for a long time, until my dad started calling my name because he couldn't find me.

Sayer Wesley had just kissed me. Sayer Wesley had just kissed me after I'd risked my life to steal his necklace and been promised to the syndicate. And all I could think about was doing it again.

I didn't care about working for Roman or that Atticus was probably going to try to kill me anyway or how pissed my dad was going to be. Not when I had Sayer to think about.

Not when I had decided that Sayer wasn't supposed to be in my life, he was supposed to be gone already. Yet here he was, carving out a permanent place for himself in the brotherhood.

And in my heart.

Chapter Seven

Present Day

"Mommy, can we get ice cream?" Juliet asked excitedly as we walked main street Wednesday evening.

I'd felt too cooped up in our apartment, too imprisoned by close walls and a life that felt like the lie that it was. The weather was cooling down, so we wrapped up in warm cardigans and scarves and headed for supper at our favorite diner. Then I tucked her little hand into mine and we strolled the sidewalks like tourists, browsing gift shops and T-shirt stands.

"I don't know," I hesitated. "I only buy ice cream for little girls with manners."

Realizing her mistake, she started bouncing on her toes. "Please, Mommy. Please?"

She had the sweetest voice, a little raspy and a whole lot innocent. I never wanted to forget how she said her words with childish excitement that melted my heart. "Oh, good." I smiled. "You're a little girl with manners. Whew."

She grinned at me. "Does that mean we get ice cream?"

"That means we definitely get ice cream."

The building with the ice cream and candy shop was old, whitewashed brick walls and creaky wood floors. There was a wraparound deck out the back door with little tables where you could watch the live music at Foote's Rest, the outdoor BBQ joint next door.

We grabbed our double scoop cones and headed out there to enjoy the sound of bluegrass music and an open sky where stars were just starting to make their appearance for the night. The mountain peaks had started to blend in with the backdrop overhead and the crisp air made us snuggle close together while we ate our treats.

"Jules?" I asked when she'd made it to the cone part of her dessert and I didn't have to keep cleaning her up every other bite.

"Hmm?" she asked as she crunched down on the waffle cone.

"What would you think about going on a trip?"

"With Aunt Francesca?"

I nodded. "Yeah. What if the three of us went someplace new?"

"When?"

"Soon," I told her. "I think we need an adventure in our lives."

"I do too," she agreed. "We should take me to the horses."

Her comment caught me off guard, but I should have been expecting it. "Um, I was thinking of an adventure with a car." And a million miles away from this place.

Maggie had thrown the flower away before I'd been able to get a second look at it, but I'd shown the note to Francesca. We had both been freaked out. Even days after, the memory of opening that box sent a chill down my spine.

I had the urge to run. The need to run fast. But it wasn't that simple.

Frisco wasn't DC It wasn't easy to drum up new identifications for three people, especially when one was a child. Plus, we needed to move money. We had a big stash of cash, but we'd be leaving behind a significant amount in bank accounts. And there were other things. Stupid things. Like an irrational attachment to this place and what little friends I'd made and the mountains.

This was where Juliet had been born. This was where we'd carved out a life for ourselves.

I just wanted to be absolutely sure before we left all of this behind that we *needed* to leave it all behind.

After the nightmares Francesca and I had abandoned in DC, this place felt too close to utopia to turn our backs on.

Still, I wasn't an idiot. I had our go-bags packed. I had enough cash to last us a while. And Frankie and I had a plan to get out of town at a second's notice. If another package showed up, we were gone. We wouldn't even open it first.

Feeling on edge, I scanned the people eating, drinking beer and watching the band on stage. The lead singer had paused their set to take requests. Currently they were singing *Piano Man* by Billy Joel, which was only slightly awkward since they didn't have a piano. But it was always a crowd favorite, and this crowd seemed to especially love it.

"You promised to take me to the horses," Juliet reminded me. "You said Jesse would let me ride the big ones this time."

I had said that. But I hadn't really meant it.

Jesse and I had met at one of street carnivals Frisco threw every couple months. He had been there representing the ranch, in charge of the ponies for the kids to ride. Juliet had been terrified at first. Which was fine with me. I was in no hurry to help her conquer that particular fear.

But then Jesse had come along and somehow appealed to the courageous, brave, independent little girl inside her. He'd coaxed her onto one of his gentle ponies and then given her three rides in a row— effectively pissing off all the other moms and kids and every tourist in Summit County.

Afterward, he'd invited us out to his ranch so Juliet could keep riding. He had claimed that he didn't want her to regress. She lived in Colorado. It was wholly unacceptable to be afraid of horses.

I knew he'd been flirting with me. But I also knew his reputation around town. I also knew my indomitable will.

I just hadn't been anticipating how charming Jesse would be. Or how much I would genuinely like and respect the guy. Our friendship had developed naturally.

And so had his relationship with Juliet.

Which usually I appreciated. Just not right now. Not when I was trying to get us the hell out of dodge and she was reminding me how stupidly and sentimentally attached to this place I'd gotten.

"You're too little for the big ones," I argued.

Her expression turned stubborn in all of one second. Her button nose wrinkled and her chin jutted out. "Jesse said I'm just big enough."

"Jesse is not your mother. He doesn't get to tell you what to do. That's my job."

"But he can sweet talk your mama into seeing it his way."

77

Juliet and I swiveled at the same time. Jesse was standing directly behind us, his hands resting on our chairs. "Jesse!" Juliet squeaked in elation at the same time I hissed, "Holy shit!"

Jesse's brows furrowed at my curse word in front of my daughter. I wasn't a perfect mom, but I did try to keep colorful language at a minimum when she was around. When I was her age, I could cuss with the best of them. I was trying to save her from that childhood—the one that lacked innocence and naivety and wholesomeness.

"You scared me," I told him by way of an explanation.

He grinned back. "I didn't mean to sneak up on you. I saw you two sitting over here and came to say hi, but then you were talking about me. So..."

I raised an eyebrow. "You eavesdropped for a while?"

His smile turned guilty. "Just a little bit."

This man! Unbelievable. "Your penance is to explain to this darling little girl that she is too small for the big horses."

"Wh-what?" His big man hands dropped helplessly to his side and he looked totally crushed. "But she's not—"

"Jesse Hasting..." I warned.

Before he could turn his puppy dog eyes into weapons of mass destruction, the singer started another request. Juliet started jumping up and down and squealing, "Mommy! Mommy! It's your song!"

Jesse lifted his head and stared at the musician, listening while the beginning bars of "Sweet Caroline" came to life over the speakers.

His low laughter was sincere when he looked back at me. "Sweet Caroline."

The audience echoed a boisterous, "Ba, ba, baaaa!"

I smiled and it felt surprisingly nostalgic. "Yep. I was named after a Neil Diamond song."

"Oh, you were actually named after this song?" Jesse asked, his dimple popping out.

"Yes. Yes, I was. My dad was a big fan. 'Sweet Caroline' is his favorite."

"I'm named after him too," Juliet added.

Jesse gave her his full attention. "Who? Your grandpa?"

"No, Meal Diamonds," Juliet corrected him.

"Juliet." I went on to explain to Jesse, "It's another song by Neil Diamond. Not as popular. But just as good."

He nodded. "Yeah, I know Juliet. Another of your dad's favorites?"

My lips lifted in something that was not quite a smile. "No."

I didn't like to talk about my dad. And I really didn't want Jesse asking questions about him. But I could sense where this was going. The door had been opened. His curiosity had been piqued. Now he would want to know if my dad was still alive. And did I ever go visit him? And what brought me to Frisco to begin with.

I stifled a groan. People were so obnoxiously predictable.

But Jesse surprised me by saying, "You could have gone with 'Cherry.'"

I stared at him and blinked. "You really know your Neil Diamond."

He shrugged. "It's either country or oldies out here. Growing up I preferred oldies."

For some reason that made me like him even more. I pictured a teenage Jesse, white T-shirt and dirty Levi's, skinny arms and a six-pack of abs—because he couldn't help it—with Neil Diamond playing on the radio in his old truck. Goose bumps pulled the hair on my arms to standing. What would my life have been like if I would have met Jesse as a kid?

Away from DC?

Away from the life?

I closed my eyes briefly and imagined myself as a teenager. My heart kicked and shame fizzled through my blood, snuffing the oxygen out of me. Jesse would have hated me as a teen.

I would have eaten him alive.

"Jesse, when can I ride the horsies?" Juliet demanded. Her chin dripping with chocolate ice cream.

Tilting my head, I stared at my brave, courageous, disobedient child in mortified awe. "Juliet Leighton. You cannot be serious."

Her innocent eyes widened with confusion. "I am serious, Mommy. I want to serious ride the horsies."

Giving Jesse a helpless look, I bit my lip to keep from laughing.

"Your mama said no to the big horsies. Remember, Jules? And unfortunately, she's the mom, so we have to do what she says."

Juliet's lips thrust forward in a pout. "You don't got to do what she says. She's not your mama."

Jesse chuckled, his laugh like a warm fire on a cold night. This man was trouble. The kind that made me envy how easy normal life could be. Usually I was better at keeping my guard up, at maintaining a safe distance between us. But tonight I didn't have the willpower for it.

It took work to stay away from Jesse. At first the pain from my past had been so fresh, that I didn't have room for Jesse in my life. But now life had settled down and there were too many empty moments of my day to think about how lonely I felt.

And how long it had been since I got laid.

I wasn't even sure if I remembered the mechanics of the whole ordeal at this point.

But it wasn't just about my more basic needs either. I hadn't been intimate with a man in the same amount of time. I hadn't been held or touched or told how beautiful I looked in my little black dress. I hadn't been the center of someone's attention or felt the constant buzzing of butterflies as we peeled back the layers and got to know one another.

This reconsidering of my boundaries had more to do with loneliness than horniness. It was easy to turn down a date when I convinced myself it was just about the sex. It was harder to turn down Jesse Hasting when I realized the components of my life that were missing were the ones I needed the most.

And tonight, he smelled so good. He was wearing a fuzzy lined flannel shirt and well-worn jeans and I had the craziest urge to wrap my arms around his waist, under his jacket. I wanted to press my body against his and let him remind me that I wasn't just a mom, but that I was a woman too. That I wasn't just a girl with a past, but a woman that had a future here.

Here specifically.

The mountains had worked their mysterious magic on me. I didn't want to leave Frisco.

I didn't want to run again.

I didn't want Juliet to have to run with me.

"How about this, Juliet. How about you let me take your mama out on a date this weekend and I'll see if I can't sweet talk her into letting you try out one of the big ones. Does that sound like a plan?"

Juliet's entire face lit up, her smile brightening the dark night with pure, innocent glee. "That sounds like a plan!"

Jesse turned to me and waggled his eyebrows. "How about you, Caroline? Does it sound like a plan to you too?"

"You're unbelievable," I told him. If only I hadn't been smiling.

He leaned in. "A little birdy told me you enjoy art."

I raised an eyebrow. Where was this going? And who had told him that?

Jesse nodded down Main Street. "I don't know if you heard about the new gallery opening this weekend? But Friday is opening night and I'd love to take you, Caroline."

Sucking my bottom lip between my teeth I tried not to look happy or flattered or interested. Juliet climbed on my lap and I pulled her against me, wrapping my arms around her tiny waist. She turned her face and kissed my cheek. "Please, Mommy? Please go with Jesse and talk about the big horses?"

I slowly shook my head at Jesse. This was impressive. He'd managed to con me—the con! I was trapped between my relentless affection for my daughter and his stupidly adorable dimple!

Plus, I really did want to go to the gallery opening. The name had caught my attention first. The DC Initiative.

It reminded me of home. The good parts of home.

I'd asked around about it in town and apparently the owners were wealthy business guys from back east. A few years ago, that would have freaked me out and sent me into a tailspin of panic until I met them. But after spending some time in Summit County, I was familiar with wealthy people moving here from either coast. They bought up rental properties and tourist shops like they were playing Monopoly. They never lived here permanently, but they sure managed to make a whole lot of money from a distance.

The DC Initiative was apparently another east coaster trying to make a quick buck by offering the tourists a bit of culture. It was supposed to be part fine art gallery and part swanky cocktail lab or something.

I'd also resigned myself to the realization that it wasn't going to be kid friendly and I would have to wait a very long time before I got to check it out.

Jesse's offer was a dangling carrot in front of a starving bunny.

"I don't know," I told him. "I'd have to find a babysitter and on Fridays we usually do—"

"Aunt Francesca could watch me!" Juliet offered. "We can do pizza night without you one time." She turned to face me with folded hands in the prayer position. "Please, Mommy. Please, please, please!"

Well, it was true. Francesca could watch her. Whatever social life she'd attempted when we first moved here had fizzled a couple years ago. Her schedule was as exciting as mine. Which meant she would have nothing going on Friday night except for a date on the couch with Juliet and me.

Jesse held up his hands in a similarly pleading pose. "Please, Caroline? Please, please, please!"

I dropped my head back so I didn't have to look at these two traitors in cahoots. "Ugh," I told the stars, feeling my resolve crumbling. "You two are bad influences on each other."

"I'll have you home by ten," Jesse added, sweetening the pot. "So you don't miss all of movie night."

My eyes narrowed. "You've been talking to Francesca?"

"She thought this was a great idea when we ran into each other at the grocery store the other day," he said quickly.

Rolling my eyes, I gave up completely, "I bet she did."

I breathed deeply through my nose and gave into Jesse and myself for maybe the first time in five years. "Okay, Jesse. I'll go with you. Thank you for inviting me."

His smile deepened, turning me into a melty pile of goo. "Thank *you* for finally saying yes. We're going to have a great night." His expression turned teasing. "In fact, it's probably going to change your life."

My smile disappeared. I knew he was kidding, but his words hung in the air with a permanency I didn't like.

I didn't want my life to change. I liked my life the way it was.

Chapter Eight

"What am I doing?" I felt the panic start as a pinpoint, but quickly blossom into painful streaks across my chest.

"My hair," the most precious giggle answered my question. "But I think you forgot."

I looked down at the mass of dark curls wrapped in my fingers. Juliet tipped her head back and wrinkled her button nose at me. "Did you forget about me?"

I smiled at her. It was impossible to look at her porcelain skin, sprinkling of light freckles and dark, blue eyes and not smile at her. She was the most beautiful thing I had ever seen. And I could hardly believe I had some hand in creating her. "Never! I could never forget about you. I made you, you know. You're ingrained in my brain."

Her shrewd eyes narrowed. "Then maybe you forgot you," she concluded. "Because I've been sitting here forever!"

"Okay, okay, Miss Thing. Sit still. I'm almost finished."

"I have been sitting still," she grumbled.

Her attention turned back to the TV, and this time I tried to focus on braiding her hair. My fingers weaved through her thick, soft strands as I pulled at it gently.

Before Juliet was born, I didn't know how to braid. I didn't know how to do most female rituals. But it was funny what having a child forced you to learn.

"Mommy, are you an alien?"

I looked down at her again as I tied the hairband around one braid and moved onto the second. The question did not even faze me. "If I'm an alien then you're an alien."

She giggled making that squealing sound that always made me laugh too. "I mean, are you an alien tonight? You keep forgetting to listen to me!"

I leaned over and pressed a kiss to the top of her freshly washed forehead. "I'm sorry, Jules. I'm sad that I'm not going to tuck you into bed tonight. It's making me spacy."

"Don't be sad, Mommy. Just stay with me. Jesse can watch the movie with us and you can talk about the big horsies here."

I finished her second braid and spun her around to face me. "I would love to stay home and watch the movie with you." The roaring panic stretched to my fingertips and made them tingle. It reached up to my shoulders and neck and pulled my muscles tight.

I glanced at my phone on the kitchen counter. Maybe I could still cancel? Would it be rude to call him while he was probably already on his way?

As if in answer to my silent questions, the apartment buzzer blared through the room. I dropped the hairbrush on my toe and nearly fell backward in surprise.

"We need a different buzzer," I told Juliet while she watched me with an exasperated expression.

I wobbled over to the voice box in three-inch heels. "Hello?"

"Let me up!" Francesca shouted into the box. "I forgot my keycard."

I buzzed her up and unlocked the door so she could let herself in. I turned around to find Juliet twirling in happy circles with her arms spread wide. "The pizza's here! Finally!"

I leaned my hip against the island and crossed my arms. "Oh, have you been waiting a long time?"

She stopped twirling and matched my pose with arms crossed and eyebrows raised. "Mommy, I'm starving to death!"

Her adorable attitude calmed some of my racing nerves, but just barely. I walked over to the microwave and checked my reflection in the glass.

I'd pulled my dark hair into a pretty, sophisticated bun low on my neck and applied more makeup than I had in years. I used to keep my hair chin length, in a bob that was low maintenance and flattering. After I had Juliet, my hair had changed enough that a new hairstyle was in order. Besides, I had wanted to shed my East Coast look and change it up. Not just because it was safer this way, but because I didn't want to remember the person I used to be. Frankie had done the same thing—only she'd finally been able to chop hers short.

My little black dress was way too little and tight and short, but Francesca swore my unattractive bits remained hidden and my boobs were safely tucked away thanks to the high collar and long sleeves. Juliet had saved me from a lot of things, but she'd also helped me lose some pieces of me that I hoped to find again, like my before-baby body and sex appeal.

I hadn't dressed up in years. I spent most of my life in yoga pants and thermals at home, and what could only be described as hiking chic when I was at work—tunics and leggings paired with my oh, so stylish hiking boots. I didn't go anywhere else. My life with Juliet, raising her by myself, was simple, but also busy. There wasn't much time outside of our necessary routine.

Which was how I liked it.

I liked to control every last detail. I lived for routine and repetitive structure. I was at my best when things were mundane and predictable.

Francesca swept into the small apartment with all of the vivaciousness and energy of a woman possessed. In an alternate reality, Frankie was the kind of girl that would be quickly climbing her way to the top of a corporate ladder right about now. She had the focus and drive to command huge companies. And the ruthless instinct to run the rest of them out of business.

In our current life, she had been raised to head another kind of business empire. And had we stayed in DC, she would have excelled in the role her uncles had designed for her. She would have kicked ass.

Which was just one of the many reasons we had to get out of there. For Frankie's sake.

To be honest, she was a little lost here. She liked her management position at the Lodge, but I could tell she was bored. She was bored with our whole life. Not enough to want to go back to DC, but enough that I had been worried about her lately.

She was used to constant activity and a high level of authority. Here she was low level management without friends or a social life or a purpose. She was trying to be happy. She was trying to be thankful. But I saw the struggle. And I understood it. If I didn't have Juliet, I could imagine myself just like her, afraid to try because it would mean potential exposure, afraid to make friends because she didn't trust anybody. Afraid to be happy because the other shoe could drop at any moment. Purposeless, listless, rudderless.

But she was trying. For us.

"Whoa, Mama!" Francesca whistled when she took in my evening ensemble. "You look… you look like…"

"Like I'm trying too hard?"

Her dark eyes narrowed. "I was going to say like a woman. A real, live woman."

I turned back to the microwave, wondering if I should wipe off some of my fire engine red lipstick. "I think it's too much. He's going to think that I'm… that I'm…"

"Into him?" She smiled at our game, but panic tightened my chest.

"I can't do this."

Francesca picked up Juliet and plopped her on a high barstool. "You can!" she sing-songed to me.

"I'll just stay home," I decided. "I'll hang with you two."

Frankie and Juliet glared at me, twin stares of impatient judgment. "You're not staying here with us," Francesca insisted. "We plan to misbehave for the next four hours, eat way too much candy and stay up long past our bedtime. You'll ruin all of our fun."

Juliet looked up at Frankie like she was an angel sent from heaven.

I turned around and leaned back on my hands, pressing them against the cool granite counter. "Frankie, I'm serious. I can't do this."

She smoothed her hand down Juliet's braids before looking over at me with a solemn expression. "Caro, you can. You've been hiding yourself for too long. You can't lock yourself in this apartment forever."

I stared at my little girl and knew that I could. Knew that I probably should. The world was an insidiously dark place. I knew more than most how many dangers lurked in the shadowed places. I could easily stay locked in this apartment to keep her safe… to save her.

To save me too.

Frankie walked over to me, deliberately blocking Juliet from my sight. She rested her hip on the kitchen island and softened her voice so Jules couldn't hear everything.

86

"It's just one date," she reasoned. "It's not a marriage proposal. He won't even expect sex. You're just going to an event that you want to go to anyway. That's all."

"I'm freaking out," I whispered to her. "I can't feel my face."

Her lips twitched with a gentle smile. "You didn't take something trippy did you?"

I glared at her. "Of course not."

She leaned forward. "I wouldn't blame you. Jesse is..." She trailed off to fan her face with her hand.

Her enthusiasm for my date did not help me settle down. Nobody was more aware of how long it had been since I'd been on one of these. And even back then... it wasn't...

Well, it wasn't this.

"I'm too old to date. Shouldn't I be trolling the internet or resigning myself to my bedside drawer? This is ridiculous!"

"Oh my God, Caro," she growled and laughed at the same time. "You're twenty-five! You're hardly facing a midlife crisis! Most girls our age are out every night."

My gaze flickered back to Juliet. Determination mingled with the hysterical lunatic inside me. There was nothing I wouldn't do to protect my little girl.

And I just didn't know if dating while she was so young was the right decision for her.

"Yeah, well, I'm not most girls."

"You're right," Frankie agreed seriously. "You're so much better."

I returned my focus to my best friend of my entire life and smiled at her. Besides Juliet, she was the only family I had left. I would be lost without her.

"This is why I keep you around," I said. "I need you to boost my self-esteem before I leave the house."

She rolled her eyes and pulled out her cell phone. "You keep me around because I babysit for free and order enough pizza for you to eat when you come home."

"Those things are also true." My smile died when the buzzer once again blasted through the room. "Oh my God, that's him."

"You look hot, Caroline. Go have the best damn night of your life." She slapped my butt as I shuffled to Juliet. I let out a squeak while Jules laughed at our antics.

"I love you, munchkin. Be good for Aunt Francesca or she'll eat all of your pizza."

"I'm always good for Aunt Francesca!" Juliet insisted.

"So it's just me that gets the attitude?"

She smiled a smile that reminded me of my dad and I immediately wanted to lock her in her room for the rest of her life to save us all the trouble. "It's just for you, Mommy. I know you love me the most."

"This is true." I kissed her nose and squeezed her tightly.

When the buzzer shrieked again, I reluctantly let her go and grabbed the clutch I'd bought earlier today that went perfectly with my dress. I hadn't had anything more than an old Target tote and a hiking backpack lying around my apartment. I knew Jesse wouldn't mind if I showed up in jeans, an old T-shirt and a Duct tape wallet, but if I was going to do this, I was going to do it right. No more hiding behind the single mom version of me. Or the blending into the wall version. Jesse had gotten to know me over the years, maybe not all of me, but enough to want to take me out on a date. So out of respect for him and our friendship and these real, but terrifying feelings I had for him, I was done hiding.

At least in the existential meaning of the word.

In every other area of my life, I was still very much, very necessarily hiding.

I jabbed the button with my freshly painted nail and said, "Be right down!" I didn't give him a chance to respond before shouting "I love you" a few times at Juliet, then hurried through the door.

I cursed my heels on the ride down the elevator. Before Juliet, heels had been like second nature to me. I had lived in them. Now I was like a fawn just learning how to walk—Bambi ice skating with Thumper. My old self hovered over my shoulder, silently judging me.

The elevator doors opened and I had to take a steadying breath at the sight of Jesse waiting for me. He stood hovering underneath the awning outside, avoiding the light rain falling on this autumn Colorado night.

I waved to Jesse when he caught sight of me through the clear glass. He shot me a bemused half-smile and I second-guessed this decision for the millionth time. What was I doing? I concentrated on not tripping on the wrinkled rug beneath my towering heels and leaned too hard on the push bar.

The door flew open and I careened dangerously from the building and would have face-planted on the rough concrete if Jesse's large hands hadn't been there to catch me.

"Whoa," he murmured in that deep baritone drawl that had drawn me to him the first time I met him. "Are you okay?"

I blinked up at him, trying to find the answer to that question. His handsome face stared down at me in concern, but amusement twinkled in his brown eyes. "Sorry," I squeaked. "I'm a little unsteady in these shoes."

His eyes traveled the length of me, taking their time in a sweet kind of perusal. They finally found my shoes and one corner of his mouth kicked up in a crooked smile. "I can see why."

"I haven't worn heels in a long time," I explained unnecessarily.

"Do you want to change?"

I shook my head, embarrassed that we were still talking about my walking problems and that he still held me so tightly in his arms. "I'm sure I'll remember how they work. Like riding a bike, yeah?"

The other corner of his mouth joined the first in a genuine smile. "Honestly? I have no idea."

He finished setting me upright and moved his hands to my shoulders to make sure I was steady. "I would have come up to get you."

I took in the chiseled lines of his jaw and his strong Romanesque nose, the subtle curl of his golden-brown hair. His strong, corded neck looked so startlingly tan next to the white of his crisp oxford. "It's okay," I hurried to explain. "This is better."

"Not ready for me to be up in your space?"

I shook my head. I was suddenly afraid that I'd offended him. Had I managed to ruin the night before it began?

That might set some kind of record.

"It's okay," he assured me smoothly. "I get it. You're being a good mom."

I breathed a sigh of relief and some of the panic that had been threatening to choke me all night eased. I didn't let anyone into my space. Where Juliet and I lived was as much of a secret as I could manage it to be. I used Maggie's on the Mountain for my address for everything. Not even the daycare had my real address. Phone number yes, but not place of residence. I wasn't listed in the phone book or on the internet. Frankie was the same way. We were not ever careless with where we lived.

We were just as vigilant about Juliet. Maybe people saw us around town, but I didn't advertise our life for any reason. We only invited a small, select group of people to get to know us—mainly it was just Maggie and Jesse for me. Frankie had a couple friends at work, but nobody she would bring back to our apartment.

Jesse and I had eased gently into friendship and stayed there for two years before he started pursuing me so intently. I trusted him as a friend. And I had tried to make sure we stayed firmly in the friend zone. But there was an attraction between us that I couldn't deny anymore. And Jesse had obviously stopped denying it a while ago.

So here we were. On a date. He was looking better than I had ever seen him. He was calm and so cool—like he always was around me.

And I was trying not to flail my arms and run around in circles like a chicken with her head cut off.

I was jumpy about relationships for good reasons. My experience with men was either highly manipulative and predicated on lies or it was intensely codependent. When it came to men, I couldn't trust myself to make smart decisions.

Jesse was a nice guy, but even after our long friendship, I still wasn't sure I knew that much about him. As sweet as things had started with him, I couldn't help but anticipate everything eventually going south. I was a pessimist waiting for the sky to fall, for Jesse to finally wake up and realize I wasn't a catch—I was a walking disaster.

And I was an expert at running. Even if I stayed in Frisco, there were ways to run from Jesse and cut him out of my life entirely.

"Should we go?" he gestured toward his sleek black truck parked along the curb.

There was a short time in my life when I would have turned my nose up at a truck like Jesse's. I would have expected something sporty. Something insanely expensive. I was used to men obsessed with money and nice things and having everything they wanted. Legally or illegally, it didn't matter. I had been a part of a lifestyle that needed shiny things to prove their value. And maybe I had bought into the lie too. But I was free of that life now. My attention had shifted to things that had meaning.

Like the heat of Jesse's hand on my lower back as he guided me along the sidewalk and the heady scent of his cologne. I listened to the low rumble of his smoky voice and let myself be present in this conversation only.

Those were the things that mattered. For the next few hours, those were the only things that mattered.

He opened the door for me and waited while I climbed up into the truck cab as gracefully as possible. I slid all the way in before he closed the door behind me. When he had crossed in front of the truck and taken his place in the driver's seat, I finally found the courage to speak again.

"This is an interesting concept, yeah? Half-restaurant, half-gallery, half-bar."

Art was my one weakness. It always had been.

And it always got me into trouble.

He smiled at the road as he drove thirty-five miles per hour through zero traffic. "That's three halves."

"This place must be magic then."

He turned to stare at me for a long moment, the truck idling at a stop sign. "Magic, huh?"

I licked my dry lips and tried to breathe evenly. "Just an idea."

"I like that idea, Caroline. And I like you. I'm glad you finally said yes."

"Me too."

My heart punched the inside of my chest at the same time my belly flipped. One of my internal organs calling the other a liar. A cheater. A thief. The other simply responded the way any woman would.

I don't live in DC anymore, I whispered to my heart.

It shriveled two sizes to teach me a lesson. You might not live there, my heart whispered back, but I never left.

In a few more minutes we'd traveled the short distance of Main Street and pulled up in front of a sleek, white-washed brick building vibrant with people and opening night excitement. The light rain cast a dewy glow around the renovated structure, softening the edges and giving it a picturesque quality.

The place was packed, especially for Frisco. People milled all around the building, on the sidewalk in front of the building, around the side, huddled under table umbrellas in a charming little courtyard complete with quaint iron tables and a pergola covered in climbing flowers. The windows to the building were cracked open, spilling out the sound of music and laughter and buzzing chatter. Golden light lit up the inside, illuminating the pieces hanging on the walls and on free-standing displays around the open design space. Waiters hurried back and forth from the bar to the tables to the kitchen and back again.

The setting was perfect.

Completely perfect.

Jesse parked right on the street, down from the main entrance. He hurried around the front of the truck and opened the door for me, helping me down the significant jump to the ground. His hand landed on my waist once I'd hit the ground. "You okay?" he asked, his gaze dipping to my shoes.

"I'm great," I told him sincerely. "This place is amazing."

His smile stretched. "Let's go have some fun, Caroline." He looped my arm through his and led me to the entrance of The DC Initiative.

I relaxed against him, finally letting myself open up and enjoy this perfect evening. The occasional raindrop felt like a familiar kiss on my exposed skin. I took a deep breath and decided to enjoy tonight no matter the cost.

I had to start enjoying my life and stop looking over my shoulder constantly.

It was time to start forgiving myself for the decisions I was forced to make. It was time to bury the dead and find happiness in the land of the living.

Still, my feet faltered just before the front door, a gust of something ominous twirling through me. My mouth dried up as I faced the restaurant-gallery and acknowledged that letting Jesse take me inside would irrevocably change who I was as a person.

It would change every single thing about me.

It would truly be a step in moving on—a step I had once assumed I would never be able to take. Until now.

Until this man.

"Ready?" Jesse asked, his eyes twinkling with promise for the night.

"Ready," I answered, finally... finally feeling ready.

Later I would realize what an absolute idiot I had been.

Chapter Nine

My entire body relaxed inside the gallery. There was so much to see, so much to examine, that I could have ignored Jesse for the entirety of the night.

I had always loved art. Before Juliet, it was the one vice I'd let myself indulge in. I didn't want the fast cars or the jewelry or the stacks of cash—although I had access to all of it. I just wanted the pretty paintings. The abstract ideas brought to life on canvas by the mix of creative genius and a simple paintbrush.

"Wow," I whispered while we waited for the hostess to notice us. "This place is crazy."

Jesse grinned. "This is your thing?"

I nodded. "Oh yeah, this is my thing." The majority of tables were placed along the outer walls by the wide, open windows and the pieces by an artist I didn't immediately recognize hung toward the center. White partitions were placed strategically throughout the space, making it seem like there were separate rooms, but also open at the same time. Everything was well lit and modern, the art showcased with hanging spotlights and the tables set away from the brightest lights.

To the left, a long bar stretched the length of the wall. I recognized one of the bartenders from around town. She was dressed in a black dress kind of like mine, mixing a fancy cocktail. All I wanted to do was get a drink and peruse the paintings. Forget about the date. Forget about dinner. Just give me alcohol and whoever this artist was—because he was fabulous.

The hostess was about to finally acknowledge us when one of the waiters rushed over and whispered something in her ear. She frowned, looked down at her seating chart and then at me. Her eyes narrowed as she continued to listen.

I turned toward Jesse, feeling self-conscious, and discreetly tugged at the hemline of my dress.

He must have felt the weird vibe too, because he turned to me and slipped his hand to my waist. "When I called, they said they didn't do reservations."

Before I could say anything, the hostess called out to us. "How many?"

Jesse turned back to her. "Two."

She looked down at her seating chart as if she hadn't been studying it awkwardly for the last five minutes. "It will be about twenty minutes before a table opens up. You're welcome to the bar in the meantime. We encourage you to grab a drink and enjoy the art on display."

"Is that okay?" Jesse asked sounding a little unsure. I could tell this wasn't his element. I didn't know if it was the gallery part or the swanky bar aspect. Frisco was a pretty chill town and the restaurants and bars reflected that atmosphere. Jesse's nightlife leaned more to Foote's or the nearest German beer joint rather than expensive cocktails and fussy food.

"It's what I've been dying to do since we walked in the door," I told him honestly.

His expression relaxed. "All right then. Let's get a drink and browse."

The hostess waved us toward the bar with a sneer I couldn't decipher. Her behavior was strange enough to make me wonder if I knew her from somewhere. Had I somehow offended her without realizing it? "Do you know her?" I asked Jesse. Maybe he had dated her before. Maybe she was pissed that he was here with me.

"Never seen her before," he replied.

"Hey, Caroline," Cass greeted me as we slid up to the bar. I knew her from Juliet's preschool class. Her son Max was the same age as Juliet.

94

I shook off the weird vibes from the snobby hostess and focused on the pretty bartender. "Hey, Cass. I didn't know you worked here."

She passed a couple drinks off to a waiter and turned her full attention to us. "Yeah, I applied as soon as I heard they were hiring. I was over at Mick's before. But this is better. Closer to home and they're really great about working with my schedule so far."

"That's awesome. It's so hard to find that."

She nodded. "Yeah, the owners are pretty much the best. And isn't this place amazing? This is seriously the coolest bar I've ever been in. They wanted to bring the East Coast to Colorado. I think they pulled it off."

"They did," I agreed although I felt a little weird about how much Cass was gushing about her bosses. She was a single mom like me and we'd bonded over raising kids alone. She was a tough cookie. Her ex had been a real piece of work from what I'd gathered, although she rarely talked about him. The point was, I had never heard her compliment anyone before, except for maybe her son Max.

"Anyway, you're obviously here to drink. Let me help you with that."

"To see the art," I clarified. "The booze is a bonus. Oh, and this is Jesse. Jesse this is Cass. Our kids are in school together."

"The horse guy," she nodded familiarly. "I know you."

The tips of Jesse's ears turned red and I had the pleasure of watching him squirm. "Uh, yeah, horses. The Hasting Ranch outside of town."

Cass's eyes widened. "Ah." Shooting me a sly grin, she nudged a drink menu in front of us. "Well, nice to meet you, Jesse. Take your time deciding on what you want. But to be honest, I make a fucking awesome mojito."

Her reaction embarrassed me for some reason. The Hasting Ranch was well known in Summit County and clearly well off. But Jesse didn't exactly own it. And even if he did, his money was not what finally got me to say yes.

I knew what it looked like though. Cass was a single mom and I knew she was struggling. She worked late shifts when her mom could watch Max. And she struggled to pay the preschool fee every month. She saw me and assumed the same thing.

But I didn't need Jesse's money.

I had my own.

Maybe it wasn't the fortune it had once been, but it was enough for Jules and me.

Although I did take her up on her raspberry mojito and she was not lying. It was amazing. Jesse grabbed a pint of beer from a local brewery and we left the bar to browse the exhibits.

Now that we had settled into the venue, conversation with Jesse grew a little strained. At first we just awkwardly stood in front of a painting, taking in the details silently.

Which was fine with me, but I could feel Jesse getting more and more awkward. I ignored him at first. The painting was breathtaking. A woman's silhouette stood in the center, her body raised up on her tiptoes, her face covered by a long hood. Her toes just barely touched the surface of the water, making it ripple in every direction. Her head tilted to the side and her arms were stretched out. It was mesmerizing. Was she in pain? Or something otherworldly altogether? The background was an interesting mixture of dark sky and exaggerated stars. And in the corner of the piece, the initials swirled together in a way that I couldn't read.

I squinted at them anyway. I felt at home with this painting for some reason, at peace. She wasn't in pain, I decided. She was offering something. A gift.

"It's really beautiful," Jesse murmured when I continued to stare at it.

"Do you see the artist's name anywhere?" I asked him. "I can't find it."

He looked around. "You think these are all by the same person?"

"I think so. Look at the detail, the way the bodies are formed, it's all in the same style. It's an installation by one artist. I just don't recognize any of the pieces."

"You're really into art then?" Jesse asked, sounding surprised. "Do you paint too? Or just appreciate?"

We moved over to the next painting. Another woman, her face only partially covered this time. I blinked at it for a long moment. The woman seemed familiar. I couldn't put my finger on why, but there was something about her face that I recognized.

"I just appreciate," I finally answered Jesse's question. "I mean, I've definitely tried my hand at painting before. Like when I was younger. But I struggled to come up with my own voice."

"What do you mean?"

I tore my eyes from the woman half submerged in the same lake from the last painting. This time her hood had slipped back, only

96

covering her eyes, as she tipped her head back and gasped for one last breath.

Focusing on Jesse, so I could give him my full attention and stop being so rude, I said, "I just never found that original voice inside me, that unique story I had to tell. I got good at copying other artists, replicating what had already been done. But I could never seem to paint something original."

"I find that really hard to believe. You're so... comfortable in your own skin."

My cheeks heated faintly. "Do you mean weird?"

He chuckled. "No, that is not at all what I meant. I mean, you're so confident. So completely sure of who you are. I can't picture you struggling to know yourself. Even in painting."

His compliments soothed some of my old insecurities that I hadn't realized had surfaced until now. "I was younger," I explained. "And truthfully, I didn't really know myself. I've grown up a lot since coming to Colorado. Having a kid will do that to you, I suppose."

"What brought you to Frisco?" His question was so natural that I couldn't even blame him for it.

I had been the one to bring up my move. I had basically opened the door for him. But I still didn't want to answer it. Not even to someone like Jesse who I mostly trusted.

Taking a sip of mojito to stall, I turned back to the painting. This was why I shouldn't date. This reason right here. Where could this even go?

I should have played this out better. I should have thought of every scenario, of every possible outcome. Where was my due diligence?

Sure, I could make this up as I went. I could answer every one of his questions with a lie. But then that would be our relationship—a storybook of lies and half-truths. I could maybe even remember them all and keep them straight, but then Jesse would never fall for me. He'd fall in love with the girl I told him I was, the girl I made up to give him pretty answers that wouldn't get him killed.

I couldn't even get naked in front of him without having to explain the orthodox cross tattooed over my right breast or the puss in boots on my left hip. Symbols of my old life, of my old position as a thief. I was *bratva. I was bratok*, a soldier. I was not Russian by blood, but in every other sense I was one hundred percent Volkov.

But I hadn't played this all the way through because I never thought I'd actually say yes to this man. The fact that not only had I said yes to a

97

date, but also managed not to think about what would happen beyond it said I was seriously losing my touch.

Goddamn, Caro.

It wasn't like I could keep seeing him. I could never be the girlfriend he wanted, expected. I would never open up to him and tell him about my past or what brought me to Colorado or why I had a go-bag stashed in the trunk of my car and cash hidden all over my apartment. I couldn't even answer easy questions honestly, like where were my parents? And why did we never go visit them? Or stupid questions, like, where did you go to elementary school? Do you have Facebook?

I licked dry lips and mumbled the inane excuse I'd given Maggie once upon a time. "I just needed a change of scenery."

He stepped closer, no doubt struggling to hear me. "Really? That's why you moved here?"

I should have known a flippant, canned response wouldn't be enough for Jesse. He wanted a peek into who I really was and what made me make life altering decisions. He wanted to know me, *really* know me. But he could never know the truth. And not just because I was afraid of scaring him or that he would call the police or even that he would judge me. He could never know about my past for his sake. For his protection.

Meeting his gaze again, I threw myself into the lie, the con, the game I could play so easily. He wanted more from me. Well, here was more. "I fell in love with the mountains. It was like love at first sight for me. I wanted to live somewhere with depth and soul and… personality. I thought, why the heck not? I asked Francesca if she wanted to come with me, which of course she did. We threw everything into my car and headed out here. It's been the best decision I've ever made."

His lips stretched into a sweet smile. He believed me. "I agree."

Something about his blind trust took a dig at my heart, tore away at the hard layers I'd built around my callous outlook on life. It made me hate how convincing I was, how good at the game I'd always been. Jesse Hasting was so much better than me. He was the kind of good I would never be. It wasn't fair of me to hold his attraction. He deserved better than me.

A waitress walked by and I latched onto the opportunity to change the subject. "Excuse me." I touched her shoulder before she could speed away. When she turned to me, I gestured at the painting. "Who is the artist? I can't seem to find a name anywhere."

She smiled the same kind of adoring smile Cass had at the bar. "He's one of the owners," she explained. "He and his partner wanted to open with his installment."

Awe swelled inside my chest as I took that in.

"Is he an artist by trade?" Jesse asked before I could. "Or businessman?"

The waitress's smile deepened familiarly. "He claims to be a little of both." She looked around the floor, but we were in the center of the gallery and most of our view was blocked by other paintings and the guests wandering around. "He's around here somewhere. I'll point him out to you if I can find him."

My heart kicked a warning in my chest. A feeling of fear slithered through me, leaving a greasy trail of slime in its wake. I noticed another painting and that same vaguely familiar woman stared back at me from the center. It wasn't just a connection to the emotive work or the artist in some intangible way. I knew this work.

I knew this artist.

"What's his name?" Jesse asked, completely oblivious to the panic kicking my adrenaline into drive.

"Augustus Oswald."

Augustus Oswald.

Augustus.

Oswald.

I knew an Augustus. And I knew an Oswald. Father and son. Only I knew them as Gus and Ozzie.

Oh shit.

Oh shit, oh shit, oh shit.

Taking a step back, I prepared to run. But still some stupid, stubborn part of me refused to accept this as reality.

This couldn't really be happening. They couldn't have found me.

The note. The box with the Dahlia. Mistakes. Coincidences. A cruel twist of meddling fate. But not intentional.

Except I knew better.

The old Caroline would have already been gone. I would have thrown Juliet into the car and not even glanced back at this sleepy town.

I would have been halfway to Mexico by now. Or the moon. Anything to get away from the possibility of being found.

I'd gone soft over the five-year lull. Mushy. I was a marshmallow parading around like a shark. Only marshmallows didn't have instincts and they didn't know how to bite back if they were attacked. They were gooey and useless and not alive.

Holy shit, was I about to not be alive too?

"Oh, there he is." The bubbly waitress pointed across the gallery.

I refused to look.

"Which one?" Jesse asked.

"The one in the hat." I would have bet my kidney that it was a stocking cap. "Our other owner is around here somewhere too," she explained as if letting us in on a secret.

Partner?

I had assumed marriage partners before. Like they were together—partners. But now I realized I had assumed wrong. So very wrong.

I couldn't breathe. I legit couldn't breathe. My lungs started making a wheezing sound and my throat had all but closed up. This couldn't be happening.

I turned my back on Jesse and the waitress and in the opposite direction of Augustus Oswald—such a bullshit name by the way—and scanned the gallery for an escape. But I couldn't see anything! My view was blocked by paintings and dividers and reminders that I had made grievous mistakes in my past—mistakes that I couldn't outrun forever.

The reckoning day had come and I was the least prepared I had ever been.

"You stupid marshmallow," I whispered to myself, clutching at my chest in case the sudden pain there turned out to be an actual heart attack.

"Are you interested in buying a piece?" the waitress went on. "He'd be the one you talk to. Then they'll ring you up at the front."

"Thanks," Jesse told her. "We're still browsing but—"

"Jesse, I don't feel good," I blurted, telling the entire, one hundred percent truth. "I think I'm going to be sick."

His hand landed on my shoulder. "What's wrong?" he asked, sincerely concerned.

I struggled to suck in a breath, to fill my lungs with the oxygen they so badly needed. "I need to go home. I need to go home right now."

"O-okay." Jesse's hand dropped around my waist, helping me forward. But it didn't feel like help. It felt like an anchor slowing me down, holding me back from the escape that I desperately needed.

I wanted to push it off, push him away and just run. And run. And run. And never look back. I winced, feeling my fear like a physical pain. Like a bullet wound in my gut, a knife in my back.

I was almost surprised when I didn't fall down and start bleeding out right here, right on the cool concrete floor.

"I'll get you home, Caroline," he murmured next to my head. "Everything's going to be okay."

No, it wasn't. Nothing was ever going to be okay again.

"Right now," I croaked. My legs felt like jelly and my mind was static-y and savage, wild with too many thoughts all clambering to be heard. This was the exact opposite reaction I should be having.

I was usually so cool under pressure, so collected. I was a goddamn genius when it came to getting out of sticky situations. Francesca and I had escaped the Volkov *pakhan* for God's sake.

But now? When I needed to be in control, my most inventive? Now I was crumbling like a coward.

Fear was overpowering me, giving me away and if I didn't get my shit together in the very next second, everything was over.

All of it.

My new life. My sparkling future.

My daughter.

Finding strength buried somewhere deep down, I latched onto it and inhaled another shaky breath.

You have a spine, I reminded myself. Use it.

"Caroline, seriously, you're scaring me," Jesse murmured gently. "Are you going to be okay? Do I need to get help?"

"I'm okay." And as I said the words, I decided they would be true.

I would get out of this.

I would get Juliet out of this.

But then my past reached out from the dark tomb I'd buried it in and grabbed ahold of my present in a chokehold. All of the demons I had been running from, hiding from, crashed into my safe haven present in a fiery collision that jarred my body, mind and soul.

"Caro?" a voice called across the gallery.

We were still in the center of the restaurant, white partitions displaying art on every side of us, half hiding the other patrons, half isolating us out of sight from everybody else.

The familiar voice called again. "Caro, is that you?" It was deeper than I remembered, more cultured, more masculine. And yet it still had that raspy edge to it that reminded me of my childhood and sneaking around warehouses and stealing candy from gas stations.

"Is he talking to you?" Jesse asked, sounding truly perplexed.

I stood up straighter. My face was white, drained of all the blood and color and life I'd spent five years pouring into my body. Now I was a corpse, ready for judgment and punishment.

"I think so," I told Jesse.

Without acknowledging the man approaching us, Jesse asked in a low voice, "Do you know him?"

"I think so," I repeated.

And then he was directly next to us. Past meet present. Life meet death.

It had been good while it lasted.

But it was over now.

Everything was over.

"Caro, I can't believe it's you!"

Lifting my chin in defiance, I turned to face Gus. The sight of him was a slap in the face, a punch in the throat, whatever other analogies there were for feeling completely beat up at just the sight of someone. It was Gus. Gus was here. Right here. I could touch him if I wanted to. He was here and I was here and my heart hurt looking at him.

I wanted to scream and run away and cry all at once. He'd had the advantage of seeing me first. He'd already collected himself. Or maybe he was a better actor. But I started shaking. It was all I could do to keep standing. After all this time, after everything I had done to ensure we never saw each other again... here we were.

Our gazes collided and I thought I was going to be sick. Something sharp and hateful flashed in his eyes, gutting me to my very core, calling out my worst sins.

Betrayal.

I had betrayed him.

"Oh my God, Gus," I said in disbelief, letting real emotion warp my tone, my voice hoarse and strained with the effort to speak. "I can't believe it's you."

His smile was wolfish, knowing. "I bet you can't."

"What are you doing here?" I asked politely, when I really wanted to scream, WHAT ARE YOU DOING HERE????

There was a weighted beat of silence before he said teasingly, "Wouldn't you like to know?"

"Do you know each other, Caroline?" Jesse asked bluntly.

I swiveled to Jesse, remembering that he was here. Oh God! I needed to get him out of here. Fast.

His arm was still across my back, his hand resting on my hip. Gus tracked the subtle touch with a not so subtle raise of his eyebrows, causing all the color that had drained from my face to return with hot, red vengeance.

"Caroline, who's your friend?" Gus asked, still casual, still nonchalant, still frustratingly adjusted.

I could not speak. I mean, I tried. But the words would not leave my mouth. They lodged themselves in my throat and tried to strangle me to death.

There was no way in hell I could introduce Jesse to Gus. Or Gus to Jesse. Or that this was really happening and not one of my worst nightmares. I had to be still asleep.

Right?

This was a nightmare??

Right?!?

So instead of introducing the two men that had zero business ever meeting each other, I flailed silently and tried not to pass out.

"I'm Gus." He thrust out his hand and waited for Jesse to shake it, which meant relinquishing his supportive hold on me. "An old friend of Caro's."

"I'm Jesse," my date said, finally taking hold of Gus's hand. "This is some surprise. Caroline has never mentioned you."

"It's a pleasure to meet you, Jesse. *Caroline* is funny like that. She probably hasn't really mentioned anyone to you though, right? She's private, this one. Secretive." He winked at me like this was all in good fun.

But this was the opposite of fun. This was so fucking not fun.

He looked so different than I remembered him. It was almost hard to reconcile the gangly twenty-two-year-old I'd left behind with the twenty-seven-year-old man in front of me. There were traces of him in the face, the boyish mischief that he could never hide, the floppy mop of dark hair. The signature beanie. The smile.

But he was so different too. Broad shoulders and muscled arms. His jeans were stylishly ripped, expensive, nothing like the torn, well-worn jeans he'd sported as a kid because he hadn't cared one way or the other what he looked like. His sweater was expensive too. Cashmere. The Gus I knew from before never wore anything but T-shirts that said stupid things meant to be funny.

The only thing familiar about his style was a leather cuff that used to be Atticus's. It was worn and lined with age. The initials AU were etched into a gold medallion in the center. A chill slid down my spine. Was that his business partner?

Was it Atticus?

And if so, what in the hell were they doing here?

If they meant to kill me, why had they gone to so much trouble to set up a gallery? They were using fake names, obviously, but why go through all this effort?

"We haven't spoken in years," I quickly told Jesse in answer to Gus's comment. "It's been... Er, how long has it been, Gus?"

"Five years," he said plainly. "It's been almost exactly five years."

Trying to laugh off the sudden flatness in Gus's voice, I turned to Jesse without taking my eyes off Gus. He might have once been as close as a brother to me, but I didn't trust the man. Not even a little bit. "Five years. It's hard to believe it's been so long."

Jesse bought my reassuring smile. I watched the questions he'd wanted to ask me click into place inside his head. He turned to Gus. "You know Caroline from back east?"

Gus's eyes narrowed suspiciously, realizing the same thing I did. Jesse saw this as an opportunity to find out about my past. And no matter what I had done to Gus, he did not appreciate an opportunist. Even if Jesse was relatively harmless.

Gus ignored his question, jerking his chin in hello to someone behind me. "Look who I ran into?"

My stomach dropped to my toes. Instinct screamed at me to run. This was it. Get out. Get out of this place. Out of this town. Out of this freaking country!

Instead of doing any of that, I turned to greet the newcomer at the same time Jesse did.

If seeing Gus after all this time felt like a kick in the face, turning around to find Sayer Wesley was worse than that. So much worse I didn't have an adequate way to describe it. I felt turned inside out, strung from the ceiling by my toes so all my secrets could shake out of me and land on the floor below. I felt exposed and transparent and broken in half.

Here he was. Alive. And free. And standing in front of me. And all I wanted to do was disappear.

"This is a surprise," Sayer greeted smoothly, without any speed bumps of shock getting in his way.

My mouth fell open at the same time my heart just gave up and quit beating. I was dead.

This had to be death.

Gus had stabbed me in the back or shot me in the head or did *something* irreparable to me to cause death. And I was currently bleeding out all over his art gallery floor.

This could not be real life.

Sayer was here.

Sayer was standing in front of me.

Sayer was out of prison and here in Colorado. Within touching distance.

My gaze traveled from his mouth up and over his nose to those blazing blue eyes that created an ache inside my soul so deep I could have sworn it tore me in two. And that's where I stayed, trapped by the cold, lifeless nothing staring back at me.

Held hostage by the one man I never expected to see again.

By the boy I'd fallen in love with when I was ten years old. The boyfriend I had let change the entire course of my life.

By the father of my daughter—the daughter he had no idea existed.

Chapter Ten

Ten Years Ago

The middle of January and I didn't have a freaking coat. Figures.

I used to have a coat.

It had been a nice coat. Long and puffy and so warm. Now, in the middle of winter, in the middle of a job, I didn't have one.

I wanted to punch something.

"Where's your coat?" Gus asked as he hopped up on the retaining wall next to me.

My jaw quivered as I tried to fight the biting wind in a battle of wills. "Whichever whore my dad brought home last night ran off with it."

"His taste in women has definitely declined over the years," Atticus consoled in that way of his that was not at all consoling. "Which is saying something since I thought your mom was about the dirtiest piece of trash he could have drummed up." Atticus smiled at Gus. "I mean, talk about bottom of the barrel."

"Shut up, asshole," Francesca growled. She was shivering too, but only because she barely weighed a hundred pounds. It didn't matter how bundled up she was, she needed more meat on her bones. "That's an ugly fucking thing to say." She sashayed by him, reminding him that her ass was about the only non-boney part of her body. "Besides," she taunted, "if we want to talk about slutty mothers, yours is always top of the list."

"Geez, Frankie," Gus groaned. Atticus and Gus's mother was still very much married to their father. Much to all of our surprise, since she hadn't been faithful to her very dangerous husband in a long time. I assumed every time Gus and Atticus went home they were surprised to see their mother still there, still breathing.

It wasn't that Ozzie was faithful in return. In fact, it was probably his lifetime of infidelity that had pushed her into the arms of other men. But Oz was *derzhatel obschaka* to the most powerful Russian syndicate in DC. And she was just arm candy.

Aging arm candy.

Atticus's expression flattened, turning into that cold serial killer psycho we all knew and loved. And then he turned that cruel glare on Frankie. "It's not a good idea to talk about my mother."

She didn't flinch. "So talk some shit about my mother. Get me back. I dare you."

Atticus turned away, knowing he couldn't say a damn thing to Frankie. Let alone, her deceased mother, the favorite sister of our bosses. "I don't know why you're here anyway, princess. You don't belong with us."

"Who's us?" Gus asked. "The working class?"

Atticus pushed off the retaining wall and walked away. Throwing an, "Exactly," over his shoulder.

"What's wrong with him today?" I asked needlessly.

Neither Gus nor Frankie answered. Something was always wrong with him. He was always pissed about something. Or everything.

Lately, though, I had an idea of what it was. He had it bad for the pretty, untouchable, angry-at-the-world princess. And she'd just insulted his mother.

Sayer crossed the street, headed in our direction. His long legs ate up the distance with purpose and speed, making the rest of the world appear in slow motion. He had his hands thrust into his pockets and a plaid scarf tucked around his neck.

I lost my breath watching him move toward us. I had never seen anyone more breathtaking than Sayer. He couldn't be human. I refused to believe he was a mere mortal.

And in the five years I had known him, he had done nothing but prove me right.

Fallen angel. That was my current theory.

108

He walked right up to me, stepping between my legs and rubbing his hands over my biceps. I sank into his warmth, needing as much of it as I could get. "Where's your coat?" he demanded in a much firmer, more possessive way than Gus had.

With him this close, smelling like cigarette smoke and spearmint and this new soap he'd started using, I lost the ability to form coherent sentences. That or my brain had gotten frostbite. "Uh…"

"Her dad's lucky lady of the night ran off with it," Gus explained for me.

Sayer frowned, his freakishly blue eyes darkening with concern. His hands moved over my neck and up to cradle my face. I loved the way his callouses scratched against my jawline and the way his fingertips disappeared into my hair. "You going to buy a new one?"

"O-of course." I licked dry lips and wished I had the courage to tell him to get on with it. Despite how much I loved his attention, I really was freezing.

"Tell him the truth, Caro," Frankie demanded.

I bit back a growl, hating how much I'd told her on the subway. "There's nothing to tell him, Frankie. I got it covered."

Frankie rolled her eyes at me. "Her old man ran off with her savings."

"Frankie!"

She gave Sayer a look. "All of it."

I dropped my face into my frozen fingers. "It's not a big deal. We have a job right now, don't we? I can wait until we get paid."

"How much did he take?" Sayer demanded.

I shook my head. I wasn't going to tell him that. The amount was sickening. I felt like puking every time I thought about it.

Sayer dipped his head and held my gaze. I wanted to look away so badly. I really did. But I couldn't. He had this frustrating way of hypnotizing me. And getting the stupid truth out of me.

It would be easier to lie if I could look somewhere else. Anywhere else.

But I couldn't.

And I couldn't lie to him. Which seriously rubbed me the wrong way.

Frankie said it was because he was always touching me. She claimed it was way harder to lie when you were turned on.

Obviously she was an idiot.

It wasn't even like his touches were sexual. He just… I didn't even know what it was about him. But when we were together, his hands were on me. His arm was around me or he was holding my hand or he'd pull me into his lap in front of his entire crew and just expect me to sit there like it was the most normal thing in the world.

And maybe it would have been if I was his girlfriend or if he'd admit he liked me or something. But I wasn't and he hadn't.

He'd kissed me once, five years ago, when I was ten and he was thirteen. But that had been the last time.

Now that I was fifteen and he was eighteen and we were both official employees of the Volkov, he'd kept everything between us completely platonic.

Except for the affectionate touching.

And sometimes intense looks that made my knees buckle.

"A lot," I finally admitted to Sayer.

"Her college money," Frankie added.

I was going to punch her later. She was always complaining about being treated differently and how everyone was scared of her. Well, not me. I was definitely going to throat punch her.

"Fuck, Caro," Sayer growled, jumping back from me.

The urge to cry pricked at the backs of my eyeballs, but I refused to let the tears fall. It was a hell of a lot of money, but I should have put it in the stupid bank. I should have hidden it better. I should have had it better protected.

Instead, I'd left it where anyone could find it. Yeah, fine, it was in my apartment, in my room, hidden away in a spot that I thought only I knew about, but my dad was in trouble. I knew that he was. He acted like everything was fine, but I knew he'd started gambling again.

Which was a dangerous thing to do for a bookie and an addict.

"I'm going to get it back," I announced to Frankie and Sayer and Gus for good measure. "He's going to pay me back."

Sayer unzipped his coat and pulled it off his body, wrapping it around me. I closed my eyes against the sensation of warmth and his scent still lingering in the lining. "Here, at least take mine for now."

"Then you'll freeze," I pointed out weakly.

He shrugged. "I've been through worse."

He always said that and we all believed him. Whatever Sayer had gone through before he joined the syndicate had been hell. He never talked about his life before Fat Jack had found him on the streets. He'd wormed his way into the syndicate by helping the *bratva* steal an entire container of Irish guns. But it was something you could tell about him just by looking at him, by watching him climb the ranks of the brotherhood faster than any Six had in the history of organized crime.

He was our brigadier, our *avtoritet*. And we were his *boyeviks*, his soldiers. And we knew in another few years he would make *vor*. Sayer's eyes were on the top. It was only a matter of time before he got there.

It was why Atticus hated him so much. Sayer had stolen Atticus's fame and glory, making it his own and leaving Atticus in the back with the rest of us that didn't want to be here.

"We'll talk about the money later," Sayer promised. I nodded, praying he would forget all about it. I could handle my dad without him. I didn't need the help nor did I want it. To the group he said, "They're ready for the hurrah. We need to hit tonight."

Frankie leaned forward. "They want us to break into the mayor's house?"

Unfazed, Sayer added, "And rob him."

"Are you out of your mind?"

"They want it cleaned out. Nothing trashed. No signs that we've been there. They just want it all gone." He rubbed the side of his jaw. "Also, there's a dog."

We all shared a look. I hated dogs. Especially stealing them.

"And what do we get out of it?" Gus asked.

"Your usual cut."

We all winced. We were paid well, but not enough to risk breaking into the mayor of DC's house and stealing everything of value.

Besides Sayer and Atticus, the rest of us were here against our will. Gus was forced into the life by his father. Frankie demanded to be given jobs, but only so she could escape the pretty prison her uncles had designed for her. And I had been sucked in when I'd stolen something for Sayer.

Sometimes I hated him for that day as much as I loved him.

And I did love him.

I had loved him since he kissed me that same day. Hate and love always at war within me for this boy that could talk me into anything.

It was messed up. I knew that it was. But I also knew I couldn't do anything about it. I had been trying for five years. And yet here I was, secretly smelling the warm coat wrapped around me.

"We'll meet at the usual spot at nine tonight," Sayer continued to order. "Gus and Frankie, you'll stick with Atticus. Caro, you're with me."

I ignored the I-told-you-so-look on Frankie's face. She was convinced he loved me too.

But what she didn't understand was that boys like Sayer and Atticus and Gus didn't fall in love. They screwed around. A lot. Maybe they married eventually, but only to get a pair of sons. Nothing changed for them though. They never stopped screwing around. And they really didn't fall in love.

Just ask any of our fathers.

Gus jumped to the sidewalk. He shoved his hands into his pocket and tugged on his knit beanie. "I got work to do then. I'm assuming there's security?"

"He's on the Italian payroll," Sayer explained. "The bosses aren't happy that he won't play ball."

"That's why he wouldn't take the girls last weekend? The congratulatory gift?" Atticus asked from the outskirts of our circle.

Sayer nodded. "He's been in office for two weeks. Long enough to figure out how things work."

Atticus shrugged, agreeing with Sayer. Meanwhile, acid reflux burned in my throat. I reasoned that if the mayor was already working with the Italians, he knew what he was getting into. If he'd picked a side in the ongoing war for the underbelly of DC, then he knew there would be repercussions. He knew nothing in his life was safe or protected.

Maybe he didn't expect Russians to hit his house two weeks into his term. But he should have.

These people didn't play fair.

And they sure as hell didn't play nice.

We'd been working on this job for a lot longer than his term. We'd known who was going to win the election long before it had actually taken place. Last summer, we'd all been given our roles. Gus had gotten a job at his landscapers and mowed the yard every week. Atticus had volunteered at his campaign office. Frankie and I had gotten to know his daughter by hanging out at the pool where her and her friends always went. And Sayer had run point. We knew the ins and outs of his life. We knew when he'd be home and when he'd be gone. And we knew the layout of his house.

It would be a clean hit. We'd get in. We'd get out. We'd take everything from him, even his dog, sending a clear message to reconsider his allegiances. From there, his circumstances would get progressively worse until he complied.

I felt sorry for him. Yeah, he'd sided with the Italians, but what choice did he have? DC was thick with crime, infested with it. You couldn't enter a public office at any level without having to deal with some crime syndicate or gang intimidation tactic—it went on and on. At least the Italians were significantly subtler than say… the Irish. Or us. The Ukrainians were trying hard to get a foothold here and they were brutal savages. Mexicans, Rastas, Yakuza… everybody was here. Everybody wanted a piece of the pie.

It was true that most everyone was smart enough to lay low, to let gang violence and rising crime cover up the organized activity, but that didn't mean DC didn't have its fair share. And why wouldn't we?

DC was the most corrupt city in the country. Politicians came here already half twisted toward evil. Then there was the "donor crowd." The top one percent. Already so perverted by money that they didn't care where it went as long as their agenda was accomplished. The lobbyists. The police. The fucking mayor. DC was a cesspool.

So yeah, we laid low because we didn't want to piss off the FBI, but we ran this city.

Gus mimicked typing on the computer. "I'll see what I can do about the security system then."

"That would be great," Sayer answered. "I'll be right behind you."

"Frankie, you going back to your house?" Atticus asked. "I'll give you a ride."

"I think I'll just hang with Caro," she answered.

We hadn't had plans, but I knew she didn't want to be alone with Atticus. He freaked her out.

He freaked all of us out.

"Whatever," Atticus mumbled, turning around and heading in the opposite direction of Gus.

"Nine," Sayer called after him.

Atticus replied with his middle finger in the air.

Sayer rubbed a hand over his face. "He's such an asshole." Looking at Frankie he asked, "Has he always been an asshole? Or is it something that's getting worse with age?"

"He's always been an asshole," Frankie answered. "But what do you expect being the first son of Ozwald Usenko? Like father, like son."

Sayer shrugged. "Ozzie's not so bad."

Frankie and I stared at him. Oz regularly beat the shit out of Gus and Atticus until they were old enough to fight back. He forced both of his sons into this life. Maybe Atticus had gone willingly, but Gus had never wanted this, never wanted to be a part of any of this. And he was a cruel bastard to his wife.

113

The only decent thing Oz had ever done was take Sayer in when he had nowhere else to go. But everybody knew that was because Roman had ordered it. Gus and Sayer were close to the same age. It made sense to everyone but Oz.

Another clue to Sayer's messed up life before the syndicate.

"All right, see you ladies later tonight. You going to be okay?" Sayer's question was directed at me.

"Fine," I answered quickly. "Here, let me give you your coat back."

"We'll go shopping for a new one," Frankie suggested. Then with a sly smile she added, "Maybe we'll run into those guys at the mall again. This time you have to give that one your number though. He was so hot, Caro."

Sayer's blue eyes flared. "What guy?"

Oh my God. I was going to kill Frankie. Kill her. This was so embarrassing. And it was only going to get worse. My bright red cheeks were about to catch fire any second, then I would start Sayer's coat on fire and then I would just die. I would just burn up and die from humiliation.

"What guy, Six?" Sayer demanded using the nickname he'd had for me ever since we were ten.

"Oh, just these prep school guys we met at the mall last weekend," Frankie prattled on. "One of them was so into her. He was like obsessed with her."

"Frankie, enough," Sayer growled. "I asked Caroline."

I licked dry lips. Nobody ever used my full name. Ever. Unless it was Sayer. And only occasionally. Like when it was just the two of us. Or right now… when he was obviously pissed off.

"Caroline," he repeated firmly.

Clearing my throat, I fumbled with the zipper of his coat. "Like she said, just these prep school guys. They were just messing around. We don't even know their names."

"You're into them, though? Or the one guy? The *hot* guy?"

Could his glare get any more intense? I was surprised it hadn't sliced me in two by now. "I'm not into him. Geez, I don't even know him."

Sayer stepped closer to me and it wasn't sweet or protective or nice. He was trying to be intimidating. He was trying to be the tough guy our bosses paid him to be. "And that's what you want?" he pushed. "You want to get to know this prep school kid?"

I glared up at him briefly before I turned back to the zipper, struggling to get it down the frustrating seam. Argh! I was only ever a fumbling idiot around him. And right now it was pissing me off! "Maybe. He seemed nice. And bonus, I'm pretty sure his plans tonight don't include breaking and entering or grand theft."

Sayer grabbed my wrist in a tight grip, stalling me from ripping his coat off and throwing it in his face. "Yeah, but yours do. Don't forget that when you're playing rich kid in the city."

I was so mad I could have sworn I was about to breathe fire. He had hit all my insecurities. All of them. I wasn't even interested in that stupid prep school kid. To be honest, he'd been a pretentious asshole and I didn't like the way he leered at me. That's why I hadn't given him my number. Or even my name. Frankie had only brought him up to get a rise out of Sayer.

Only it had backfired on all of us.

"Don't worry about me, Sayer. I can handle myself. The job comes first, right? Always?"

His jaw ticked, the silent anger vibrating through him. Everybody knew Sayer was the *pakhan's* errand boy. He would do anything for them. This job was his life.

This job was all he cared about.

Not Frankie. Not Gus. And certainly not me.

"You better be there tonight, Six. On time. Or so help me god, I'll—"

My chin wobbled, betraying me. "What? Tell on me? Report me? Maybe they'll fire me and I'll finally be free of this godforsaken place."

"Don't fucking talk like that. You know the consequences."

I bit my tongue to keep from saying something I regretted. I did know the consequences.

Death.

A bullet between the eyes.

"I'll be there tonight," I hissed. "You don't have to be such an asshole about it though." I finally got the zipper free of the fabric surrounding it and yanked it down. "Here, take your coat."

Sayer stepped back, the dragon inside him retreating. "Go to the mall. But you better wear that fucking coat." He took another step back. "Frankie, don't let her take it off."

"That's the dumbest—"

He ignored my outrage. "See you tonight, Six."

"I hate him," I told Frankie when he'd walked away. "And I hate his nickname for me."

She jumped down from the wall and bumped her shoulder with mine. "You're such a liar."

115

I sighed, hating the most that she was right. "Why does he have to make things so difficult though? Why can't he just be a nice guy and ask me out?"

"Because you would be bored by a nice guy. You'd never waste your time with someone uncomplicated or upright. You can fight it all you want, Caro, but you were born for this life."

I turned to my friend. She had a baseball cap on over her braided long hair. "Yeah, well that makes two of us."

Her expression flattened. "Let's go find those prep school guys. We'll stash his jacket in a locker. I won't tell if you won't."

Smiling at her idea, we headed for the mall. We even stashed the jacket and found some guys to hang out with. They weren't the same prep school kids, but they might as well have been. Because the outcome was the same.

I didn't give out my number.

I didn't find anyone capable of keeping my attention.

And the entire stupid time I kept thinking about the coat and the boy it belonged to and that even though I wasn't actually wearing his coat, I was so wearing his coat.

And I didn't think I'd ever be able to take it off.

Not in the way that mattered.

As messed up as Sayer Wesley was, I was as entangled in this game of ours as he was. As long as Sayer was in my life there would never be anyone else.

The next day, I rolled out of bed in the early afternoon, exhausted by our late-night success at the Mayor's. A new winter coat was waiting for me in the living room with a note from my dad. He felt bad for losing my other one. Oh, and he would replace my college money as soon as he could. I didn't need to worry about anything.

Only my dad didn't do shit like that... ever. This had Sayer's hand written all over it. He'd intervened. He'd stuck up for me to my dad. He'd somehow convinced Leon to do the decent thing.

So yeah, I did have something to worry about. I had Sayer to worry about.

I had my weak, infatuated heart to worry about.

Chapter Eleven

Present Day

" $\mathcal{I}$ t's so good to see you," Sayer said sounding so pleasantly surprised, my skin prickled with warning. "Imagine us running into each other after all this time. Here of all places."

I gaped at him. My mouth literally dropped open and my tongue lolled.

Okay, maybe I didn't have a lolling tongue. I had managed to retain some of my motor functions.

Not many.

But some.

While I stood there internally flopping on the floor like a fish out of water, he stepped forward and pulled me into a hug. A hug? What was happening?

"That's what I said," Gus agreed. "Of all the places in the world, we run into our old friend Caro in the middle of nowhere Colorado. It's just so surprising."

He didn't sound surprised at all, the asshole.

Sayer stepped back and I realized I hadn't even been able to feel him touching me. I was too numb. Too shell-shocked. I hadn't smelled him or stolen his wallet or patted him down or done any of the things I should have been doing.

Oh my God, my wallet! I took another step back and ripped open my clutch.

Breathing a sigh of relief at the sight of my wallet, house keys and lipstick, I snapped it shut again and returned my gaze to Sayer fucking Wesley.

"Caroline?" Jesse asked, obviously concerned with the state of my mental welfare.

"She's so surprised to see us," Gus teased. "Look at her. We've blown her mind."

There was a hard edge to Gus's voice that made me nervous. He was so good at pretending, at playing the con. So much better than he used to be. It was only because I knew him so well that I could hear it. Every word, every mannerism laced with fury. Betrayal. Outrage.

It should have made me want to run away. It should have made me afraid.

But all I wanted to do was cry.

"She can't even introduce us to her friend," Sayer added. "Don't be so rude, Caroline." He chuckled at his joke, prompting Gus and Jesse to laugh with him.

I still hadn't gained control of my facial muscles.

"Sayer Smith." He reached out his hand to Jesse. I flinched at the old name. The old alias. Smith had been our inside joke.

His words echoed through my head from long ago. Let's just run away. Go somewhere new where nobody can recognize us. We'll be the Smiths. We'll blend in. We'll disappear.

Back when our futures had been so entirely entwined.

Back when I couldn't imagine a life without him. Wherever that meant we ended up. Whatever that meant we ended up doing.

Jesse eyed me before shaking Sayer's hand. "Jesse Hasting."

Sayer nodded. "Hasting. Are you connected to the Hasting ranch outside of town?"

"That's mine," Jesse confirmed. "My dad and I run it."

Sayer smiled easily, familiarly. Dangerously. The look was so him, effortless and confident, friendly and beguiling. He used his charm as a weapon. To lay traps. To win. "Thought so. That's a great operation you got out there."

"Interested in horses and cattle, Mr. Smith?" Jesse asked, rightfully suspicious.

118

"Not really. But Gus and I did our research on the town. We know the ins and outs. On paper at least. It's nice to be able to put a face to the name we've heard so much about."

Each of his words had a double meaning, a secret agenda. My heart hammered inside my chest, a desperate drumbeat that threatened to pound right out of my body, through bone and sinew and flesh.

Jesse smiled. "Small town gossip?"

Sayer nodded.

Jesse's smile disappeared. "It's funny though. We heard nothing about the two of you before tonight."

The steely look in Sayer's empty blue eyes didn't change. "We know how to keep a low profile." Then he laughed, as if this were the most natural conversation in the world. "There will be plenty to gossip about after tonight though. I'm sure."

I struggled to swallow. Was that a threat?

Gus refocused on me. "What about you, Caro? What are you up to these days?"

There was a long awkward silence while I struggled with what to do. If they had been asking around town about me and people I hung out with, i.e. Jesse, did they know about Juliet too? Did they know she was Sayer's daughter?

How much did they know?

How much could I lie about?

I cleared my throat and shook myself out of the zombie-like stupor I'd fallen into. There were higher stakes at play than my life. I had a daughter to protect.

A daughter I would do anything to save from this life.

Sayer represented everything that I was desperate to keep Juliet away from. I would never go back.

I would never let Juliet get sucked into that vile world.

I was out of practice and rusty. But I remembered the basics. Organized crime and conning was once a way of life for me.

I could lie with the best of them.

And with so much on the line, I would lie my freaking ass off. Until I believed the words spewing from my mouth and the pretty illusion I conjured. Sayer could kill me later. Sayer could torture me and drag me back to DC and let Roman kill me. But I would never give Juliet to them.

And if all else failed and I didn't make it back home, Frankie would know what to do.

"I'm a manager at one of the local resorts," I explained. "It's nothing like back home. The pace here is so easygoing and my job is so much less... restricted. But I love it. I love the change of pace."

Sayer's jaw ticked and my smile became more confident. He was pissed. He didn't like that I'd recovered. Or that I'd no doubt confirmed all of his groundwork.

I ignored the satisfying feeling of still being able to read him even after all this time.

"That's great," he said, his smile turning forced. "That sounds great."

I held his gaze, confessing the truth. "It is. I love my life here." Jesse put his arm around my shoulders and squeezed. I wasn't sure if he sensed my need for comfort or if he felt responsible for my happiness, but his warm touch was comforting.

Sayer's jaw ticked again and those blue eyes flared for the first time—the way they used to. Darkening and brightening all at once. I sucked in a breath as old feelings I had worked relentlessly to bury clawed at their internal grave, desperate to resurface.

He's dangerous, I told them. He's one of them.

He's here to kill me.

He's here to take away everything.

It's Sayer, they hissed in return, addicted to his voice, desperate for his touch, weeping from the separation.

"A tour!" Gus announced, his boisterous voice slicing through the sudden tension. "You need a tour."

"Oh, no," I rushed to decline. "That's okay. We were actually leaving."

"Caro, come on," Gus pushed. "We haven't seen each other in five years and you're in a hurry to get out of here? What kind of assholery is that?"

"I, uh, no, you're so busy and we couldn't impose—"

"It's already happening," Gus insisted. "The tour is happening. I won't take no for an answer." He spun around, as animated as I remembered him. "This is the gallery. Our current installation is kick ass as you can see. Our artist is a real talent. Young, handsome, a legit genius with the brush."

Jesse shot me a confused look. "Aren't you the current artist?"

Gus grinned. "Oh, right. It's probably best if we move on. You can ogle my work later." He started walking toward the bar. "I'll even give you the friends and family discount, Caro. Six percent off."

120

I ignored the dig. "Wow, Gus. I don't know what to do with your generosity."

"Right? That's what everyone says."

We followed after Gus while he pointed out the inanest shit ever. There's a table. That's one of our chairs. Look at the light fixtures over the bar. That left Sayer to follow behind us. I hated that I couldn't keep my eyes on him. I hated that he had the advantage and the perspective and all the things I wanted. In an effort to get out of tonight alive, I had to play the con they'd started without my permission. Which meant I couldn't let Jesse in on any of it.

I could have run from the building screaming like it was on fire, but Sayer and Gus had found me. They weren't going to let go or give up or walk away. At least not without a fight. So all that would have done was lead them straight to Juliet.

But along with playing my role in a game I didn't know the rules for, I had to keep Jesse safe too. He couldn't know any of this. He couldn't suspect anything was wrong.

Jesse was a good guy and he would do what all good guys did—he would try to help me.

Only his help would only hurt. And probably get us both killed.

When Gus started skirting the back of the gallery near the kitchen, we turned a corner and I took the opportunity to glance back at Sayer. His gaze was already on me.

"You okay, Six?" he asked with that cruel, distanced smirk twisting his mouth.

No. I wasn't okay. I turned back around.

"More art," Gus was saying. "That's the kitchen." We approached a doorway. Gus stepped into it and as we followed after him, we realized it was a darkened hallway leading to a stairwell headed to the basement. "Okay, enough with the boring stuff. Let's get to the cool part."

I froze, causing Jesse to bump into me. "What's down there, Gus?"

He was already halfway to the bottom. His cat-that-ate-the-canary grin did nothing to soothe my nerves. "It's a surprise."

Shaking my head, I took a step back. Sayer was right there. His muscled chest grazing my back. "I don't like surprises," I told them.

Sayer's hand landed on my hip. His fingers wrapped around the bone, squeezing tightly, cradling intimately. "You'll like this one, Caro. I promise."

121

I couldn't hide the fear anymore. Pleading with my eyes, I appealed to the more sensible of the two men. "What's down there, Gus?"

"Aw, come on, old friend, you've made it this far. Don't chicken out now," he goaded.

That was a direct reference to me running from DC.

I knew I should never have agreed to this date with Jesse. I could make an argument that this was his fault. His idea. Only I'd gone along with it willingly. Like a stupid lemming. Or a suicidal sheep. I just needed someone to blame. Resisting the urge to bang my head against the brick wall, I ignored Sayer's punishing squeeze and followed after Gus. If for no other reason than to escape Sayer's touch.

He was the same as before. But so different.

The Sayer I knew before was long and lean, the way runners were built. His shoulders had been narrow and his waist tapered. And even at twenty-three, his face had held onto some of the boyishness of his youth.

Now he was all muscle. His green hooded sweater did little to hide his ripped physique beneath the expensive material. His shoulders had broadened, with all this new strength of course, but with age too. He had stepped into manhood and gripped it with two fists.

All traces of boy and teenager and young man were gone. In their place was a deliciously stubbled jaw and raw, untamed power. He towered over me, taller, stronger, meaner. And unlike before when his body had been a shelter for me to run to, the safe haven I counted on for protection, it was only cruel distance now. There was an invisible space between us that stretched across oceans. Continents.

Worlds.

Sayer Wesley had gone to prison as the person I trusted most in this world and come out a stranger.

He wore his five years in prison like new skin, flexing the hard-fought years with bared teeth and shredded muscle. There was no softness left in him, no gentle touch or understanding ear. Only anger. Only hatred.

He was at once utterly beautiful and every nightmare I had ever had come to life.

I decided not to look at him again tonight. Not even if his plan was to kill me. It hurt too much.

At the bottom of the steps, there was a short hallway that led to a supply room that had the door propped open and another door that was closed. This was it. This was the empty room where they were going to kill us. The people upstairs would pause at the sound of gun shots, but the loud pop music would disguise the gunfire to make them think they were hearing things. Gus and Sayer would shove our dead bodies into barrels of acid and then close the door behind them before rejoining the party like nothing had happened.

And I would never be heard from again. My dead body would eventually be dumped, but nobody would be able to identify the body because I'd be turned into human soup. Caroline Valero would just fade away into oblivion, another unsolved homicide that nobody cared enough about to demand justice.

Or something along those lines.

It was possible I'd been binging too much *Luther* lately.

When Gus put his hand on the doorknob, a sudden surge of panic gripped me and I latched onto Jesse's hand, squeezing so tightly my fingers went numb.

"You're going to love this, Caro," Gus exclaimed, some of his familiar optimism slipping into his tone. He pushed open the door and we were led into an office.

I breathed with instant relief. Having expected an empty room with soundproof walls and a drain in the middle of the floor, modern, efficient desks and filing cabinets and plush leather chairs were a welcome sight.

My gaze fell on the safe in the corner of the room immediately. Old habits and all that. Thick, heavy and a brand I was unfamiliar with, I couldn't help but be intrigued. Instantly, I wanted to find out what was in it. The dormant thief in me itched to know what secrets they had locked inside that impossible box. It was big enough for me to walk inside and stand up in, so it must be filled with useful trinkets and titillating information.

But it was also too obvious. And since Gus was involved, there would be cameras and security and measures taken to keep all their dirty little secrets secret.

Scanning the ceiling, looking for cameras, I finally figured out why they brought me here.

"Son of a bitch," I hissed under my breath. I felt Jesse's surprised gaze on me so I gave a halfhearted effort to cover up my reaction. "That's quite a painting." Then hated myself for drawing attention to it.

"Oh, yeah? You like that?" Gus asked with a smug grin. "That's one of our older pieces. We've been hanging onto it for a while. You know, waiting for the right opportunity to display it."

"Are those diamonds?" Jesse blurted, checking out a long counter of displayed jewelry.

I spun around while Gus explained something about being a collector of fine things. The room backed up his claim. There was an antique cigar box worth thousands. A Rembrandt and Leighton worth so much more than that. There was a little black journal that was absolutely priceless, containing an accomplished job ledger from a notorious hitman. Extravagant jewelry and a priceless sculpture and all of my sins stockpiled in one reckless room.

The Leighton especially, the Fisherman and the Siren, which I'd managed to steal on a dare after a night of vodka and bad decisions when it was on temporary display at a gallery in DC, had my name written all over it. I doubted Jesse was up on his FBI lists, but to me it felt like my name was splashed in red paint all over it. That's the painting that would send me to prison.

That's the one that would upend everything.

Hell, everything in this room would just add years to my sentence.

This was like my own personal dragon's cave. While working for the syndicate I was given jobs, assignments in which I would steal, con and coerce my way through. And while working for the syndicate my moral compass had swung a little too freely. I was good at my job. Really good. Which might have led to my hobby. Over the seven years I worked for the Volkov family, I was able to amass quite the collection.

All of which I entrusted to a certain associate of mine to keep hidden—away from my father's sticky fingers.

What I hadn't realized until the moment it mattered most, was the associate I'd entrusted to keep everything safe for me also had sticky fingers. Sayer had lied about where he kept everything. He'd safeguarded his own fortune by stealing mine.

When Francesca and I ran, I had cash, but none of the truly valuable items that would have given us complete financial freedom. And kept my name clear.

Now here they all were. These things were mine. All of them. I'd stolen them fair and square. And Sayer, the bastard that he was, had not only tracked me down and interrupted my peaceful existence, but he'd chosen to flaunt all of my trophies as if they were his own.

I was going to murder him.

Okay, not really. But as long as he didn't murder me first, I was going to get back every single thing of mine and rub his nose in it. Then Juliet and I would be gone for good.

Chapter Twelve

"What do you think, Caro?" Gus asked, still grinning like the foolish idiot he was.

I met his gaze and told him the truth. "I think you're showing off."

"This is quite the impressive collection," Jesse added neutrally. He could sense the obvious tension in the room. But he was a civilian, a nice guy that only knew nice people. He could not fathom the bad blood between us or the origin of the priceless items in the room.

Normal people didn't automatically assume everything surrounding them was stolen. Or that the girl they had a crush on used to work for the Russian mafia and had the reputation of being a high-class thief. That was fantasy to the everyday person. Fiction.

Gus shrugged. "Honestly, I inherited most of it."

I blinked at him, still shocked at his unabashed arrogance. "Is that so?"

"The lady everything originally belonged to up and died."

"She died?"

Gus held my gaze, "Well, she's dead to me."

I rolled my eyes and turned to Sayer, hopefully appealing to a more levelheaded moron. He held his hands in the air and walked further into the room. "We're not here to pick a fight, Six. We're hoping for your opinion. We're wondering how much this is all worth?"

The door clicked closed with a sort of ominous finality at the same time I said, "I don't know why you think I'd know the answer to that question."

The room went dark, and a red light came on over the door.

"What the hell?" Jesse asked.

"Oh, no," Gus sighed, not sounding worried in the slightest. "Sayer, you forgot again."

The previous dread flared through my belly. Holy shit, this was the moment! Goodbye, cruel world. "Forgot what?" I asked all even tones and false bravado.

"The security system," Sayer explained, his voice sounding like it had been dragged across a gravel road. Now that his face was cast in shadow, I imagined a raging monster coming to life inside him. A monstrous beast fueled by the love of his life disappearing, abandoning him to prison and crime and hell. "We've taken special measures to keep this room secured, but the door has been acting funny since we got the system installed. It keeps locking us inside." He let a heavy pause settle over us. "The only way to get out is for someone to open the door from the other side."

I ground my teeth together to keep from screaming in frustration. "You're kidding."

Sayer's face was cast in darkness, but I felt his gaze crawl all over my skin. "Afraid not."

My mind spun, desperate for an exit. This was a recipe for disaster. If Gus and Sayer weren't planning to murder us, then I didn't want Jesse finding out any of my secrets. Fine, if we were being held at gunpoint or Sayer had handed us two shovels and ordered us to start digging our graves, I might have fessed up to Jesse. He would have a reason to know then.

But since Gus and Sayer had yet to start screwing on their silencers, I decided to spare Jesse the information that would likely lead to his later demise. Yes, it was dangerous for Juliet and me, but also for him. If the *bratva* had come back into my life, I needed to do whatever it took to save Jesse from that world. I needed to do for Jesse what I couldn't do for Sayer all those years ago.

"Call someone," I ordered, pointing at the desk phone. "Call your hostess."

"The line isn't set up yet," Gus answered.

Son of a bitch. I stormed over to a phone and picked it up. Sure, enough there was nothing but empty sound. I made a fool of myself crawling around on the floor, groping in the darkness to test the jacks. Then I did it to the second phone. Nothing.

Kneeling in the middle of the office in my little black dress, I remembered my cell phone. I yanked open my clutch and pulled it out. No service.

"Are you serious?"

Sayer leaned forward on one of the desks, his bigger, brawnier arms flexing in the glow of red light. Where had that muscle come from? "Dead."

I shook my head, hating that I was so easily distracted. "Wh-what?"

"Dead serious," he clarified. "That's not going to work down here."

"Damn it."

"Eventually, they'll notice we're missing," Gus said. "Maybe."

"Hopefully," Jesse echoed. "Has this happened before? Will they realize you're locked in down here?"

The guys shrugged, turning their attention to me rather than Jesse.

I felt them circling like a pack of lions. Like a pack of angry, starving, asshole lions. What were they doing here? And why had I walked so stupidly into their trap?

I was not a naïve gazelle hanging out at the watering hole. I was a lion in my own right. Queen of the fucking jungle.

They couldn't have known I would show up here on opening night. Let's operate under the assumption that they moved to this town with the express purpose of confronting me. They wouldn't have opened up a business if they planned to kill me tonight.

If this was a hit job, they would have found me, rolled into town and grabbed me, finished the job and then left again.

No, they were up to something. This was a con. And obviously a long one. Another one of their games.

They were here for a reason. Yes, the reason was probably me. Or Francesca. But either way, they weren't going to hit and run this one.

Which meant their cover was as important as mine.

"Serendipity, right, Caro? That we would run into each other here of all places." Sayer tapped the desk with his knuckles. "After all this time."

Serendipity was the name of one of our old cons. We would run into each other in the middle of a party and make a big scene, hugging, laughing, I would start to cry. Then we'd ask someone to take a picture

127

of us, and while I was showing them how to use my phone, I would steal their wallet or their hotel key card or whatever.

"Yep," I mumbled, struggling to stand again in my too short skirt. "Serendipity, Sayer." Only this time I was the mark.

Jesse reached out his hand and I took it, grateful for the help to my feet. He seemed to sense something was wrong, because he pulled me close to him and dipped his head to ask, "You okay?"

"Claustrophobic." I blurted. It was a lie. "I'm starting to freak out." Truth.

Gus plopped into a leather chair and spun around in it. "Relax, kids. Someone will notice we're gone soon enough. In the meantime, let's catch up."

No. Not happening.

Using the darkness to my benefit, I scratched my head in a stressed-out way and moved over to the door. Jiggling the handle, I checked out the lock. Whew, not complicated. A simple enough mortise lock. Automatic, but not impossible.

I turned around and pressed my back against the door, bending the bobby pins I'd just retrieved into the right shape. Ideally, I needed something more substantial than bobby pins. I wanted my set of curtain picks or at the very least skinny Allen wrenches.

Now that my fingers were busy, I felt like I could relax a smidge. Besides, I needed a little misdirection for Jesse's sake. "It really is good to see you guys after all this time. How's everybody else? How are your parents, Gus? Atticus?"

"My dad passed away four years ago," Gus responded with short, clipped consonants. "I thought you knew that."

"I didn't know." There was true emotion in my face and heaviness in my heart at his words. I truly had not known.

Gus had hated his dad. Ozzie was a real and true asshole. But I still felt sympathy for his loss. Maybe even more so because he had never had a good father or someone that really loved him. Maybe I felt it more for him because I knew what it was like to be used by my father and thrown into a world I wanted no part of.

"Sorry to hear that," I told him sincerely, even if I disguised it with a brusque response.

"Yeah, well, I'm not," Gus muttered. I realized I had taken him out of his mental game, made him emotional when he hadn't wanted to be.

"What about Atticus?" I asked, pushing buttons I knew would continue to throw him off. Or at least I hoped they would. "What's he up to?"

Gus and Sayer shared a look. I knew they hadn't meant to give themselves away and were counting on the darkness to disguise it, but they didn't quite manage. Before I could say anything the lock clicked open behind me and my hand slipped on the handle, thrusting it open before I was ready.

I laughed openly. I still had it! Bonus, when the door opened, the lights came back on. I wasn't prepared to see every stolen thing surrounding me again, but it was so much easier to keep an eye on Robin Hood and his merry band of one when I could see them.

Jesse stared at me. "How'd you do that?"

"I just pulled on it. The door wasn't locked."

"Yes, it was," Gus insisted. "It's been locking me in here all week."

"Well, this time it wasn't," I argued. "As soon as I put pressure on it, the thing opened right up. Crazy, right?" I slipped my bobby pins into my purse and hoped nobody noticed my hair was a little looser than before.

Gus stood up, pretending to be super surprised. "I tried it. It was locked. Seriously, Caro, how did you do it?"

Were they trying to catch me in a lie in front of Jesse? Silly boys. Tricks were for kids. I had moved onto something called illusion. And I was so much better at it than these two circus clowns.

"You must not have tried hard enough." I gave him my best sympathetic smile. "Good thing I was here to save the day."

He stared at me. "Good thing."

"Well, we need to get going," I told Sayer and Gus, mustering up enough courage to look them both in the eyes. "I have, er, Jesse and I have other plans to get to. It was nuts running into you though. Here. In Frisco."

Sayer's glare was all over Jesse, and I wasn't convinced we were going to make it out of here alive after all. "You guys have other plans?"

His words had a hard edge to them, the double blade of a knife. He sounded jealous, but I knew that was wrong. Sayer didn't reveal his emotions or let them slip out accidentally. If he wanted me to hear jealousy, then he had done it for a purpose. He was setting a trap, laying the foundation, engaging the mark. Making me question every decision I'd made in the last five years and doubt myself.

No, Sayer wasn't jealous. He was playing his game.

I grabbed Jesse's hand and tugged him toward the staircase. "Bye, guys," I called after them. "Thanks for the tour."

"Nice to meet you," Jesse called back as I all but dragged him up the stairs.

We made it to the sidewalk outside before I found the courage to speak. "That was weird, wasn't it? Was it just me or did you think that was super weird?"

Jesse looked down at me, coming to a stop on the passenger side of his truck. His lips twitched before letting go of a charming smile. "That was really weird," he agreed. "I think those guys are on drugs, Caroline."

Laughing at his assumption, I shook my head. "Drugs? Really?"

"Well, you explain it. Then getting locked in that basement office? I thought one of them was going to pull out an ax and start chopping us into pieces."

I had expected a version of that scenario too, to be honest. But Jesse didn't need to know that. So instead, I laughed at his joke and told another lie. And another lie. And I continued building the stack of cards that had always been my life. "Don't worry. You're safe. Sayer and Gus are mostly harmless. I think bumping into me surprised them." Taking a steadying breath, I said the one truth I knew would make sense to Jesse. "Sayer used to have a thing for me, you know, back when we were kids."

"Ah," Jesse nodded. "That makes sense." He leaned forward, forcing me to look up at him. Our bodies were perfectly aligned even though we weren't touching. I could feel his body heat, see a million stars overhead framing his handsome face. I could smell a wood burning stove and crushed autumn leaves and fresh mountain air. And this moment was perfect. This would have been the moment that had pushed me firmly into head-over-heels territory with Jesse.

Only Sayer was back. And here. And in my town and very suddenly my life. And... the moment fell flat.

I didn't know if Jesse sensed me pulling away or if he never intended to kiss me anyway, but he pushed through the moment by reaching around me and opening the door. "I don't think your friend's thing for you is in the past. He seemed pretty into you still."

It wasn't possible to take those words seriously. For so many reasons. Anger bubbled inside me, like lava trickling down the side of an active volcano. Slow, constant and destructive. Like all of my feelings for the past five years.

130

But I couldn't share any of that with Jesse. Instead, I shook my head and waited for Jesse to move around the front of the truck and climb in. "Thanks for being a good sport tonight. Sorry, our plans were kind of derailed."

He turned to me, leaning back against the door. "Do you still want to grab a bite to eat?"

I let my gaze float over Jesse, appreciating him and his friendship and the Colorado cowboy he was. He was all solid muscle and tall, unrelenting frame. I pictured him on one of his horses, cowboy hat on his head, looking like he belonged on the cover of a grocery store romance novel. I should want to go to dinner with him. I should want to finish this date.

But after crashing into my past like it was a brick wall and I'd been driving a hundred miles an hour, all I really wanted to do was go to bed.

"Don't hate me," I whispered, just barely making the excuse audible. "But that whole ordeal kind of wore me out. I don't think I'd be any fun at dinner."

Jesse leaned forward, his eyes deepening with concern. "That's okay, Caroline. I can take you home."

His simple acceptance made me feel even worse. "Sorry, Jesse. I... Well, to be honest, I used to have a thing for Sayer too. We ended badly. Seeing him tonight?" I turned and stared out the windshield at The DC Initiative glowing in the night, alive with movement and people and all the ghosts of my past. "I had hoped I would never see him again."

Jesse sat there for a few long minutes, watching me watch the gallery. I couldn't find the courage to look at him again, to let him see the raw emotion spilling out of me. It was too much. All of it was too much.

And what I wanted to do—take a hot bubble bath and psychoanalyze every single jaw tick and raised eyebrow and minute detail in an investigative report of what the hell Sayer Wesley was up to—I couldn't do. I didn't have time to get lost in the past or even deal with the present. I needed to think about the future.

I needed to think about Juliet. And Francesca. And I needed to figure out how the hell to get us out of this town.

Jesse drove me back to my apartment and walked me to the lobby door. We said goodbye as friends, and I hoped we would be after the weirdness of tonight wore off. I took the elevator up to my floor and let myself in.

131

Juliet and Frankie were asleep on the couch while movie credits played on the TV. The lights were dim save for the small spotlight above the sink. The windows were open, letting in the cool autumn breeze.

I moved over to the kitchen sink, lifting my face to the smoky air that floated through the open window there. It curled around my face and caressed my hair before sinking into my skin, grabbing hold of my bones and reminding me of how much I'd let this place get into me. I'd let it change me. Save me. And now the thought of leaving it, this city, this life...

It hurt.

I hurt.

I threw my clutch on the counter and noticed the note immediately. I would try to figure out when exactly he'd slipped it inside later. I had been paying attention the entire time. As soon as I saw Gus, I was hyper-aware of his movements and Sayer's.

The white corner of the paper stuck out of the side pocket, proof that they still had the skills to pull some things off.

I pulled out the note and found Sayer's familiar handwriting. Ache and anger bloomed side by side.

I know this is going to be difficult for you, but don't leave town, Six. Not if you know what's good for you.

I made a groaning sound. Cliché much, Sayer?

"What's that?"

I sucked in a sharp breath and stifled a scream. I hadn't heard Francesca approach. She was just very suddenly there, looking like a horror movie apparition with her sleep-wild hair and smudgy eyeliner.

Her brows drew down over how I huddled against the counter, cradling the loathsome note I wanted to burn. "They're here. They found us."

She tugged the note out of my hand, her finger ice cold as it brushed mine. "Who?"

I met her terrified gaze. "Sayer. Augustus. They're here. They opened the gallery."

She looked down at the note, reading it and rereading it and rereading it. "No."

"I saw them, Frankie. I talked to them. They locked Jesse and me in their basement office and—"

She held up a hand. "Start at the beginning. Tell me everything."

So I did. I told her how the art gallery was amazing and how Jesse and I were having a great time when suddenly Gus showed up. I told her about Sayer and how he'd changed and how he hadn't changed. How I'd unlocked the basement door and how Jesse totally picked up on the ex vibe between Sayer and me. And then finally, how I found the note.

"But we're going to leave anyway, right?" Francesca demanded. I could see the wheels turning in her head. She was counting her money and pooling our resources. She was driving through Colorado to Wyoming and up to Montana and maybe straight on to Canada. She was crumpling the note in her hand, already dismissing it. "Caroline, tell me we're going to leave anyway."

"Y-yes, of course. Obviously. Frankie, we're leaving. We can't stay."

"But."

I rolled my eyes. "But we can't leave tomorrow. We have loose ends that need to be tied up, and we need to get our resources—"

"Caroline, that's not our deal. We promised each other that if we ever got a whiff of the brotherhood sniffing around, we would be gone. No attachments. No reasons to stay. We'd just get up and go."

I felt her frustration. It was the same as mine. And she was right! We needed to go. We needed to go fast. For Juliet's sake.

But. There was always a but. "They'll follow us, Frankie. They found us this time, they'll find us again."

"Caroline," she hissed.

"They opened a gallery. Okay? They're not here to kill us. They wouldn't have set up shop in our town if they had come to handle us. They're meeting business owners and spreading their names around town. They're stockpiling witnesses and leaving all kinds of money trails. Frankie, I don't know why they're here, but it's not to kill us. At least not yet."

Her eyes bulged. She looked like a porcelain doll standing in the middle of the kitchen in her silk pajama shorts and tank top. She had that delicate eastern European look. Russian genes that should have given her a career in modeling. But her looks meant nothing to her. Her family history and genetics meant even less. The only thing Frankie cared about was her freedom.

Fuck everything else and the whole goddamn world.

"If we're going to leave, Francesca, we have to do this right. We have to pull everything. We have to take everything. We have to start completely over. New names. New identities. A new country. New everything. Give me a week to get it all together. Two tops."

She glared at me. "And what about Juliet? This is a bad idea, Caro."

133

I waved the note in front of her face. "What would you have me do?"

She turned away from me, chewing on her thumbnail. "Does he know?"

Realizing she was staring at the couch where my daughter was stretched out and sleeping soundly, I had the strongest urge to take everything back. We wouldn't wait. We would leave tonight. We would run tonight.

"No," I whispered, but I felt the truth in my words. I didn't know how I knew that he didn't know, just that I was right. I felt it in my bones, in the depths of my soul. Sayer came to play a game with me. If he had known about Juliet, he would have come to wage war. "Not yet."

Frankie nodded, accepting our plan, even though I knew she didn't want to. Without saying another word, she disappeared into her bedroom, and I had no doubt she spent the rest of the night packing and repacking her go bag.

As for me, I scooped Juliet into my arms and took her to my room. I tucked her under my covers and then kept my eyes on her the entire time I got ready for bed. Finally, I crawled next to her and pulled her into me. Breathing in the sweet smell of her shampoo, I finally let myself relax.

Sayer didn't know about her.

Sayer wasn't going to find out about her.

I would dodge him for a week, get my assets together, say my secret goodbyes and then leave.

Forever.

Except when I closed my eyes I saw the words from his notes, the ones calling me out for my past sins, the ones throwing my necessary decisions in my face.

I know this is going to be hard for you...

He had no idea how hard it was for me to leave DC five years ago.

And he had no idea how hard it would be for me to leave Frisco now. And not just because I loved this sleepy little town.

Sayer Wesley was back in my life. And for better or worse, I was going to leave him all over again. Only this time I had a bad feeling I wasn't going to survive it.

Chapter Thirteen

*T*uesday morning felt like a miracle. I had not only survived the weekend, but I'd survived a hell of a Monday. And not just because my past had come back to haunt me.

No, Monday had been bad because Mondays were usually bad. And because the occupants of cabin four had clogged the toilet, not bothered to call us or fix the issue, and then flooded the master bedroom. Then cabin seven had broken the picture window in their living room—shattered it. Let this be a lesson about teenage boys and canoe paddles indoors. And cabin eleven had jacked up their hot tub with wild, drunk sex.

Ah, the glamorous life of a resort manager. I couldn't even remember what wild, drunk sex was like. But I did clean up after those participating in it quite often.

As the manager, weekends were beyond obnoxious to work, but nothing was ever as bad as a Monday morning because nobody fessed up to their mayhem until checkout.

It was the reason Mags didn't mind me taking weekends off. She figured I would have to deal with all the crap come Monday morning anyway—literally.

She was so lucky she had me.

But did she really?

What would happen to Maggie's on the Mountain if I just suddenly disappeared?

I stared down at my little black book of local handymen. She would find someone else. Probably the very day I didn't show up.

That was how Summit County worked. Everybody wanted to live in ski country. It was a twenty-something's dream come true. I would leave and then a gorgeous blonde from like Switzerland or Norway or something would roll into town and just walk into the office and stand behind the desk like she always belonged there. Maggie's reaction would be a shoulder shrug and a muttered, "That seems about right." And all of Frisco would move on in happy merriment.

"Plumber," I said out loud. "I need to find a plumber."

My phone buzzed in my pocket and I pulled it out immediately, stabbing at the number code so I could read the text. It read, Still alive. Still in town. Still think this is a stupid idea.

Francesca's text made me smile. The text also made me breathe a sigh of relief. Frankie had Juliet today since her job at the swanky Lodge at Blackburn didn't have a regular schedule like mine. She also didn't have a boss that checked out cowboys with her or gave her the weekends off. But she did get corporate benefits and better health insurance and free rooms at any of the sister resorts around the world.

She also made almost twice as much as me. And she didn't have to work until Thursday this week, so I was taking full advantage of her time off.

I tapped a quick reply into my phone, you're the best!

To which she replied, any sign?

Frankie and I had done our own covert ops over the weekend. Taking turns, we both scouted out The DC Initiative. From a distance, of course. Sayer and Gus spent the remainder of their weekend at their gallery and restaurant. We both witnessed them making nice with the locals and schmoozing the out of town guests. They seemed friendly and open and kind to their mostly female employees.

That said, we couldn't see a ton of what they were doing sitting in our dark cars on side streets, peering through binoculars at night time. But nothing we saw screamed of shady behavior.

Which was exactly how we knew something crazy was going on.

First things first, Sayer and Gus had been breaking rules and the law for as long as we'd known them. I had known Sayer for fifteen years, and Gus longer than that and there was not a time in either of their lives they weren't working on a scam, coming up with the next scam or reaping the rewards of a scam. They were thieves. Criminals. Con-artists. *Bratva*.

It was in their blood.

Secondly, Sayer had only been released from prison recently. I didn't make it a habit to search for him on the internet. I didn't want to ping the wrong watchdog and get someone on my trail. But I had my ear to the ground enough that only a few short months ago, I knew for a fact, he still hadn't been able to win parole.

Third. And this was probably the most important point. Frankie and I had abandoned them. We'd straight up run away. I had my reasons with Sayer, but leaving Gus behind had been an asshole move on our part. We had always planned to escape, the three of us, together, united.

But when it came time to go... Gus was on Sayer's side. Gus was moving his way up the ranks, set to take over his dad's job as bookkeeper. He was learning the ropes and the ins and outs of the business. He was gaining notoriety and respect, along with stacks and stacks of cash.

We had to ask ourselves if we knew for sure that Gus would come with us. We couldn't take the chance that he would even waffle for one second. When it came down to it, we felt as though he would rather stay with the brotherhood, and his biological brother and Sayer.

As for Sayer?

Nothing, Six. Do you understand that? Nothing could make me leave them. They're the only family I've ever known.

What about me? What about the family you're going to start with me?

They're my brothers, Caro. I won't. He'd sucked in a deep, final breath. *I can't.*

I had Sayer's answer. I didn't need to ask him my question. He'd been super clear on what to expect.

Maggie walked out of her office, ready to spit nails and breathe fire. "Move that family coming in today to the king suite. Tell them it's a complimentary upgrade. And then let's just freaking hope and pray that they don't want to extend their stay. With three rooms in the shitter, it's going to be a miracle if we can get through this week." She put her hand on her forehead and spun toward the wall with a pinned map of the cabin layout on it. "I have no idea how hard it is to pull a sex toy out

137

of a hot tub jet, but I'm hoping the repair is simple and straightforward."

"And cheap," I added. "We also need it to be cheap."

"Son of a bitch," she growled.

At Maggie's look of frustrated helplessness, I rushed to assure her. "We're just close to the end of our repair budget for the month. We have some saved for a rainy day though. If we go over this month, we'll be okay."

She cocked her head and breathed out slowly. "You're sure?"

"I've been running the numbers with the estimates I've received so far. Barring no hidden problems, like black mold in all the bathrooms, we should be okay. More than okay."

Her lips tugged up into a reluctant smile. "Is that your subtle way of telling me 'I told you so?' I can admit it, the emergency fund was a good idea. I don't really need a new car anyway. Or new clothes. Or hell, that vacation to Cancun I promised myself I'd take before I turned sixty."

I did not smile back. "You should always have a backup plan. Sometimes it pays to have three or four."

"*Careful Caroline*. What would I do without you?"

Her question was said jokingly, meant to bring me out of my depressed funk. But her words twisted the blade in an already open wound. What would she do without me? She couldn't run this place by herself anymore. She'd only just started to relax. "Go bankrupt?" I suggested, only half-kidding.

She bobbled her head back and forth, considering the answer. "Yeah, well good thing you're not going anywhere."

The door to the office jingled, throwing Maggie's words right back in her face. Sayer stood in the doorway, bringing the chilly October afternoon with him. Thunderclouds rolled overhead and lightning streaked across the sky. Unlike Jesse that walked into this office framed in golden light like an angelic halo, Sayer walked into this place with fire and brimstone on his heels.

For a heavy, pressurized minute, all I could do was stare at this man that used to be my entire world. He was even more shocking to behold today. Friday night he had been all crisp lines and glossy revenge. Today he was casual in a long-sleeved Henley and low-slung jeans. His bigger, better, prison-bulked arms were huge compared to the gangly things I remembered from our youth. His shoulders were broader. His jaw somehow more defined, more unforgiving. And of all things... he was wearing glasses.

They should have been out of place on his face. He was the quintessential tough guy. He used to beat people up on a regular basis. He'd just gotten out of prison. The black-framed hipster glasses should have been one hundred percent ridiculous on that face. Yet... somehow, they only added to his allure. They made him more mysterious. Even more different than the boy I ran away from five years ago. He was so terrifying my stomach flipped with nerves. And lust. Mostly nerves. "What do you want?" The words were out of my mouth before I could temper them.

Maggie cut a glare in my direction. "W-welcome to Maggie's on the Mountain," she stuttered. See? Even Maggie of the Mountain was scared of this man. And she was the toughest broad I knew.

Sayer ignored her. "A room," he told me, answering my question. His crystal clear blue gaze, only magnified behind those lenses, tore from mine to inspect the dated office. "Or a cabin, I guess. Whatever it is you rent out here."

"We're booked," I answered quickly, lest Maggie get any ideas.

His eyebrows rose skeptically. "You're booked?"

I couldn't answer immediately. I was having trouble catching my breath. Why was he here? How had he found out where I worked? Had he decided today was the day I died? Had he finally got the kill order from the *pakhan*?

Maggie let out a groan of a sigh, not worried about the terrifying man on the other side of the counter at all. "We are unfortunately. Three of our cabins are out of commission after the weekend. The situation has left us in somewhat of a bind. We're scrambling to find cabins for everyone through the week."

Sayer seemed undeterred by our answer. "What's wrong with them?"

Maggie looked back and forth between us. "Do you two know each other?"

I said, "No," at the same time Sayer said, "Yes." Which blew my cover.

It was hard to admit, but I had managed to play it smoother at the gallery. Tucking my hands into my pockets, lest I truly give myself away by smacking my palm to my forehead, I tried to recover while Sayer stood smugly across the desk, waiting for me to dig my own grave. "We used to," I said. "It's been... a long time."

"It's been a long time since you've seen each other?" Maggie filled in. I nodded. "But now you, Mr. ..."

139

"Smith," Sayer supplied.

"Mr. Smith, would like to rent a cabin from Caroline—the friend you haven't seen in awhile?"

One side of Sayer's mouth kicked up into a smile, and my heart squeezed as if two invisible fists were around it. Why was looking at him so difficult? Why did this hurt so much? Why wasn't I more afraid?

I should be more afraid.

I should probably be begging for my life or something.

But I couldn't bring myself to do it. Sayer wasn't a killer, at least not the Sayer I knew. And if he was going to book a room, that meant he probably wasn't going to throw a black hood over my head, toss me in the trunk of a car and drive me back to DC.

At least not yet.

My fear temporarily receded, making plenty of room for my raw frustration. "Mr. Smith showed up to be a pain in the ass, Maggie. He doesn't really want a room."

Sayer stepped up to the counter, pulling out his wallet. "Mr. Smith would like a room. Mr. Smith even needs a room." His gaze found mine again, all sincerity and openness. All lies. "Gus and I will kill each other if we go one more day in the same hotel room. As fun as it's been living out of a suitcase, I need my space until I can find something permanent."

Permanent.

The word was a gut punch.

I sucked in a sharp, silent breath and reinforced my nerves with steel. If it was a game of wills he wanted, well, I didn't need five years in federal prison to build the muscles to play. I was born with them. "It's like Maggie said, Mr. Smith, we don't have anything available for you. But there are other resorts elsewhere on the mountain that would be happy to take your money." I leaned forward on my elbows, flashing Sayer a confident smile. A smile that said, you can't rattle me, hotshot. You can't show up after five years, looking like this, sounding like sin, and wearing glasses for God's sake and get into my head.

I'm tougher than that.

Stronger.

Meaner.

Fucking determined.

His gaze dropped to my smile, the way it used to. With my new resolve bouncing around my head, I forced my face to keep it in place. "I don't want to go elsewhere on the mountain, Six. I want to stay here."

140

"Well, we don't have a cabin available."

"Well, maybe you should one." Then he looked over at Maggie and added, "Please."

"Maggie—"

She ignored me. The traitor. "Here's the situation, Mr. Smith—"

"Sayer." He smiled gently at her again, completely freaking wooing her. "Please call me Sayer."

Maggie's smile was uncertain, like she hadn't been expecting a first name.

No, it was more than that. She hadn't been expecting a first name like that.

Nobody was, I wanted to tell her.

We were all caught off guard.

It was Sayer's first breach of your defenses.

Damn him. What was that saying about old dogs and new tricks? Well, maybe the old dogs didn't *need* to learn new tricks. Maybe their old tricks worked just fine.

Maggie quickly recovered, "Here's the situation, Sayer. I have three cabins out of commission. The first is flooded from a backed-up toilet. The second is littered with broken glass and freezing from a shattered picture window. The third is in working order, save for the hot tub, which has a rubber dildo shoved into one of the jets. The cabin itself is fine, but we're hesitant to rent it out to paying guests. We don't want them to feel awkward when they find out the reason the handyman has to have access to their deck." Sayer's lips twitched with the effort not to smile. "If any of those accommodations seem habitable to you, you're welcome to them. I'll even throw in a twenty percent discount until whichever of the problem rooms you rent is repaired. How does that sound?"

A respectful smile stretched across Sayer's face, reminding me so fiercely of our daughter that my knees nearly buckled. "I'll take the cabin with hot tub issues."

"You won't be able to use it," I quickly reminded him. "Until we can get it fixed and that could be... months."

Maggie slipped in a quick, "Days. It will only be a few days."

He addressed Maggie, "I'll survive."

I gave it another shot. "Most of our guests demand a working hot tub. That's one of their favorite features."

He tilted his head and glared at me. "Caroline, I haven't been in a hot tub since we snuck into that Italian party six years ago and locked ourselves in the Don's room. I think I'll manage a few more days."

Throwing caution to the wind and one last ditch Hail Mary, I turned to Maggie. "He's been in prison for the past five years. That's why he hasn't had access to any hot tubs."

Her jaw hardened and she fully fixed her attention on me. It was like a wall went up between her and Sayer. Whatever charm he'd laid on her fizzled away, and she was herself again. "Did he go to prison for hurting you, Caroline?"

I could have said yes. I could have lied. She wouldn't have let him stay then. She would have made him leave. And not just her resort, but the whole freaking mountain. She probably would have escorted him to the border of Colorado and kicked his ass to the other side.

But that particular lie tasted like ash and died on my tongue. I couldn't make myself say it. I couldn't make myself stoop to that level.

He had never put his hands on me without my consent or mutual desire. He had never done anything to my body that I didn't absolutely want him to do.

Fine, he'd broken my heart into a million little jagged pieces. But that wasn't exactly punishable by a court of law.

"No," I confessed quietly, reluctantly. "He's never put his hands on me."

She immediately relaxed, the invisible barrier of her desire to kill him disappeared and a patronizing smile replaced her granite expression. "Well, then we all have our pasts. Don't we, Caroline? Judgmental isn't a good color on you."

Sufficiently chastised, I turned away so I could roll my eyes at the window and pull out a map and a keycard and all the other things I needed to exchange with Sayer.

"Why don't I handle this," I told Maggie, "and you call the repairman so Mr. Smith can have a working hot tub in no time." She narrowed her eyes at me, not liking that I was trying to get rid of her. She wanted to eavesdrop, the nosey Nelly. "I mean, it's been six years. Don't make the man wait longer than he has to."

Maggie shook her head but grabbed the little black book of business contacts I'd left on the counter anyway. To Sayer she said, "It was a pleasure to meet you, Sayer Smith. I truly hope you enjoy your time here. Please let my manager, Caroline, know if you need anything. She can be very helpful when she remembers to take the stick out of her ass."

Sayer coughed in surprise at the same time I hissed, "Oh my God, Maggie!"

"See you in a bit, darlin'." She was absolutely unapologetic. "Make sure you walk Sayer to his accommodations. We wouldn't want him to get lost on the way."

"Oh, I'll walk Sayer to his accommodations," I mumbled to the reservation page on my computer. And then I'll push him off the side of the mountain.

"I'm sure I can find my way," Sayer offered after Maggie disappeared into her office. "I know how to read a map."

"I'll need some information before we get to that part," I clipped out instead. "And a credit card."

He blinked at me. "I'll transfer money in the morning."

"You know how this works, Sayer. I need a card for the file." Meeting his gaze again, I searched for truth or obvious lies so I would know which truths he was trying to hide. "Unless you don't have a card? Maybe you don't have one that matches your driver's license?"

He pulled out his wallet and thumbed a card from the slot. "Is there room service?"

I took the credit card from him, careful not to touch any part of him. My eyes quickly scanned the raised font reading Sayer Smith in plain letters.

So what? He had managed to get a new identity, and it came with good credit. If anything, it just proved my original theory—Sayer knew how to survive.

"No room service. But there are delivery apps that will pick up anything in town and deliver it to your cottage. We're a ways from town though. It doesn't always arrive hot." Switching gears, I got back to work mode. "How long will you be staying?" I asked, for the sake of the computer screen. I couldn't go to the check-in page until he answered. I wasn't being nosey. Okay, I was being a little nosey. "I need to know for the computer."

He leaned forward, resting on his forearms. "For the computer."

"I'm trying to check you in, dummy."

"I forgot how ballsy you are," he said to his hands, head bowed. "How reckless."

I pushed the rolling chair back. "Okay, I'm over the mystery man bullshit, Sayer. Either threaten me or kill me or do whatever it is you're going to do to me. But let's stop whatever game this is because I'm over it."

His half-smile was cruel, vindictive. His gaze never left mine, daring me to look away. "You think this is a game? That after five years, I show up here to... tease you?"

His words were so hollow, spoken with no emotion. It was the hardness that stabbed at my heart, the wall between us so wide and tall and unbreakable that hot tears pricked at the backs of my eyes. I hadn't thought that. After what I did to him, I would never think that. But the way he said it... like I was my fifteen-year-old self, dropping hints and flirting with him. Like he was eighteen again, chasing me around the back alleys of DC and beating up all the other boys that tried to talk to me.

Infusing my voice with mettle and moxie and ice, I told him honestly, "No. No, I don't think this is a game. But you're here for a reason, Sayer. And since I can't possibly guess what it is, you need to just tell me."

He made an amused sound in the back of his throat. "You left me, Six. Vanished. Disappeared. There was no note or phone call. Gus didn't even know what the hell happened. One day you visited me and you're all, 'I love you, Sayer. I would do anything for you, Sayer. I'll wait for you forever, Sayer.' And then poof." He smacked the counter, making me jump at the sudden sound. "Nobody can find precious Caroline fucking Valera. Not even her old man. And what can I do about it? My girl is gone. Fucking gone. And I can't do a goddamn thing about it."

"You—"

He had no time for my excuses. "Do you know how frustrating that is, Six? How infuriating? The only person you've ever loved disappears out of the fucking blue, and you're stuck in prison like an asshole, helpless. Totally helpless. I lost my fucking mind thinking the worst had happened to you. I went insane. That darkness..." He ducked his head again, hiding whatever memories reflected in his eyes. "You can't understand the depth of that darkness, Caroline. Won't ever understand it."

I was nothing but a slow-beating heart, struggling desperately not to make any noise, or movement or be anything but invisible. "Sayer," the word was a whispered apology that he deserved.

His head snapped up, almost as if he just remembered that I was here. "Then I show up in this hole of a town and here you are. Not dead. Not kidnapped by Italians or Irish or a crazy fucking serial killer trying to get to me. You're just here. Working and living and dating. And normal.

Happy. Fucking adjusted. I'm not here to play games with you, Caro. I'm here to live out a dream I once I had with a girl I once loved." He leaned forward, holding my gaze, twisting it, squeezing it, crushing it. "Me being here has nothing to do with you because not everything is about you, Caroline. And after all this time, I am not about you at all."

I wanted to say something smart in reply; cutting, soul-ripping. But nothing came out of my mouth. Not one cruel response wandered into my head. I could do nothing but gape at him like a fish out of water, gasping for breath. I tried to console myself by believing I deserved that. I did. He was right. I had left him without a single word of where I was going or that I was going to be all right.

He had no idea that anything was wrong. That I needed to leave. That I had to.

And despite what he believed of me now, I had done the right thing.

But I could never tell him that.

"Six weeks," he said.

I just kept staring at him, only barely getting the feeling back in my appendages. "W-what?"

"Put me down for six weeks. To start."

Remembering what I was doing and why he was here and that I had a job to do, I entered that into the computer. "The cabin isn't available for six weeks. I can give it to you until... Next Thursday."

He rapped the counter with his knuckles. "Make this easy on yourself, Six, and figure it out."

Glaring at the computer and biting my bottom lip until I tasted blood, I fiddled around with the computer. "Six weeks? All right, that will be twenty thousand, three hundred and eighty dollars."

He didn't flinch. "Don't forget the dildo discount."

It was all I could do to keep from screaming. "I'll refund you the difference after the repairman comes."

He leaned back, standing up straight. His shoulders relaxed and his face did something too—but it wasn't relaxed. It was... I didn't know what it was. "Make sure you include an itemized receipt when you do."

Since Sayer showed back up in my life, I had been afraid that he was going to murder me. What I hadn't considered was me murdering him. That should be a concern for everybody. "For tax purposes?" I taunted him.

"Obviously."

And kudos to him because he sounded serious.

I finished entering his information and locking down his rental for the next six freaking weeks. I would have to do some rearranging later to figure out the rest of our calendar and upcoming reservations. It was going to be a giant pain in the ass. But I already had a feeling that Maggie was going to side with Sayer anyway.

It had nothing to do with guilt over the way I left things with him five years ago.

Nothing at all.

Because that would be really stupid of me. And dangerous. And basically, shooting myself in the foot.

I didn't have a choice with this one. If Sayer wanted to stay here for six weeks, fine. At least then I could control what he saw of me. Juliet never came to work with me anyway. Problem solved.

Besides, Sayer could hang out for six weeks if that's what he wanted or for the rest of his life or whatever. It wasn't like I was going to stick around.

I ran his card for half the amount of his total stay, for the deposit and made two room keys for him. Pulling out a resort map, I highlighted his path from the main office to where his cabin was located. He'd gotten my favorite cabin. It was isolated from the other cabins, up the mountain a bit. He'd have privacy and quiet—which was something I knew he would appreciate.

"You can call the office if you need anything," I told him the same way I would tell any guest that same information. Granted I was as pleasant as a rock, but still, he couldn't turn me in for not doing my job. "If you need more towels, or a wake-up call, or directions around town, just let us know. We're happy to help." I highlighted the number to the main office on the side of the map.

He leaned forward again, bringing us close very suddenly. We still had the counter between us, but I had been leaned over with the highlighter. Now he was all in my space, his head barely brushing mine, his hands stretched out beside mine. "A wake-up call," he murmured in that low, sandpapery voice of his. "I'm going to need a wake-up call every morning."

I struggled to swallow the boiling anger. "You don't really want that."

"You offered," he pointed out. "Every morning."

"I'll make sure Maggie knows."

"From you, Six. Seven o'clock. Every morning."

I pushed up on my hands, desperately putting space between us. He smelled like… He smelled differently than he used to. It was distracting. "Sorry, I don't get in until eight."

Plucking the map from the counter, he took a step back. "Not my problem."

This time I let him see my eye roll. "You're going to have to get it from someone else, Sayer. I can't help you."

"Ballsy. So fucking ballsy when I know so very much about you."

My heart dropped to my stomach. Another thinly veiled threat. How long was I going to have to put up with this? "I thought you weren't here to play games. I thought this was just some kind of catastrophic coincidence."

He shrugged. "This isn't a game, Six. This is your fucking life. Don't be stupid with it. Wake-up call at seven. Every morning."

Remembering his note from the other night, I held his glare. "And if I run?"

"Well, that would be pretty goddamn stupid, yeah?" His hand landed on the door to outside. "But, I don't know, I guess try it if you want. I'm up for seeing what happens if you are."

His casual attitude and ambiguous threat sent a chill skittering over me. I felt turned inside out by this man. He wasn't supposed to have found me, by coincidence or not. In one breath, he gutted me with memories of my past and the way I used to feel for him and how badly I'd hurt him. And in another I was terrified for my life, my daughter's life, for this life we'd carved out of nothing and made into something worth protecting. Instead of giving into the fear that curled around me like a slowly tightening snake, I defaulted to the professional in me. "We'll let you know when the repairman will be out to look at your hot tub."

Sayer's expression finally broke, his lips lifting in a barely amused smile. "You do that, Six." He pushed the door open. "Guess I'll see you around then."

I nodded. I guess he would see me around.

And I would see him.

And call him every morning at seven.

I waited until he'd pulled out of the parking lot in a brand-new Jeep Wrangler—apparently he was going all in with this whole Colorado life—before thumping my forehead on the counter and closing my eyes against the press of hot tears.

What had I gotten myself into now?

147

And how was I going to get out of it?

Chapter Fourteen

Ten Years Ago

Frankie walked quickly across the back yard to plant herself at my side. "He's here," she whispered discreetly. "He just walked in with my Uncle Alek."

"Francesca," my dad beamed next to me, excited to be in such proximity to my friend. "You're looking lovely tonight. Growing up to favor your ma, you know that?"

My cheeks flushed on my friend's behalf. Francesca hated drawing attention to herself and she hated being put on display for parties like this one. But her uncles would not tolerate her baseball cap and tomboy look tonight. She did look like her mom in her designer mini dress that had a big bow on the right hip—which was a good thing for her since the entire *bratva* hated her deceased dad. Her hair was down in loose curls and fell almost all the way to her butt. She had even put on makeup tonight, something I'd made her repeat on me when I got over here earlier.

"Th-thanks, Mr. Valero," she mumbled.

"Call me Leon, honey. How many times do I gotta tell you? Nobody calls me Mr. Valero unless they owe me a lotta money."

She lifted her face and attempted a smile, "Leon."

One of her uncles called her name from across the yard, and she snapped to attention. "Please excuse me."

I watched her weave through party guests, careful not to touch anyone. When we were on a job, she was like a ghost. She could slip through a room unseen, unnoticed. But here, she didn't stand a chance. She wasn't just on display. She was the focal point of the room. The poor orphaned princess. Her uncles' pride and joy. The future of the Volkov dynasty.

She had male cousins. It wasn't like the syndicate was going to be entirely left to her. Her uncles had wives and sons and other family to step in. But they had also made a promise to Frankie's mother. They were to give her a future, keep her close to the family, make sure she was taken care of for the rest of her life. She didn't have a choice. The syndicate was her life.

It would always be her life.

My dad put his arm around me, ducking his head so we wouldn't be overheard. "That girl okay?"

"She's fine," I replied automatically. My dad squeezed my shoulder, demanding truth. "She hates being the center of attention," I shared, confessing it like it was a secret. "These kinds of things make her uncomfortable."

He relaxed, letting out a good-natured chuckle. "Yeah, what is it about teenage girls, huh? These things make you uncomfortable too."

Was it so surprising that being at a house with thieves, murderers, drug dealers, sex traffickers and all manner of lowlife scum would make me, a fifteen-year-old girl, uncomfortable? Apparently.

"I feel out of place," I said, shrugging off his heavy arm. He smelled like booze and cigarettes and the girl he'd brought with him as his date tonight. "There aren't that many people here my age."

"Lucky for you, I've heard there's a job tonight. You can get out of here soon enough."

Only my dad would be so excited about a job for me. The fact that it would be highly illegal and dangerous didn't bother him at all, even though I doubted he knew any of the details. He didn't have my clearance level—something that equally made him proud and drove him crazy. I strained my neck and tilted it to the side, cracking the bones and releasing some stress.

"I haven't heard anything," I argued. And I hadn't. We were supposed to be celebrating Dymetrus's birthday. The whole gang was here. A girl was supposed to jump out of a cake later and I had been curious about the finer details of that for a week. Was it a real cake? Or a plastic one like what you'd see on TV? Would she be covered in frosting? Would she be only covered in frosting? Because gross.

I wasn't usually invited to shindigs. The little parts Frankie and I played were usually purposefully overlooked. I was paying a childhood debt, and Frankie got to do whatever Frankie wanted. We reported to Sayer and Atticus and nobody else. They told us what to do, and we did it. That was it. That was our part. They paid us enough to keep us from wanting to take a piece for ourselves. We were Sixes; we were the *bratok*, soldiers with a specific purpose. But tonight, we got a piece of the cake.

Only I wasn't going to eat any of it if a woman jumped out of it.

"Here comes the kid. He'll tell you." My dad's attention moved to a cluster of young guys walking toward us. They moved through the crowd as one unit, the other, older guys stepping back, out of their way. Sayer was at the front, Gus and Atticus behind him like the wings of a fighter jet.

It was ridiculous how much respect they commanded, how much influence they had. Gus and Sayer weren't even out of high school yet. Atticus was an asshole. But they'd somehow built this untouchable reputation without being killers, without dealing in women, drugs or weapons.

Money talked. And Sayer brought in a lot of money.

He caught my eye from across the decorated backyard, jerking his chin in a command for me to follow him. I thought about looking away and pretending I didn't see him. I could probably pull it off. I wasn't always looking at Sayer. I looked at other things.

Sometimes.

"That's your cue, kiddo." My dad nudged me with his elbow.

Letting out an agitated sigh, I looked at my dad. "Aren't you supposed to protect me from this kind of stuff?"

He let out a bark of laugh. "Protect you? Honey, I'm proud of you." And then his eyes truly teared up. The bastard. "Who would've thought my daughter would be able to do what you do? I knew taking you on all those jobs when you were young would pay off. I saw the potential in you from day one. Now look at you. Think of your future, Caro. Don't say I never did nothing for you. Cause you keep this up and you won't gotta worry about nothing, baby. You'll be set for life."

Yeah, right. Life in prison maybe. "Do you know how screwed up that is, Dad?" I asked calmly.

His smile stretched. "I think you meant to say thank you."

"Unbelievable." I turned around, knowing better than to keep Sayer and Atticus waiting. "I'll see you later."

"Probably not going to be home tonight though," he called after me, and I decided it was better if I didn't know why.

I slipped into the crowd the same way Frankie had, silently, stealthily, smoothly, clocking pockets and purses as I went. For being criminals, these people had no idea how to keep track of their crap. There was so much to take—so much there to be stolen.

They assumed they were safe here, surrounded by their brothers and their weapons. But these were the moments we waited for. The game had begun.

My fingers were light as feathers. A roll of cash peeking out of the side pocket of trousers, a money clip just barely visible in a back pocket, by the time I'd reached the other side of the party, I had three hundred bucks. I divided the money and slipped it into the cups of my bra. The extra padding wouldn't hurt either.

Sayer raised his eyebrows as I approached, having caught the tail end of my heist. I shrugged one shoulder and silently dared him to bring it up.

"That's a dangerous game, Six."

I looked away. "No more so than the job tonight."

"You don't know what the job is yet."

"Is it legal?"

His lips twitched. "You have a death wish, is that it?"

We were standing under a tree that had twinkly lights wrapped around each of its branches heavy with the green leaves of summer. There was a band playing some kind of polka music near the house. Women were flirting, and men were laughing. The warm breeze smelled like expensive perfume and July moonlight.

Sayer had dressed up for the night, in a white collared short-sleeve shirt and black shorts. His hair had been styled with actual product and pushed back from his face, tamed into staying in place. He was dangerous. And beautiful. And he was going to ask me to do something that I didn't want to do.

After I said yes, I would blame the magic of the night and the three hundred bucks hidden inside my bra.

But Sayer had a kind of magic all his own. He stepped closer to me, trailing his finger over my bare shoulder. Dad had said I needed to dress up, that this was a big deal. So Frankie had let me borrow one of her

152

designer things. A strapless emerald green dress that was too short and too tight and too pretty for me—the degenerate daughter of a bookie.

"It's not a death wish," I told Sayer. "It's more like a... get me out of here wish."

He stepped closer, dropping his voice so we weren't overheard. "Where would you go, Six? There's nothing out there that's better than this. You'd be bored. You'd hate it."

Frankie said the same thing to me all the time. I don't know what that said about me. I just knew what I felt and that was hatred for this life, for what we did, for what we stood for. I watched my dad struggle through life at the lowest level. He was either gambling or wishing he was gambling or regretting gambling. He was either asking people for money or making people pay him money or trying to figure out how he was going to pay someone off. He drank too much and smoked too much and slept around way too much.

There had to be more to life than this. There had to be some kind of peace in living a normal, legal, safe life.

I had to believe that. Because I could not live like this forever. I could not be my father. I could not grind out the next thirty years hopping from one job to the next, living in shitty apartments, always looking over my shoulder.

Or worse. What if I got caught? By one of our marks? Or the police?

How the hell would I survive prison?

"I'd love it," I argued with Sayer. "I'd get a normal job and a bank account and a library card. I'd even go to church."

His head moved back and forth. He didn't believe me. "Yeah, where? Where would you live this normal, *boring* life?"

I thought of the most normal place I could, the most boring, the most unexciting, the most even-paced place in all of existence. "The Midwest," I said confidently.

He laughed this time, low and truly amused. It made my stomach flip. It made my heart flutter. It made me question all of my dreams about the Midwest and want to throw them away.

"The Midwest? Any place in particular? Or are you just going to grab the next covered wagon and see where you end up?"

"Don't be an asshole." But I was trying not to laugh.

"No, it's cool, Caro. I get it. Why stay here and get rich beyond your wildest dreams, when you could go there and live amongst the corn and cows."

I smiled against my better judgment. "Exactly."

"I'm not even sure they have cable."

"They have cable," I said confidently. Although I wasn't one hundred percent sure about that.

"No fast cars."

"They have those too."

"No museums."

"Where do you think the Midwest is? The moon?"

His smile was wicked, his blue, blue eyes full of the devil himself. "I just want you to think this all the way through. I want you to weigh all your options. Make a pros and cons list."

"I'll be sure to do that."

He took another step closer to me, his chest almost touching mine. "You're too pretty for the Midwest, Caroline. Too daring. Too independent. They wouldn't know what to do with a girl like you."

I struggled to think straight. "You think I'm pretty?"

His head dropped so that his lips were at my ear. "I always think you're pretty, but tonight you're making it hard for me to breathe."

Now I couldn't breathe. He lifted his head, showing me the truth in his eyes, the conviction in his expression. "Promise me you won't leave, you won't head off into the sunset until you say goodbye. It would kill me. You know that right?"

"Sayer..."

His jaw ticked, the muscle popping out a warning that he was serious. "Promise me. Don't just leave. At least say goodbye."

"I promise," I said quickly. "Of course. Of course I'll say goodbye."

He nodded once, moving his tongue slowly over his bottom lip. His hand lifted, landing along my jaw. His fingertips dug into my hair and his palm curved around my face, holding me tightly. His head dipped, and I knew this was the moment. He was going to kiss me. He was finally going to kiss me!

"Are we going to do this or what?"

Wrong.

This was the moment I was finally going to murder Atticus.

"Yeah," Sayer called back. "Yeah, we're going to do this."

An hour later, Gus had dropped us off two blocks away and we were creeping toward a four-story Victorian row house in Georgetown. Atticus let out a low whistle.

"Quite the piece of real estate," he mumbled.

Sayer ducked, so his head was lower than the hedges in the back yard. "Jealous?"

Atticus shot him a look. "Nah. It's only a matter of time, Wesley. Only I'll get it a hell of a lot sooner than fucking Fat Jack. And I'll know better than to get greedy and piss it away."

Childhood had made my loyalties stronger than I realized, because I added, "We don't know anything yet. We're just supposed to look around. There might not be anything."

Sayer and Atticus stayed quiet. Their silence said enough though. Nobody but me thought Fat Jack was innocent. The *pakhan* wanted us to take a look around his house while he was at the party. They wanted evidence before they took action. They wanted us to come up with a reason for his suspicious behavior.

I felt sick.

"We'll start in the basement," Atticus whispered as he clipped the lock on the back gate. Somewhere in the neighborhood, Gus used his computer magic to shut off the security cameras posted around the house.

"We'll start upstairs and meet you in the middle," Sayer confirmed.

And that's what we did. The boys let me pick the lock on the back door since I had the gentlest touch, and we separated. Frankie with Atticus. I stayed with Sayer.

Up we went, creeping up three flights of stairs to the master bedroom on the top floor. My nose wrinkled at Fat Jack's sense of décor. Okay, it wasn't like my two-bedroom apartment with my dad was anything to brag about. But I never understood why men with money always went for the black silk sheets.

"I should have guessed," I told Sayer. He raised his eyebrows, having no idea what I was talking about. "A mirror above the bed. Because why wouldn't a man that looks like Fat Jack want to watch himself get nasty?"

Sayer chuckled darkly. "I don't know, Six, maybe it's for educational purposes. Maybe he's trying to improve his game."

I wrinkled my nose, struggling not to gag. Fat Jack was three hundred pounds of bubbling anger with a vodka-reddened nose and deep-set dull eyes. He had no soul, no sympathy, no reason to look out for anybody but himself. If he could find girls willing to come back here with him, their needs were the last thing he was concerned about in that bed.

"I've never understood the silk sheets though," I whispered as we made our way around the room, looking for clues and evidence and anything damning. "Aren't they slippery? I'm picturing Fat Jack like a greased pig in that bed." I shook my head quickly, trying to rid myself of the mental image. "Scratch that. I'm not picturing Fat Jack at all. Ick."

I felt Sayer's gaze on me from across the room. "You've never, you know, messed around on silk sheets before?"

Giving him my back, I picked up the edge of a picture frame, my hidden fingers curled under the sleeves of my cardigan. I'd brought it in case I got cold tonight, but it doubled for fingerprint protection in case of last minute jobs.

My cheeks flamed red and I wanted to jump off the balcony just off Fat Jack's room. Was Sayer serious? Had I ever messed around on silk sheets? The real question was, had I ever messed around at all? No. The answer was definitely no. And it was all his fault.

Not that I felt like a huge chunk of my life was missing because nobody had ever brought me back to their sleazy den of iniquity and slid me around on their slippery bed while they watched their technique in the mirror overhead. But, still. It was the principle of the thing.

Instead of saying any of that to him though, I lied. Because that's what I did. I was a liar that lied for a living, to stay alive, to pay off some stupid debt to the syndicate. "That's what I'm saying," I told him. "I think they're more work than they're worth. Not to mention tacky."

Sayer's voice was devoid of his previous humor when he said. "I didn't realize you had so many opinions about silk sheets."

I glanced at him over my shoulder as I moved to rifle through some papers on a desk in the corner. "It's not like I'm high maintenance about the whole thing, I just draw the line at self-indulged assholes. That's all." Oh my God. What was I even saying? I blamed Sayer. He shouldn't have made it sound like he had so much experience on silk sheets. It was annoying. And gross. And turned the normal female inside me into a green-eyed jealousy monster.

"Those are some high standards, Six."

I spun around, glaring at him across the room. He had moved parallel with me, near a dresser in the corner. The room was crowded with our unsaid words and frustrated feelings and the constant push and pull. Or maybe that was just me.

"Do I need high standards?" I asked, knowing it would piss him off.

"Are you serious?"

I shrugged as I walked over to a locked side table near the French doors leading to the balcony. "Oh, you're one to talk, Mr. Judgmental. Didn't you go home with Crystal what's her name last Friday? Obviously you were exercising your incredibly picky decision-making skills."

156

"You're awfully mouthy tonight, Caro."

He'd moved to stand next to me. I could smell him again, feel the frustration rolling off him. And it took everything in me to keep from gloating. It was nice to get under his skin. He was always under mine and in my head and pushing into my decisions and plans and better reasoning. He was always there, constant in everything I thought or did or wanted. And I was tired of it.

Tired of him.

I squatted down and did a little magic with the locked drawer using a hairpin and an Allen wrench. It popped open, and I smiled at it. I hated this too. This life. This specific skillset I didn't ask for. Yet, I would take this every day over Sayer. I understood this job, these things. I could see the problem and figure out how to solve it.

Sayer was something else entirely. I didn't know how to pick him open. I didn't know how to con him into playing my game. I didn't know how to take what I wanted from him and leave the rest.

Because it seemed like he just kept taking from me. Or I kept giving to him. Either way, I wasn't getting anything in return, and I hated it.

"I'm always mouthy." I popped back up to check out the contents of the drawer and found Sayer even closer than before. I turned to look at him. "But the point remains. My standards are my choice. As are yours."

Those blue eyes that were my absolute downfall found mine and held on tight. "I didn't go home with Crystal Kanstanova last Friday, Six. Nor have I ever gone home with her. Think what you want of me, but I do have high standards. And she doesn't come close to meeting them."

I sucked in my bottom lip and nibbled on it, ignoring the way the two internal fists that had been squeezing my heart relaxed. But the game between us was still going. I couldn't let him see how much his words affected me or how desperately I wanted to be the reason he hadn't taken Crystal home. She'd been all over him last Friday at the club where the *bratva* spent most of their time. And she dressed like a total slut. I wasn't saying that to be mean. It was just a fact. She was all nip slips and whale tail. It was like her thing, her signature. "I suppose you want me to acknowledge what an upstanding human you are now?"

Sayer's eyes darkened. "I want you to acknowledge what's between us, Caroline. Fucking admit you have a thing for me. I'm tired of chasing you."

I slammed my finger in the drawer. Hissing a curse, I spun to face him. "Is that what you think you've been doing? Chasing me?"

One side of his mouth kicked up. "Since I was twelve years old in an alley I didn't belong in with three dollars to my name."

"Sayer," I whispered, his name like a plea and a prayer, like a desperate demand for more.

"Are you really this blind? You think this was Roman's idea?" He motioned back and forth between us. "That he wanted a team of kids? Six, I've been fighting to be with you since the day you saved my life. My standards are fucking high. I only want the girl that's totally out of reach, that's so much better than me it's embarrassing. I only want the one girl I should let go." He stepped closer to me. "So she can move to the Midwest and have her corn and cows and normal life."

I shook my head. "I-I'm not better than you."

His chin jerked once. "You are. So much better. So much better than anything on this goddamn earth." He dipped his head so that his forehead rested against mine and he lifted both hands to cup my face. It was the closest we had ever been. Butterflies took flight in my stomach and my appendages started to tingle. I had to close my eyes against the sensation, against the heady bliss of Sayer's words and his touch and his body so very hot against mine. "And I know you can do better than me and this life and that you probably should get whatever it is you want so badly, but Caro, I'm going to ask you to stay here. Stay with me. Be with me."

Sayer was three years older than me, eighteen to my meager fifteen. It wasn't that much of a difference, but it had always felt like the difference between being a grown-up and a little kid. Sayer was this big man in the syndicate. He was older than his age, so much tougher and smarter and wiser than he appeared. And I was just this little girl playing at a chance to be around him. I didn't want the syndicate life, but I hadn't had a choice. I didn't want to be good at stealing and lying and cheating, but I didn't have a choice. Sayer had every choice in the world and yet he chose this life.

He could have done anything with his life and he picked the syndicate.

That was how I felt now too. I had never had a choice in loving Sayer. I just had. Always. Since the day I met him, he had been it for me. I couldn't even get myself to pay attention to other guys. It was always Sayer for me.

But he had all the choices in the world. He could have anyone. Be with anyone. And yet, he wanted me.

He wanted me.

"Like as your girlfriend?" I asked because I was fifteen and that was the only thing I could wrap my head around. A distant, more mature part of my brain told me he wasn't just asking for me to be his girlfriend, that his perspective was bigger than mine, more permanent. But I had never had a boyfriend before, let alone had a boy who said things like *that* to me. This was new and uncharted territory. Besides, like I said, Sayer was the only one I wanted, the only one I cared about. I didn't stand a chance.

Sayer's chuckle cascaded over my skin, warming me and pulling goosebumps up at the same time, making my heart race and my blood rush in my veins. "Yeah, Six. You want to be my girlfriend?"

I nodded, giggling a flirty sound I had never made before. "Y-yes. Yes, please."

He caught my words with his lips pressed against mine. I gasped at the sensation, those too-soft lips a heady contrast with the hardness of his body, the rough feel of his hands, the grit of his personality. His mouth moved against mine slowly, carefully.

Sayer might have been my first boyfriend, but he wasn't my only kiss—I had managed to get a few of those in since the first time he kissed me when I was ten. For practice's sake. Boys from school under the bleachers or behind the track mats in the gym. I had no idea what I was doing with someone like Sayer, but I at least wasn't a total amateur when it came to kissing.

Or at least that's what I thought.

But kissing Sayer wasn't just kissing a boy—it was kissing a man. He was all of my dreams and fantasies and desires packaged into one perfectly gorgeous, perfectly dangerous man of my dreams, and I could have spent the entire night just learning the contours of his lips and how they fit against mine.

His teeth caught my bottom lip and then his tongue was there to soothe the nip, coaxing me to open my mouth wider and let him explore me more completely. He tasted like spearmint and everything I'd ever wanted. With my eyes shut tight and my hands tentatively clutching his crisp shirt, I let him lead the kiss just praying I was not making this a horrible experience for him.

Was this going to be the shortest relationship in the history of relationships? Was my bad kissing going to send him running? It was all too much.

I pulled back, gasping for breath and my scattering confidence. His head dropped to the curve of my neck, his breath heating the bare skin there, making me shiver.

He felt the chill run through me and his hands were immediately around my waist, tugging me against his warmth. "Are you cold?" he whispered.

"N-no."

His head pulled back so he could see my face. "Repulsed then?"

His candid question pulled a nervous laugh out of me. "Intimidated," I whispered. "You're terrifying."

He brushed his nose against mine. "You're delicious." Then his mouth was on mine again, and this time it wasn't slow or soft or careful. This time his kiss was hungry. Demanding.

His mouth moved over mine quickly, our lips and tongues tangling together with need for each other, unrestrained want. My hands stopped being shy, smoothing over his chest and stomach, wrapping around his neck and pressing my body against his.

He didn't hold his back either, letting them explore the curves of my waist, the side of my breast, the top of my ass. He didn't go straight to ripping my clothes off, but the feeling was there, the desire. On both sides.

It had felt like we'd been playing this game for five years. This fire between us had been building and building and building and we'd just been adding fuel without bothering to contain it or tame it. And now there was no stopping it. We'd built this pyre, and now we would have to burn at its mercy.

Which was fine with me.

I'd gladly give into the flame to be with Sayer, to stay with him.

When he pulled back this time, we were both flushed, our lips swollen, our eyes dark. His smile was satisfied, cockier than I had ever seen it before.

I struggled to swallow against the lump of emotion in my throat. "Wow," I whispered.

"Knew it was going to be good, Caro. I shouldn't have waited so fucking long."

Blinking against the blinding beauty that was painful in its intensity, I had one clear, resounding thought. I'm going to lose my virginity to this guy.

And the thought after that—He's going to get me to give up running away. And I don't think I care.

I would have gladly handed it over that night had we not been in the middle of Fat Jack's bedroom in the middle of a job.

I stepped away from Sayer, anxious to untangle myself from those dangerous thoughts and my reckless heart. This was what we both wanted. For now. There was no way we would last. We were young. I was really young. And we wanted different things.

This would be good for both of us. I would get over my insane infatuation. And so would Sayer. We'd let this run its course and then we could go our separate ways.

It was almost like this had to happen for us to be able to grow up. Sayer had needed me when we were kids and he needed this now so he could thank me or get over me or whatever. And I needed to see this through so I could move on too. I needed to get Sayer out of my system so that someday I could at least find a way to be attracted to other guys. Sayer couldn't be my only option forever.

This would be good for us.

And until we were over each other, we would have fun exploring the childhood crushes we'd had on each other. I could get rid of my V-card in the process to someone I trusted. He could trust me not to cheat on him or give him an STD. Win-win.

"There's something behind the—" I left Sayer and walked over to the wall behind the master bed where a map of the world had been artfully hung in a chestnut frame. I stepped up onto the bed, ignoring the wrinkled sheets and pillows I was ruining.

I pushed the picture back against the wall, releasing the spring. The picture sprung forward, revealing a safe.

"Oh, shit," Sayer murmured, coming to stand beside me. "How are we going to open that?"

It would have been a serious problem if we'd have had to. I could pick a standard lock, but doctoring a safe was an entirely different beast. Besides, this wasn't a Walmart brand. This was a pain in the ass.

But thankfully, Fat Jack was a moron. "Like this." My fingertips still hidden behind the sleeve of my sweater, I pulled the unlocked safe open.

Sayer's surprised snicker was all I needed to feel amazing, but what we found inside the safe was enough to give us serious credit with the bosses.

His laugh quickly turned into cursing the asshole that lived here. "Holy shit," Sayer rasped. "FBI. Is he fucking serious? The brothers are going to string him up by his toes and castrate the bastard. This is bad."

My skin felt itchy all of a sudden. I closed my eyes and remembered all the commercial vans lining the streets as we'd made our way here. "We need to go." I grabbed the files, tapping them into a hasty pile. "Sayer, now."

We shared a look and then jumped into motion. We grabbed Frankie and Atticus from the main floor and hightailed it out of the house, sprinting through back yards and down side streets until we felt safe we weren't being followed.

We headed back to the party and handed over the information. We spent the rest of the night laughing and kissing and sneaking vodka drinks and ignoring the fact that after tonight, we would never see Fat Jack alive again.

Chapter Fifteen

Present Day

I stepped out of my bathroom and glared at my phone where it was still plugged into the outlet by my nightstand.

"This is stupid." I didn't know if I was talking myself or the phone.

The clock read 6:57. My hair was half styled and I was wearing a bra, matching panties, and my thin, short-sleeve robe. It was time to call cabin eleven and give Sayer his first wake-up call.

I loathed the idea. Everything inside me rebelled against it. I mean, how long was I going to let this guy hold me hostage?

Granted it was only Wednesday morning, but I was already annoyed.

And yet I couldn't risk the fallout should I not follow through with Sayer's request. Would he turn me in to the *bratva*? The Colorado police? To the ГBI? Who was he working for these days? And how much danger was I in?

See? There were too many unanswered questions to play this one loose. I was just going to have to suck it up and deal with it. Besides, it was only a wake-up call. I was still safe at home even. This was part of my job.

I cleared my throat in preparation of making the call. And then I cleared it again. "Stop being stupid, Caroline, just make the dumb call."

I closed my eyes and prayed that it would keep ringing, that he wouldn't be mean enough to answer, but—

"Hello?"

Uh... Uh... Blank.

"Uh..." I pinched my nose and forced my brain to ignore the sleepy way he answered and the weirdness of hearing Sayer's voice on the other end of a phone call after all this time. "Uh, this is Caroline with your daily wake-up call."

Stupid. Stupid. Stupid. Most of all was my groggy voice from my still sleepy body. I wanted to sound professional on the phone. Firm, yet sophisticated. Instead, I sounded like I'd just rolled out of bed and I needed to be quiet so my gentleman lover didn't overhear.

Which would have been fine if I had a gentleman lover!

"You sound like you're going to launch into the airplane safety speech, Caroline." He emphasized my name. His words were cutting, meant to be harsh. "Try it again."

"You want me to try to wake you up... again?"

"Yes." He sounded fully awake now. I could hear him moving around on the other end.

"I'm not going to—"

"One more time," he ordered. "With feeling."

I sunk down on the edge of my bed, taking a handful of comforter in my hand and crushing it in my grip until my knuckles turned white. With all the energy of a cracked-out chipmunk, I pasted on a fake smile and singsonged, "Good moooorning!" with as much pep as possible. "Time to wake-uuuuup!"

He sighed heavily, like he was disappointed in me. "Yeah, that's not working for me."

Juliet appeared in my doorway, rubbing her sleepy eyes with one hand and holding her blankie in the other. I quickly threw one finger over my lips, warning her to be quiet.

She made a whimpering sound and I flung open my arm for her to cuddle into. She hated mornings. She would much rather stay up late with me than drag herself out of bed every morning for school or daycare. Weekends were our favorite because we both loved to sleep in.

Running to me, she threw herself into the curve of my body and laid her head on my chest. I smoothed her hair with my free hand, praying she would stay quiet enough that Sayer wouldn't know she was there.

"You can't be serious," I argued with Sayer.

164

He was unapologetic. Even though it sounded like he was pouring himself a bowl of cereal. "I'm paying for this, Six. You better make it good."

I dropped my head back and ground my teeth together in frustration. Fine, if he wanted to play games, we would play games. Only on my terms. Using the raspy-ness in my voice to my advantage, I dropped my volume and turned up the sex appeal. "Rise and shine, sleepyhead. It's 7:07 on this gorgeous Wednesday morning. We're expecting sunshine and temps in the mid-sixties today. Should be perfect weather for whatever evil deeds you have planned." I was all breathy and tempting sexpot when I finished with, "Now it's time for me to get dressed, so I'm going to hang up the phone, but if you need anything else, go ahead and bother someone else."

Quickly pushing end with a trembling finger, I tossed the phone to the other side of my bed and crushed Juliet against me. My entire body was shaking and it took everything in me not to start crying.

I couldn't keep doing that every morning. Was he insane? Had prison made him crazy?

"Who was that, Mommy?" Juliet's voice was muffled because of how tightly I was hugging her.

I relinquished some of my hold and took her rosy-cheeked face in my hands. Her bright blue eyes were soft with sleep and her dark hair curled around a face that was a perfect mix of her father and me. "No one," I whispered, trying to hide the emotion still lingering in my throat. "Just someone at the resort that needed help waking up."

She yawned wide and flopped back against me. "I need help waking up too."

My heart swelled, despite the trauma of having Sayer back in town. I knew I deserved his torment. I had been waiting for it for a long time. But what he would never understand was that it was worth it.

This daughter of mine was worth it.

I had promised Sayer my forever. I had sworn to never leave him, to always wait for him, to make it work for us no matter what. And I had meant everything I said. Juliet was the only thing on the planet that could have made me break those promises. She was the only thing worth destroying everything I had with Sayer and my old life.

And she would always be worth it.

"You do need help waking up," I whispered into her hair. "How about we try a banana to start with? Do you think that would help?"

165

"I think a donut would help better," she suggested, sounding so sincere I couldn't help but laugh.

"Oh, really? You need a donut this morning to get moving?"

She dropped her head back, blinking up at me. "Well, it couldn't hurt."

I threw my arms around her again and laughed harder. Where had she come up with that? I blamed Francesca. Like usual.

"You're right. It probably couldn't." She was so tiny, so fragile, so... perfectly sheltered from this awful world. I didn't know how I was going to save her this time. I didn't know how I was going to get her out of this mess I'd created. Only that I was. I wouldn't let her get wrapped up in my sins. I wouldn't let the poison of my past taint her childhood—or any part of her life. We were going to get through this. I was determined. Even if that meant becoming the criminal I left behind. Even if that meant dredging up old ghosts I had meant to keep buried.

Even if that meant leaving Sayer one more time.

"Okay, how about this. If you brush your teeth until they sparkle—I mean, do a really good job—we'll make time to grab a donut before school. You good with that?"

She nodded enthusiastically. "Yes!"

I kissed her forehead, unable to let her go just yet. "Love you, sweet Juliet."

She kissed my chin. "Love you too, sweet Caroline." Then she turned around and threw her hands in the air, singing loudly, "Bah, bah, baaaaah!" before running off to brush her teeth and get dressed.

"Worth it," I whispered again. "So, worth it."

An hour later, I walked into Maggie's on the Mountain with a dozen donuts in one hand and two coffees in the other. Maggie stood behind the counter sorting newly arrived keycards and filling out their corresponding paperwork.

"You're an angel of mercy." Maggie sighed when I opened the box of donuts.

I set her large latte down in front of her. "There's an extra shot in there just for you." I opened the box of donuts. "And an apple fritter."

Her eyes narrowed. "What did you do wrong?"

"What?" Avoiding her scrutiny, I got busy hanging up my jacket and stashing my purse in the file cabinet. "I had some extra time this morning. I thought I would be nice."

"You never have extra time in the morning," she reminded me bluntly. "Are you quitting? Did someone else offer you a better job?

166

Because it might pay more, Caroline, but not everything is about money, you know."

I laughed off her accusations. "I'm not taking another job. Although that Marriott in Breck won't stop calling me."

"Corporate assholes," Maggie mumbled under her breath before she turned back to me. "Okay, so what is it then? What do you want?"

She was unbelievable. "Why do I have to want something?"

"Caroline…" she warned while retrieving her special donut.

Letting out a whoosh of nervous breath, I gripped the counter with two hands and made my request. "You know my old friend that's staying here? Sayer?" She nodded, not noticing the strained way I said old friend. "He doesn't know about Juliet. And I would like it to stay that way please."

I had been expecting an easy-breezy, "Sure, no problem!" But instead I got a frown and a skeptical, "Why?"

My chest pinched. I thought, "Why can't you just make this simple for me, Maggie?" Instead, I went with, "Why what?"

"Why don't you want your old friend to know about your daughter, Caroline?"

Okay, so maybe she did notice the way I talked about Sayer. I rushed to keep my foundation of half-truths stable. "Because we used to date. And it didn't end well. It would be weird if I just sprung it on him out of the blue. It's something I'm planning to bring up eventually. I just want to do it slowly and carefully and make sure I protect Juliet."

"Why wouldn't Juliet be protected if you just told him about her?"

Goddamn her curious nature.

"I don't know." I floundered like this was my first rodeo and I hadn't thought my build-up all the way through. I had of course. I always had the foundation in place. But she was frustrating me this morning and my anger was clouding my judgment. "She would be fine, I guess. I just… I don't know. I'm trying to preserve his impression of me, okay? He was my last serious boyfriend before Juliet. I just don't want him to think… I don't know what I don't want him to think, but I do know that I would like to be the one that tells him. Eventually. When I'm ready to tell him. All I'm asking is that you don't bring her up in the next six weeks unless I tell you it's okay."

Her analytic expression didn't change. "Six weeks?"

"That's how long he's booked the cabin for."

A slow, smug smile stretched across her face. "Huh."

I waved a hand in the air and busied myself with organizing pamphlets for local attractions near the door. "No."

"What?" Maggie was all feigned innocence and doe eyes.

"Don't start with me."

"I didn't say anything."

"Yeah, but you're thinking something. And it's obnoxious."

"My thinking annoys you?"

"Magdalen."

"What?"

The desk phone rang interrupting the circling of our conversation. Maggie picked it up and answered with a short, "Front desk."

Over the last few years, I'd helped Maggie turn her resort around. Before me, she'd been bleeding money. She always had enough rentals thanks to the touristy area of Colorado she was located in, but she had been making inefficient decisions and not managing well. The problem was that she had too much business for just her to handle. There were too many guests and too many problems and too many balls to juggle—which was always surprising to me given Maggie's less than winsome personality.

"Sorry to hear that," Maggie told the phone. "I'll send someone over with them immediately." She hung up and that smarmy smile came back. "Cabin eleven needs towels, Caroline. Apparently housekeeping didn't stock the bathrooms after they cleaned on Sunday. Do you mind running some over there for me?"

I suppressed a sigh. "They probably didn't think we'd be renting it out until after the repairman dealt with the hot tub."

"I'll deal with them," Maggie strategized. "You deal with the towels."

"Can't you make them deal with the towels? Isn't that their job?"

"Scared of cabin eleven, are we?"

"No," I told her. "I'm scared of towels. It was on my resume, I'm sure of it."

"Stop being difficult."

"Stop playing matchmaker."

She pulled out a stack of white bath towels, hand towels and washcloths from a cabinet behind her and set them on the counter, nudging them toward me. "I'm not doing anything of the sort. And I resent the accusation. I have my life to worry about, Caroline. I don't need to worry about yours and the many men you date."

I started to wonder if she had been abducted by aliens and sent back as a robot. "The many men I date?"

Her lips twitched, but she held onto her poker face. "Are there not many of them? There seem to be many of them lately."

"I think you're having a stroke, Maggie. You don't know what you're saying."

She finally laughed. "You're so easy to rile up."

I grabbed the cart keys and towels for Sayer. "I'll remember this when Billy Bob comes back through for his 'extended layover.'"

She stood up straighter. "His name isn't Billy Bob. It's Bruce. And don't put it in quotations like that. You make it seem sordid."

It was my turn to smile victoriously. "Isn't it sordid? I thought that was the whole point." She patted her bright red cheeks, so I had to keep going. Obviously. "Come on, Mags, you got a hot trucker boyfriend that likes to keep things spicy. Ain't no shame in that game."

She glared at me. "Don't keep cabin eleven waiting now."

"I'll be back in a few."

"Take your time." Always with the last word.

I pushed through the door making a quick escape. She had no idea what it meant for Sayer to be here, at her resort. Thankfully. I cared enough about Maggie to keep her in the dark.

But that also meant playing this game so she never found out— which was turning out to be harder than I thought it was going to be. And I had anticipated hell.

Hopping in one of our little ATVs we used to get around the resort, I headed out to face the devil himself.

I temporarily forgot about the monster in cabin eleven on the short drive to his cabin. I loved the mountain in the morning. The clouds clung to her side, dusting everything with hazy fog and making the golden light glitter where it broke through. And it was so silent. There was reverence. A quietude that even the tourists understood. We tiptoed through the early hours, soaking up every second of the splendor.

By the time I pulled up to Sayer's cabin, I had marginally settled from the shock of seeing him Friday night, yesterday, and from calling him this morning.

Not that I was less afraid or that I'd stopped planning to get Juliet and me out of this as fast as possible. But I wasn't as jumpy. The shock of seeing him after all this time when I had truly believed I would never see him again had faded.

Or I had at least stopped denying the reality of what was happening.

Sayer was here. Sayer was in Frisco and at my resort and in my life. And didn't appear to be going anywhere.

169

Curling up in the fetal position until he disappeared again wasn't an option. So it was time to face the crisis and figure it out. I was rusty, but I knew the game as well as anyone. I could be smarter than him. I could be faster than him. I could be more inventive than him.

I just had to get over my bad attitude and start trying.

Scooping up the towels from the passenger seat of the ATV, I headed up the rock path to the front door of his cabin. Our cottages were picturesque against the mountain backdrop. With wrap around porches and log cabin siding, they were about as adorable as could be imagined. They reminded me of little Lincoln Log cabins with their slanted green roofs and painted green doors.

Sayer better fucking love his accommodations.

The door was cracked and swung wide open when I knocked on it. I leaned back, not expecting for Sayer to have left everything open. There was only silence that greeted me. He was nowhere to be seen in the front room or adjacent kitchen.

"Hello?" I called out.

No answer.

I knocked again and yelled, "Hello!" louder.

Still no answer.

Looking to the right, I saw that his Jeep was parked in the driveway, so he should be home. Besides, I might not have had one single conversation with Sayer in five years, but I knew the man well enough to know he would never accidentally leave his front door open.

The man was paranoid.

Like me.

It was what the job had done to us, made us always look over our shoulder and assume everyone we met had ulterior motives.

I took a tentative step inside. "Sayer?" I called out. Still no answer.

Okay, so I had two options. I could assume he was just fine and leave the towels on the bench next to the door. I could leave before he noticed me and avoid talking to him altogether.

Or I could pretend to be concerned about his well-being and take a look around. Discreetly, of course.

And noninvasively—lest he try to get me fired.

I went with option two.

Carrying the towels sandwiched between my hands, I stepped all the way inside Sayer's rental cabin and kicked the door quietly closed behind me. I didn't find any of his belongings in the front room save for two pairs of discarded shoes—a worn pair of running shoes and a newer, nicer pair of dress shoes. There was also a book on the coffee table by an author I didn't recognize. It looked like nonfiction.

So Sayer was boring now. Interesting.

Tiptoeing into the kitchen, I found more of the same—interesting if I were doing a character study on how Sayer had changed over the last five years, but useless for investigational purposes. There was a six pack of local beer on the counter and English muffins. A look in the fridge revealed eggs, bacon, stuff for sandwiches, a marinating piece of meat, a Caesar salad kit and a flat of bottled water.

Huh.

I had never seen Sayer so much as make a peanut butter and jelly sandwich before. When he lived with Gus, he let their housekeeper make all of his food and later, when he'd moved out on his own, he only ate out or bought meals that could be microwaved.

Lack of culinary skills was one of his more tragic traits in my opinion. He'd never been domesticated, never had someone to make him meals or show him how to make his own. Once we became an official couple, I'd cooked for him as often as possible to remedy that, but he had never once shown interest in learning how to do it himself.

There was a laptop on the table that caught my attention. Looking around, I stepped closer to it. It was closed and didn't look like it was on. I nibbled my bottom lip and weighed the consequences of snooping. I would have to turn it on probably and that would take time. And I didn't know what I was looking for exactly. I doubted he kept files labeled *Sayer's Devious Plans* open and ready for my perusal.

A sound at the back of the cabin drew my attention and I decided to wait for a better opportunity to explore his computer. He would have to go into work, wouldn't he? And I had master keys to all of the cabins.

I would break in later and find all the secrets he thought he could keep from me.

Skipping the second bedroom for now, I headed straight for the master suite. I heard movement, but couldn't see anybody from the hallway.

"Sayer?" I called out in a half-hearted effort to get him to finally answer me. When he still didn't, I walked in and prepared to face him.

Only nothing could have prepared me for what I found.

Which was Sayer buck naked.

Oh my God.

The door to the bathroom was wide open. I turned the corner to set the towels on the edge of the king size bed and caught sight of him in all his nude, muscular, holy-hotness glory through the mirror over the dresser. It provided a perfect view of the bathroom and the opaque glass that walled the shower did nothing to give the man privacy.

His head was bent under the shower and he had one arm braced against the wall while he ran the other through his hair, rinsing shampoo out. My mouth watered and I had to swallow quickly to keep from drooling.

I had his profile, a straight side view of his rippling back, those ridiculously toned arms and sides that tapered to a narrow waist, corded with muscle. And then there was the lower half.

I must have made a sound because his head snapped up and his gaze targeted me. *Busted.*

"What are you doing?" he demanded with such force it caused me to back up a step.

"I, uh, I brought you towels." I lifted them as proof. "I didn't mean to... Uh, I called your name, but you didn't answer so I thought I would... Here are your towels."

He shut the shower off, still facing me, giving me a giant view of his giant... umm, ahem. "Well, you might as well bring one here."

Was he serious? I all but threw the towels on the bed and started backing up. "I'll just leave them here for you."

"Caro." He stilled me with just my name. "I'll drip all over the floor. I just need one."

"Oh my God," I hissed at the stack of towels as I picked one up. This was crazy. I should have run away. But I didn't.

With trembling hands and a flopping stomach, I walked a towel into the bathroom where he still stood bare-ass naked.

"It's not like you haven't seen it before." he reminded me as I tried to look anywhere but at his body covered in droplets of water and surrounded by steam. The scent of his soap left a heady aroma in the room. His presence seemed to take up ninety-nine percent of the space.

I had seen everything before. We'd been naked together more times than we'd been clothed—or at least that was what it seemed like to my teenage hormone-rattled mind. But I wasn't sure I had ever seen this before.

How did that happen?

He was twenty-three when he'd gone into prison, barely a man, barely a grown up. But he'd come out the full package of manhood.

Literally.

172

Finally finding the wherewithal to look at the ground, I held the towel out in front of me and shuffled toward him. His toes wiggled as I approached, catching my attention. It didn't seem possible, but they had also changed in our time apart. They were hairier, more masculine looking. They shouldn't have also gotten more attractive. That didn't seem fair.

I looked at my feet hidden in black Merrells. Had my feet changed? Aged? Were they prettier? Or just older looking?

"You've changed." His low voice echoed in the long but narrow bathroom.

I decided not to take the bait. Instead, I wiggled my hand holding his towel, reminding him to take it.

He reached for it, our fingers brushing in the exchange. It was like a lightning bolt had rocketed through me. Such a simple touch, but not at all simple in the same breath.

My head snapped up and I found those brilliant blue eyes that had always signified my downfall. He was watching me, waiting for me to lift my gaze to his.

They were like locked doors. I couldn't see past the surface. I had no idea what was hiding behind them. Only that something was. Only that he was doing his best to hide as much from me as possible.

And it nearly broke me.

I didn't leave Sayer because I stopped loving him. I left him because I found someone else that needed my love more. And the temptation to tell him that made my knees lock and my hand reach out to steady myself against the wall.

But I couldn't tell him. He was still working for the Volkov. He had to be. Otherwise he'd be dead and not here. There was no way to leave the brotherhood other than death. Forty years in the future, they'd let him retire. But he'd just spent five years in prison for them. And on top of that, he had been one of their most successful soldiers ever. They would never let him go.

Consequently, he could never know about Juliet.

Because I would never take her back to DC to live that life. And I would never give them leverage over my life by revealing my daughter.

They could all burn in hell, because we had gotten out and we planned to stay out.

"What are you doing here, Sayer?" I was breathless with anticipation and too many emotions and crippling fear.

He secured the towel around his hips, making it possible to breathe a bit easier. Maybe his nakedness had something to do with my inability to catch a full breath...

"This was my idea, Caro. Do you really not remember?"

I remembered. I remembered everything. But that idea was a plan for both of us. A hypothetical escape for when we got out of DC.

But he never planned to leave DC. He'd made that abundantly clear. He'd always intended to stay. And to work for the *bratva*. I had been the idiot to fall for his lies. For his game.

I pulled my mustard cardigan tighter around my chest, hiding the scoop-neck navy blue tunic and all of the pain pinned to my exposed heart. "So what, you're really here to put down roots? To run your bar and pay your taxes and stay out of trouble?" I waved my hand around the bathroom, my expression wrinkled with intense frustration. "This is all about getting on the straight and narrow?"

He scrubbed two hands over his face, hiding an elongated sigh. When he looked back to me, he looked ancient, worn and dragged through an eternity of something horrible. "You have no idea, do you? You have no idea what I've been through the past five years or how fucking hard prison is. You have no idea how many times I had the shit beaten out of me or dodged attempts at my life. You have no idea what the last five years have been like for me because all you think about is yourself.

"But that's fine. That's totally fine. That's your right. You can do that if you want. But let's talk about that. You. Let's talk about how you left me, since we still haven't really addressed the fucking heartbreak I went through. You didn't show up and you didn't show up and you didn't show up and then finally I woke the fuck up and started asking around about you. Did someone take my girl? Did something happen to my girl? But nobody knew. Fucking nobody. Then they started asking me the same questions. First your dad, which was fine. I can handle Leon Valero. But then the bosses showed up, Caro. Just imagine what I thought when they came to visit me, asking for your whereabouts. And then the FBI came. 'Where's Caroline Valero? Where the hell is Caroline Valero?' Nobody seems to know. Least of all me, the asshole trapped in a federal penitentiary with zero chance of early parole.

"So yeah, Caroline, by the time I got out, I was tired. Tired of the life. Tired of fighting every day just to keep breathing. Tired of it all. So I grabbed the only person I had left in this world and we made our way west to set up a life I had only dreamed about. And then what happened? You fill in the blank."

When I didn't immediately respond, he growled, "Go on, Six. Fill in the blank. What happened next?"

I wiped at tears I only just now realized were falling. But there was fire in my voice when I bit back, "I don't know, Sayer. I can't fill in the blank because I don't know what happened next."

"I found the girl everybody's looking for. The girl that promised she would stick by me through all the shit, the girl that swore she would never leave me. She was here all along. Had I thought that my ex-girlfriend was going to take my dream and turn it into her own without so much as a postcard to deliver a proper fuck you, I would have handed over that information a long time ago. The brothers? They can have you. The FBI too. I don't care what you're doing here Caroline, but whatever it is has nothing to do with me. And the same goes for my business here. It doesn't have anything to do with you. So stay out of it."

He was warning me to stay out of his business? Hilarious.

"Did you just bring a whole bunch of trouble into my life, Sayer? Is an army going to come looking for you and find me instead?"

Something flashed in his eyes. Something I couldn't decipher. But it was sharp enough that I didn't trust his next words. "My business with them is settled. If they come here it will be for you. Not me."

"Your business is settled, huh?"

"Settled."

"Then what's with the note? What's with the cabin? If you want a life of peace and quiet why do you keep causing chaos in mine?"

His jaw ticked once. Twice. His tell. But what was he telling me? "You've somehow managed to stay under the radar for five years. The note was a favor. You run now and they will find you. They have not stopped looking. They won't ever stop looking. At least not for Frankie. You run again and it's only a matter of time."

"Frankie's not with me."

"Don't pull that shit with me. I know better."

Chewing on my bottom lip until I tasted blood, I decided it wasn't worth it. Clearly Sayer had done enough research on me to know the basics of my life here. It wouldn't have taken anything to find Frankie once he found me. I just had to hope that he hadn't discovered Juliet yet.

175

"Do I have your word that you're not going to bring the hounds of hell down on me? Can I trust you not to run back to your brothers and give all this away?"

His head tilted and for the first time since we'd started our conversation I noticed the elongated scar across his middle. After all these years, he had never told me how he'd gotten it. He'd never shared his secrets. And yet I was the one surprised when he turned out to be a liar. Silly, Caroline.

"Do you trust my word?" he asked.

I lifted my chin and stared him down until I couldn't see straight. I stared until I knew I was seconds from breaking down in tears, until there was no breathable air between us anymore. "No," I answered him simply.

Before he could say anything else, I spun around and fled the bathroom. I noticed his glasses on the bedside table and that was the last straw. There was something about seeing them that broke me.

My reaction was stupid. So stupid. I should be scared for my life. I should be angry he was staying in Frisco. But there was something about that tiny weakness that dug at my armor. When did he get glasses? How bad was his vision? Was it simply because he was closer to thirty? Or was it because of something that happened to him while he was in prison?

I covered my mouth to stifle the sob that would not wait and ran to the ATV. I got out of his driveway and down a secluded access road before I had to pull over. I covered my face with my hands and finally let the tears fall.

It hurt to see him. *So much.* He had every right to rail at me, to throw my sins back in my face. But *damn*, it hurt.

And this place. Oh God, this place.

I had never given him credit for this town. Not once. It had been my idea. I had been the one that wanted to run away to some obscure place in the middle of America. I had been the one that decided on the mountains. I had been the one that had researched whether or not we could hide here.

"So if you're off the whole Midwest corn and country kick, what about Frisco?"

"Where's that?" I slung my bare leg over his naked thigh and pressed my body closer to his, loving the feel of us fitted together like this. Our feet rubbed together, teasing and enticing and comforting.

"Colorado," he said simply. "It's the one with the mountains."

176

"I know Colorado has mountains."

I felt his smile when he kissed the top of my head. "I just like the sound of it. Frisco. It's got to be a real cowboy town, yeah?"

"I didn't know we were looking for a cowboy town," I laughed. I'd started tracing the lines of his stomach with my pointer finger, following the length of his raised scar, enjoying the way he squirmed but let me have my way.

He lifted up, looking down at me with the devil in his eyes. "You're in love with a cowboy. Of course he wants a cowboy town."

I tried not to laugh. "Oh, really? You're a cowboy, huh?"

I squeaked from surprise when he ripped his arm out from underneath me and pounced like a jungle cat. He straddled my waist, keeping his weight elevated. He leaned over me, slowly pushing my arms over my head by sliding his rough palms along them.

I shivered, anticipating what he was going to do next.

"Oh, I forgot. You're the cowboy."

I raised an eyebrow. "Do you mean cowgirl?"

His smirk was wicked. "Do you mean reverse cowgirl?"

I shook myself out of the memory, knowing it didn't lead anywhere helpful. Fine, Frisco had been his idea. But he'd never mentioned it again. Not even once. And after that night, we'd talked about leaving less and less until he was finally arrested and there wasn't talk about leaving ever again.

Frisco wasn't his to claim. Not even a little bit.

I dried my tears and headed back to the office. I saw him leave a little later in his Jeep, the tires kicking up dust in his wake.

That was it, I determined. The last time we needed to speak. He'd said his piece. And I didn't have anything more to say to him. So if he wanted to set up a life here, that wasn't my problem. He could do his thing. And I would do mine.

Until I figured out how to get us out safely.

Then I'd go find a town that was truly mine. A town that had nothing to do with Sayer or my memory of him or our past.

And that would be that.

Chapter Sixteen

I managed to avoid Sayer for a week. Well, avoid wasn't quite the right word. Maybe ignore would be better because I still had to see the bastard every day at work.

It wasn't like we were forced to interact, but I couldn't exactly pretend he didn't exist either. Especially since I had to call him every morning to wake him up.

And he found lots of reasons to come to the office. He needed more towels. He was forever out of towels. It got so bad that I had to interrogate the housekeeping staff whether or not they were replenishing his supply. And when they promised that they were, I made them start counting the towels they gave him just to make sure he wasn't stealing them for some mysteriously nefarious reason.

Once his Wi-Fi wasn't working correctly. We discovered later that a chipmunk had chewed through some wires behind his cabin. Another time he needed to remind me to refund him the hot tub discount. He stopped in to grab activity pamphlets and cups of free coffee and replace his keycards that he kept too close to his stupid cell phone.

He was everywhere I was. And under different circumstances, I would have thought it was on purpose. But the way he glared and growled at me, and tried to speak to anyone that wasn't me, I knew he didn't want anything to do with me. He was just obnoxiously high maintenance.

I mean, how hard was it to remember to put your keycard in a separate pocket than your phone?

Not hard.

He was smarter than that. This was a man that I'd once watched convince a Ukrainian enforcer he'd accidentally gotten lost in the Ukrainian section of town—inside the Ukrainian weapon's warehouse.

When the office door jingled, I was already working on an exasperated sigh. What now? Was it the Wi-Fi again? Had another ninja chipmunk managed to sever his contact with the outside world in an effort to trap him in his cabin and demand he get naked and take a shower?

No? That was just my sleazy fantasy?

Okay, then. Moving on...

"Hey, there," a rich, warm voice called my attention out of my flustered silence. I lifted my gaze to find Jesse standing across the counter.

My smile was relaxed and genuine after I switched gears mentally. It only took three seconds. Ten seconds tops. "Hey, stranger. Haven't seen you in a while."

His smile wobbled and I mentally kicked myself for making him feel awkward. We hadn't talked much since our date was derailed. He had texted the next day to make sure I was okay and we'd shared some random texts since then, but he hadn't asked me out again. And he hadn't made an effort to see me.

I didn't know what to think about my current reality. And to be honest, I hadn't really had time to think about my thwarted date with Jessie. Since that fateful Friday night, my thoughts and actions and decisions had been focused solely on Sayer. I'd even somehow let Gus slip through the cracks. I was pretty sure he was following me around town. I kept seeing a black Mercedes creeping behind me, but since I never had Juliet with me during those times nor was I doing anything particularly interesting other than random errands, I had let it slide. I should probably say something to him though. Maybe offer to log my activities for him and save him the trouble.

"Things have been crazy at the ranch," Jesse explained not quite looking me in the eye. "We're getting ready to go to auction."

His excuse made me feel funny, rejected in a way I hadn't felt in a very long time. He didn't owe me an explanation and I wished he hadn't given me one. It would have been better for him to pretend like nothing was weird between us. But acknowledging it shed light on it. Now I was embarrassed and flustered. I wanted to kick it all back under the rug.

I swiped my hand through the air. "Oh, no worries. I mean, that's cool. Auction sounds... busy." Holy crap, put the words back in my mouth. What was wrong with me?

Jesse took mercy on me and nodded. "It is busy."

"I've been busy too," I blurted when the silence had stretched between us for longer than three seconds. "So busy."

"Oh, yeah? You got a lot going on?"

I let out a puff of air that forced my hair out of my eyes. "Yeah, I do. Work has been... swamped." As a matter of fact, before Jesse walked in I had been trying to stack the new keycards into a tower. It was a truly frustrating endeavor because of how slippery they were. "And, you know, getting ready for Halloween has really, uh, taken up a lot more time than it should have."

He laughed. "I forgot about Halloween. What are you going as?"

I plopped my chin in my hand and tried to relax. This was Jesse after all. I needed to chill out. Gosh, ever since Sayer showed up I had been acting like a crazy person. He'd gotten under my skin and started bringing out the worst in me within seconds. Was this always how it had been? Had I been too infatuated to see it? Had he always brought out the shady in me? My baser instincts? The dangerous criminal?

"A bank robber," I told Jesse. "Juliet's idea."

He laughed because of how absurd that idea was. Who robbed banks anyway? Oh, wait...

Okay, I had never robbed a bank.

Bankers, sure. But not an actual bank.

Sayer's Jeep pulled up outside and I wrinkled my nose. I didn't want to deal with him right now. I was trying to have a conversation with Jesse. Argh! Why did he have to ruin everything?

"So auction is a big deal?" I asked him, vaulting the conversation away from Halloween and Juliet and my life.

His attention was on Sayer. "Yeah, it is. We're buying and selling this year, so it's a great big effort to make it all run smoothly."

Out of the corner of my eye I watched Sayer jump down from his Jeep. He was back to businessman in gray dress pants and a blue sweater that would bring out the already vivid color of his eyes. His short hair was pushed to the side, styled to stay in place. And he was wearing his glasses again.

I focused harder on Jesse, realizing I hadn't even paid attention to what he was wearing. "Oh, I bet."

Jessie was wearing a button-up plaid shirt and jeans. If Sayer hadn't walked into the office, ruining the entire morning, Jesse would have been one of the hottest guys I'd ever seen. I mean, who could resist plaid?

But alas, Sayer was here. And no matter what our history was or if he was trying to kill me or not, impartially speaking, the man looked delicious.

You know, from an objective perspective.

"Good morning," Sayer greeted as he entered. "Man, it's cold out there today."

I was slightly taken aback because he hadn't said more than two pleasant words to me since I'd seen him naked last week—and he'd subsequently berated me.

"M-morning," I mostly whispered, which ended up being better for my self-esteem when Jesse said the same thing louder and with more confidence.

Then the two men proved we were in some kind of alternate reality and not real life by shaking hands.

What just happened?

"How's it going?" Jesse asked Sayer.

"Good." Sayer responded casually, nonchalantly, normally. "How are you? How's your dad?"

"Good." Jesse was comfortable and at ease. "He's going to meet us down there if that's all right?"

"Oh, yeah, that's no problem." Sayer tilted his head toward his Jeep. "Should we go?"

"Sounds good." Jesse waiting a beat and asked, "Do you want me to drive?"

"No that's all right. I can drive. It will help me get a feel for the area."

"Okay, let me grab the paperwork out of my car then."

"Sounds good."

Jesse turned to me with a soft smile. I was pretty sure I looked like a cartoon character after that exchange, complete with my mouth hanging open and my eyeballs bugging out of my head. "Can I call you later, Caroline?" I nodded because I couldn't seem to make words form.

His smile stretched and he held up his hand to wave goodbye. "All right, then, talk to you later."

"Bye, Jesse."

Sayer walked over to the counter, giving Jesse his back.

Some of my sanity returned and I tilted my head to stare at him. "What the hell?"

His eyes cut to mine. "Excuse me?"

"What the hell are you doing with Jesse? What is going on?"

His expression hardened, the corner of his jaw ticking with fury. "It's none of your business, *Caroline*."

"Stop it," I hissed. "Stop saying my name like that, like it's some sort of crime against humanity or great offense to you. Caroline is my name. It's what people are supposed to call me!"

He made a sound that said he didn't entirely agree with me.

"And what are you going to do with Jesse? Seriously, I have a right to know. You better not hurt him. Or worse! Sayer, are you going to kill him? You just got out of prison and I don't think that would be a good—"

"Are you kidding me? Have I ever killed anyone before? God, Caroline, what kind of monster do you think I am?"

I took a steadying breath. I hadn't really thought he was going to kill Jesse. But it doesn't hurt to ask questions. There was no such thing as a bad question, you know. "I just don't understand why you two are going anywhere together. You guys have nothing in common."

He leaned forward on the counter, resting his forearms in front of mine. He'd scooted intentionally close, trying to get into my head. But I wasn't going to let him. I was stronger than those glasses and that smell and the heat of his body. So much stronger.

"We have you in common," he taunted. "Maybe we're going to compare Caro to Caroline. Maybe we should swap details." His head dipped, bringing his mouth close to my temple. His voice was rough, deep and smooth and hard all at once. "Do you make that sound when he nibbles on your ear? Are you still greedy with your mouth? Does he know where you like his fingers—"

"Stop." I was breathless, and furious and blind with rage. "Enough."

He pulled back, that cruel smirk I was getting used to twisting his mouth. "Don't tell me you're shy now, Six? After all we've been through?"

"It's not like that with him." There was enough grit in my voice that his eyebrows jumped. "We're friends, asshole. Just friends. We've never

183

so much as kissed goodbye, so whatever you're planning for him today needs to end. He's innocent. He hasn't done a goddamn thing to you."

"You're so full of shit," he snarled. "You showed up at my gallery in a sexy as sin dress hanging all over him. Yeah, I'm so sure he hasn't hit this."

My eyes were going to start shooting fireballs any second. I could feel them burning behind my eyelids, ready to raze this bastard of a man. "Enough, Sayer. I get that I hurt you. I get that you're pissed off. But Jesse and I aren't anything but an awkward first date interrupted by my ex-boyfriend showing up to ruin the night. Not that it's any of your business. I'm only telling you this so you'll leave Jesse the hell alone. He's not some vendetta for you to settle. He's innocent."

Sayer tapped the counter. "You did so much more than hurt me, Caro. You showed me who you really are."

"You're such a prick." Emotion roared through me, drowning out reason and logic and sanity. "You don't even know what you're talking about. You want to blame me for leaving you! But you won't even own up to your part! What you did!"

"What did I do, Six? What did I do to you?"

You chose the brothers over your pregnant girlfriend, over your child. I sucked in my bottom lip, unwilling to let him keep getting to me. "Doesn't matter now."

He nodded, pursing his lips thoughtfully. "You're fucking right about that." He stepped back from the counter, tucking his hands into his pockets. "But for what it's worth, I'm not taking Jesse out into the woods to murder him. He's selling a piece of property. I might be interested in buying it. I know this is hard for you to wrap your judgmental mind around, but I'm not here to ruin your life. I'm here to start my own."

I had nothing to say to him. He could tout that lie all he wanted, but I would never believe him. There was something else going on with him. Sayer Wesley didn't just accidentally stumble into my life and decide to be a law-abiding, upstanding citizen.

He held my gaze, his blue eyes icing over with hatred. "And you know once upon a time, you would have supported that."

I bit back all the things I had to say on that matter.

He jiggled the keys in his pocket and switched topics. "I'm expecting a package today. I'm not sure if they'll drop it off here or at my cabin. Just wanted to give you a head's up."

It took everything in me to remain politely professional. "I'll be on the lookout for it."

His jaw ticked again. "I'd appreciate that."

I watched him walk out of the office to his Jeep. I prevailed with a calm outer appearance resembling a statue, but inside I was on fire. My heart slammed against my breastbone, punching and kicking and screaming in frustration. My blood rushed and my adrenaline spiked and it was all I could do not to cry. It wasn't even like I felt like crying or I was moved with sadness or anything. It was the surge of emotion desperate for an escape, desperate to release any way that it could. My brain bellowed in fury and my heart thudded in heartache, and my eyes were just desperate to rid myself of it all. I didn't want to feel like this anymore. I didn't want it to be this hard or this hurtful or this harrowing.

Sayer pulled out of the parking lot with Jesse in tow. I scrambled for my phone, yanking it out of my pocket and pushing dial before I could take another breath.

"Hello?" Francesca answered on the third ring.

"I can't do this," I told her. "Let's go. Let's leave town."

"Tonight?"

"Right now." I couldn't seem to catch my breath. "I can't do this anymore, Frankie. I don't want to be around him anymore. It hurts too much."

"I ran into Gus today," she whispered. I heard a door close. She was at work, so she must have shut herself away. "He showed up at the front desk, asking for a meeting with me."

"Are you okay?"

"Yeah." She let out a slow breath. "Yes. I will be." I didn't bother pointing out that she was contradicting herself. I could relate. "I knew they were here. I had seen them. So it wasn't so much of a shock as it could have been." She was silent for a few beats before she admitted, "He gave me the same thinly veiled threats Sayer gave you. Don't leave town and all that."

"So what are you saying?"

"I don't know. I don't know if it's a good idea. Do we have other identities? Do we have enough cash? We can't make a mistake. We can't mess this up. They can't find us again."

I agreed. "I reached out to my guy, but I haven't heard anything yet. That either means he's dead or he's working on it."

She made a wincing sound. "I hate not knowing. I need a game plan."

185

The pain in her voice made my heart hurt. "We're going to get out of this, Frankie. I swear to you, we will never go back."

She sniffled, but she was able to relax a little when she said, "So we're not flying out of town tonight like bats out of hell?"

"Standby," I told her. "Let's not count anything out yet."

"Caro, I'm not sure if I've ever told you this before..." She sniffled again, stalling, making me worry about what she was going to say. "I just wanted to say thank you. Thank you for getting us out. Thank you for giving me these five years. You don't know how much they've meant."

She already sounded defeated. Or maybe she hadn't totally given up, but she was preparing herself for it just in case. "They're not over, Frankie. We're still out. We're going to stay out."

Her voice dropped to a whisper, signaling an interruption from work. "I've got to go. Love you."

"Love you too."

I hung up the phone and spent the rest of the day thinking about a whirlwind of escape plans and what if scenarios. By the time the FedEx guy showed up I was sick with nerves, but hell bent on leaving town with an infallible plan in place. This wasn't a game. This was the real deal and I needed to execute it perfectly.

The FedEx guy lifted his chin in greeting as he carried a few packages inside. Maggie's was his last stop of the day, so he never showed up until close to five. We were friendly but I had yet to learn his name or give him mine.

"What did you order?" He walked with the stack of packages held as far away from him as possible.

"I don't know," I chuckled. "I just sign for them. I don't know what Maggie orders." Which wasn't exactly true. I did a lot of the ordering for the resort, but I couldn't think of anything that I'd gotten recently that would smell bad.

He dropped the packages in front of me and I got a whiff of what he meant. Stifling a gag against the rotten smell wafting from the cardboard boxes, I quickly signed for them. "Oh, something is definitely wrong with one of them."

"Maybe something spoiled," he suggested.

"Maybe."

As soon as he retrieved his stylist that I used to sign for the packages, he was already backing out of the office, anxious to get away from the stinky package. "All right, see you tomorrow."

"Bye," I said to the closing door.

Sayer mentioned he was expecting a package today. Was that the stinky one?

I quickly rifled through the deliveries, setting aside the majority as Maggie's for the resort. There was nothing for Sayer in the pile. Not for Sayer Wesley or Sayer Smith or any of his other identities that I knew of.

But there was a box for Caroline Baker.

It was the same size as the dead dahlia and the return address hailed from the same town in Ohio. Was this what Sayer meant? The package he wanted me to look out for was for me? What a grade A asshole.

And surprise, surprise, it was the one that smelled.

I grabbed the nearest box-cutter and took the package outside. Whatever was inside wasn't going to be a baked good with nice intentions gone bad. It smelled like death and decay and something putrid.

Had I gotten a horse's head after all?

Slicing open the packing tape only intensified the stench. I covered my nose with the collar of my blouse and sucked in a sharp breath of courage before opening the lid.

I promptly turned my head and gagged, barely stopping myself from puking my lunch into the bushes. When I thought I had sufficiently recovered, I accidentally inhaled through my nose, caught another whiff of the godawful smell and gagged again.

Pinching my nose closed with two fingers and breathing exclusively through my mouth, I turned back to the box filled with fish guts. It had taken me a minute to figure out what they were, but I eventually found the chopped off heads. Six of them. The bottom was lined with brown butcher paper and the shiny side was slimy with the blood and guts and rotten pieces of rancid fish.

But six of them? Six dead fish? It was hard to misunderstand the message.

The problem was, I knew there would be a message in there. Somewhere in the carnage was a note meant for me.

I grabbed a stick from a few feet away and mentally readied myself to face the smell again. It took me a minute of poking around to find the rolled-up piece of paper wrapped in cellophane. And the worst part was that I had to retrieve it with my bare fingers.

Using the box cutter to tear off the slimy cellophane casing, I wiped my dirty fingers in the grass and unrolled the note. I didn't know what I expected it to say. I mean, hadn't Sayer said everything to me the other

187

day? And again today? And every time he opened his mouth? It wasn't like he was exactly going easy on me.

So I didn't understand the point of this box and the note. Unless he was just purely torturing me now. He apparently wasn't finished with his sadistic game of cat and mouse. He wanted blood. He wanted revenge.

He wanted me on my knees.

But he wasn't going to get it. My promise to Francesca was real. We were going to get out. We were going to survive. We were never going back to DC again.

I read the note one more time.

Sixes that Snitch get the Fishes.

It was like a Dr. Seuss poem for the villains of the world, but not hard to interpret. Sixes—me and Frankie—that snitch—leave/tell/abandon the life—get the fishes—death/dead/swim with the fishes (the oldest mob line in the book).

The box made me furious. My hands were trembling and I'd stopped gagging at the smell as I marched my way across the resort, stomping over stone trails in a warpath of fury. I reached cabin eleven in just a few short minutes and chucked the box onto the porch. It rocked back and forth but didn't tip over. Which only made me madder.

I was just about to storm the porch and kick the box sideways when Sayer pulled up behind me. The growl of his engine fueled my rage and I waited not so patiently for him to exit his vehicle. Jesse wasn't with him. Who knew where Jesse was. I wouldn't have put it past Sayer to lure the poor unsuspecting, innocent Colorado cowboy into the woods and chop him to little pieces. He was a sadistic bastard.

"What are you doing here—" he started, but I had no time for his pretend innocence.

"You've gone too far." I swung my arm toward the box on the porch. He just blinked at me, acting as though he didn't know what I was talking about. "You're package came."

He stared at the open box, his eyes narrowing, his jaw ticking. "That's not my package."

The sincerity in his voice was the final straw. I walked over to him and hit him in the chest, my hand meeting rock hard resistance. I didn't care how strong and tough and scary he was. The note was crushed in my fist, evidence that he'd taken this game too far.

188

"This isn't funny anymore, Sayer!" I shouted in his face, hitting him again. "I'm so sick and tired of you fucking with my mind." I hit him again and then threw the crumpled note in his face. "I left you. Fine. There! I said it. And I'm sorry I did it. Okay? Does that make you happy? I'm sorry I left you. I knew it was a shitty thing to do. I knew you would be devastated. And I did it anyway. My reasons are my own, but know this—they were way more important than your poor me feelings of abandonment. I knew what I was getting into with you when we were kids. And I knew what I was getting out of when I left. Both were worth it to me. Do you understand? Both. So I'm sorry that you hate me now. I'm sorry that you can't let go of us or what happened or the bullshit between us. I'm sorry you're so fucking vindictive over the whole thing. But you need to let it go!" I was shouting and shaking with anger, but then all of a sudden it drained out of me and I could barely whisper my next demand. "You need to let me go."

He stared at me, his jaw ticking and his eyes blazing. Pure, raw fury vibrated from him. My back was to the siding of the cabin before I knew what was happening and my hands were pinned to my sides, locked in his relentless, crushing grip before I could think to fight back.

"Can you let go, Caro? Have you let go of us? And all the bullshit?" His body pressed against mine, trapping me against the house and his chest. It was all I could do to breathe, let alone think rational thoughts or continue my argument. His head dipped, bringing our faces closer together. I could feel his breath on my lips. His hands gentled their grip on my arms, but didn't let go. My heart hammered so hard I knew he could feel it, I knew it mirrored his, mimicked his, chased after his. "Can you let me go, Six?"

His mouth was on me before I could answer. Bruising, punishing... defeating me. I was so shocked I could only stand there and let him kiss me.

But that didn't stop him. His lips moved over mine in a way they never had before. This wasn't the sweet, gentle familiar Sayer I'd fallen in love as a kid. This was a man that had spent five years in prison alone, abandoned, hardened. This was his shocking transformation on display. His muscled arms and broad chest. His darker, more serious eyes and the hard, chiseled jaw. This was the man that had gone through hell and survived.

"Come on, Caro," he growled against my lips, grasping and shaking my arms roughly at the same time. "Fight back."

189

My mouth responded before my brain could figure out what he meant. On a gasp, his tongue was in my mouth, coaxing me to kiss him, reminding me how explosive we were together, seducing me into a world I did not want to go to.

But I couldn't help it. Had I let him go five years ago? No. No, I hadn't. And how could I when he was embedded so deep beneath my skin.

Sensation rocketed through me, sparking my tattered nerves alive in a way they hadn't been in five years. I could feel him everywhere. His hard, merciless body pressing against mine, his thick, muscled thighs cradling mine, his rough, calloused hands holding my arms. His lips against mine, fighting, warring, worshiping.

A whimper tore out of me, as weak as my own will. And still I kissed him back. I let his tongue tangle with mine and my lips move against his and my teeth scrape against his soft bottom lip the way I knew he loved. Still, my thighs parted so one of his could wedge between mine. And still my breathing faltered and my stomach flipped and my heart tore in two.

Divided in half by want and need, past and present, life and death.

His thigh pressed against my core, sending desire spiraling through me. I hadn't let anyone touch me like this in so long. I hadn't wanted a man like this since Sayer. The intensity of the feeling was so sharp it hurt.

He let go of my arms to wrap around my waist and pull me closer to him, pressing me against all of him, letting me feel all of him. My hands were in his sweater, clutching it for stability. But I wasn't pulling away.

Not even one inch.

A car drove by on the road behind him and it was a jarring enough sound to bring us back to our senses. He set me on the ground, apparently I'd been trying to climb him. I relinquished the grip I had on his shirt. He plucked off his wayward glasses and slipped them into his pants pocket.

But that's as far as he went. He didn't step back. He didn't remove his leg from the intimate place between my own.

His expression was cocky, full of satisfaction. "I guess that's you letting go?"

If I didn't think he'd lock me in his cabin to teach me a lesson, I would have punched him in the smug face. "Move," I growled, my throat raw with unshed tears.

His mouth lifted in a half smile, but he raised his hands in surrender and took a step back. "It's fine, Caroline. Don't be so upset. It's not you. It's just all that bullshit between us."

I ground my teeth together, hating him all over again for throwing my words back in my face. I wanted him to feel like this, like I did. I wanted him to feel this awful and lost and ruined. I wanted to wreck him the way he had just destroyed me. "I feel bad for not giving you a warning before, Sayer. So here it is—your big, obvious head's up. I'm going to leave again. Not today. Not tomorrow. Not any day that you can predict. But I am going to leave again. And this time, when I go, you'll never be able to find me again."

I pushed by him, not waiting for his mean reply and headed back to the office. He didn't try to stop me and I didn't turn around to see if he even cared. I had other things to worry about. Like keeping my promise to leave him. And getting Francesca and Juliet out of this town and away from him and the world he belonged to forever.

Chapter Seventeen

*I*t took all the strength I had to get up to go to work the next morning, and I hadn't been able to bring myself to give Sayer a wake-up call. I knew there would be consequences, because he was a vindictive son of a bitch. But they were worth it. Even Juliet saw how drained I was from having to face him every day—although she didn't understand the reason why.

"Mommy, are you sleepy?"

I looked down at her and saw Sayer looking back at me. She had his blazing blue eyes, his expressive eyebrows, his sly smile. I hated him just a little more every time I looked at her. Their similarities used to make my chest pinch with nostalgic regret and a healthy amount of guilt. Now I wanted to kick him in the shins for lending my daughter his looks.

He didn't deserve her.

I closed my eyes, trying to relax a bit but saw him there too. My thoughts strayed to him pushing me against the cabin again, trapping my hands in his, pressing his thigh between mine. His lips were all over me. Softer, slower... and this time they didn't stop.

"Fine," I half shouted. "I'm fine. Sorry, Jules. I just need a cup of coffee."

Francesca shot me a look from the couch. She was working nights the rest of the week, so she got to lounge in her pajamas until lunch. And then she got to go to work where her ex-boyfriends didn't stalk her or bother her or try to make out with her.

"Why are you looking at me like that?" she demanded, cradling a big cup of black coffee in her hands.

I shook my head back and forth, trying to brush off the weirdness that seemed to cling to me this morning. "Like what?"

"Like you want to push me off the balcony."

Reaching for the coffee pot, I brushed off her accusation. "I need coffee."

"You said that."

God, I was losing it.

"Are you okay, Caroline?"

I hadn't told Francesca about Sayer mauling me yesterday. Part of me felt like I already knew what she was going to say and I didn't want to hear it. I knew it was a bad idea to kiss Sayer. We were so on the same page about that.

Another part of me wanted her shocked empathy. I wanted her honest reaction that I couldn't get past. That kiss had completely and utterly stunned me. Where had it even come from? I would have been less surprised had he started strangling me. Or pulled out a gun. Or wrestled a black hood over my head and thrown me in the back of a windowless van.

But a kiss? With tongue and groping hands and sizzling heat? Uh, no. Until yesterday, I would have sworn with my life that those days were over between us. So where had it come from?

It wasn't like it was this grand gesture to get me to go out with him again. It wasn't even a kind kiss. It was cruel and savage and completely, one hundred percent wild. There was nothing seductive about it, other than it had been a very long time since I had been kissed like that. There was nothing even remotely gentle about it. It was not a request for us to get back together. It had been a punishment of some kind.

Although I had yet to suss out the whys and whats of it. There were plenty of other ways to punish me.

The skanky side of me shivered in anticipation.

That was so not what I meant, ho-bag.

Oh my God. I needed a mental health day.

"I'm fine," I lied. "Just tired." Turning around, I met her gaze, not even meaning to manipulate her. It was just part of it—part of who I was. "The last couple weeks have been exhausting."

She raised her coffee cup to me in a toast of solidarity. "Agreed." When Juliet ran back to her room to get some toys for her backpack, Francesca walked over to the kitchen island, trying to be secretive. "Any word on new identities?" she asked softly.

I shook my head, adding just the right amount of creamer to my coffee, turning it a rich caramel color. Black coffee was for the birds and the guilty—or so my dad used to say. Which was apparently Francesca. She preferred to chew her coffee. "Not yet."

"We should leave anyway," she murmured.

Juliet bounced around her room, looking for a doll to pack for school. I watched her from where I leaned against the island and felt my plan cracking, finger length fissures like a spider web along the edges, making it fragile and weak. "Juliet needs new records, Frankie. She needs a valid birth certificate and social security card. We could maybe make it, but how am I going to send her to school next year without some kind of paper trail. Immunization records, hospital and doctor's records. Frankie, all the records. I don't even know how to start the process without them. I can't show up in a new city and not have at least birth records. They'll call CPS. They'll take one look at me and assume I kidnapped her from a nice, punctual, two-parent family. I can't risk it... I can't risk losing her because we weren't careful."

Francesca made a growling noise. "So many more details this time around."

"I know."

"What are we going to do, Caro?"

I shook my head. "I don't know."

"I'm going to ask around at the hotel. There are some girls... I don't think they're students. You know what I mean?"

"Fake visas?"

She nodded. "Something like that."

"Okay. Do it. Our only other choice is to run with cash and hope we can get these particulars sorted when we land somewhere."

Neither of us liked that option. There were too many variables, too much potential for getting caught.

Frankie's hand landed on mine. "Do you think it's just the Volkov or do you think we need to worry about the feds too?"

Leaning forward, I dropped my voice even lower. "Frankie, I don't know. Sayer says it's innocent. He says he's trying to start over. I don't trust him, obviously. But whether or not he's telling the truth, I do know trouble follows him wherever he goes. And if he's hanging around here, it's only a matter of time before trouble finds us too."

"How do I look?" Juliet asked from her bedroom doorway. She was wearing black and white polka dot leggings beneath a purple paisley skirt and a bright pink sweater. Her ringlet curls clung to her face thanks to the static of her sweater and she had a red rain boot in each hand, ready to slip on.

"Beautiful," I told her, absolutely meaning it. "Are you ready?"

"Yep!"

"K, kiddo, grab your jacket and your backpack and meet me by the door."

She obeyed and I turned around to pour my coffee into a thermos. "Ask around at work, Frankie. See what you can come up with. In the meantime, let's keep an extra low profile. I am confident he doesn't know about Juliet yet and I plan to keep it that way." Only I wasn't confident. I just didn't have any other options. I put my hope in Sayer's silence. He hadn't mentioned Juliet yet. He hadn't tried to see her yet. I had to believe that meant he didn't know about her. He'd changed a lot over the years, but I knew him well enough to expect absolute hell if he ever found out that I'd been keeping his daughter a secret from him for five years.

Frankie sighed, pulling her knees to her chest. "I'll have to cancel all my weekend plans. That will disappoint so many of my friends. Oh, wait. You're my only friend and I didn't have any weekend plans. So, keeping an extra low profile shouldn't be a problem."

Her tone made me pause. Turning around to my moping best friend I set my coffee down and gave her my full attention. "Do you regret leaving?"

She took a deep breath and stared at her toes. "I regret who my uncles are. I regret that my mother died. I regret that my father had to die for her. I regret that I have to live in fear and that I won't ever have a normal life and that I can't ever just be... free of that world. But I don't regret leaving. Not when it meant washing my hands of the bloodshed and the trafficking and the drugs. I just couldn't... I didn't want to be a part of any of that."

"If we had stayed though... do you think we could have turned things around?"

She laughed, but it was dark and slightly hysterical. "And what? Turned them into a charity? No, Caro. My cousins would never have let that happen. If we would have stayed, I would have lost my soul to the *bratva* and you would still be paying off your dad's debts. And just imagine—" She tossed her head to the side, indicating Juliet. "Imagine her life. Imagine how much they would have demanded from her. We did the right thing. It's okay to be a good person. It's okay to fight to stay a good person. Don't let Sayer make you feel bad for leaving. You did the best thing for your family."

I grabbed her hand and squeezed. "And you did the best thing for you." She lifted her eyes, gratitude shining through. "We have each other. That's the only kind of normal we need."

She nodded, but didn't add anything else. And I got her silence. I got her mood. It was hard to live remembering everything we'd left behind.

It hadn't all been bad. We had a life in DC. We had family. And protection and danger and excitement. We'd been respected. We'd been taken care of.

We'd also been sheltered from the worst of the syndicate. We were thieves. We were con artists. We didn't have to deal in the hardcore drugs and the trafficking of women and young girls and the killing. When conflict broke out with other families or with gangs, we went into hiding. When the news reported overdoses and underage girls in strip clubs and murders, we pretended like they had nothing to do with us.

We took the money and gifts given to us by the family and lived for each new adventure. It was crazy to think about where we would be now if I hadn't gotten pregnant. Juliet was the wake-up call we needed to get out.

We had been out for a long time... and we were never going back.

I left Frankie to take Juliet to her preschool. It was only a seven-minute drive, not too far from Main Street. We held hands as we walked inside and talked about worms and bugs and all the little things on the sidewalk that fascinated four year olds. I checked her in with her amazing teachers, Miss Beth and Miss Harmony, and headed to work.

This used to be my favorite drive. I loved leaving town and heading up the mountain, winding around the twisting roads. But now it felt like a march to my funeral. Someone honked behind me and I realized I was going painfully slow—even for mountain roads.

By the time I got to work, I was already a tangle of nerves and trepidation. What was Sayer going to do now? Would he tell Maggie all

197

my secrets? Or worse? Were Roman, Aleksander and Dymetrus going to be waiting for me?

I had to figure this out. I had to devise a freaking game plan.

Maggie was in her usual spot in the office when I arrived, thumbing through a book. She didn't even look up when I walked in. Seeing her leaned over the counter, glasses perched on her nose was so familiar that my heart hurt. This woman had somehow become such a big part of my life even though I'd made a concerted effort to keep her out of it.

I was supposed to be hard. And callous. And totally willing to give up every comfort to keep Juliet safe. And I was... kind of. But the thought of leaving Maggie or having her find out my dirty secrets killed me. I felt the same about Jesse.

Yes, I had bigger things to worry about than their good opinions, but the thought of them thinking badly of me still stung.

I wasn't the criminal to them. They didn't use me for my skills or my connections or what I could get them. They genuinely liked me.

I didn't want to lose that.

Or them.

"Must be a good one," I said to Maggie when she still hadn't looked up at me. "Let me guess, the duchess is destitute so she agrees to marry the wealthy duke that doesn't want to settle down, but needs a wife to give him a legitimate heir?"

She still didn't look up. "That was last week's. This duke is enamored with the idiot. He's totally in love with her and she has no idea."

"Well, then he's not doing a very good job of showing his affection."

"Pride," Maggie murmured. "He's an arrogant asshole."

I laughed. "Aren't they all?"

She sighed wistfully. Maggie's romances were the one thing that could distract her from work. She was all slave driving workaholic until she started a regency romance. Then she would lock herself in her office for days at a time while I took care of business for her.

I didn't mind. She needed more breaks. If she wanted to get lost in her romances occasionally, more power to her.

"I need to run into town," she told me. "I have to go to the bank and the hardware store and meet with my accountant."

"And probably take a long lunch so you can finish that book."

She tapped the book on the counter. "Wouldn't that be nice?"

"Go for it," I encouraged. "I've got things here. Just be back by three-thirty so I can grab Jules."

"You sure? Cabin eleven came in this morning to complain about his wake-up call? He said he never got it."

I busied myself with restacking the outgoing mail. "That's weird, when I called this morning nobody answered. He must have slept through it."

"You didn't put him on the automated system?"

"I will today. He wants a personal call every morning, but that is too far above and beyond the call of duty."

She grabbed her jacket from the office and stopped by the counter to pick up her book again. "Honey, is everything all right between you two?"

A cold splash of panic trickled through me, but I kept my expression curious when I asked, "What do you mean?"

She raised her eyebrows. "I mean, there's a hell of a lot of something going on between you two and I can't decide if you're welcoming it or running from it."

Unexpected laughter bubbled out of me. Did I sound crazy? I was running from it. I was running as fast as I could from it. But to Maggie, I added a shrug and said, "Can't a girl do a little of both?"

Her eyes narrowed. I'd executed my lie perfectly. There had been no quaver in my voice or nervous glancing around. I had delivered my lie with every ounce of confidence I possessed.

She still didn't believe me.

"All right, darlin', if you say so."

"Have fun in town," I teased her. "Enjoy your duke."

She paused at the door, halfway inside and halfway outside. Shooting me a wink I was not expecting she said, "You too." Then she was gone and I was left foundering and furious and trying not to text her a hundred messages correcting her.

By the time Gus pulled into the parking lot out front, I wasn't even surprised.

Let me clarify, I wasn't surprised to see him. I was a little concerned to see that he drove a red Subaru Forester and not a black Mercedes sedan.

"Cabin eleven," I told him as soon as the office door jingled. "Here's a map." I pushed the directions across the counter that I had hastily prepared for him.

His eyebrows jumped to his hairline. "Huh?"

"Sayer's cabin," I said slower, "is number eleven. This map will show you how to get there."

He matched my tone and speed. "I already know where Sayer is staying. So I don't need a map."

Oh.

"Well, why are you here?"

His top lip curled. "Do you mind telling me what I ever did to you? Fuck, Caroline. We used to be friends. Now the stick up your ass is so big, I can't even get a hello out of you."

I blinked at him. "You're not here to rekindle our friendship, Gus. I'm not an idiot."

He made a sound in the back of his throat. "You are, in fact, an idiot. But that's a different discussion." He walked over to the counter, setting his hands carefully on top of it. "We should talk for real." He glanced over his shoulder.

I was torn between interrogating him and covering my ears with my hands and running away before he could say anything else. The old Caro jerked to life inside me. This was my opportunity. Gus had never been a good liar. It was why he'd moved to technologies when we were kids, and later accounting. Sayer was a locked box and a master manipulator. I couldn't trust anything he said. But I might be able to get something out of Gus.

"All right, Augustus, let's talk. Have you been following me around town?"

He tugged at his stocking cap and shrugged. "I got a business to run, Caroline. I don't have time for that."

"What about before you launched your bar? I mean, you knew we were here, right? That's why you came. You came to interrupt our lives for some stupid reason. So how long did you follow us around and dig into our shit?"

His eyes bugged. "Do you know what you did to Sayer? When you left? Do you know how much you fucked him up? Caro, he went outside of his mind. He did things that he should never have done. Made a lot of enemies. Because of you. Because you disappeared."

This was not where I wanted this conversation to go. "So that gives you the right to stalk me?"

He pulled back, staring at me incredulously. "He thought someone took you. The Italians... the Ukranians... Fucking Irish retaliation or some shit. That's the only explanation he would accept for two years. Think about that for a second. Stop thinking about yourself and put yourself in his shoes—in prison. He went fucking berserk in there. He went after each family until he'd exhausted his resources. He had me go after them on the outside. He tapped Roman's resources all over the city. He got desperate and started trading his collection. Priceless pieces. Trophies. All of that fortune you two had amassed over the years, dwindled to what you saw in our office."

"Everything in your office was mine."

He made a face. "Exactly."

"You're saying Sayer only sold his pieces? Not mine?"

"Ding ding ding. Maybe you're not a total idiot after all."

"Why would he do that, Gus? It doesn't make any sense. That was his future. He only had to get out of prison, and he was set for life."

"Are you clueless? He thought someone had taken you. He was going to move fucking heaven and earth to find you."

"Why did he give up?" At the look Gus gave me, I rephrased the sentence. "I mean, why did he stop thinking I was taken? You said he looked for me for two years."

Gus looked away. His casual shrug wasn't as convincing as he probably wanted it to be. "You'll have to ask him that question. I just know the plan switched."

"And you do whatever he does?"

He pulled back, shaking his head at me. "You've known since we were kids that I wanted nothing to do with that hell hole. I've always wanted out. I finally got my chance." His snarl was cruel, tortured and completely honest. "Sayer and I got out together. He wouldn't have left without me. And I wouldn't have left without him."

Guilt. So much of it I nearly choked on it. "Good thing you waited until he got out of prison then."

He made a humming noise. "Good thing."

We noticed Sayer at the same time, walking up the gravel drive. I only had seconds left with Gus to get what I could out of him. "Hey, answer a question for me."

"What?"

"If your dad's dead, how are you here?" His expression didn't give anything away. "I mean, how did you get out? Don't they need you back in DC?"

His expression softened, turning curious and more... gentle. It was disconcerting. I immediately put my guard up.

"Caro, the operation in DC was shut down."

My spinning mind screeched to a halt. The earth and time and all of space tripping over their feet, slamming to a stop right behind me. One colossal rear-end collision after another. What? What did he say?

"Say that again?"

"The entire upper echelon of management was arrested. Did you not see it on the news? Roman, Dymetrus, Aleksander, the two spies... all of them. It was a giant FBI takedown."

"H-how is that possible?"

"There's nothing left in DC."

While I stood there dumbfounded and completely upended, Sayer walked into the office. My glare turned to him. He didn't think this was a piece of information I would want to know? He didn't think mentioning it might have been helpful? When he was practically dry-humping me against his cabin?

And then—*and then*—he had the nerve to speak.

"Did you forget something this morning, Six?"

My mind was too jumbled to figure out what he meant. "No?"

"My wake-up call," he bit out. "At seven. That's what I'm paying for."

I chomped down on my bottom lip and contemplated the best way to dispose of a body. I glanced up at the security camera that focused on the front office. I couldn't have witnesses. "Can I, uh, talk to you for a second? In the back?"

He raised his eyebrows and I noticed he was without glasses today. I wanted to know what the deal was with them. I wanted to know if he was wearing contacts now and when he'd gotten them and how bad his eyesight was and why I even cared. *Good grief.*

"Lead the way."

I was surprised he was so willing to follow me. Maybe he didn't realize how murderous I was. Or maybe he thought his big, tough muscles could protect him. But he was about to find out that hell hath no fury like a woman left in the complete dark!

Pushing open the door to Maggie's office, I gestured for him to go walk inside. He did. I shut the door behind us and glanced around for the closest weapon.

He took a seat on the top of Maggie's ultra clean desk, his legs spread wide, a boyish smirk tilting that wicked mouth of his. "Got something on your mind, Six?"

My hands were perched on my hips and my toe was tapping a hole through the floor. "The DC syndicate is shut down?"

His head dropped back and his fists gripped the edge of the desk. I heard him growl, "Fucking, Gus," at the ceiling.

I didn't know what to think of that response. But I clung to my anger and decided to push for answers until one of us broke.

202

"Sayer, what the hell? You didn't think that maybe you should have led with that when you rolled into town? You didn't think that was maybe something I would want to know? Are you kidding me?"

He straightened, crushing me with that furious gaze of his. I thought he was going to yell at me again, but his careful words were ice cold, not explosive. "It's not exactly a secret. It was all over the news."

"I watch the news, Sayer. I never saw anything about it." But had I been watching the news recently? I'd kind of let that slip. I'd been busy at work. And national news wasn't necessarily something I wanted my four-year-old to see. So maybe I'd been slipping.

Maybe I hadn't been quite as on top of things as I should have been.

Sayer lifted one shoulder. "Regardless, it was there."

His lack of angry engagement let some of the air out of my fury. I was still pissed. And paranoid. And freaking irritated. But I was less... ragey. "So that's how you got out? They went to prison. You got early release. And now you're in retirement?"

"Something like that."

I tapped my fingers against my hip bones, trying to decide if my next question was worth it, if I even cared. After I'd sufficiently chewed my lip and worn holes in my jeans, I huffed out a breath and gave into my curiosity. "And my dad? Was he one of the guys arrested?"

Sayer watched me for a minute without answering. We were yin and yang, total opposites. I was nothing but nervous energy, a ball of frenetic electrons that couldn't sit still or be still or do anything but wait in uptight anxiety.

And he was nothing but calm. His body was relaxed on the desk, his expression reserved, thoughtful. His hands still rested on the desk, not fidgeting, not moving, not trying to convince himself he didn't care.

"Listen, I don't have a lot of love for your dad," he told me.

"Yeah, me either."

"But." I stopped wiggling and blew out a steadying breath. Sayer continued, "Before Gus and I left there were rumors that he was in debt in a big way. Severed hands kind of big way."

A nervous flutter circled in my hollowed belly. The *bratva* were brutal with people that crossed them or didn't live up to their promises. A bookie that couldn't settle his own debts would be high on their intolerance list.

Which meant they would take a hand.

Depending on how bad his debt was, they could take both.

"So is he okay now that everyone is gone?"

203

Sayer's head bobbed back and forth. "He didn't necessarily owe the Volkov money, Six. He had debts all over town."

"If he didn't owe the *pakhan* money, why would they take his hands?"

He looked away. "Shame? They're embarrassed of him? He'd dragged their name through the dirt. I don't know, Caroline. Why do they do anything that they do? All I heard was that they wanted their pound of flesh and planned to get it. Then... I don't know. There was a deal or something. Leon figured out how to pay them some other way."

"But now he doesn't have protection. Is that what you're saying? The *bratva* is gone and my dad is on his own?"

"The bosses were pretty much done with him before they went away. It's possible that he hasn't had protection for a long time."

There was a moment of insanity where I thought about going back to save him. Again. Just a tiny pinch in my gut that felt sorry for him because he was my family. I wondered how much he owed. Did I even have enough to cover it? Some of it? Surely I could cover some of it. Just enough to get the whole city to stop breathing down his neck.

"Stop," Sayer ordered.

I looked back to him. "What?"

"Stop trying to figure out how to rescue him. You can't."

"You don't know—"

"Think it all the way through, Caro. You'd have to resurface. You'd have to step into the open. The *bratva* is spread out, but they're not dead. And the *pakhan* are locked away for now, but how long will that last? Think of the consequences. You knew what you were doing when you left five years ago. He is not worth stepping out of hiding to save. You know that."

I couldn't believe what he was saying. "He's my dad."

"Yeah? And I was the fucking love of your life and you didn't save me. Don't you dare throw this away for that piece of shit. He's used you your entire life. You're not going to let him use you now. Not after you got out."

He was right. And I hated him for it. "You should have told me sooner."

"Because we're being so open and honest with each other?"

His snide comment reminded me that I did want him to be open and honest with me. The information about the Volkov was easily searchable, so I doubted he was lying about that. But there was more I wanted to know. Was he seriously out? Or was Colorado his attempt to lie low? What did he really want here? How did I get all my stuff back? When was he going to leave?

I decided to change tactics. Nagging him clearly wasn't working. But there were other ways to kill a man. Like with kindness. Running a hand through my hair, I let out a puff of air. "Thanks for telling me." I let real emotion roughen my voice and tears fill my eyes. I was a wide-eyed puppy begging for attention. "Thanks for being honest."

His laser eyes moved over me, taking me in, noticing every small detail. "Come here," he demanded.

Why was on the tip of my tongue. But contrite girls weren't paranoid, they were compliant. I stepped toward him, slumping my shoulders and giving him the best poor me I could manage.

He hooked his finger in the pocket of my jeans and tugged me into the space between his legs. He pulled me closer, until I was pressed against him, his inner thighs, his abdomen, the space between those two places.

Sayer captured my gaze in his, a prisoner held hostage by the enemy. I tried to take a step back, fear nipping at my resolve to stay in character. He tugged me back against him.

"Don't stop now," he murmured, his voice throaty with promise and vengeance and a dare. "You want something. Now isn't the time to back down."

"I don't," I whispered, my voice choked with fear. "I shouldn't have—" I couldn't finish my sentence. What shouldn't I have done? Any of this.

Any of it starting with when I was a little girl before Sayer even showed up.

Sayer's nose brushed along my jaw causing a shiver to work its way through me. I needed to disentangle myself from this mess. I needed to get out of here and Google a few things.

"Don't give up, Six. You're so close to getting what you want." He nipped at my ear, quickly soothing the bite with his tongue.

I bit back a weak whimper, refusing to let Sayer get the better of this exchange. Yes, he was the boy I had fallen in love with and had never really fallen out of love with. Yes, his body felt amazing pressed against mine, all hot, hard man and dirty promises. Yes, I was finding it hard to step away from him and shake off his hands and the crazy power he had over me.

But. But I was good at this game too.

Sometimes.

Er, I used to be.

He reclaimed my attention by pressing a wet, slow kiss to the hollow of my throat. My hands fell on his shoulders, clutching at his shirt. I needed help balancing. Standing. Thinking.

Empowerment, I internally hissed at myself. Independent. Free. You are more than your feelings.

Swallowing a big dose of my pep talk, I dropped my cheek against his. He kissed the underside of my jaw and I took the opportunity to move my lips to his ear.

He stilled, freezing with the anticipation of what I was going to do next. Not wanting to disappoint him, in a vindictive way I moved my lips over the shell of his ear, letting my tongue taste and give and drive him crazy.

I pulled his earlobe between my teeth and had the pleasure of feeling his hands grip my waist, holding me against him with a helpless grip. When his jaw muscle ticked against my chin, I took that as a sign.

I kept my voice breathy, soft, feminine. He had recently gotten out of prison. I mean, it probably wouldn't hurt to remind him that I was a woman and that he had been locked up for a very long time. "What are you doing here, Sayer?"

He leaned his head back, keeping our bodies close. His eyes had darkened with want, his face was an open book. He was going to tell me.

This was it.

"I wanted to redeem myself," he said.

My blood rushed so loudly I almost couldn't hear him. "You do?"

He nodded slowly. My fingers curled into his shirt.

And then he leaned in and let his lips touch mine. It wasn't at all like yesterday. He wasn't rough. He wasn't punishing. This time he was achingly sweet. Careful and gentle and considerate.

His tongue brushed over my bottom lip until I opened my mouth for him, a Pavlovian response from years of life with him, of old habits and remembered need.

He kissed me like I was breakable and delicate and his. He kissed me like he couldn't stand being apart for a second longer. He kissed me like I was his breath and he needed me to keep living.

Our mouths were a symphony, a chorus in unison. We were striking art and perfect sound and a homecoming of touch.

It didn't take long before he'd coaxed me to kiss him back. My resolve and fury and years of hurt didn't stand a chance in the reality of

206

his mouth on mine. Leaning into him, I took more, deepening our kiss until he made a growling sound in the back of his throat.

His teeth captured my lip with more pressure, reminding me of the veiled strength that hid behind this careful kiss. We deepened together, at the same moment, breaking in the same tangle of tongues and taste. I pressed into him, letting all of my body feel all of his. My arms were around his neck, desperate to hold him close. I gasped a sound that was an invitation for so much more. This wasn't enough. I wanted more. I needed more.

I needed him.

Which was, of course, his plan. He pulled back, separating our mouths, and then scooted back so there was space between our bodies too. His eyes were half-lidded, dark with the same need I felt coursing through my body. But his smile was all smug victory. "For yesterday."

I was a gooey pile of lust and desire. His words made no sense to me. "Huh?"

"Redemption," he repeated. "I kissed you yesterday to prove a point. But I was angry and got carried away."

My head was still wrapped up in the kiss we'd just had. If I had any less willpower, I would be leaning forward right now with an open mouth, trying to continue what he started. "You got carried away?"

His half smile was triumphant. Conquering. "I did."

My anger returned and I took a few steps back, needing separation. "So what was that?"

His smiled kicked up a notch and a wicked look flashed in his eyes. "Five years without sex, Caro. That's what it was."

"Are you punishing me?"

He leaned forward, as casual and relaxed as I had ever seen him since he'd shown up in Frisco. "I wouldn't really call that a punishment. You seemed pretty into it."

"Are you serious?"

He jumped off the desk and prowled toward me. I took quick steps back, afraid he was going to punish me again. But more afraid I wasn't going to be able to tell him to stop.

"You can ask for more, Six," he murmured, pulling the thoughts straight from my addled brain. "I won't tell anyone."

My back hit the closed door. His hands came up on either side of me, bracing his body just an inch from mine. "You're a bastard," I told him.

"You're the one trying to get in my head. You're the one playing games, Six."

I pushed against his chest and he captured my hand and held it against his rapidly beating heart. "This whole thing is a game to you," I accused. "Since you walked into town, you've been up to something. Spare me the high and mighty scolding."

His head dropped to hide his dark smile. "You really are a piece of work."

"Then give me something real." I'd meant to demand it, order his truth from his lips and then throw it in his face. But my words came out as a plea, a broken beg.

He lifted his head again, his blue eyes shining with raw, unfiltered openness. "It's not a secret why I'm here, Caroline. Try and listen this time. I had an opportunity to get out of a life that had taken a lot from me and not given enough in return. I took that opportunity. I found a quiet life in a quiet town where I can do the things I like without being bothered by my past. If you find that threatening, I'm afraid that's your issue."

"You told me not to leave town," I reminded him. "More than once. You said people would find us."

His jaw ticked. "The brotherhood is finished. That's true. But there are certain people out there that blame that on me. They would hurt you to get to me."

Where is he?

Found you.

The box of fish guts from Ohio.

The floor dropped out from beneath me and I slumped back against the door. The black Mercedes. It wasn't Gus or Sayer. I was being followed.

Juliet.

My only thought. My only motive.

I focused back on Sayer, the source of so many of my problems. I wanted him gone. I wanted him as far away from me as possible. And if I couldn't get him to leave this city, then I would be the one to go.

I pushed him away from me and yanked open the door. "Get out," I hissed at him, breathless with concern for my daughter. I had paid the ultimate price to get her away from that world only to have Sayer bring the world straight to her. "Go away."

Something dark flashed in his eyes. In any other circumstance, with any other man I would have said he was surprised. But I knew that wasn't true with Sayer.

208

It was a different emotion. Something more sinister. Something more calculated.

He snorted, but didn't fight me. Although he did throw out an annoyed, "If you think that's smart."

When he was halfway through the door, I had to get the last word in. I was compelled to say something by the evil, vindictive demon inside me. "They should know by now you're over me."

He paused, dipping his head and looking at me out of the corner of his eye. "Yeah, I'm over you. That's why I keep kissing you."

Then he was gone, leaving me to reel and fight for breath and try not to pass out.

There was someone after Sayer. There was someone after me to get to Sayer. My peaceful, idyllic little town was no longer safe.

I was sucked back into the world I had fought so hard to escape.

And not just me, but Juliet too.

The door to the office jingled. I heard car doors slam and Gus's Subaru drive away, but I couldn't bring myself to leave the office. I couldn't bring myself to move.

Because on top of everything, overshadowing the danger and exposure and life-threatening risk, was Sayer's last words to me.

That's why I keep kissing you.

It was time to leave. I had to get Juliet and Frankie and get the hell out of here. Because even if my body survived this time, my heart would not.

Chapter Eighteen

Ten Years Ago

"Be careful tonight," Frankie warned on the other end of the
phone. Her sigh was bone deep and full of emotion. "I should be going
with you."

"Yeah, well you have more important things to do tonight. I can take
care of myself. You don't need to worry about me."

"Don't call what I have to do important. It's not."

It was. But I wasn't going to argue about it with her. Instead, I played
dumb. "Aren't your uncles taking you to a dinner tonight?"

"With some politicians," she groaned. "They're going to dress me up
like a doll and put me on parade."

"And..."

"And teach me how to wine and dine my way into partnerships." Her
voice dropped, taking on her uncles' Russian accents. "Not everything
should be obtained by threat and intimidation, you know." She made
another frustrated sound. "You wouldn't believe these people, Caro.
You wouldn't believe how easily they give up their morality for the
promise of just a little bit more power. It's disgusting."

"Yeah, well maybe you should casually bring up the container of
human beings your uncles got last week."

"I swear they wouldn't care. They'd pretend to be deaf and blind."

"Is the mayor going to be there?"

"Yeah, apparently the life of his dog is more important than thirty underage girls."

My stomach tightened, threatening to empty itself of my lunch. "They can't do this forever."

"They can. And they will."

She was right. As long as the Volkov had a foothold in this city, they would run girls and more—drugs, weapons, black market everything. And if something happened to the Russians, ten other crime families would be there to fill in, pulling politicians and lobbyists and policemen and all of the supposedly upstanding citizens into it with them.

Maybe the people hanging out to the right of legal didn't know the extent of the depravity, but only because they didn't want to know. They wanted to live their shiny, happy, wealthy lives with clear consciences. As did the rest of America. It was easier to pretend that human trafficking didn't exist than to do something about it. It was easier to pretend the fat diamond on your engagement ring wasn't a blood diamond, that little kids didn't die so you could have it than to pick a less popular stone for your wedding band. It was easier to assume drug overdoses and gun violence happened to other people than to recognize how far the dangerous tentacles of the underworld reached, how they choked and strangled and imprisoned all of society to their whim.

I wasn't judging. I was part of the problem. Maybe I didn't deal in humans and illegal substances directly, but my department funded a lot of the other happenings in the *bratva*. If all sin was the same, I was as corrupt and depraved as the rest of my thieves-in-law.

"Be safe," I told her.

"Oh, hey, Caro." Her voice dropped, catching me right before I disconnected our call.

"Yeah?"

"They're going to make Sayer a brigadier. I heard them talking about it over lunch. They want to keep moving him up. They talked about him becoming one of the two spies someday."

"What the hell, Frankie?"

"I thought you should know. This job is a test."

She couldn't have led with that? I pressed my palm to my forehead. "Thanks for the head's up."

"Are you going to help him?" Her voice dropped even lower. "You could… sabotage."

She didn't know what she was saying. The *bratva* was everything to Sayer. He would kill me if I messed up a chance like this.

And yet the temptation was there…

"I need to go, Frankie. I'm going to be late."

"Bye, Caro."

"Bye."

We hung up our call and I tucked my slider Sidekick into my purse. I finished my makeup, taking extra care to make it perfect. I was supposed to pass as a college girl tonight, a little extra attention to detail was called for.

Twenty minutes later, my chin-length hair was straightened, my makeup was perfection and I'd managed to squeeze into my gold strapless minidress with chain detail across the waist. Slipping on a pair of stockings and my favorite hand-me-down Louboutins from Frankie, I admired myself in the mirror behind my door.

Boom. Nineteen.

I grabbed my crossover purse and left my bedroom, hoping to sneak out before my dad saw me.

No luck. He was hanging in the living room with his usual crew, Vinnie and Brick. Steeling my courage, I walked through on my way to the front door. They catcalled and threw out lewd suggestions until my dad told them to shut up.

"Where you going, Caro?"

I hesitated by the coffee table covered in shot glasses and vodka bottles. "Work," I told them.

The three of them whistled again, but it had the tone of respect this time. "See that, boys, my daughter's doing important things. Very important things. She's moving up." My dad's words ran together thanks to too much drink. He rubbed at his bleary eyes and red nose, unable to focus on me.

"It's not a big deal," I said quickly, lest they start asking for details. "I'm just meeting Sayer."

The three of them made more guffawing noises. "Now there's a fucking cockroach," Vinnie slurred. "That kid can suck my big, hairy balls."

My dad's eyes narrowed on his friend. "What's your problem with the kid?"

213

"The little shit is the reason Fat Jack is gone, dummy. He's a fucking spy."

"Who?" Brick asked. "Jack?"

"No," Vinnie grunted, then his head bobbled back and forth as he thought about it. "Yeah, fine, Jack. But that kid too. He's got his eyes on the top and he'll do whatever it takes to get there, including stepping on all of our heads on his way."

I should go. Gus was waiting for me. But this drunken conversation had taken an interesting turn. "Fat Jack had it coming," I reminded Vinnie. "He was snitching to the feds. What did you think was going to happen to him?"

Vinnie waved a meaty hand back and forth. "Psssht. He was staying out of prison. When those federal bastards put you in their sights you got to do what it takes to keep 'em from locking you up. The *bratva* can't protect you behind bars. It's up to you to stay outta that hell hole."

"What are you saying, Vinnie?" I demanded.

"I'm saying Jack was giving them bullshit. Just enough to keep them off his back. He wasn't doing nothing to hurt the brotherhood."

Brick nodded, his eyes mostly closed. "S'true. But the bosses don't care. All that matters is if you're a snitch. Tell one secret or all the secrets and you end up the same." He tilted his head and looked at me with squinting eyes. "Dead."

I swallowed. We all knew that to be true. If the *pakhan* heard you were simply approached by the feds, they punished you—reminded you where your loyalties should lie. If they had reason to believe that you were cooperating with law enforcement that meant... something worse. And significantly more painful.

Fat Jack was dead because of what Sayer and I had found in his house.

"Let Jack be a lesson to all of us," my dad said, bolstered by the tragedy of his friend. "Keep your hands clean."

"And your nose cleaner," Vinnie finished for him, although I murmured along.

I had always found that particular saying a bit of an oxymoron. Their hands weren't clean. They were covered in blood and greed and lawlessness. But I understood the sentiment. It meant don't steal from your thieves in law and don't go sticking your nose where it doesn't belong.

Head down. Focused on the job. Eyes on the prize.

"Jus' be careful is all I'm saying," Vinnie warned me. "Don't let the little prick catch you talking to the feds. Don't matter that you're fuckin' him. He's only loyal to the *pakhan*. Nobody else."

My cheeks were bright red and I avoided my dad's eyes, even though they were glassed over. I wasn't sleeping with Sayer. We'd been together all of three months. And while I was pretty confident things were headed in that direction, we weren't doing that... yet.

"Whatever," I mumbled weakly. "I'm not the one you have to worry about talking to anybody."

My dad poured more shots of vodka. "Go on, Caro. Don't keep 'em waiting on our behalf. Go do what you need to."

I rubbed my hand over my chest, hating the way it pinched for my dad and his pathetic friends. "You guys going to be okay?"

Dad jerked his head toward the door. "We're just saying goodbye to Jack, baby girl. Then we're not going to talk about him again."

"Never again," Brick agreed.

That only made my heart hurt more. Guilt coiled in my gut and whispered to change my plans for tonight. I shouldn't go. Who knew what else I would find.

Who knew who else would have to die because of what I found.

My phone vibrated in my purse. It was probably Gus wondering where I was. Shit.

"Bye, Dad," I told him.

"Love you, sweet Caroline."

"Love you too," I told him even though he was already in another ruckus round of toasting and shouting about the friend they could never mention again after tonight.

Jack had been a snitch. The bosses had built a case proving his guilt and then made an example out of him to anyone that was thinking about opening their mouths.

It had started the night Sayer and I found the info about the feds. And now it was common knowledge among the *bratva*.

Don't open your mouth. Not unless you want to be strung up by your feet with your tongue cut out and your nose chopped off, left to choke to death on your own blood.

Because of me.

I hurried downstairs and out on the street. A black town car waited on the curb—my ride. I threw myself in the passenger seat, anxious to get away from my dad, his sad friends and my racing thoughts.

"Bout fucking time," Atticus growled.

215

I did a fast double take, my heart jumping to my throat. "I thought Gus was picking me up."

He pulled out onto the street and pressed a heavy foot down on the accelerator. "Gus had other shit to do."

"I didn't know you were on this job."

"Don't you ever shut up? Shit, Caro, not everyone wants to hear your whiny voice all day long. Save it for your boyfriend."

"Don't be such an asshole."

His hand slammed down on my knee, slapping it so hard I let out a surprised screech. Then his fingers were digging into my knee, crushing and gripping until my eyes watered and I was afraid of ruining my makeup.

I grabbed his hand, trying to peel it off. "Let go, Atticus."

"You should be careful who you call names." His strong fingers pressed harder, making me breathless with pain. Out of options, I sunk my fingernails into the back of his hand. He slammed his foot on the gas, driving like a maniac through darkened streets, unconcerned with my efforts to get him to back off. "Apparently you need me to teach you a lesson, little girl. Somebody's got to teach you some manners."

"If you rip a hole in my stocking, I will kill you," I hissed at him. "You're going to ruin my cover."

"Then say you're sorry."

"What?" I blinked back tears, he was going to leave bruises.

His words slowed like he was talking to a small child. "Say you're sorry. I want to hear how fucking sorry you are."

"Let go of me."

He did, but only to slam his fist down on my kneecap, making me double over. "Say you're sorry, Caro, or I'm going to do it again."

"I'm sorry," I said quickly, hating myself for giving in. But I knew he wasn't going to stop until I did.

I should never have gotten in the car with him. I should have paid closer attention. But I'd been shaken up by what my dad and his buddies had been saying.

If Sayer knew I was riding with Atticus instead of Gus, he would be pissed.

Atticus retracted his hand and put it back on the wheel. "Good girl."

Bile rose in my throat. We couldn't reach our destination quick enough. He didn't try to speak to me again, and for that I was grateful.

Atticus had never liked me. Part of me still thought he held a grudge for one time when I'd managed to steal a hundred bucks from him in the middle of his crew—before I had my six pin. He'd caught me and taken me before the bosses to have me punished, but Roman had sided with me.

Atticus had never liked me, but after that I was irredeemable to him. And he tried his hardest to find subtle ways to torture me. He never did anything crazy enough to alert the *pakhan* or throw a job. But when it was just the two of us, he made my life miserable.

It was fine. I punished him too. By keeping him as far away from Frankie as possible. He was obsessed with her. He always had been. And as her friend, I couldn't blame the guy. She was drop dead gorgeous and set to inherit a huge chunk of the syndicate ruling class. But she was also smart enough to see straight through him.

And I did whatever I could to remind her of his awfulness.

We both avoided him whenever we could. Unfortunately, the bosses didn't share our opinion. They saw his ruthless sociopathic skills as an asset. He hadn't risen in the ranks quite as fast as Sayer, but he was still one of the shining stars. And a regular favorite of the brothers.

"You're walking in with me," Atticus ordered when he pulled up to the valet at the Mandarin Oriental Hotel.

I was pretty sure we were supposed to meet up with Sayer first, but I wasn't in the mood to argue with Atticus. Besides, I needed to know I could walk okay after what Atticus had done to my knee. If Sayer saw me limping around, the night wasn't going to end as planned. We so didn't have time to deal with that fallout.

The valet opened my door and I stepped out of the car on shaky legs. My knee was sore, but not too bad. I just needed it to keep from swelling for now.

Atticus handed over the keys and the two of us walked into the stunning hotel, with golden light and gleaming marble floors. The posh atmosphere made me feel small, tiny compared to the wealth and resources of the upper echelon. I wondered if Atticus felt it too. We were just kids from the wrong side of the tracks—thieves, criminals, wild things that didn't understand elegance or better society.

We followed signs leading us to the grand ballroom without another word spoken between us. We both knew the job. And the mark. There was nothing else to say to each other.

"Tickets?" the matronly woman dressed in a Chanel dress cluttered with shiny strips of sequins and feathers asked.

Atticus and I produced our tickets, stolen well in advance for tonight's shindig. She looked them over with a wrinkled nose and distaste written all over her pudgy face, but eventually she marked us off and gestured toward the ballroom.

We continued not to speak as we entered the annual party celebrating DC's law enforcement. The room was swamped with Secret Service, DEA, ATF, and plenty of FBI. And lawyers and judges and politicians and journalists and on and on and on.

Sayer would turn anyone in that spoke to FBI?

That was going to be a problem tonight, since that was my assignment.

My heart fluttered in my chest, just knowing the kind of legal power that surrounded me in this room. These people were my enemies, I reminded myself. And after Fat Jack, now more than ever.

"Fuck me," Atticus murmured as soon as we'd walked through the doors.

That was exactly how I felt. Surrounded by wolves and lions and sharks all at once. "Let's mingle," I suggested, anxious to get away from him as well.

We parted, heading out in separate directions to case the party. I clocked a few other Sixes posing as wait staff as I worked my way around the room, but I didn't see Sayer anywhere. My fingers tingled, wanting to fidget, but I kept my cool, my perfectly comfortable disposition. I could pretend to be from money. I could be a convincing socialite. Easy peasy.

"Are you looking for someone?" a deep male voice asked as I stretched over a table to grab the non-fishy looking canapes hidden out of reach.

I landed back on my heels, ignoring the twinge of pain in my knee. Lifting my gaze to find a young, striking man standing there, I gave a demure smile and said, "A friend. My date."

His smile was wide and only made him more handsome. He had all the classic good looks of an American quarterback. He was like a walking billboard for apple pie and sweet tea. Blonde hair, movie star light blue eyes, square, trustworthy jaw. And a fed. You could always tell by the Men's Warehouse suits and scuffed dress shoes. Secret Service were significantly better dressers. And ATF were significantly worse.

Then there was the government look about them. This was a trait that was harder to define. Something in their open smiles and paranoid eyes. They were all trust me with all of your secrets, so I can write them down and give them to my boss. We'll be best friends until I raid your house and seize all of your assets.

"Is he your friend? Or your date?" the man asked, chuckling warmly.

"Both," I grinned. "Shouldn't he be both?"

"Ah, smart girl," the agent agreed. "Which one of you has the connection to this lot of hooligans?"

"He does," I admitted quickly, needing him to hear unabashed truth in my words. Why would I have a reason to lie anyway? I was just a vapid undergrad meeting her new boyfriend at his dad's event. I didn't know what was going on. Was I listening to the wrong conversation? Oh, so sorry. It was so easy to get lost here. Where's the ladies room again? "His dad is with the bureau."

"Oh, really? Me too."

Duh. I smiled at him. "No way. That's so cool. I have to admit, I'm fascinated by everyone here tonight. I'm taking a constitutional law class this semester and I have so many questions."

His eyes turned flighty with the sudden urge to flee. "Yeah?"

"Yes," I answered energetically. "Like income taxes for starters. Illegal, right? So what is the deal with them? Also, mandatory check points. How is it not a blatant violation of our rights to set up checkpoints and allow cops to search every car that goes through without probable cause?"

"I, uh, I—"

"And what about the Patriot Act—?"

He held up a hand. "I'm going to stop you right there. I'm off the clock tonight. Sorry."

I shot him an apologetic smile. "No, I'm sorry. I got carried away."

Before he could say anything else, warm hands slid around my waist and pulled me back against a solid chest. "There you are," Sayer murmured, his lips brushing my ear. "I've been looking for you."

I tilted my head back so I could check him out in the crisp tuxedo he'd gotten for the event. I suddenly found it hard to swallow. Had anyone ever looked so good in a tux? My legs felt like Jello and I was confident I was three seconds away from combusting. Clearing my throat, I tried to focus on the potential mark. "I've been grilling poor Mr..." Looking back to the agent still standing awkwardly near us, I repeated. "Mr..."

"Payne."

"Excuse me?"

His smile was shy, self-deprecating. "Mason Payne."

I recovered, barely. "Nice to meet you Mason Payne."

"And you too...?"

"Carolyn Cook. This is my boyfriend, Sawyer Prior."

Mason reached for Sayer's hand. "Nice to meet you."

"Likewise," Sayer said. "Thanks for keeping my girl company."

"It was an accident," Mason admitted on a laugh. "I thought she was someone else."

"Oh!" I pretended to be offended, all of us laughing at the mistake. "Well, thanks anyway. I appreciate your attempt at answering my questions."

"No problem. You two have fun tonight." His smile stretched and I mentally predicted his next words. "But not too much fun."

Sayer's laugh was forced, tested by this agent that was kind of flirty, but also kind of suspicious of us. "Is there such a thing?"

Mason laughed again, a more hollow sound, and then left us to ourselves. Sayer turned me in his arms so I could throw mine around his neck and greet him properly. We kissed hello, neither of us willing to forget the people standing around us.

"You look lovely tonight," he breathed against my temple. "No wonder you have feds hitting on you."

Vinnie's warnings crawled over my skin, pricking at my ability to brush off his compliment. "Creepy feds," I whispered. "I'm a minor."

"Something to remember when I try to defile you later," he chuckled.

My stomach flipped and I wished I could see his eyes to know if he was serious. I used my vantage point to scan the room, hoping nobody was looking at us.

"Should we dance or something?" I asked Sayer.

His body tensed, his shoulders going completely stiff. His head whipped to the right, and to the left. "What the hell?"

I pulled back, desperate to see what he saw. Fighting to keep my casual smile, I asked, "What?"

"Is that Atticus?"

Atticus stood across the room, deep in conversation with one of the senators that worked closely with the syndicate. "Yes," I told Sayer. "I thought you knew he was going to be here. He drove me."

Sayer's gaze cut to mine. "He drove you?"

Shrugging it off like it wasn't a big deal, I said, "He made it seem like he was supposed to be here. He had a ticket."

"That he probably stole from Gus," Sayer growled.

220

We watched Atticus finish his conversation and head to the doors. Was he already leaving? "I should have texted you, it's just that he's technically my boss and—"

"It's not a big deal, Caro. You couldn't have known. It's just something I'll have to ask the *pakhan* about."

"Hey. What are they doing?"

Sayer followed my gaze to a cluster of feds looking our direction. They were speaking in low tones and subtly nodding our way. They were clearly talking about us and trying not to make it obvious.

News flash, morons, you're basically on broadcast. It didn't matter that they were dressed to the nines tonight. They were always on the job. They couldn't disguise their asshole tendencies.

"We should move," Sayer suggested.

He took my hand and led me to the outer edges of the crowd. We passed a guy with an ear piece hanging around his neck. The radio said, "Gold dress. College age."

Sayer glanced at me. "I'm not feeling this party."

My heart kicked in my chest. It could have been a total coincidence. But if life had taught me anything, I knew there was no such thing.

Everything happened for a reason—and usually that reason was so Fate could piss all over you.

"I'm not either," I told him. "I think I'd rather go... anywhere else."

He leaned in. "Let's do that."

We detoured right before we got to the outer fringes of the crowd. There were two more men with earpieces moving to block the back exits. "This way," Sayer instructed.

Our steps were purposeful and our movements subtle, we were blending in, staying under the radar. Sayer slouched so he didn't stand taller than the rest of the mingling people.

An FBI agent pushed through the crowd in front of us, Mason Payne following directly after him. The two agents caught sight of us, surprised that we were right there. We took the advantage and about-faced, slipping in and out of designer dresses and hand-tailored suits, disguising ourselves in the crush of the rich and powerful.

"Don't let go," Sayer said over his shoulder.

I didn't respond, but it wasn't like I was even entertaining the option. My heart was in my throat, a last-ditch attempt to abandon the sinking ship that was my body. Oh my God.

Why were they chasing us?

What did they know about us?

"Faster," Sayer urged. We crossed a wide-open area, temporarily exposing ourselves, before we ducked into the kitchens.

"Shit," he growled when he barely missed running into a server balancing two trays stacked high with replacement hor d'oeuvres.

"Come on," I urged him. "We have to get out of here."

"You can't be in here!" someone shouted. "Hey! You need to leave!"

"Spoiled brats," someone else snarled.

Oh, if they only knew.

The door to the kitchen banged open behind us, someone screamed and dropped a platter. "Caroline Valera," a vaguely familiar voice called from the middle of the commotion.

"Go," I ordered Sayer, pushing his back.

"Valera stop!" that same voice shouted. I realized it was Mason.

My new FBI friend now wanted to arrest me. Oh, how quickly the fickle of heart fade. And here I thought we were going to be bffs.

Sayer and I turned a corner and took off sprinting. I managed to catch a room service cart on the way and tip it over. We burst out of the kitchens into back hallways. The sudden quiet was jarring. We sounded like a stampede as we raced through carpet-muffled corridors, my frantic breathing amplified to my sensitive ears.

Slowing our pace, we shuffled quickly toward a metal door near the emergency exit. Hitting the push bar, we burst into the stairwell and took them two at a time. I had no idea where we were going or why we were fleeing upward, deeper into the labyrinth of the hotel, but I trusted Sayer. And he seemed to know exactly where he wanted to go.

"This way," Sayer ordered.

We pushed through another door and I realized we were on one of the top floors. "We need to go back down," I reminded him. "That's where all the exits are."

"They'll already have blocked those. They'll be waiting for us. Don't worry, I've got a backup plan," Sayer said quietly, slowing his pace to casual, unconcerned with things like the FBI and getting caught. His arm wrapped around me, pulling me to his side. But we kept our faces focused on the carpet, out of sight of peeping security cameras. "Do you trust me, Six?"

"I do," I told him immediately. That wasn't even a question.

He reached into his pocket, pulling a keycard still wrapped in the paper packet. At the end of the hallway he found the room it belonged to, smoothly sliding it in and out of the electronic lock. The door clicked open and Sayer ushered me inside.

I tripped over nothing when the inside turned out to be a suite. "What is this?" I asked breathlessly.

The door closed and I heard him fiddling with all the locks, securing us inside. "A surprise?" he suggested on a quiet laugh equal parts hopeful and nervous. "I had been hoping we'd check off all the d's first though."

Turning around so I could look at him, I walked backward into the luxurious room. "The d's?"

Half his mouth kicked up in a sweet smile. "You know, drinking, dining, dancing. The plan was to sweep you off your feet and then pretend to get lost until we ended up here. I've been looking forward to tonight for weeks." He let out a frustrated sigh. "I should have known the FBI would get in the way."

I smiled at his disappointment, for some reason feeling incredibly special that he had put so much thought into this night. "The FBI ruin everything."

He winked at me. "That they do." He paused, before adding thoughtfully, "They'll be expecting us to leave though. I'm sure they'll have the exits blocked and the hotel won't hand over security footage until they can come up with a warrant. We'll be safe here tonight."

Forcing my gaze from his, I absorbed the extravagant room that was ours for the night. The muted fabrics were highlighted with golden accents so that they matched the cream and gold furniture, and there were windows on every side. Wide, tall, stretching windows revealed the city at night and all the glittering light dancing from historic building to shimmery water to stoic monument.

He'd picked the most beautiful room for us. And after imagining the evening he had planned, I knew I truly would have been swept off my feet. I was halfway there now and we'd just outrun the feds.

Pressing my hands to my stomach, I tried not to think about why Sayer would go to all these great lengths. I was nervous now for an entirely different reason. Anticipation buzzed inside of me, a swarm of bees without a place to land. My fingers started trembling, so I hid them behind my back, unwilling to share my weakness. I was supposed to be resilient, unflappable, completely cool under pressure. And yet with just the opening of a door, Sayer had managed to completely turn me inside out.

"What was that down there?" I asked because it was easier to change the direction of my thoughts than come to terms with what this room could mean.

Sayer frowned. "I don't know."

"They knew my real name," I said unnecessarily. "They recognized me." I held his gaze, opening mine up so he could see all my truth, all the things I wouldn't hide from him. "How, Sayer? Why me?"

He shook his head. "I don't know. I'll make a call. See what I can find out."

Before he could do that though, I started shaking. And it wasn't the quivering of a nervous virgin on the potential night of her deflowering. No, this was full body quaking from nearly getting caught by federal agents.

It was the first time I had ever been made. It was the first time an FBI agent knew me by name. It was the first time I had ever had to face the consequences of my lifestyle.

"Hey," Sayer murmured gently. He rushed to me, pulling me into a tight hug against his body. I wrapped my arms around him, absorbing his strength and steady nerves. "Hey, Caroline, it's going to be fine."

I hugged him harder, crushing my body as close to his as was humanly possible. "I've never talked to them before, Sayer. Other than the recon we did before tonight, I have never even seen them. How did they know me?"

One of his long fingers nudged my chin, lifting my face to look at his. "I believe you. Okay? You're safe. You're not in trouble."

His soothing words did nothing to calm my racing nerves. "What if they arrest me? What if they have something on me?"

His blue eyes blazed with conviction. "They won't." His frown returned. "They don't. I'll figure it out," he promised. "We'll get to the bottom of this. And if by some miracle they have a tiny piece of evidence against you, we'll make it go away. It won't be hard. You're going to be fine."

I felt sick. All I could think about was Brick and Vinnie's warnings. "How do you know?"

"Because I'm not going to let anything happen to you. I promise you that, Six. As long as I'm able, I will protect you from every bad thing. You don't have to worry about anything. Ever. I will do whatever it takes to keep you safe."

His words wrapped around my heart, cradling it back to reality. His promises seemed impossible. Except I believed him. There was conviction in his tone, raw truth in his eyes. Sayer meant what he said. Every single word of it. "How can you say that? We've only been going out for—"

224

"You think my feelings started when we kissed?" His eyebrows drew down over his eyes. "You think my feelings started a couple months ago? Come on, Six, I've been after you since the first day I met you. Since you saved my life and gave me something to live for."

"Sayer, I didn't—"

His fingers pressed against my lips. "Caroline, before that day I was lost. I was living on the streets, afraid of dying every single day. Afraid of dying that day when your dad and his friends were done with me. And then there you were, so fucking pretty my chest hurt just looking at you. And you didn't just give me the courage to get through the day, you gave me the tools I needed to get off the streets. To stay off the streets. To keep living. To live *for* something. You saved my life that day, but you also saved my soul. You gave me the brotherhood, yeah. But before that? You gave me you. And since that day you've been it for me. My world. The one thing I'm living for above everything else."

I couldn't speak. I didn't want to speak. I just wanted to spend the rest of the night absorbing those words, playing them over and over and over in my head until I finally convinced my heart to believe them. How... how did he expect me to recover from that?

"I love you, Six. I think I've loved you since that alley. I think I'll always love you." I bit my bottom lip and tried to steady my breathing. I was desperate to hold myself together, to keep from crumbling in a heap of awe and emotion and hope. How did I get to have this man's love? How did I get to love him back? How was this my real life? There had never been a job that compared to this moment. No surge of adrenaline or priceless trophy or singular moment in all of history that was as special as this one. He mistook my silence for rejection. Glancing down at the carpet, he asked, "Is it too soon to say all that? I meant to wait..."

"It's not too soon," I whispered, barely finding my voice. My frozen fingers cradled his face, coaxing him to look at me again. "It's not." I had to swallow a deep breath and dig for courage, but finally I was able to confess my truth. "I think I've loved you from that same day. I think I've always loved you. I can't remember a day when I didn't. Before you I was miserable and angry. And then there you were and it was like I had finally found..."

"Something to live for," he filled in, his words making permanent homes in my heart, filling my soul with a satisfaction I had not known existed.

I knew he'd just confessed he loved me, but the insecure girl in me had been expecting rejection anyway. Instead, I got the most beautiful boy smiling the most beautiful smile. All of Sayer relaxed in a way I had never seen from him before. He was warm and bright and radiating peace all at once. It was like my confirmation of love had given him access to a whole new part of him, a piece he hadn't even realized he'd been missing.

His head dipped to meet my lips already on their way to his. His kiss was tender, slow, achingly reverent. His hands landed on my shoulders and slid down my arms, carefully caressing my body as he went.

There was so much sweet worship in this kiss that I didn't know if I'd be able to survive it. I had never been touched like this before. Never been kissed like this.

His mouth was all warm seduction as he moved over mine. I was a fluttering heartbeat of consent as he moved us to the bedroom, stripping pieces of our clothing as we went. Our shoes were left in the entryway. His jacket over the back of the couch. His belt on the floor by the bathroom. His shirt and my dress at the foot of the bed.

He laid me back on the puffy comforter and slowly stripped my stockings off me. I lay there in my strapless bra and miniscule panties and waited breathlessly for him to cover me with the warmth of his body.

He came down on top of me like a boy that had been given the best gift of his life. His eyes alight with true love, his hands trembling with the sacredness of the moment. His mouth moved over my body, tasting every inch of me, kissing and licking and adoring me as though he'd never had something so wonderful before.

The rest of our clothes quickly disappeared and we were left naked and desperate for each other. I still trembled. I couldn't stop myself.

I had never been this far with a boy before. I had never been this intimate or exposed. And yet, he took care of me as we explored uncharted territories carefully.

His fingers dipped inside me first, taking me to a precipice I didn't know existed. And just when I thought I couldn't hang on for a second longer, he changed tactics. I watched him put a condom on without taking a breath.

"Have you done this before?" he asked, his gaze holding mine captive.

I shook my head. "No."

His expression softened, deepened, his entire body going taut with anticipation. Then he was hovering over me, whispering promises and I love yous and pushing inside me slowly. There was the break, the release of the barrier and a wince from me while he kissed my breasts and my collarbone and all the places he could reach, soothing the ache and creating a new one all at once.

"Sayer," I whispered, needing him to move, to do something other than drive me to the edge of insanity. "Love me," I begged shamelessly.

His head lifted and our gazes collided, finding each other in the darkened room, refusing to let go.

"Always," he swore. But he didn't move right away. Instead, his mouth pressed against mine, searing that promise to my lips, making it permanent.

When at last he lifted his hips, only to drive them deeper inside me, I gasped at the sensation. I didn't know something like this existed... I didn't know it was this good.

We were a tangle of lust and something deeper, something eternal. My breath hitched and continued to hitch until I finally tumbled over the edge of blinding light. My legs were wrapped impossibly tight around his waist and my fingernails dug into his back without realizing it. He chased after me, moving fast, hard, deep.

"Oh, God," I gasped. And that same beautiful symphony of light and sensation and the tightening of every last muscle happened a second time.

When I came back to earth, he was still over me, and in me, watching me with unfiltered awe all over his face. My laugh was shaky, self-conscious, nervous... "Wow," I whispered.

I was all rubbery limbs and warm muscles, but he was as serious as always, observing me with that same sharp instinct. "I will never be the same," he said, his voice roughened gravel. "You've done something to me that can never be undone."

I didn't have the strength to be as serious as him. Instead, I lifted up on my elbows and kissed the corner of his mouth. "I'll be gentle."

He finally rolled over, pulling me into the crook of his body. I laid there listening to the heavy beat of his heart and smiled at a victory I had never known I wanted. "I don't need you to be gentle. I just need you to stay with me. Don't leave me, Six. I won't survive it."

I pressed my hand over his heart, loving the feel of him like this, so wide-open, so absolutely familiar. But I knew what he meant. I wouldn't survive it either. Not after this.

227

Not after *that*.

After we'd cleaned up, we found each other in bed again. I curled into him, loving the feel of his naked body against mine—even when we weren't doing anything but cuddling.

"It feels safe here," I whispered to him. The feds might be looking for me, but I was untouchable in this room. If they had an arrest warrant, I would face them in the morning. But here with Sayer I was safe. And it wasn't just them that I wanted to hide from. It was all of it. The *bratva*, my dad, the job. I just wanted to stay here with Sayer forever. "I don't want to leave."

His fingertips stroked my back, running up and down my spine, lulling me to sleep. "We will always have this, Six. We don't need a room for this."

I closed my eyes and drifted to sleep knowing he was right. We were connected at the deepest level now. We'd been on this trajectory since the day we met. Tonight had been a fiery culmination of everything between us. Fireworks and explosions and the melding of two hearts that formerly belonged in two different bodies. Now I held his within me. And he owned every inch of mine.

I knew we were young and it was impossible to tell what the future held for us. But I also knew my heart. It would never belong to someone else.

I was Sayer's. Forever.

Chapter Nineteen

Present Day

I looked down at the text Frankie sent me, all my emotions bubbling over with righteous indignation. This was highway robbery.

The dollar amount for three new identities stared at me, eyebrows lifted in mild disdain. It seemed to ask, "What?" in that teenager tone of some of our resort guests that drove me crazy.

"You're what," I told the identities. "You're too expensive."

The number didn't change. Son of a bitch.

It was almost the end of the day, but this couldn't wait. I pulled my purse out of the filing cabinet and reached my hand into the hidden pocket, retrieving my emergency track phone. I didn't trust cell phones or text messages or really any kind of smart technology.

Like I said, paranoia was my best friend.

I texted Frankie from my real cell asking if we could talk.

Innocuous enough, right? But she would see the code. Five minutes later when she replied with a curt, *Sure*, I knew she had her own track phone and had settled in a secured location.

I slipped my normal cell into my purse, and slammed everything away in the metal cabinet taking the burner to the bathroom. I dialed her number from memory and counted the rings until she answered.

"Why is it so much?" I asked on a raised whisper.

"Juliet," she answered immediately. "You were right. You need a lot of paperwork for kids."

"We don't have enough, Francesca. Not for that amount."

Something banged on the other end of the phone. She hit something. Or kicked it. "They're coming for us, Caroline. We have to do something."

Cash.

This was a cash flow problem. We had money. We had assets. But we didn't want to trip any wires or alert any unnecessary authorities. We had to leave Frisco discreetly or people would start looking for us. Maybe not many, but enough to start a snowball effect that could land us in serious trouble.

Maggie, for instance. Jesse. Juliet's preschool and daycare teachers. Our landlord—especially when we left a whole bunch of shit behind.

If we had rock solid identities, none of it would be a problem. We'd lay low for a while and reemerge in a brand-new town as brand new people.

But we didn't know these counterfeiters. We were putting blind trust in strangers, which sat wrong with me. I wasn't going to chance everything else too.

So what we needed was cash.

Or something of value that we could turn into cash.

"The office, Frankie. Sayer's office. It's flush."

"Caroline..."

"Come on, it's perfect. And it all belongs to me anyway. They stole it from me." My tone hardened with conviction the more the plan developed in my head. "I'd just be reclaiming what's rightfully mine."

"This sounds like a terrible idea," she warned.

"What other options do we have? Give me another solution and I'll gladly take it." Although that wasn't entirely true. The more I thought about getting all of my things back, the more I liked the idea.

It was mine anyway. Sayer had no claim to it. The fact he had it in the first place was a good reminder he had never trusted me like he claimed to. He had never believed my promises. He'd used me, manipulated me and then counted on my trust in him to pocket a hell of a lot of insurance.

"We could do something here. In town. Something fast but low maintenance. Like a laundromat or something."

"You want to rob a laundromat?"

"Or the till here. I could just walk out with it today after I get off. They're insured. The Lodge would be fine."

"No way. You're crazy. Come on, Frankie, think this all the way through. They would catch you on camera. And as soon as word hit DC, whatever's left of the syndicate would come for us. We have to be smarter than that. We can't make mistakes."

"Sayer will know that it's you," she argued.

"But he won't send an army after us. If anything, he'll come after me himself. Just him. Just me."

"And Juliet?"

That made me pause. What would Sayer do if he found my daughter... our daughter? "Give me something else then. Anything else. I'll take it. I'll do it. Whatever it is. Just tell me what to do, Frankie. I'm out of options." My voice was a ragged whisper. I could feel the exhaustion all the way to my bones. It was a painful, intolerable thing, like a clenched fist on the jugular of my soul. I wanted to escape just so I could find somewhere new and take a nap.

I just needed to catch my breath.

When Frankie spoke again, she was resigned. We both knew the answer. It was dangerous, but it was possible. And nobody in Frisco got hurt.

"What do you need me to do?" she asked.

"Where is the guy? Where can we get the papers?"

"Denver," she whispered. "He said a week."

"Set it up then. We'll leave tonight and lie low until the papers are ready. As long as they're in process we can live off cash for a week. That will give us time to fence the goods and come up with enough to pay him."

"Tonight?"

"Can you pick up Jules? I'll meet you at home. Have everything packed up and ready."

I guess all of my leave in good standing, don't raise questions philosophy was thrown out the window. But with Sayer's basement office calling my name, it finally felt like we had a solution.

"Sayer will never forgive you for leaving him twice, Caro. Are you sure you're up for this?"

She was right. Sayer would never forgive me. And if I ran off with all his cash, he might never give up looking for me either.

But that was a risk I was willing to take.

I would be smarter next time. I would never let my guard down. I would never get comfortable.

"Frankie, can you pick Juliet up tonight or not?"

"I can get her," she agreed. I could feel that she wanted so say something more. Whatever it was swirled in the air between us, clogging up the line, stifling all the breathable air.

"Be ready to go," I ordered, cutting her off before she made me question myself.

I hung up our call and slipped it into my pocket. It was so much smaller than my other phone, I barely noticed it.

"Hey, Mags," I called, stopping by her office in an effort to implement my plan immediately. "I got a call from daycare and they said Juliet is super sick. She started throwing up earlier today."

Maggie's expression immediately fell with concern. "Oh, no. Is she going to be okay?"

I waved a hand in the air and furrowed my brow. I needed to be concerned but not overly so—this was just the flu. And I was a veteran parent. "Yeah, she'll be fine. She just caught a bug or something from school. It's that time of year when all the little kids start wiping their snot everywhere."

"Do you need to go?"

"I called Francesca and she's going to grab her since she's closer, but I'm wondering about tomorrow. Her daycare's policy is twenty-four hours without a fever. And she's throwing up and who knows what else is wrong with her. Would it be possible to get the day off? I know that puts you in a bind but—"

"Oh, stop," she ordered. "We'll be just fine for one day." She pointed a finger at me. "Just make sure it's only one day though. Otherwise things start to fall apart and I'm too old to deal with all that."

My smile wobbled, despite my years of training and my ability to lie. I didn't want to do this. I didn't want to hurt Maggie or leave her. "It might end up being two days. Or even a week. You know how these things hang on."

She sobered and moved closer to me. "Are you worried, darlin'? She'll be okay. It's just the touch of the flu. Nothing that she can't handle." I was full-fledged crying now, weeping like a complete moron and total guilty party. "Oh, no, Caroline. Did I say something to upset you? I'm so sorry."

I moved around the desk and met her halfway, clearly concerned for me. I threw my arms around her neck and started sobbing against her shoulder. She hesitated, but eventually hugged me back. It was the first time we'd ever embraced. Neither Maggie nor I were the touchy-feely types, so there had never been anything more between us than an occasional high five.

Realizing how strange I was acting, I pulled back and started wiping my eyes. "Sorry," I hiccupped. "I don't know what came over me. Sometimes the single parent thing is really hard." And I started crying all over again, because that was true but it was also a lie. And I found that I didn't want to lie to Maggie. I didn't even care about protecting her. I wanted to confess, to spill everything just so she could give me guidance. I'd survived five years on Maggie's good, wise advice and it sucked that the time I needed it the most I couldn't ask for it.

"Caroline, you're worrying me."

Laughing nervously, I took another step back. "I'm PMSing or something. I'm acting like an idiot."

"Are you sure you're okay? Is there something you want to talk about?"

Yes. So much. "I'm really okay," I promised her. And it wasn't a total lie. This was hard. This was unbearable. But saving Juliet would make it worth it. Keeping Francesca away from her psychotic family of criminals would make it okay. "I've just been stressed lately and I keep everything bottle up. That was the cathartic release I needed."

Her frown deepened. "You're a terrible liar."

I wasn't. I was the best liar. Which meant I could lie myself out of this situation too. "I'm going to go check on cabin ten. They called earlier to say their dishwasher was acting funny. I'll find out if we should call the handyman or if it's a simple fix. Then I'll take off for the night, okay?"

She still had that concerned look on her face. "You'll call me if you need me?"

"Of course. Thank you for offering."

I was halfway through the door when Maggie added, "Give my love to Juliet. Tell her when she gets better you two can take me out to dinner."

Her suggestion made me smile. "Oh, wow, Maggie, that's so generous of you."

She smiled and her brows relaxed, transforming her face from drill sergeant to stunning. "If you're good, I might even let you take me to a movie."

My head tipped back and I laughed a real, genuine sound that I was beyond grateful for. "You're so full of it."

It was her turn to laugh. "You love me for it."

Heading toward the front door, I was grateful for the natural opportunity to reply, "I do love you for it. Very much."

By the time I stepped outside, I felt marginally better. Maggie and I were parting on a good foot. On Friday when I still hadn't shown up for three days, she might hate me. And I wouldn't blame her. But today we were as good of friends as always. And I would remember this goodbye for the rest of my life.

I did what I said I was going to do. I drove the ATV to cabin ten and talked to the guests about their dishwasher and what it was doing. I could see Sayer's Jeep up a short hill at the end of this driveway. And when I left cabin ten, Gus's Subaru had joined it.

They were both there. Now was my chance.

I hurried back to the office and got it ready for the rest of the week. I wasted precious seconds organizing and scheduling and writing To Do Lists for Maggie and making sure she had access to all of our different passwords. I just wanted her to be set up for success. I didn't want her to lose me and flounder because she didn't know our social media passwords or how much we paid the paper goods delivery guy.

When all was said and done, I pressed a kiss to my palm and laid it on the tall, worn counter. This place had been a second home to me for five years. I was going to miss it as fiercely as I would miss Maggie.

Driving back to town with the mountain in my rearview mirror felt like a death, like I was watching someone die. So I focused on the drive ahead, refusing to watch the life behind me fade.

I got back to town near six o'clock. The sun was hovering low over the peaks of the distant mountains and the sky was darkening quickly. The temperature was dropping too, giving the air a bite, smelling of possible snow.

After driving around the block three times, I parked in an alley between two resort hotels just off Main Street. I left my Murano unlocked and circled around the block so I could walk down the main road and enter the DC Initiative through the front door.

I was dressed for work, but not sloppy, so I hoped I didn't draw too much attention in my black, distressed skinny jeans and thick gray cardigan. The hostess seemed to turn up her nose at me, but I didn't get the vibe that she was watching me in particular, at least no more than she was judging the world around her as a whole.

234

"I'm just going to have a drink at the bar," I told her, flying by without slowing down.

Cass was bartending again and I was grateful to see her. I should have been ducking from any people that could spot me, identify me, testify against me, but there was something about seeing a familiar face that calmed some of my frantic nerves. Besides, I'd only been in here once, I didn't exactly have the place perfectly cased.

"Hey, mama," she greeted me as I slid onto a bar stool. "What brings you in tonight with no date and no kids?"

I smiled weakly. "That exact reason? I need some me time."

She nodded enthusiastically. "Can I get an amen?" She held up a bottle of gin and a bottle of vodka. "Pick your poison?"

I pointed at the gin. "Lime and tonic please."

"You got it."

Fiddling with my purse straps, I made a show of pulling out my phone to check it and then tucked it away when there was nothing. "Hey, Cass?" She raised her eyebrows indicating that she was listening even though she was in the middle of my drink. "Last time I was here, Sayer and Gus took Jesse and me to the basement. Is it only the office down there? Or are there other rooms? I was so like, shocked by their office, I can't seem to remember anything else of what I saw."

She laughed. "Right? I can't believe they have all that stuff just lying around. But I guess it's secured and neither of them have permanent homes right now. So maybe it's the safest place for them? Who knows."

"You've seen everything?" Great, all I needed were more witnesses that could place the Leighton to a specific place, city, state with me.

"I mean, I didn't get a special tour..." She lifted her eyes and gave me a poignant look. "But I've been down there to have meetings and talk to them and whatnot. There's a diamond necklace that I'm fairly confident weighs more than me that belongs in the Tower of London."

The diamond necklace had once belonged to an Austrian empress. I'd lifted the shiny bobble from a Russian ambassador during a job. It had been very dangerous and very secured. It had taken months of planning and a huge amount of luck. We'd been sent in for documents. I came out with a necklace, a matching pair of earrings and tiara. I remember feeling entitled to them after nearly getting caught and extradited to Russia. "No way," I feigned awe. "I didn't see a diamond necklace! I was too overwhelmed to take any of it in."

Her smile turned conspiratorial. "I've heard rumors that there's an entire drawer of expensive jewelry. It must be worth millions."

It was in fact, worth millions. Millions and millions and millions. But most of it was too dangerous to fence. There were only a few pieces that wouldn't be tied directly to me and in those, there were only a few pieces that would get their actual value in cash.

Austrian diamonds were pretty and fun to brag about. But the street value for them was atrocious. Nobody appreciated history anymore. But more than that, there was greater risk with getting caught. Online databases and technology advances in CSI made everyone a little more cautious about getting involved with a hot item.

"Aren't they afraid someone's going to steal it all?" I asked Cass.

She shrugged. "Actually, no. They're maybe the nicest people I've ever met. I think if you needed money or something, they'd just hand it over to you. You wouldn't even have to steal it." She glanced around and leaned in. "Last week, I had a really bad day. Get this. My ex showed up in town and tried to take Max away and when I called the cops, he tore my apartment apart and then he stole from me. All of my money. Not only did Gus and Sayer give me the week off, they still paid me."

"That was nice of them." I didn't mention that this business was probably a money laundering front and they were most likely washing money through her. Nor did I mention that they probably went after her ex and made sure he was never going to come back. Because that would upset her.

I was a good friend like that.

This also explained the gooey stars dancing in her eyes for Sayer and Gus. I would too if they'd cleaned up my mess like they did Cass's. Instead, they showed up and made mine bigger. They took the mess of my life and tripled it, quadrupled it, fucking blew it up until all I could see was a mess and all I would have time for was mess.

I laid a ten-dollar bill on the bar. "Where's your restroom?"

She pointed toward the back where I already knew it was. "Thanks, Cass."

"Hey, let's have a playdate soon," she suggested. "Max would love to get together with Juliet."

"Sounds like a plan," I smiled, hiding the sadness in my eyes. "Juliet would love that too."

We said official goodbyes and I walked toward the back, pretending to look for the restrooms.

It didn't matter where I was walking because I slipped down the stairs as soon as I was hidden behind the art display dividers. I crept down them slowly, remaining as inconspicuous as possible. Nobody seemed to notice me or my snooping. Which was a good thing because I planned to do a lot more of it.

At the bottom of the stairs, I took my time opening doors down the corridor and listening for anyone that could have followed me. I found the supply closet and a janitor's closet, and lo and behold, an emergency exit to outside. It led to a stairwell that resurfaced in an alley.

I went back to the supply closet, found a box cutter and snipped the wires connected to the push bar on the door just in case an alarm went off when I opened it. I tucked the box cutter into my pocket and headed for the office.

It appeared to be locked, which I had suspected it would be. But it seemed to be a more complicated system than the first time I was here. It wanted fingerprints and a key code. I didn't have the right fingerprints, nor did I have time to figure out the right code.

Damn it. I was just about to try to box cut my way through the door, when I noticed there were no lights on the keypad. I pushed my pointer finger to the scanner and nothing happened.

The lock system would be highly sophisticated, eventually, when they set it up. Currently, it was absolutely useless.

Smiling at my good luck, I pulled out my old set of curtain picks and quickly worked the mortise handle. It clicked open with a satisfying tick and I walked into the office with dollar signs cha-chinging in my eyes.

No, it was more than that. To say I was excited to make money was not the whole truth. It was the satisfaction from the job, the thrill of the hunt and spike of adrenaline.

I stood in the dark in the middle of the office, my blood rushing and a smile on my face, realizing something crucial. Oh, my god, I'd missed this. I felt more alive than I had in weeks... months... maybe years. Everything was suddenly in color again. Not just black and white or muted tones, but vibrant, effervescent, neon hues.

I wanted to believe I was all upstanding citizen and righteous moral compass, but the truth was, I was a criminal. To my very core. This was the life I had been raised in, the only truth I had ever known.

Caroline Valera was good at lying, but she was very good at stealing.

Tonight would not only be my vindication, it would be my redemption.

Moving immediately to Sayer's desk, I flipped his lamp on and surveyed all that was available. I opened my big purse and started dumping things in it. Jewelry and a signed rare baseball, a collection of very old, very gold coins, whatever I could find that I thought would fetch a decent paycheck. I pulled the Leighton off the wall and set it near the door. It was mine. The hitman's handbook too. And a Faberge egg that could have terrible consequences if anyone ever found out it was me that took it.

More, my greedy thief's heart whispered.

It's yours anyway, my better, usually moral side agreed.

He stole it from you.

Scanning the office, my eyes fell on the safe. I walked over to it and slid my hand along the top.

"What are you hiding?" I asked it. I could never have unlocked it without help. It was big and bulky and complicated—all the things I hated in a safe. And it was by a brand I didn't recognize which meant I couldn't even wing it. I had no idea how it was built or the secret to cracking it. It was a total and complete enigma.

Except it wasn't locked.

I noticed the crack at the top when I ran my fingers over it. Gripping the large handle, I pulled. It opened. Haha! Hello, secrets.

Although part of me had to wonder how juicy these secrets were if Gus and Sayer didn't even bother locking the safe behind them.

But when the door was open, I couldn't decide if I wanted to know them after all. I had been expecting more valuables, maybe files they didn't want other people to find. I wanted something from Sayer's time in prison or Gus's stint as the bookkeeper for the *bratva*.

Instead, I got one manila envelope. In the entire safe, just that one, thick, ominous envelop. And if the titling wasn't a warning then I didn't know what was. I started to question my entire time down here.

Where were Sayer and Gus? Didn't they have a restaurant to run?

Had no one noticed me come down here? Was it really that easy?

No. On all of the jobs I'd ever been on, not one had been this easy.

In fact, we could say this was too easy.

Which meant something was wrong. This was a trap.

Caro.

That's what was written on the envelope.

Simply, understated Caro written in Sayer's handwriting.

I couldn't shake the paranoid feeling that I'd just walked into something that I wouldn't be able to walk out of, but I had to see what was inside the envelope. I mean, I was already planning on leaving tonight. There was nothing that could keep me in this town. Nothing that would entice me to stay. No matter what Sayer had been able to gather on me.

There was no reason to be scared of a paper. Or an envelope. Or what was in it.

"Just do it," I ordered myself. Shaking my head, I snatched it up and wondered why it was so heavy. I meant to drop it in my purse and get the hell out of there. I meant to maybe just burn it before I ever knew what was in it.

But that wasn't what I did.

And how could I have? This was my life. I deserved to know what Sayer had done.

Chapter Twenty

The contents of the folder lay before me, overlapping, covering and revealing at the same time. It was exactly how I felt. Laid out, half of me completely exposed and the other half totally in the dark, utterly clueless.

There were recent pictures of me from before Sayer rolled into town. I read the timestamp and tried to think about my life back then. That was before the DC Initiative had even started renovation.

It was before Sayer had come here.

He'd hired someone to find me, take pictures of me. There I was walking out of the grocery story. There I was at work. There I was picking Juliet up from daycare.

My guts twisted together. He knew about her then. But did he know she was his? He'd never brought her up. Not even once.

Then there were printed emails with his PI. Have you found her? Sayer had asked. Maybe, his PI typed back. I'll keep digging, but I found someone that matches the description. I want a picture, Sayer demanded. Not yet, his PI tried to reason with him, let me be sure.

Sayer had been unrelenting, Now.

That was the end of that email thread. I didn't know what happened next, other than Sayer must have gotten some kind of confirmation because there were pictures of me everywhere. With Jesse on his ranch, at Foote's with Francesca, with Maggie and two coffees between us and big smiles on our faces.

More correspondence, this time folded neatly in short, white envelopes—communication of some kind, only without addresses or return labels or stamps.

They weren't even sealed.

I grabbed the closest one and pulled out the letter.

Caro,

Where are you? What did I do? Why did you leave? When are you coming back?

I need you to come back.

I just need you.

Sayer

My heart twisted in my chest, wringing out like a wet sponge. It wasn't dated, but I could guess when he'd written it.

I opened another letter that seemed to predate the first one.

Six,

I'm starting to worry. I haven't seen you in two weeks. I expected you a while ago. Are you in danger? Is something wrong? Did I do something to piss you off?

I don't say this enough, but I love you, Caroline. You are the best thing that has ever happened to me. Without you I don't think I could face the next ten years. It's unbearable in here. And worse without you. You're the only thing that keeps me breathing. The only thing that keeps me sane. From the day I met you that was true.

You saved me when we were kids. And I'm a selfish bastard because I need you to save me again. Payne says the charges are going to stick. All of them. What am I going to do?

I'm sorry, Caro. For whatever I did. For every single thing. Please forgive me. Please come see me.

Please don't leave me.

Sayer.

It hurt to breathe and my hands were trembling. But I still opened the next one. And the one after that. And the one after that.

Did I ever tell you my dad was a cop? Crazy right? Considering the line of work I ended up in. Although it's not so out of the question if you know the whole story. If you know that sometimes the people pretending to be the good guys are really the worst of them all. So, maybe it's not that surprising that I joined the syndicate. They never beat the shit out of me. They never put their hands on me. Or locked me in a basement for days without food. Or did unspeakable things to my mom until she couldn't stand her life anymore, until she didn't even care enough about me to keep living. The only silver lining to my mom killing herself? Was that my dad did too shortly after.

Which was good news for me until the fucking system got ahold of me. Foster care? More fake good guys taking advantage of little kids. To be fair, there were a few good homes near the end, but the damage was already done and I was too wild to settle down.

That's when you found me. I was a feral dog living on the streets, so close to death I felt it every day. Then Caroline fucking Valera shows up and breathes life back into me, finds me a home and gives me purpose. Do you know that you rescued me? Do you know that you saved my soul?

I was dead before you, Caroline. Don't make me live without you now. I don't know how. I don't know how to do anything without you.

Come back to me.

Come home.

Take away this constant pain.

Breathe life into me once again.

Tears started falling and I was helpless to stop them. How could I? He had never told me about his past and it wasn't for lack of trying on my part. I had asked him endless times about what his life was like before the syndicate, before me. He would never talk about it. He'd get that blank look on his face and clutch the key around his neck.

How could he not have told me? How could he have kept all that a secret for so long?

I pressed a hand to my cracking chest in a failing attempt to hold it together.

Six,

I should hate you. I want to hate you. The three hardest years of my fucking life and you're nowhere to be found? I thought we were in this together. I thought we had a deal—the whole death do us part kind of thing.

But you're gone. And everything is falling apart here. And I don't know what end is up, down or fucking sideways.

You better have a good fucking excuse. Don't you think I at least deserve to hear it?

Come back and give it to me.

Goddamnit, just come back.

I read through all the letters except one. They weren't in any particular timeline and some of them were so angry I couldn't do anything more than weep over them. He had a right to be mad. He had a right to hate me. But every single letter ended in him asking me to come back despite how he felt.

He mentioned his past more and more. How awful his dad had been. How he'd been abused. And then abused again in two different foster care homes. He had just started to believe he was free from the constant physical pain from someone that was supposed to love him when it turned to sexual pain from someone who was supposed to protect him. He had run away from the system only to face constant danger of both varieties on the streets.

He credited me with getting him away from all of it.

I didn't deserve the gratitude. I had helped him trade one hell for another.

But he didn't see it that way. It was no wonder he hadn't been bothered by the *bratva's* dealings. It was no wonder he was so loyal to an organization that had given him new life, given him the means to take care of himself, to be independent.

It was no wonder he didn't want to leave.

There was one letter left. I was the most afraid to open it. I'd saved it for last on purpose.

Because unlike all of the letters before it, this one had an address. Sayer had written every letter but this one from prison, when he hadn't known where I'd gone, when he didn't know how to find me.

But this letter was addressed Caroline Baker with my Colorado address. My home address.

This was the letter he'd written when he finally found me.

Fear stopped the flow of tears, although my cheeks remained wet as I was too focused on the letter to wipe them dry. Pulling it from the envelope, I noticed it was on a different kind of paper and written with a different color of ink. Everything about it showed the change in Sayer, no longer the prisoner, no longer wondering what happened to me.

Caroline Baker,

No wonder it took me so long to find you. I didn't expect you to use something so familiar. Something you've used before. And Frisco of all places? Did you intend that to be a slap in the face? I honestly can't tell. I don't know how to read you anymore.

I don't know you anymore.

You've been gone for five years. Does it feel that long to you? It feels longer to me. But maybe that's because I was the one rotting in a prison cell while you moved on with your life. Maybe you don't think about me at all anymore. Maybe in light of your new, life you've forgotten about me completely.

I wish I could forget. I wish I could forget the way you used to look at me, as though I were your very reason for existing. I wish I could forget the way you would smile in that secret way, a thousand hidden thoughts locked away in your brilliant mind that the rest of us were left only to guess. I wish I could forget the way you talked to yourself or nibbled on your lip or laughed at everything Gus says.

I wish I could forget the Mandarin, Fat Jack's, the warehouse when we were kids, and every single time I've touched you and wanted to touch you and thought about touching you. The way you feel. The way you smell. The way you taste. The way you lie with such skill, that even I believed you. Even I thought you were telling the truth. I wish I could forget you, Six. More than I want my next breath, I want to forget you.

It would be so much easier. I could move on with my life. I could save the syndicate and tell the FBI to fuck off.

And if I can't forget you, I wish I could just hate you. Everything would be so much simpler if I could hate you.

But I can't do that either. So I'm going to stick to doing what I can do. Which is to give you the life you want. I'm going to make sure the syndicate never bothers you again. I'm going to give the fucking FBI what they want so they leave you alone forever. And I'm going to quit this obsession I have with you. I'm done, Caroline. I'm letting you go. If you can forget me and move on with your life, I can too.

Consider this my resignation from your life forever. Good luck to you, Six.

You're truly free now. Just like you always wanted.

Sayer

I hiccupped a sob and realized for the first time that I was crying. His words were knives in my chest, stabbing at the suddenly empty place where my heart used to be. I hadn't expected something like this. In my best-case scenario, we just never saw each other again. I didn't have to hear these words. I didn't have to face this truth. I just wanted an ambiguous ending to our tragic love story so I could fill in the blanks myself.

I bent over, crushing the letter in two fists. Why did it hurt this badly? How did he still have this power over me after all this time? Why hadn't it faded? Why hadn't I moved on?

And what really sucked, I mean, what really hurt more than anything was that I had been lying to myself this whole time. I had been the mark in my own stupid game. I'd been the one conned. Duped. Made to look like a fool.

"Turn it over."

I jumped at the sound of Sayer's voice behind me. Habit made me glance at my purse and the Leighton propped by the door.

Okay, maybe it was more than habit. I didn't want to face him, not after reading his real thoughts, not after seeing them all in cruel, heartbreaking ink.

"Turn it over, Caroline."

I finally looked at him, starting at his shoes and working my way up, over low-slung jeans and a navy-blue cardigan over a gray V-neck. Finally, I braved beyond his shoulders. That long corded throat, the square jaw, those full, masculine lips, the blue, blue eyes and all that dark hair. Why did he have to look like that? Why couldn't all ex-boyfriends just turn into toads the second things were over? So many bad decisions could be avoided in the world if women only had to face toads they were in love with and not the real men that represented their heartbreak and lost hopes and dreams and wasted orgasms.

Well... maybe we didn't regret the orgasms.

"What are you doing here?" I demanded, my voice hoarse with the buckets of shed tears.

He shot a pointed look to the crumpled letter in my hands. "Damn it, woman, turn the paper over."

246

Something in his tone convinced me to do it. He had sounded almost... playful. And he managed to pique my curiosity enough to do as he said.

The letter was a mess, crumpled and damp from my tears. And yet there was his writing again. He'd continued his thoughts.

"Oh, good," I whispered to the paper. "More rejection."

"Just read it."

That was a lie. Not all of it, but damn, a lot of it. Starting with "this obsession." This isn't an obsession, Six, this is love. And it's deep and wild and forever. I can't stop. And I can't quit you.

So yeah, I'll give you all the other shit you want. But I'm not going to step back. I'm not going to stop trying. I'm not going to let you go.

I'm coming for you, Caro. And when I get to you, I'm not letting go. Never again.

You're mine. And I am yours. Let's give up this game and stop lying to ourselves. You own my heart, Caroline. It's yours. Come claim it.

I got to the end only to reread it immediately. And then again. "What is this?" I asked him, my voice a raspy whisper.

"Truth," he said simply.

"You came here for me?"

His mouth lifted in that half smile. "Wasn't it obvious?"

"You took down the syndicate?"

This time it was a half-hearted shrug. "Payne wanted names and places and locations. He wanted every single thing I remembered. So he got it. As long as I didn't have to testify." He walked further into his office, pretending to examine something on Gus's desk, but I knew it was because he was uncomfortable. He needed to move. This conversation made him restless. "It took five years, but he was able to get everyone on something."

"You stayed in prison to work with him?"

"Secretly of course. You won't find my name in any of their paperwork. Or on some fucking WITSEC list or CI database. That was the deal. Mason asked his questions, I gave him answers. We took them down slowly, but permanently. Payne's happy and I'm finally free."

My one word question burned my tongue like a hot coal I was desperate to spit out. "Why?"

"Come on, Six, you're not this dense."

247

No, not dense. Afraid. Cowardly. Weak. "F-for me?" His eyes darkened meaningfully. "You did all of that for me? Risked your life? Betrayed your brothers? Gave up DC for me?"

His brows drew down. "Are those supposed to be difficult choices? When it comes to you, Caroline, there's only one choice. There's only you."

"Sayer..."

He stood there, hands tucked in his pockets, waiting on me to get it. To fully get it. But it wasn't that simple. It wasn't that easy.

"You're telling the truth?" I had to ask. I had to hear it from his lips.

His bright blue eyes intensified, turning a shade that couldn't have been human. They were too beautiful. Too otherworldly. Too bigger than life. Just like Sayer. And all those things he'd done for me.

"No more lies, Caro. There's no reason for them. Just truth from now on. Starting with, I love you. And if you never tell me why you left or why you didn't talk to me first or what you've been doing for the past five years, I will still love you. If you tell me everything and I hate all of your answers and wish I could change them all, I will still love you. If you walk out of this building right now because you can't stand the sight of me and you want something different or you're already married or something that keeps us apart. I will still love you. I will always love you."

I was out of my seat and wrapped around him faster than he could blink. But he was ready to catch me. His arms were around me at just the right moment. Our mouths collided, kissing with the kind of hungry desperation that made me want more, made me addicted with just one taste of him.

We devoured each other, unable to be sated with small, polite or PG kisses. Our clothes started disappearing next. First his glasses—they had to go for obvious reasons. Then his cardigan and my cardigan and my shirt and his shirt. We toed off our boots without breaking apart, which wasn't easy. I stumbled backward and he followed me, his feet tripping over his half-discarded shoes. My butt hit the desk and I half wondered if he'd orchestrated the movement, because his hands were already on the back of my thighs, lifting, kissing, ripping off what was left of our clothes.

His buckle was impossible. I hated it. After several unsuccessful tries, I tipped my head back and growled at the ceiling, making him chuckle darkly.

"I thought you were over me?" he whispered in my ear, his breath hot and enticing and familiar all at once.

"Never," I told him, swore to him. "I could never be over you. No matter how far I ran or how long I managed to hide. I would always, eternally come home to you."

He pulled back, letting his gaze find mine. "I came to you."

Resting my hand on his bare chest, I said, "You came to me so I could finally come home."

"Say it, Caro. Let me hear it."

I hesitated. It wasn't because I wanted him to suffer, but I needed him to feel the words, know how serious and honest they were. And I hadn't said them in a while. I was rusty. They were difficult words to say. They were all of my trust and hope and fears and insecurities and future and past and dreams and goals and aspirations all in one little sentence. They were everything and all of me and both of those things at once.

It wasn't something I wanted to say flippantly or on command. I wanted to mean it. I wanted to swear it.

I wanted it to be my oath and creed and life's purpose.

"I love you, Sayer Wesley. I never stopped loving you. I will never stop loving you."

His hands cradled my face, gentle and unyielding. "I went through the seven circles of hell to hear you say that, Six. It was worth it. Every damn minute."

Tears pricked at my eyes again, but when his mouth connected with mine, I forgot all about them or about the sorrow, the heartbreak and years apart. Everything became about this moment, this touch, this man with his hands on me and his mouth on me and what he was doing to me.

With one hand, he managed to finally undo his buckle. My jeans were gone next, ripped off my legs and turned inside out. And then his, so that we were finally stripped down to only underwear.

I'd seen him naked recently, but not like this. Not when his muscles were flexed and rippling because of how he had to lean over me. Not when his corded strength was coiled for me. Not when his rough hands caressed my thighs and my breasts and parted my legs so he could explore the center of me.

Yet while I was ogling him, I was highly self-conscious of how I looked as well. While all of his changes were for the better, mine were not as kind. He had bigger, stronger arms. I had stretch marks on my abdomen and wider, childbearing hips. He had turned his body into muscle. Mine had gone soft from too many pizza Friday nights and ice creams with Juliet and not enough time found to exercise. And yet next to him, I didn't hate my rounder body or matured features. Next to him they felt right, designed to be this way, complements of each other in a way that I would never have expected.

Neither of us were the same, but I preferred it that way. We weren't the same as before. We had changed and grown and suffered and hurt and faced this world and all its hardships. So it was okay that we weren't the same naïve kids. It was okay that we weren't kissing as those people we used to be. We weren't them anymore.

We were new versions of us kissing in a new version of passion.

And to be honest, I preferred this one.

His fingers circled and coaxed and created a delicious ache that was soul deep. It spread through me like ripples on water, making my limbs tingle and my core tighten. It had been so long since my body had been brought to this point by someone else.

I had been asleep for the past five years and Sayer was determined to wake me up.

He leaned over me, swiping everything off the desk behind me and leveraged my body so his fingers could reach deeper. I gasped at the sensation, the fulfilling feeling of him finding the most sensitive part of me.

"Fucking missed this," he murmured against my temple. He trailed kisses down the side of my face, the corner of my eye, my jawline, the column of my throat. His lips caressed the top of my breast, and with his free hand, he nudged my bra to the side so he could close his mouth around my nipple and suck.

I let out a gasp of pleasure, encouraging him to suck harder, longer. His tongue flicked and swirled and then his teeth scraped in a way that drove me crazy.

Squirming, I tried to sit up straighter, tried to find some position in which I had more control, but with clever pressure from the fingers still moving inside me, he coaxed me to lean back further, dominating my body and my senses and my desire.

"Let go, Caro," he ordered in that deep, growly voice. "Give in."

I leaned back on my hands, spreading my legs wider, tilting my hips for his benefit. His fingers moved in and out slowly, pressing deeper each time, bringing me closer and closer each time. Then his thumb pressed that sensitive bud right where I needed him the most, right

250

when I needed him the most, and he gave my nipple another long suck, letting me feel his teeth and tongue and all the wicked heat of his mouth.

And there was nothing left for me to do other than obey his command to let go. Lights burst behind my eyes and my entire body arched and tightened and became something else entirely. He didn't stop moving his fingers or driving me wild with what he was doing to my breasts. I was at his complete mercy, totally and completely his.

When I came back to myself, my appendages were warm, limp with satisfaction, but still his fingers moved, refusing to let my desire go to sleep. I reached forward, wrapping my hand around him, caressing the hard length I had missed for far too long. He shivered at my touch, a full body tremble that revealed his own need.

"Better not," he murmured with a wicked half smile. "It's been a while."

I nibbled on my bottom lip, wondering just how long. He tugged my underwear off and stepped between my thighs.

"Are you clean?" he asked, his voice only slightly more coherent than before.

"There's been nobody since you," I promised him.

His eyes darkened and his hands landed on the insides of my thighs, spreading my legs wider. "No one?"

I shook my head. "I couldn't." Looking down, unable to stand the intensity in his gaze or the fear that swallowed my heart whole, I said, "It's only ever been you, Sayer."

He nudged my head up with a hand under my chin. "There's been no one for me either. No one has even entered my thoughts since you."

My eyes bugged. I hated to ruin the moment or call him a liar, but come on! Boys were different than girls. I loved sex, but my body had been perfectly happy to go into asexual mode when I didn't have the trust and safety of a committed relationship. Frankie didn't seem to have that problem, but I'd been with the same man since I was fifteen. I wasn't exactly prepared to go out into the world and find my sexual freedom.

But Sayer was this gorgeous, healthy, virile male. How could he have possibly waited for me? Especially after I hurt him so deeply? After everything I put him through, it seemed that at the very least, revenge sex was in order.

"How?" I demanded of him. "How has there been no one since me?"

251

His hand cupped my jaw, his thumb brushing over my cheekbone. With all the sincerity and raw, genuine truth, he held my gaze and said, "Because it felt like cheating. And I couldn't. No matter how angry I was or frustrated or lost... I couldn't make myself be unfaithful to you. I had no desire to be with anyone but you. So yeah, it's been a long fucking five years. But it was worth it, yeah? Because now it can be you." He slid his boxer briefs down and pressed himself against me. His mischievous smile came back and he leaned over me, forcing me to lie back on my elbows. "Also, prison helped."

I couldn't help but laugh, knowing he was still telling the truth.

I wrapped my legs around his back and trembled at the intensity of the pleasure. "Then we have a lot of time to make up for," I whispered, turned on all over again by this incredible man that had remained faithful to me after all this time.

He slid into me without another second's hesitation and I gasped for breath at the full feeling. "Oh, my God," I moaned, trying to wrap my head around his size and hardness and heat. "Oh, God, Sayer."

"Worth it," he murmured against my breast. "So fucking worth the wait." He shivered again, and stilled like he had to acclimate to the sensation. I was thankful for the second to get used to him as well. I needed to process this, us, that we were doing this again after so much time, after I'd run from him and after he'd chased me until he found me. In my racing thoughts, I was still flipping through his letters and trying to reconcile his presence in my town and in this office and inside of me.

But then he started to move and I forgot everything I was trying to work through. I pretty much forgot the entire English language. We ceased speaking and flirting and treating each other gently in favor of treating each other much rougher—but in the good way.

My heels dug into his back as he drove me closer and closer to that blissful edge all over again. I threw my arms around his neck, lifting my body up for an incredible new angle. He made a delicious sound in the back of his throat and I moaned something I didn't even understand. It sounded like more, and he did not hesitate to deliver.

He pulled back, taking in my face, and the way I gasped for breath. My fingers dug into his shoulder blades as I held onto him, letting him take as much as he wanted from me. As much as he needed.

"So fucking beautiful," he murmured. "You're mine, Caroline. You always have been." He pressed in deeper, making spots dance in my vision. "You always will be."

"Yes," I agreed, my voice nothing more than a pant. "Always. I will always be yours."

His hands dug under my ass, lifting me to a better position for him. I let out a loud cry of pleasure as he went deeper and deeper until I couldn't keep my eyes open anymore.

"I love you," he murmured against my cheek. "I will always love you."

I barely found the sanity to respond, but my words were still truth, my lies were dead and buried. "I love you too," I told him, feeling it to my bones, to my soul, to the very ends of me.

We came together in an explosion of fireworks and passion, our bodies slick with sweat and sex. He didn't leave me. Instead, he continued to press into me, wrapping his arms around me in the tightest hug. He buried his face in the crook of my neck, pressing gentle kisses there.

He stayed like that for a long time and I soaked up every second of it. My arms firmly around his neck, my cheek resting against the top of his head, my legs still languidly wrapped around him. It was heaven. It was healing. It was everything I had been missing since the day I left him.

"Gus is going to kill us," he murmured against my skin.

I looked down and laughed. We were definitely on Gus's desk. Sayer's sat untouched across the room, littered with the letters that had changed everything.

"He just might." Realizing that in order for Gus to be pissed off, he'd have to know that we had sex on his desk, I blushed fiercely. "Oh, God," I groaned. "Let's not give him all the dirty details. Maybe you could just tell him there was a problem with his desk. Like a chemical spill or something."

His laugh shook his chest, prompting him to hold me tighter against him. I savored the moment, relishing every second of his skin against mine. I had always loved this feeling. The raw heat of him. The feel of his hard muscle beneath soft skin. His chest against mine, his heart beating in tandem with mine.

"I don't know that Gus would believe a chemical spill ruined his desk."

"He should," I said practically. "Depending on the chemical, they can be very dangerous."

He laughed again and we had another few minutes of perfect peace, tangled together. But something shifted in him, quieted. I was suddenly afraid of what was next.

He pulled back and I was startled by the serious look in his eyes, especially since I mostly felt like a limp noodle with zero strength to stand up or stay awake or even sit here by myself without his support. He'd taken everything out of me in the very best way.

Apparently, I'd done the opposite to him and infused him with energy. The intensity inside him was practically vibrating his whole body.

His voice pitched low, gravelly and sincere. "I don't expect us to just pick up where we left off, Six. But we're together now, yeah? That was you finally admitting this is real between us, that we belong together... that we still love each other."

"Y-you want to be together?"

His expression darkened. "In my head, we never parted. You know, since you didn't have the guts to break up with me."

"Are you picking a fight?" I almost laughed. He was absurd.

"I'm trying to get on the same page," he countered. "I don't want to guess at what you're thinking. I want to hear the words."

I thought about Juliet. I thought about all that I'd kept a secret from him. I thought about why I left to begin with.

Did any of that matter now?

Juliet was my daughter. I couldn't deny the fighting instinct inside me to protect her, to want to introduce Sayer into her life gently and carefully and with her best interest always in mind. But at the same time, Sayer was her dad. Didn't he have the right to know her? To be in her life and see how absolutely special she was?

"There are things we have to talk about," I told him. My phone started buzzing in my purse across the room. I tried to ignore it. "There are things I haven't told you."

He gave me a look. "Caroline, you haven't told me anything."

"That's what I mean." My phone started buzzing all over again. "I-I left for a reason. A very important reason." The phone quit buzzing. Then started up again.

He quirked a brow. "Do you need to get that?"

The phone stopped vibrating. Only to start all over again a second later.

"Apparently," I told him. "I'll call back. It will just take a sec. We should get dressed."

He stepped back, giving me room to slide off the desk. I realized I was naked and we hadn't used protection and sex was messy. Grabbing

254

some tissues nearby, I used them as discreetly as I could while Sayer got dressed behind me.

For the few minutes it took me to dress, I felt unfairly exposed. The air grew thick with tension and weird with unsaid things. Was this what a one-night stand was like? Was it always this awkward?

No, he'd said he wanted to be together again. He said he still thought of us as a couple.

This was my issue. Not his.

I took a steadying breath and buttoned my jeans. My phone had continued buzzing, so I finally reached for it in my purse, digging past the stolen items to find it.

The daycare had called four times and Francesca had called seven. My pocket started buzzing and I nearly screamed until I realized it was my burner phone. Pulling it out, I didn't even check the caller. There was only one person who had this number.

"What's wrong?"

"Where have you been?" Francesca shouted in the phone. "Did something happen? Are you okay?"

How to answer that question. "I'm okay."

That was not the answer she wanted. "Then why the hell did it take you so long to answer?"

"Geez, Francesca, I'm—"

"Someone took her, Caro! Before I could get her, someone picked her up! The teachers had just called the cops when I showed up, but she's already gone. I don't know where she went. The cops are going to be here any second and I don't know what to tell them—"

My blood iced over with fear, turning my limbs brittle, paper thin. "Slow down, Frankie. Tell me the whole story," I whispered, sounding calmer than I ever had. It was a façade, a tool to get the information I needed. I wasn't calm. I wasn't close to fucking calm.

Sayer saw my distress and walked over to stand next to me. His hands landed on my shoulders, comforting, warming the frost, anchoring me to this planet.

"It's Juliet," she wailed, full on crying now. "She's gone! Someone took her!"

"Who?" I roared into the phone.

"I-I don't know. Sayer maybe?"

"He's with me," I answered quickly.

I felt her surprised pause through the phone. She had questions but now was the wrong time to ask them. And my answers wouldn't help the immediate problem at hand.

"What's wrong, Six?" Sayer demanded.

"The cops just got here," Frankie said. "You need to get here as fast as possible. They're going to want to talk to you."

Sayer's grip tightened in an attempt to get my attention. "What is wrong, Caroline?"

"I'll be there as soon as I can," I told her. Another layer of ice froze my hands and face and lungs.

"I'll see what I can find out here," she promised. Her voice dropped, infused with sincerity and a lifetime of surviving this bullshit. "We'll find her, Caro. I promise. She's going to be okay."

But was she? What monster had her? What were they going to do to her? What did they hope they could get from her?

How could this have happened? I picked that daycare because of their security policies. Goddamnit, I was going to murder the son of a bitch that took her.

"Caroline, you need to tell me what's wrong," Sayer demanded, taking the phone from me and closing it.

I lifted my gaze and blinked slowly at him. For a half-second I was grateful for the hell he had been through the last five years. There was no way to prepare for the information I was about to give him, but at the very least he had been toughened, built stronger, sharpened to a double-edged sword that could withstand this blow.

"You have a daughter," I told him, voice rough with unbearable agony. "And someone kidnapped her."

256

Chapter Twenty-One

Five Years Ago

I was going to die. They were going to fucking kill me.

Who takes meetings with FBI agents? Who?? Girls that have death wishes, that's who.

I remembered what Fat Jack looked like all bloated and disfigured and dead. Oh, my god, that was going to be me.

Was there a way to get word to Sayer first? They would have to kill me. That was a given. But I didn't want to be strung up by my feet. That was my one wish. Sayer would intervene on my behalf, wouldn't he? I mean, he'd of course let them kill me. But he owed me some kind of dignity after five years together, right?

I didn't want to die upside down like some twisted version of the apostles. I didn't want my tongue cut out or my hands chopped off. I didn't want to be gutted.

Mason Payne walked into the abandoned warehouse flanked by two federal goons. Some of my fear disappeared in light of misplaced pride. Was the big, bad, FBI agent afraid of little ole me?

That put a promising spin on things.

I pushed off the column I'd been leaning on and walked over to face the absolute bane of my existence. A chance meeting when I was fifteen years old had propelled me into a never-ending game of cat and mouse with this guy.

Sometimes I was the mouse. And sometimes I was the cat. Today, I was the confused snake. I thought I was in control, but this could be the day when the cat figured out how to bite me in two.

He promised this time was different, but Mason's promises meant nothing to me. Mason took lying to an entirely different level. I mean, I was a professional liar too, but his were buried treasure chests and holy grails and the arc of the covenant—pretty and shiny, but the booby traps would kill you before you ever reached the prize. They were heavy with deadly consequences and dangerously light on the reward. I didn't build houses of cards based on promises of immunity or lessened sentences. I didn't dangle plea bargains in other people's faces pretending like they were Christmas presents.

I didn't use the law to manipulate, coerce and control.

Coughing to cover a smile, I tried not to check out his clothes, which were significantly nicer than anything I'd seen him in before. And by nicer, I meant designer. The last time we'd "run into each other" had been three months ago at a fundraising party for a senate seat race. All of DC had come out in their best black tie to throw money around like it was confetti. Only Mason's best black tie was from the discount bin at a men's big and tall store. His cheap polyester and coffee-stained tie were a walking fire hazard.

Of course I wouldn't have missed an opportunity like that. The *pakhan* wanted a certain judge's cooperation in an upcoming case. And I wanted the Cartier pearls that belonged to the wife of a certain judge. I had been posing as an aid for the judge until I could get the code to his super safe and find an opportunity to break into it. The job was taking longer than I had originally anticipated.

So that meant attending a high-profile function—which I knew was a dangerous game in itself given the amount of law enforcement power present. The function wasn't all aboveboard. I'd spotted Irish soldiers near the bar and an Italian underboss dancing with his wife. There was even a South African drug lord near the food table.

But had Mason singled any of them out? No. No, he had not. And when he'd asked me to dance, I couldn't say no. He'd given me shit about him being close to finding something on me and I'd given him shit about his sense of style.

Out of the two of us, I was the only one with accurate information.

Not that I believed I was completely untouchable. But so far, I'd covered my tracks. I'd been careful. I'd kept my hands clean and my nose clean and done my due diligence with every job. Save for the one he tried to run me down at when I was fifteen.

Luckily for me, the man had no probable cause to arrest me or detain me or question me. He had nothing on me. He'd simply recognized me from a list of potential Russian-associated Sixes. And being the green little newbie to the bureau he was, had decided to take that opportunity to introduce himself with a spectacle in the most public of ways.

Now he was like a dog with a bone. He couldn't let the Russians go. It was personal to him for some reason. I didn't know why because I had never bothered to ask him and what research I had done turned up nothing on the guy. He was a straight up enigma.

"Caroline Valera," he said as way of greeting. "Nice of you to join us."

I rolled my eyes. "Did I have a choice? Because if so, I'd be happy to reschedule. I have shit to do."

"You might want to clear your schedule," he countered. "This might take a while."

Warning bells blared in my head. Run, my instinct screamed. Get out while you still can. I spun around only to find more agents had entered behind me. This was a trap.

My lip curled back. I was a cornered wolf. "What's going on, Payne? Are you going to arrest me?"

His voice softened as if trying to soothe the wild animal inside me. "Calm down, Caro. We're just here to talk."

Mason had taken it upon himself to use my nickname, like we were friends or something. He was maybe the most irritating human on the planet. But right now wasn't the time to correct him.

"Go on," I ordered, feeling increasingly uncomfortable. "Talk."

He stepped closer to me so we were only inches apart. He held a file folder in his hands and tapped it against his open palm in a nervous sort of gesture. "I'm only telling you this because we have history, okay? This is a favor I'm going to do once. That's it."

I swallowed the building panic, waving my hand for him to hurry this along. To be fair, we did have a sort of history. For the last five years I'd managed to interact with him on a semi-regular basis without giving anything up. Not that he hadn't tried. And not that it wasn't tempting sometimes.

He'd even offered witness protection at one point. That had probably been the most difficult to say no to. A new life? A clean slate? And all I had to do was put a giant target on my back by ratting out the entire operation first?

Thanks, but no thanks. That was not how I wanted to start over.

Besides, I knew without a doubt Sayer would never go for it. He was on his way to becoming a spy. There were rumors that the current two from our family were about to retire. They were old. They were making mistakes. Minor mistakes, but everybody knew it was better to quit while you were ahead. Then the way would open up for Sayer and Atticus. Gus would eventually become the bookkeeper. Our future was as good as made.

I was happy for Sayer. This was everything he had always wanted. He respected the *bratva* and in return, he was rewarded. And he deserved it. He really did. Nobody was more loyal. Nobody worked as hard or as long. Nobody could do what he did.

He was invaluable to the brothers.

He would never leave them.

And I would never leave him. When I was younger, I'd wanted a different life. But that was before Sayer. Now I only wanted a life with him. And that meant I would have to take the syndicate with him. That meant eternal entanglement with the *bratva*.

That meant more thieving.

"We're moving on the brotherhood," Mason said. "In a way you're not going to like."

Fear spread through me like frost over a window. I was clean. He didn't have anything on me. I knew that. Because if he did, he would have arrested me by now. Mason wanted to pretend like he could take me in at any second and didn't because we had some kind of dysfunctional relationship. Like he was doing me some kind of favor by letting me live my life and that meant I should trust him. I knew better.

But what about Gus? Francesca? Sayer? Had they been as careful as me in all of their dealings? Had they always covered their tracks? And recovered them? And then buried them six feet under?

"Who?" I demanded. Mason didn't drag me all the way out here to dangle empty information in front of me.

His head dipped with a meaningful look.

260

Sayer.

"He's the best chance at taking down the entire organization."

I let out a sharp breath. "If you're arresting him to make him talk it won't work." I shook my head at how ridiculous it was. "I won't. And he definitely won't," I promised. "You don't have enough on either of us to make anything stick."

Mason flinched, forcing me to doubt myself. "We have enough, Caro." Holding his hand up, he started ticking off the counts. "Grand theft, fraud, bribery, money laundering, identity theft... should I go on?"

"You have nothing real. That's all speculation," I told him, only half-believing my words. Sayer only worked with me some of the time. The bosses had him on all kinds of jobs, most of them he didn't talk to me about.

Mason's expression was sympathetic... pitying. "What's amazing to me is how white collar his crimes are. It's the drugs, trafficking and weapons we're after. But don't misunderstand, we'll get them any way we can."

My throat felt like sandpaper and I couldn't swallow. True panic pounded inside me, a firing gun that sent my heart into a dead sprint. "Why are you telling me this?"

He stepped forward—the cat cornering the poor, helpless mouse. "We want you to encourage him to talk to us. We'll give him a deal, Caro. We'll give him a really good deal. But he needs to trust us and that isn't going to happen unless he has your support."

I rolled my eyes and sniffled. "Sayer knows a good deal. If what you're offering is so great, shouldn't that be enough?"

"Sayer Wesley doesn't care about deals, offers or anything. He only cares about you. We both know that's true. He'll listen to you. He's not going to listen to us. We're on the wrong side of the law."

Tilting my head, I sized him up. "Maybe you should rethink your life plan."

His lips twitched, hiding a smile. "Maybe you should rethink your life plan, Caroline. We both know you want out. Here's your opportunity." His shrug was casual, coaxing. "Talk to Sayer. Work your magic. We'll get a chance to clean up the worst crime syndicate in this city's history and you'll get a chance at a new life, away from all this. We can help, you know. You should let us."

Damn it all. It was the lure of a fresh start that tugged the hardest. God, what would it be like to live away from this? To not have the *bratva* following us around everywhere we went? To not have the threat of an arrest or the bosses' displeasure hovering over us at all times? What would it be like to live free of crime and thieving?

But I couldn't ponder that out with Mason. "When?" I asked instead. "How long do I have?"

"I can't tell you that."

Which meant soon. "I need time to talk to Sayer. He won't be easily convinced."

"Then be more convincing," Mason countered.

I threw him the middle finger and turned around, done with this conversation and the FBI. I was done with this whole fucking day. "I got to go," I told him over my shoulder.

"Hey, Caro," Mason called after me. "This is not your opportunity to run. We have eyes everywhere. You will not make it to the city limits before we have you in the back of a van. And if you make me chase you down, I will publicize the hell out of it. Your arrest will be on every television across the nation. Everyone will know you've been corroborating with the FBI. I will go on fucking CNN and shout your name. I'm a very motivated man. If you make me chase you, the generous deals are off the table. All of them. I'll make sure you don't even get your mandatory phone call. And then I will prosecute you to the full extent of the law. For everything. I will find it all, to the last unpaid parking ticket. Your options are this: work with us and get our help, or don't work with us and experience the full Biblical-like wrath of the federal government." His voice trembled with his conviction, promising every last threat.

I believed him. He would turn the *bratva* against me and then take away the government and I would be left to fend for myself. In other words, he planned to feed me to the wolves. He was basically signing my death warrant.

He held my gaze. "If I were you, I would choose wisely."

Anger and resentment burned on my tongue and threatened to spew from my mouth. I had so many nasty things to yell at him. But this was the FBI. And he was giving me a chance to persuade Sayer. He was offering a way out. So, instead, I pushed them down and nodded. "Noted."

I left the warehouse and headed back to town. I had to walk for twenty minutes before I could find a taxi, but it gave me time to think, to sort through my feelings.

When I talked to Sayer, I would have to pin this entirely on the feds. Sayer didn't know I occasionally talked to Mason. It wasn't like I ever gave Mason anything, but Sayer would feel betrayed if he knew the agent sought me out every once in awhile.

There was a chance that Sayer wasn't the only one that would feel betrayed. The entire *bratva* would get in on that action. I knew how that scenario ended and I wasn't in a hurry to bleed out upside down.

So I'd have to be tactful. Careful. I'd have to lie.

Good thing I was so good at it.

I gave the cabbie the address of one of the bars the bosses owned. Sayer and the guys hung out there during the day to talk business and have meetings and drink vodka. All the vodka.

Vinnie opened the back door for me and I made my way to the front room. I always felt jarred by the sight of a bar with its lights on, all her rough edges exposed, the bright light glaring on the secrets she preferred to keep hidden during the night. After meeting with Mason, I could relate.

I found Sayer at a table with Atticus and Gus. They were playing cards and drinking. Typical Tuesday.

Sayer looked up and noticed me, smiling wide, his eyes darkening with secrets only we knew. The good kind. The kind that made my heart ache for the life Mason offered. The kind that made me consider that new life, away from all of this, away from these people and the ugly, terrible things we were responsible for.

"There she is," he said with that half smile that still made my belly flutter. With a jerk of his chin, he said, "Come here, Six."

I moved to him, pressing a kiss to his lips when he lifted his face to mine. His tongue caressed my bottom lip until I kissed him back, lured by the sweet temptation of his mouth. He didn't care that we were surrounded by his crew and his bosses, this moment was ours.

I gave into him. I always did. Our tongues tangled together while he tasted me slowly, intimately, too familiarly for public or this place. His hands moved to my waist, bringing me in between his legs, holding me close to him. I dropped my hands on his shoulders and tried to keep my wits.

It was impossible. This man was too much. Too irresistible. Too tempting. Too distracting.

Pulling back, I smiled down at him, lost in sharp desire and his blue, blue eyes and all the hope I had for us. "Can I talk to you?" I asked him in a low voice.

From across the table, Atticus's patience had worn out. "Are you two done yet? We're in the middle of a game."

Sayer shot him a glare. "Don't be an asshole."

"Don't make me wait," Atticus returned.

I squeezed Sayer's shoulders, hoping to regain his attention. "It's important."

"I've been looking for you," Frankie said from behind me. "Where have you been today?"

Glancing at her, I wondered what to say to her. Would the FBI relocate her too? Or would she be a casualty in the war.

I couldn't do that to my friend. I would find a way to take her with us.

"Are we playing or what?" Gus asked. "'Cause I got shit to do if this is turning into a girl's night."

Frankie smacked the back of his head. "You would be so lucky. When's the last time you hung out with a girl? Consensually?"

He folded his arms over his chest. "I don't like what you're implying. All of the girls I hang out with are there consensually. Which is why there are so few of them."

Sayer and Frankie laughed, but I felt urgency tug at my gut. "Sayer, seriously can I talk to you for a minute? Alone?"

His eyes moved back to mine, finally seeing the worry in my expression. His brow drew down, making a crease over his eyes. "Sure. Yeah. Is everything okay?"

"No," I whispered, my voice breaking with the weight of what I needed to tell him. For the first time it hit me that the feds were going to take him. Take Sayer. They were planning to arrest him. Mason had warned me not to run, but how could I not?

I couldn't let them take him. Not even for a short amount of time. And what if he didn't want to cooperate with them? Then what?

My insides started to crumble. They were a building that had just been demolished. A wrecking ball straight through my heart and now the foundation surrounding it was disintegrating, dissolving into ruin.

That wasn't an option. He would cooperate. When I laid out the whole picture, when I explained the entire plan, he would see my point of view and listen.

He stood up, his hands staying on my waist. "Okay, Six. Let's talk."

"Maybe we could go for a drive?" I suggested. And never come back. Just get in the car and leave.

He was just about to respond when someone came running from the back, the casual atmosphere exploding into frenzied hysteria. "Feds!" the Six hollered over the din of conversation. "They're outside!"

The room exploded into action. Some of the guys ran to the back, scurrying to hide drugs and cash and other paraphernalia the feds would love to find. Girls came out of the woodwork, pulling articles of clothes on and clasping their bras as they ran for the back exits. Roman walked from a side room toward the manager's office all calm and collected, a man totally confident that not one of their charges would stick to him.

Sayer pulled me against him, wrapping his arms protectively around me. Frankie moved behind the table with Atticus and Gus. And there we waited.

There was no point in running. There was no point in freaking out. The feds were here. We just had to wait and hope that they didn't have anything on us.

Only I knew differently. We would all get arrested. We would all sit in bare, isolated rooms with two-way mirrors and armed guards. We would all be questioned. We'd done this enough times before that us veterans knew we had nothing to worry about.

It just wasn't true this time. We had to worry.

Especially me.

Especially Sayer.

The feds came in their usual manner, busting down doors and shouting orders. They filled the room like a swarming hive of black wasps, guns pointed, vests strapped to their chests, helmets and visors on.

Sayer stepped back from me, raising his hands in the air, docile, compliant. I had a harder time letting go of him. Don't, I wanted to scream. Don't let them take you. But I couldn't. The second I gave away even a hint that I knew about this beforehand, I would be a traitor.

I would be Fat Jack.

I would be dead.

Once the establishment was secured—armed agents were everywhere and most of the *bratva* were on the ground—Mason Payne walked in donning his regulation navy blue FBI jacket. I glared at him, trying to murder him with just my thoughts. How dare he dangle a carrot in front of me and then rip it away just when I started to believe I could catch it.

My stomach twisted when I realized he'd probably followed me here. He'd tricked me. He'd used me. I stared at him, daring him to read my mind.

Liar. Manipulator. Asshole.

265

I would never trust the feds again. Least of all this guy.

His smile sickened me as it stretched again. He spun in one, victorious circle and twirled his finger in the air. "You know what to do, people. Round 'em up!"

And so began the arrests. They started with Roman, who walked with his head high and his shoulders squared, despite the handcuffs securing his hands behind him. He winked at Sayer as he walked by, but that was the only change to his otherwise stoic expression.

The other brothers weren't here, which was lucky. And neither were the two spies or Ozzie or my dad. But there would be plenty for the FBI. For them, this was a fantastic day.

They started moving guys from the back first, walking them out to the armored transport vehicles. We stood there with guns pointed at us, waiting for our turn.

"Is it that time of the month again, Payne?" Sayer growled.

"It's Payne's time of the month," Gus chuckled darkly. "Take some Midol, buddy. It might help with the rage raids."

Mason turned to them and grinned like the cat that ate the canary. "Laugh it up, Augustus. You've got some fun charges coming your way."

Gus's eyes narrowed and his smile turned cynical. "Looking forward to watching you try to make them stick."

Mason shrugged. That was it. He just shrugged. He didn't continue to argue or throw out ambiguous threats. He just shrugged.

The tension between the five of us shot up, our blood pressures going with it. My mind spun. Did I have anything to worry about? If Mason had used me to get to Sayer, had he also lied about charges being brought against me?

Wait, he would have needed a warrant first, right? And he couldn't have gotten one between the warehouse and now. Not unless he had the judge on standby.

Maybe he did.

Sayer dipped his head, closer to my ear. "We're going to be okay, Six. Just like all the times before, this is going nowhere."

I wasn't sure that was true. I turned fully to face him, holding his gaze and begging him to just get it. Leaning in, I dropped my voice and whispered, "Let them help you."

He jerked backward, his eyes growing wide as he let my words sink in. He didn't ask me to repeat what I said though. He just stared at me like I was a ghost.

266

Turning around, I caught Atticus's eye. He had been watching us. Shit. My heart started hammering harder, faster. I was sure he couldn't have heard us, he was all the way across the table.

Mason watched us too. He caught my gaze and raised an eyebrow, silently asking if I'd talked to Sayer. Which was really nice of him since he'd given me so much time. I wanted to punch him in his smug face. Instead, I turned to look at the wall and lifted one shoulder to scratch my ear, signaling that I hadn't.

I didn't risk looking at him again, so I didn't know if he had a reaction or a thought or a feeling of fucking guilt. But it didn't matter anyway. Soon enough it was our turn to be marched outside.

Mason motioned for his men to start with Gus, putting me at the end of the line. I didn't know if he planned it that way on purpose, or if it was spur of the moment as I walked past him.

"I'm sorry," he whispered under his breath, stepping in front of my path to fidget with my handcuffs. His head dipped and I had to strain to hear his whispered confession. "I didn't know we were moving until after you left. We had to wait for the warrant."

Fury burned in my blood, clouding my judgment. Twisting my neck, I hissed, "Save it. You're a fucking liar."

"That's amazing coming from you." He stepped back and motioned for one of the other agents to take me outside.

I didn't say another word to him, which ended up being a blessing. At the edge of the dining room, Atticus had moved behind Sayer somehow. He had eyes for Mason in a way that made me nervous for the federal agent.

We didn't speak until we were outside, but we had to wait in line while they loaded us one by one. Atticus turned to me, paranoia darkening green eyes. "What did he say to you?"

I let out a longsuffering sigh. "Who?"

"Don't play dumb, Caro. It doesn't suit you."

My expression was tired, impatient. "Oh, Payne? I don't know. Threats as usual. This time his charges are going to stick. This time I better fess up. This time blah, blah, blah."

"Did he offer you a deal?"

The truth tightened my throat. I didn't have an issue lying, especially to people like Atticus. But this time, the truth held a weight I wasn't used to. This time, the truth was scarier than ever before. "Not yet. But he will. I'm sure he'll offer you one too. Isn't that the dance with these guys?"

His voice dropped to a whisper. "You better not take it."

I blinked at him. "Are you serious?"

"Yes."

"I would never take a deal, asshole. I'm offended that you would even question my loyalty."

"I question your loyalty every fucking day, Valero. You're a snake."

That was rich coming from him. I smiled politely and stepped by him to get into the back of the truck. "And you're a dickhead."

"Everything okay?" Sayer asked, his eyes on Atticus.

"Just peachy."

"Super fucking okay," Atticus growled as the doors closed with a final slam behind us.

That was it. They dragged us to their offices, threw us in isolated interrogation rooms and picked us off one by one.

By the end of the night, most of us were allowed to go home. I caught a ride with Gus, Frankie and Atticus and we headed back to Gus's for the night. We waited for Sayer to join us, but he never did.

In the morning, they charged him with counts they planned to prosecute and I realized my worst nightmare had come true.

Chapter Twenty-Two

Five Years Ago

I signed in at the front and let them escort me through locked doors and hallways that smelled like metal and sweat. My hands balled into fists, my fingernails digging into my palms. It took everything in me not to scream. By the time I reached the visitation room, I was sick with hatred and the scent of this place.

Seeing Sayer in his prison tans was an entirely new level of frustration. This was the first time I had been allowed to visit him at Schuylkill, his new federal prison home for the next seven to ten years. I gripped my stomach and ordered my body not to wretch up the lunch I'd nibbled on during the three-hour ride to the middle of nowhere Pennsylvania.

All I wanted to do was throw my arms around him and crawl in his lap. And maybe never leave. We hadn't touched in three months—not since he'd been out on bail. That was the longest we'd ever gone without touching. Even before we had become an official couple, Sayer always had his hands on me. Holding my hand, wrapping his arm around my shoulders, finding any and every way he could to bring us together. This no-touching policy was absolute hell.

269

I blamed Mason Payne. He'd overcharged Sayer, hoping that would make him talk. It didn't. Sayer never opened his mouth. Instead, he took the sentencing, pled guilty to all accounts and faced his fate.

And why had he pled guilty? Because Roman had asked him to. Roman had wanted to send a message to the FBI—that we would not be intimidated. That we would not back down. That we would not leave.

He told Sayer it would be a badge of honor, that his sacrifice for the *bratva* would give him the respect he needed to become the next spy. Sayer had believed him.

Here we were now—Sayer in prison for the foreseeable future and me out on the streets—working for an increasingly savage crime family, arguably the most powerful and vicious organization DC had ever seen. Their growth over the past ten years was staggering. I could only imagine what would happen in the next decade. And I was without the man I loved by my side.

He immediately wrapped me up in a hug, pressing a kiss to my cheek. We stayed like that for as long as we could, pressing ourselves into each other until we were one being, one spirit, one soul. When the guard stepped forward and tapped the table, we slowly, reluctantly let go.

His eyes shimmered when I sat down across from him at the orange table. "Six," he murmured. "I've missed you."

He already looked different. He was harder somehow, made of stone more than human. "I came as soon as I was allowed," I told him, unshed tears making him blur. "I hate this," I whispered.

He reached his hands across the table but stopped short, before our fingertips touched. "It's not going to last forever."

The room was busy, inmates and their visitors huddled together in quiet conversation. I scooted closer to him and dropped my voice even lower. "What's it like?"

"Horrible," he told me honestly. "The place is swarming with fucking Italians. I swear Payne did that on purpose. He's trying to get me killed."

"Medium-security," I reminded him. "These aren't killers."

He looked down at his hands. "Yeah, maybe."

Meaning they were definitely killers that just wasn't the reason they were in prison.

"Sayer…"

His head lifted, pain and fury bright in his gaze. "I'm going to be okay, Six. I can handle these people. I'm more worried about you. Is Gus taking care of you?"

I nodded quickly. "Yeah. He's been good." Only that wasn't exactly true. Nobody had been good. Sayer's arrest had really shaken up the organization. Not that people weren't arrested all the time, but Sayer was the first of the higher ups. And he was taking the fall for everybody.

The rest of the guys were waiting for it to be their turn. Gus wasn't exactly one of them, but he had been acting strange lately and super secretive. The bosses had started his training. He was always with his dad now. And Atticus. He didn't really seem to have time for me anymore.

I hadn't even seen him in two weeks.

"Good," Sayer grunted. "He knows I'll kill him if anything happens to you. You're my one regret about this whole thing, Caro."

My chin wobbled, my voice dropping to a squeaky whisper. "So leave. Take the deal."

His eyes flared, incredulous. "You can't be serious."

My hands landed protectively on my stomach. "Sayer, I need you. I can't do this without you."

He shook his head, not catching my meaning. "You're the toughest chick I know, Six. You'll probably be running everything by the time I get out and I'll be out of a job."

He was joking, but I couldn't find it in me to laugh. Or even smile. "Didn't Mason explain the deal? He said he was going to—"

He cut me off with a smiling, "Hey, hey, hey." He discreetly glanced around before leaning in and dropping his voice even lower. "Don't bring that up here. Don't mention that name here." He let out a frustrated sigh, his jaw ticking once. "I'm not trying to be an asshole. I just have to be careful, yeah?"

I nodded once. "Yeah."

His smile was small, but there. "It's not happening anyway. You know why."

Because he was loyal to the *pakhan*. Because he would never betray his brothers. Because this was part of the life, of living in the *bratva*. This got him more street cred. This built his reputation with the bosses. There were a million reasons for him to do this.

But not one of them included me.

"Sayer, for God's sake, this isn't about them." He motioned for me to lower my voice by pumping his hands in the air which only infuriated me more. "There are other things happening outside of the... the... family." But that wasn't true. They were happening exactly inside the

271

family. His family. I just didn't know how to tell him while he was in here.

"Six, nothing." He held my gaze, clearly pissed and frustrated with me for continuing to argue with him. "Nothing could change my mind. Drop it."

I sucked in my bottom lip and tamped down a scream. I folded my arms over my chest and looked across the room. There were two men at a table staring at me. I immediately averted my gaze to another table. Again two men, one visitor, one prisoner, staring at me.

My glare moved back to Sayer. "I should go."

He grabbed my hand, squeezing it between his. "Don't be mad, Caro. I know this sucks, but... you have to know that the alternative is not a viable option. I mean, what kind of life would that be? Always looking over your shoulder? Waiting on black hoods and the blind drive to the nearest empty warehouse. You know this is the best possible scenario. We're going to tough it out. We're going to be fine."

I wrapped my free hand around my stomach, hugging myself. "I'm scared, Sayer. There's so much I want to talk to you about. So much I need to tell you."

He pressed a kiss to my temple, even though he got yelled at by the closest guard. "And you will. Write me a letter, yeah? That's probably the best way. Nothing too specific. But I can basically read your mind. I'll figure it out."

You're going to be a dad! Was that too specific?

Had he read my mind just now?

"Just wait for me," he said with a nervous smile. "Don't leave me while I'm in here."

No, he hadn't.

I finally gave him a wobbly smile. "I would never."

"You'll wait for me?"

"Forever," I promised. "I would wait for you forever."

He leaned in, his eyes glistening in a way that I had never seen before. "I love you, Caroline. More than anything."

My chest pinched painfully. "I love you too." I had to sniffle hard to hold back stupid tears. "More than anything."

His smile broke. "Stop trying to one-up me."

I just shook my head at him, not able to muster the energy to joke around. My stomach churned and I knew I was going to be sick.

"I should go."

His face fell. "Oh, right. Yeah, I guess you probably should. You'll be back though?"

I pressed a kiss to his lips, braving the wrath of the guards. "As soon as possible," I promised.

"I need nudey pics next time you come. Maybe a whole book of them."

"Why don't you see what you can do about one of those conjugal visits, hmm? I feel like that's the natural next step here. Not an entire book of me naked. Pretty sure you would get shived for it and then my poor naked self would start a prison riot."

His head tipped back and he laughed. The sound was the Sayer-before-prison laugh. I soaked up every second. "Someone's awfully cocky."

I winked at him. "Just calling it like I see it."

A warning that our time was up came over the speakers. I threw my arms around him one last time, pressing into him as closely as possible. His strong arms were around my back, squeezing me just as tightly.

"I hate that this goodbye feels so permanent," I whispered against his neck.

"It's not," he said to my temple. "This is forever, Caro."

"Promise?"

"Always."

We finally said goodbye for real. It was the hardest thing I had ever done. There had been so much I hadn't told him, so much he needed to know.

The trip home was only supposed to take a little over three hours. It took me four and a half because I had to keep pulling over to puke. By the time I got back to my apartment, I was exhausted, my throat was raw and my emotions were all over the place.

I hadn't told him.

Part of me knew why I couldn't. That ugly, smelly, scary visitation room was the very last place to make that kind of announcement. Plus, I wasn't even sure it was safe to tell him in there. If there were Italians everywhere, then they would be looking for any way to control him... to hurt him. And it seemed like a pregnant girlfriend on the outside was a pretty great way.

Pregnant.

I still couldn't believe it. It was impossible to wrap my head around.

Last night I'd stood in front of the mirror for a good hour trying to decide if Sayer would be able to tell or not. Would he see the small swell of my belly? Or the greenish tint to my skin? Would he notice that my boobs were bigger? Or that my hips had flared?

If he had, he hadn't indicated anything today.

Now I didn't know what to do or how to tell him. Hey, you're going to be a dad! sounded a little contrived. Plus, there was the reality that he wouldn't even really get to know the child until after he got out. In seven to ten years.

Oh my God, how was this even my life?

I practically crawled up the stairs to my apartment. I lived with Frankie, but I didn't think she'd be home yet. She had a dinner with her uncles and those usually went late.

Although sometimes I was wrong. My door was cracked when I finally made it to the top of the stairs. She must have just gotten home.

I shut the door behind me because I was a normal person and had a healthy fear of local serial killers unlike my roommate, and threw my keys down on the entryway table. "I need a ginger ale stat!" I called to Frankie in our darkened apartment. "And an industrial strength toothbrush. I just had the worst five hours of my life."

The light clicked on in the living room and I stumbled back, hitting the wall with my shoulder. Ow.

"Caro," Atticus snarled from the middle of my living room.

"How the hell did you get in here?" I demanded. "Where's Frankie?" I took a slow breath when I saw my dad. Vinnie and Brick were there too. And a couple of the other goons Atticus liked to work with. "What's going on?"

I had to strain to hear Atticus over my pounding heart. "A little birdy told us you're working with the feds."

Snorting a sardonic laugh, I walked past the posse of threatening men and straight for the refrigerator where I retrieved an ice-cold ginger ale—the only thing that could cure my excessive morning sickness that ironically lasted all day. And night. "Do you know what I spent my day doing today, Atticus? Driving three and a half hours to see my boyfriend, visiting him in the federal prison he's been sentenced to for the next decade. And then I drove home. Sounds pretty loyal to me."

"We know you're loyal to Sayer," Atticus barked. "But that doesn't mean you're loyal to the *bratva*. Someone's working with the fucking FBI, Caro. We think it's you?"

It could be me. It would have been so easy to make it me. But it wasn't.

274

"Well, I think it's you," I told him quickly, sternly. "But I know without a shadow of a doubt it's not me. Get your facts straight."

It wasn't me. I had played around with the idea of going to Mason, giving him whatever he wanted from Sayer. If Sayer wasn't going to take the deal, maybe I could for us both. Maybe Sayer wouldn't even have to know.

But it would never work. First and foremost, Mason wanted information that only Sayer or someone at his level could give. All I could do was incriminate myself and Frankie and Gus. The second reason was that Sayer wouldn't necessarily get the deal. If I gave up everything I knew, they might move me to WITSEC after trial, but there was no guarantee that Sayer would get released. In fact, I was pretty sure that Mason would keep Sayer forever if he could. Sayer was as guilty as the rest of the *avtoritet*, our captains, so Mason would feel compelled to punish him.

I would be without Sayer after that. And he would never forgive me for snitching. Going to the feds was not an option. No matter how enticing the deal sounded, I couldn't take it.

This time I wasn't lying to Atticus. I really wasn't working with the feds. I did, however, chat with them occasionally... Or enough to give the appearance that we were working together.

And if the *pakhan* ever found out how much that would be it for me. They'd hand me over to Atticus. I'd never see Sayer again.

And I didn't have just Sayer to think about anymore. My hand went reflexively to my belly. Protective, defensive, feral.

"Caroline," a deep, accented voice said from behind me, forcing me to turn around. It was Roman. I'd spoken to him a few times over the years, but I avoided him as much as possible. He was the scariest person I had ever known. I still had nightmares about him from when I was a kid and lied to him about stealing from Atticus.

Although I usually felt better whenever I saw Sayer wearing the necklace I risked everything for.

"H-hi, Roman."

He was flanked by Dymetrus and Aleksander, all of them equally terrifying. Equally evil.

"You say you don't know anything about the FBI," Roman went on. "And yet we hear rumors that it is because of you that our Sayer is in prison. Help us understand."

275

I licked dry lips, thankful that I had already thrown up every single thing in my stomach. Otherwise I would be emptying it here and now, right in front of the *pakhan*.

"The last thing I want is for Sayer to be in prison," I told the room full of scary men. "I love him. We were talking about getting married before he went away." My voice broke with real emotion. "I hate this more than anyone."

"We are trying to make sense of everything," Aleksander said reasonably. "We hear that you are the reason, but we see you together and feel that it is real between the two of you. That you love him. But that he also loves you. Very much. Why would someone say this about you if it is not true?"

"Jealousy?" I suggested. "Revenge? I don't honestly know. But it's ridiculous. Listen, I was raised to respect this life. I've been working for you since I was thirteen and you've always treated me rightly, fairly. I'm not some newbie Six that got scared because of a few FBI agents sniffing around." I took a deep breath and prepared to reveal some truth to authenticate my lie. "Listen, I was interrogated just like everybody else. When we were all arrested, I was one of the last that they talked to. I won't lie and tell you that I was totally cool, because I wasn't. I was nervous. I was probably pretty jittery. But I'm not a snitch. I'm not collaborating with anybody. And I know how to keep a poker face. I'm telling you, whatever is being whispered about me is all bluster. No circumstance."

Roman stepped forward, taking his place in the center of the room. It looked as though he and his brothers had been hiding in my bedroom, waiting for me to come home. I immediately felt icky. Had they been snooping?

What had they found?

"And how will we know if you're telling the truth if your poker face is so good?" Dymetrus asked.

"What do you want me to tell you? I'm not working with the FBI. I have nothing to hide from you. I have no reason to go to them. I love my life. I am grateful for what the *bratva* has done for me… for Sayer. The brothers are my family. I would never leave, never betray you."

"Caro, if you know something, if you're doing something, tell them," my dad encouraged. My eyes bugged out. I could not believe him. "If you're truthful with them, they are not unreasonable men."

My father, ladies and gentleman. The man that sells out his daughter to keep both of his hands. I pressed my palms against the small bump in

276

my lower abdomen, promising the child that I would never behave like this, that I would cherish and love and protect until the very end of me. Until I took my very last breath. I would never treat my offspring like this. I would never throw them under the bus just to save myself from punishment.

"What do they want to know?" I demanded. "Ask a question, I'll give you the answer." I turned to the bosses. "You tell me what to steal, I steal it for you. You tell me who to con, I con them for you. I've never taken so much as a dollar that belonged to you guys. I hand over everything. I have nothing to hide. I have no reason to work with the feds. Whatever you want to know I'll tell you."

Roman dipped his chin so he had a better angle to look into my eyes. I stared back, unflinching. "I want to know if you're working with the fucking FBI."

I didn't flinch. I didn't even blink. I just answered honestly. "No. I'm not working with the FBI. Nor have I ever worked with the FBI. I'm loyal to the brotherhood. To you. And I always will be."

"You swore an oath," Roman reminded me.

"I did. And I believe in it." That was my first bold face lie of the night. But it needed to be said if I wanted to stay alive.

Roman jerked his head at me. "We will be watching you, Caroline. Don't do something stupid. We do not tolerate stupid people. So far you have been very good for the *bratva*, for our... expansion in the city. But, if you turn out to be a stupid person, well... that would be a shame. It would pain me to hurt you, Caroline. It would pain your father to watch. It would pain Sayer in ways I can only imagine. Do you understand?"

He was threatening not just me, but my dad... Sayer. "I-I wouldn't dare. I would n-never. I swear it." He seemed to be waiting on something else, so I said. "I understand, Roman. I'm not stupid. I swear I'm not stupid."

"Good," Roman said. "You are such a pretty girl. I would not take pleasure in disfiguring you."

"That's not true," Aleksander laughed, as if we were telling jokes and not talking about torturing me. "You would take pleasure, brother. You would take great pleasure."

They shared a sadistic smile. "You know me well, brother. Still, she can be valuable alive. She is worth something to our brigadier. If nothing else she is the reason he never steps out of line."

He meant Sayer. Sayer stayed in line because he was afraid of something happening to me.

"That is why it is good when our soldiers fall in love, no?" Dymetrus added. "They are always so reluctant to watch their loved ones lose body parts."

I tried to swallow, but didn't quite manage. I knew their conversation was a warning, that they were reminding me of who they were, who I was and how I should behave. But they were also being honest. They would use Sayer to keep me in line. And they would use me to keep Sayer in line, no matter how high up he went, no matter how much power he had.

Because as long as I was around, they would always have leverage over him.

What about our child? If I was a liability, what about the tiny, helpless thing in my womb?

Would they clip the baby's fingers off if Sayer decided to leave? Or worse?

It took everything inside me not to double over and dry heave. This child. Oh, my god, I had a child to protect. To keep away from these monsters. To shield from this horrific hellhole.

Roman, Dymetrus and Aleksander left the apartment, their men following behind them. Atticus and my dad lingered in my apartment. I needed them to leave so I could take a long bubble bath and then take a nap for a week.

"Thanks for the vote of confidence, Dad." I slammed my half-finished ginger ale on the nearest surface. "Shouldn't you be on my side? You know, since I'm your daughter."

"I am," he said with that smarmy smile that he used on women he wanted something from. I had been a recipient of that smile the majority of my life. Usually it ended with him taking all of my money and giving me nothing but a hug and a promise that he loved me.

We both knew he didn't.

"Just give them what they want, honey," my dad encouraged. "That's how we stay alive. That's how we do this. You can't keep living if you don't keep giving."

My dad, the motivational speaker.

Because his nose was so clean.

Yeah, right.

"I saw you, Caro. I saw you talking to that tool, Payne. He knows you. And not just because he's read a file on you. He's familiar with you, which means he has a reason to feel familiar with you. And the day the raid happened you showed up acting guilty as fuck. For whatever

278

reason, the *pakhan* believe you, but it's only a matter of time before I find proof. Then they'll know what I know. That you're a fucking snitch. You're the reason behind the FBI raid. You're the real reason your boyfriend is sitting in prison."

"You couldn't find your ass with both hands," I growled at him.

His mouth split open into a crazy smile. Like actually crazy. "I know that the *pakhan* has given me permission to do the job when we have proof about you and the feds. I know that I get to be the one to extract all the little secrets you have hiding up there." He pressed a finger to my temple and shoved me so hard I stumbled trying to catch my foothold again. "I know I get to be the one to collect the pieces of you and give them to your precious, fucking boyfriend. Watch your back, Valero. I'm fucking coming for you."

I tried to speak, but all I managed to do was not pass out. I was completely frozen, my body turning to solid ice. Atticus stormed from my apartment, an avenging asshole that had no idea what the hell he was talking about.

"I'm not working with the FBI," I whispered to my dad when the door slammed shut behind Atticus.

He let out a defeated sigh. "Neither was Jack."

Oh, god, don't bring up Fat Jack now.

"Dad, can't you stick up for me? Can't you say something? You know me. You know I would never sell out the *bratva*. You know this has always been my life. I've never known anything different."

He shrugged, his face looking drawn and pale. "Caro, they don't listen to me. I'm a nobody." He rubbed a hand over his face. "You need Sayer to speak up for you. They listen to him."

"He's in prison." My chin wobbled and tears leaked from the corners of my eyes.

"That's real loyalty," my dad said. "Going to prison 'cause the bosses asked it of you. He's a good man. He's a real example."

My dad praising Sayer for his selfless sacrifice made me want to scream. "Do you believe me?" I asked him. Because it didn't sound like he did. "Dad, tell me you believe me."

He stood up and shoved his hands in his pockets. "Listen to them, Caro. Don't be stupid. Don't give them a reason to mistrust you. Don't let them be right. You know you gotta keep your hands clean."

"And your nose cleaner."

"You're a smart girl. You'll do the right thing." He walked over and kissed my cheek before moseying out of the apartment.

Twenty minutes had gone by before I moved from where I stood. I stared at my feet for twenty freaking minutes, trying to figure out what I was going to do.

The *bratva* thought I was working with the FBI. I wasn't. But Mason Payne thought we were on friendly enough terms to talk to me whenever he wanted.

It looked bad.

It *was* bad.

And Sayer was locked away for the foreseeable future and not able to help me. Not at all.

Wrapping my arms around my waist, I knew I had to do something. I knew I had to do whatever it took to protect the life inside me.

If it was just my life I was playing with, I would have been able to face it. I would have kept my hands clean and kept my nose clean and everything so goddamn clean and then faced whatever consequences came out of my decisions. But I had more to think about now.

I had more than one life to protect.

Frankie walked in the door, yanking off her heels as she headed to the kitchen without slowing down. "I hate this fucking city," she growled when she saw me standing in the middle of our apartment.

It only barely registered that she'd told me she was going to be with her uncles tonight and yet her uncles were here. With me.

"Then let's leave," I whispered to her. "Let's just fucking go."

She tottered in her bare feet. Quirking one eyebrow, she deadpanned. "You're serious?"

I grabbed her hand and dragged her out to the balcony, lest the possible bugs in my apartment give warning to the feds or Atticus or fucking Santa Claus. And out on the terrace, with the freezing DC wind biting our skin and making our noses run, I spilled everything.

I told her about Payne and his frequent visits, about the deal he offered Sayer that I didn't get a chance to share with him until after the FBI had pitched it. I told her about my visit with him today, how he will never leave the *bratva*. No matter what. And how her uncles had stopped by to threaten my life. I cried when I told her about my dad and his less than enthusiastic response. He hadn't stuck up for me. He didn't even believe me. And I told her about Atticus and his stupid vendetta against me.

"He's waited all this time," Frankie said, in shocked disbelief. "Caro, he's waited ten years to get his revenge. Ever since you embarrassed him that night in the warehouse with the Irish guns. He's like an insane spider, just lying in wait, spinning his web. He's out of his goddamn mind."

"I know."

"He'll do it." She shook her head, hugging herself tightly. "He's going to do it. You know that right? He'll find what he needs on you. He'll follow through. It's only a matter of time."

There was one important detail I'd failed to mention until now. "Frankie, I'm pregnant."

Her head snapped up, her eyes bugging out of her head. "I'm sorry, what?"

I started crying again. "I'm pregnant. I... I'm three and a half months along."

"Three and a half months..."

"The last night Sayer and I had... when he was out on bail. We... I don't know what happened. We drank too much. We must have forgotten to use protection..."

"Aren't you on the pill?" she shrieked.

I shook my head. "We've always been careful. I didn't think..."

"Oh my God. Oh my God, Caro, what are you going to do?"

I folded my arms over my chest and stared out at the city. Snow covered the tops of buildings, making the glittering lights glow with a charming kind of magic that still couldn't redeem this place.

"I'm going to leave," I told her, the words gaining conviction as they left my mouth. "I love Sayer, but he's not here. I have to do what's right for this baby."

"Think about it," Frankie warned. "If you leave, Caro, you can never come back. You can never have Sayer again. If you leave tonight, that's it. You'll have to hide for the rest of your life."

I met her terrified gaze. "I know."

We were silent for a long stretch, both of us lost in our thoughts, freezing and shivering and too afraid to go back inside. "Take me with you," she pleaded, her voice breaking with emotion. "I want to go too."

"Frankie, they will—"

"I know what they will do. Take me anyway."

"Are you sure you're up for this?"

She raised one eyebrow. "Are you sure you're up for this? At least if we go together than we have each other, right?"

"Okay..." I chewed my bottom lip, mentally calculating everything we needed, everything it would take to pull this off. "If we do this, we have to be smart about it. We can't make a mistake. We can't get caught. And we cannot come back, not for any reason."

"Hey, you're the one with ties to this city," she argued. "Not me."

We both knew that wasn't true, but I wasn't going to call her on it tonight. "Are you ready to leave tonight?"

She looked away, a mental wall sliding down over her eyes. "We need to wait until the banks are open. We need cash. We need as many assets as possible."

"I have assets," I promised. I had a whole collection of assets. I had asked Sayer to keep them for me, out of the reach of my dad's sticky fingers. But when he went away, he gave me all the keys and passwords and whatever I would need to take care of his life while he couldn't. "The morning then," I decided. "That will give me some time to get to the storage unit."

"The morning," Frankie agreed. She turned back to me, a faint smile playing on her lips. "Guess I better get packing."

"I should too. Not too much though, yeah? Just the essentials."

She nodded and then moved to the balcony door. "Oh, hey." I looked at her. "Congratulations."

Silent tears started falling again. "Thank you."

She didn't offer kind words of encouragement or shallow promises that everything was going to be all right. We both knew that it wasn't going to be. Nothing would ever be all right again.

Instead of wallowing in self-pity though, I set to work packing up my entire life into one small duffle bag and saying goodbye to the life I was supposed to have. The tears stopped as I threw myself into this escape plan.

The *bratva* would be watching me. The feds would be watching me.

That meant I would have to get creative.

I sent Frankie for the cash. She was less suspicious and had a way of charming everyone she met. I smuggled our bags down the back stairwell of the apartment building, down into the underground garage. I knew the security camera between the stairwell and the garage was broken and managed to get them in Frankie's car without being seen.

Continuing out that way, I took back alleys until I reached the subway three miles away. Then I circled around and headed to the storage unit where Sayer kept our things.

Not knowing if anyone knew about it or if I was being watched, I continued using back doors. I made it to our unit without being stopped or assaulted, so I called that a win.

I unlocked the sliding door and lifted the gate, expecting to find a treasure trove of priceless riches.

We would be set for life. We wouldn't have to worry about anything. We could pack the car with all of my things and then slowly sell them along the way. It was the perfect plan because I could only be connected to a few of the items. Most of them weren't even traceable back to me. And I wouldn't sell the obvious pieces. I'd keep those for myself.

Instead of my coveted treasure trove though, I found nothing. A few pieces of useless furniture, a filing cabinet that was empty and a box of Sayer's old clothes. But nothing valuable. Nothing priceless. Nothing worth all this fucking trouble.

"Where is it?" I gasped, trying to reconcile what I was seeing with what my brain said should be there. "Did I use the wrong key? Open the wrong unit?"

No. That was the only storage unit key I had. And it had worked. I was inside, wasn't I?

Only this was all wrong. Sayer had taken my trophies and hid them like I asked. Only he'd hid them too well because now I couldn't find them.

Had he done it on purpose?

Was this his collateral?

His way of making sure I stayed with him?

My stomach churned and I knew I was going to be sick. I needed a bathroom. I needed a breath of fresh air.

I needed answers.

My phone dinged in my pocket. I ripped it out and opened the text, half assuming it to be Sayer until I realized he couldn't text me anymore.

He wouldn't be able to text me for another decade.

Oh my God. What had I done?

Did it! The text said. Which was code from Frankie. She'd gotten the junker car we were going to use to get out. She'd found an old Toyota Corolla on Craigslist and paid cash for it out of our savings.

Our things were ready.

The car was ready.

She was ready.

We were only waiting on me.

Good job! I texted back. She knew to meet me behind the storage facility in the getaway car.

When she sent back a winky face fifteen minutes later, I knew she was on her way. We'd figured out the code last night. Today, all we needed to do was execute our plan perfectly.

If they were watching us, they would still be waiting for us to leave our apartment.

We had no intentions of ever going back there again.

She pulled up behind the storage unit fifty minutes later wearing a blonde wig. She'd grabbed our bags from her trunk back at the apartment and managed to get a significant amount of cash from our multiple accounts and three of her uncle's bars. They would see her later when they watched the security cameras and know she took the money, stole from them.

We would already be gone.

She tossed a red wig at me the second I sat down in the passenger's side. I quickly put it on and grabbed a pair of oversized sunglasses.

"Where's all the stuff?" she asked.

"Gone," I whispered. "It's all gone. It's not there. I don't know where he put it."

She frowned at me and slammed on the gas. "Cell phones," was her only response to Sayer's betrayal.

We pulled out our phones and simultaneously tossed them out the windows on either side of the car. And that was it. The end of our lives in DC. The end of our employment with the Volkov brotherhood.

The end of everything.

"Do you hate him for taking your trophies?" Frankie asked later as we drove somewhere in Missouri.

"No," I answered her honestly. "He made it easy to leave."

She nodded. That made sense to her. It just wasn't true. It didn't make it easier to leave him. It would never be easier to leave him.

I wasn't leaving because I wanted to. I left because I had to.

And someday I hoped he understood that.

Because if Sayer ever found me, there would be hell to pay for a plethora of sins.

The worst of which, he didn't even know about yet.

Thank you so much for reading Constant! This book and these characters were a story that I had wanted to write for a while. I kept putting them off and putting them off because I didn't think I had time for them and I was intimidated by the new genre and I wasn't brave enough to tell this story and on and on and on went the excuses. Then one day I sat down to write a different book and Caroline Valera decided she had something to say. And we all know Caro tends to get what she wants. This world and these characters are some of my favorites ever. And I just want to take a minute to thank you for spending your time with them. This story has been a labor of love, a reminder of why I love to write and an exciting adventure that I hope you enjoyed. Consequence, the next book in this series, is the continuation of Sayer and Caroline's story. It is another book that I didn't plan to write initially, but it pretty much elbowed its way into my head and demanded that I give Sayer and Caroline a fuller, more complete tale. So that is what I plan to do. I cannot wait to give you the conclusion to this epic love story and hope you are anticipating it as much as me! Look for Consequence, coming February, 2018!

Oh, and sorry about that ending.

Consequence, the conclusion to Sayer and Caroline's epic love story is coming!!! Look for it February 27th, 2018.

Five years ago, I escaped a dangerous life I had always wanted to leave. I got away. I found freedom. But it cost me the love of my life.

For five years I lived in hiding, protecting my most valuable secret while Sayer Wesley sat in prison paying for both our sins. I promised to love him forever. I promised to never leave him.

I broke my promises.

Five months ago Sayer found me.

Five weeks ago, I was forced to face my past.

Five days ago, someone took my daughter. They kidnapped her in order to make Sayer and me suffer. I will do anything to get her back. Even if that means coming clean to Sayer, letting him into my life and introducing him to our daughter.

All I wanted was to protect her from this life and now she's right in the middle of the chaos. Sayer is the only one that can help me. He's the only one that can get her back.

But it might mean losing him again.

Fifteen years ago, I fell in love with Sayer Wesley. Now I must pay the consequences for falling in love with a con man.

The Problem with Him coming June, 2018!

I'm over men.

I'm done with them.

Or at least the ones that work in my kitchen. Fine, one man in particular. Wyatt Shaw is cocky and condescending and so far out of his element that he doesn't know which way is up. Or how to run his brand new kitchen all by himself.

That's where I come in. Sous chef extraordinaire. Second in command. Bane of his existence. I am the reason Wyatt's doing so well as the new executive chef of one of our city's most prestigious restaurants. He has me to thank for his glowing accolades and five-star write-ups. Only if you were to ask him, he'd say I'm his biggest problem.

Despite his discouragement and bullish behavior, I've set two goals for myself.

The first? I'm going to fight my way to the top of this male-dominated industry and claim my own award-winning kitchen.

The second? I'm going to do whatever it takes to ignore Wyatt and his rare smiles and the thickening tension that's started to simmer between us.

Wyatt Shaw might be Durham's new shining star. He might be up for a James Beard Award. He might be my new boss and key to my future success, but he's also in my way.

So he can keep his smoldering looks and secret kisses. And he can be the one that figures out how to make it through service without getting distracted by me.

I'm not the problem.

The problem is him.

289

Acknowledgments

To my God, who loves me wider and longer and higher and deeper than I deserve, more than I can even grasp. Who has given me this gift of writing so that I would know Him more, love Him deeper, trust Him for everything and fall on Him when I cannot stand.

To Zach, the instigator of self-publishing, the encourager of dangerous, out-of-my-comfort-zone, totally insane projects, the voice of reason, the bringer of calm, the depthless well of patience, the cheerleader in my panic, the biggest supporter of my dreams, the love of my life. Thank you for putting up with me. Thank you for being the man that you are.

To Stella, Scarlett, Stryker, Solo and Saxon, you are the joy of my life. I do this all for you. And I know that makes life chaos. And I know I forget all of the things. But to be fair, there are a lot of you and life would probably be chaos anyway. I love you, monsters.

To mom, I told you not to read this book!!! Also, thank you for all the babysitting. And for being the woman that inspired me to be hardworking and resilient and absolutely relentless. I'm just trying to be like you.

To Holly, without whom nothing would get done. And I mean nothing. You are the best assistant on the planet. Thank you for picking up all of my scattered pieces and organizing my mess and making me appear to be a functioning adult. Thank you for not only putting up with me, but for loving my characters as much as I do.

To Katie, Tiffany and Sarah Jo, thank you for three am business meetings and laughing until we cry. Thank you for speaking my language and loving me for who I am. Thank you for being friends I waited for all my life and aspiring to be old and wrinkled and in a commune with me some day. We make the best friends.

To Georgia, Shelly, Amy and Samantha, here we are almost seven years later and I can't believe how far we've come! I knew nothing when I met you girls. And sometimes I still know nothing. But it helps to have you all to lean on. Thank you for holding my hand as I struggle through this life, thank you for offering advice and encouragement and consolation. Thank you for being incredible, beautiful, giving women that I am blessed to know. I would be lost without you all.

To Lenore, my favorite Canadian and the best beta reader ever to have lived. Thank you for getting my sense of humor and for loving the chapters of the past. Thank you for giving me reader updates so I don't give myself an ulcer. And most of all thank you for anticipating the kind of human I am and always being ready for me. You are truly a blessing. I could not be the writer I am without you. One day, I will finally get to Canada and we will have our Lenore and Rachel's Epic Canadian Adventure. #whycanteverybodybeLenore

To Amy Donnelly from Alchemy and Words. Your support and encouragement are just some of the reasons you are a phenomenal editor. I am so grateful for your editing eye and careful consideration of the entire story. You are gracious with me and forgiving and somehow put up with my hectic schedule and partial emails and chunks of books that never get finished on time. I am beyond honored to hand off something I care about so deeply to such a capable and established editor. Thank you for fixing my words, but for also keeping me sane.

To Caedus Design Co, thank you for this cover. Thank you for not listening to my opinions and doing whatever you want. You always know the best way to make a great cover. I trust you completely. And one day we might just get this whole release thing down! Although... I wouldn't hold your breath.

To the Rebel Panel, thank you for your support and excitement. I just so appreciate all of your years of encouragement. Thank you for being ready for my ARCs whenever I can get them out. One day we will all get together and I know it will be the very best time.

To the bloggers and reviewers, your help and support means the world to me. I cannot thank you enough for spending your valuable time with my characters. To especially Natasha, Vilma and Maryse who have always gone above and beyond, who put up with my last minute emails and my totally scatterbrained mind, thank you for always being there, for always crafting the most thoughtful reviews and for being some of the best people I've had the pleasure to know.

To the reader, thank you for your time. It seems a simple enough thing to read a book, but for me, when you pick up one of mine and set aside time in your life to live in it, I am the receiver of an incredibly thoughtful, sacrificial gift. I could not do what I love if you did not read my books. I could not create these worlds and these characters and these stories if you did not choose my stories. I could not live out this dream job of mine without you. So I am forever and eternally grateful for the gift you give me every single day. I hope Constant was the book you were looking for. I hope Sayer and Caroline were the love story you wanted to read. And I so hope you will come back to experience their ending.

About the Author

Rachel Higginson was born and raised in Nebraska, but spent her college years traveling the world. She fell in love with Eastern Europe, Paris, Indian Food and the beautiful beaches of Sri Lanka, but came back home to marry her high school sweetheart. Now she spends her days raising their growing family. She is obsessed with reruns of *The Office* and Cherry Coke.

Look for Consequence coming February 27th, 2018!

And The Problem with Him, an Opposites Attract novel coming June, 2018!

Other Books Out Now by Rachel Higginson:

<u>Love and Decay, Season One</u>
Volume One
Volume Two
<u>Love and Decay, Season Two</u>
Volume Three
Volume Four
Volume Five
<u>Love and Decay, Season Three</u>
Volume Six
Volume Seven
Volume Eight
<u>Love and Decay: Revolution, Season One</u>
Volume One
Volume Two

<u>The Star-Crossed Series</u>
Reckless Magic (The Star-Crossed Series, Book 1)
Hopeless Magic (The Star-Crossed Series, Book 2)
Fearless Magic (The Star-Crossed Series, Book 3)
Endless Magic (The Star-Crossed Series, Book 4)
The Reluctant King (The Star-Crossed Series, Book 5)

The Relentless Warrior (The Star-Crossed Series, Book 6)
Breathless Magic (The Star-Crossed Series, Book 6.5)
Fateful Magic (The Star-Crossed Series, Book 6.75)
The Redeemable Prince (The Star-Crossed Series, Book 7)

The Starbright Series
Heir of Skies (The Starbright Series, Book 1)
Heir of Darkness (The Starbright Series, Book 2)
Heir of Secrets (The Starbright Series, Book 3)

The Siren Series
The Rush (The Siren Series, Book 1)
The Fall (The Siren Series, Book 2)
The Heart (The Siren Series, Book 3)

Bet on Love Series
Bet on Us
Bet on Me

Every Wrong Reason

The Five Stages of Falling in Love

Opposites Attract Series
The Opposite of You
The Difference Between Us
The Problem with Him coming June 2017

Connect with Rachel on her blog at:
http://www.rachelhigginson.com/

Or on Twitter:
@mywritesdntbite

Or on her Facebook page:
Rachel Higginson

Keep reading for an excerpt from Rachel's contemporary romance,
The Opposite of You.

Please enjoy an excerpt from The Opposite of You, an Opposites Attract Novel

Chapter One

"Beautiful."

I turned my head and smiled at my best friend since fourth grade. "She is, isn't she?"

Molly pushed her dark curtain of bangs back from her eyes, revealing her heart-shaped face and determined expression. "She better be after everything I've done for her."

My heart stuttered in my chest, my pulse sped up and hammered excitedly beneath my skin. This was my baby. *My life*. And after today I was one step closer to opening. "*You've* done for her?"

Molly turned and her bright blue eyes widened, twinkling with humor. She waved her still wet paintbrush in the air. "*To* her. I meant *to* her." Ignoring my glare, she brought her paintbrush back to her messy palette and swiped the tip in the gloopy paint. "You'd be nothing without me, babe. Who cares what kind of magic you can do inside the Shaggin' Wagon? Nobody would be able to find you without my perfect signage."

I couldn't help but laugh. Molly Maverick was a ridiculous person, and the only reason I still had my sanity after the past year.

"Can we not refer to my truck as the Shaggin' Wagon? It makes me sound like a hooker."

Molly's sideways glance revealed her thoughts. "You could use some hookin'."

I turned back to the fresh paint glinting in the sunlight, my whole body shivery with anticipation. "The smell."

She snorted indelicately and paused her paintbrush midair. "What?"

"They'd find me by the delicious smell. Like little cartoon characters. They would follow their noses right here." I pointed at the ground beneath my feet.

She tossed her head back, her long black hair dancing across her back, and laughed. "If you're planning on also hooking, you might not want to advertise the delicious smells."

I poked her arm. "You're a pervert, Molly Maverick."

"But you love me, Vera Delane."

We shared a conspiratorial grin acknowledging both truths until the bright red lettering Molly had just finished painting on the side of my truck captured my attention once again. I couldn't turn away from it. Or at least not for long. There was finality in naming something. And hope. Something burrowed in the action, pulled from the decision and conviction that said, "This is mine. I claim you."

The fresh paint glistened against the silver siding. Most of the aluminum sparkled in the afternoon sun, except for the shaded part where my brand new black and white striped awning stretched along the row of windows, the frilly edges danced in the stifled summer breeze. The sliding line of windows were all clean corners and modern efficiency, but the rest of my newly acquired "wagon" winked with a kitschy vintage vibe that I liked to think mirrored my style.

She really was beautiful. Only made more perfect by the bright splash of fresh red paint. My insanely talented friend was an artist by nature and a graphic designer by trade, but her true passion was painting. And she was absolutely incredible at it.

Which was why I felt no shame exploiting our friendship. Not that Molly had taken much convincing. She was the first person I'd shared my crazy food truck idea with, and she was also the first person to offer her help when I'd returned home.

Now her retro-inspired design on the side of my truck would attract customers from all over the plaza. My most optimistic fantasy pictured them stumbling drunkenly in droves from the bars and clubs that dotted the trendy part of downtown.

Hungry droves.

Probably wishful thinking, but I didn't have much to hope for these days. My endeavor with *Foodie* the food truck was my last ditch effort to salvage the remnants of my career that had gone terribly wrong in the last few years. In fact, my truck—*my very own food truck!*—was pretty much all of my dwindled goals and remaining aspirations and savings all tied up into one final push.

If Foodie didn't make it, I failed too.

Which meant what?

I stared at the name I'd carefully picked after months of planning and dreaming and hoping and tried to picture a realistic future if this desperate venture fizzled—or worse, if it went up in flames just like everything else I'd built my life on.

I couldn't see anything beyond this truck. I couldn't imagine anything but *Foodie* working out for me. And it wasn't for lack of trying.

I thought about this all the time. Concerns, anxiety and the fear of failure kept me awake at night constantly. Most nights I couldn't stop staring up at my dark ceiling, trying to reimagine my life without food or cooking or creating.

And I honestly couldn't.

This was who I was.

Life could take everything else from me—my stable future, my expectations, my dream of becoming a noteworthy, decorated chef before I hit thirty, my last dollar... all of it.

But I would not give up on my goal of becoming the chef of my own kitchen.

I would cook out of trash cans in an alley if I had to.

Just kidding.

That was a metaphor.

Nobody would eat food made in trashcans.

"Vera?" Molly asked in that small, careful voice I was coming to realize meant she was trying not to startle me.

I blinked until the world around me came back into focus. I already knew what she was going to ask before the question formed in her mouth, so I cut her off at the pass. "I'm good."

"You spaced out," she stated the obvious, looking concerned.

I let out a sigh and told her the truth. "I'm freaking out. This is scary."

One corner of her mouth lifted in a smug smile. "This truck is going to be amazing. Your food is going to be amazing," she promised. "This city is going to be crazy for you. I predict lines down the block and hour long waits and rave reviews."

I allowed a wobbly smile that didn't feel real or honest. "Everything I've always wanted." I turned away before she noticed the tears that threatened to spill from my eyes. Sarcasm wasn't enough to mask the truth in my words. Those were the things I honestly wanted.

Or had wanted.

Once upon a time.

Before everything went to shit.

Now I wanted them again, but on a smaller scale. Instead of a gleaming, five-star kitchen, I was settling for a shiny thirty-foot galley on wheels. Instead of a fully staffed, well-oiled machine, I was giving up my original ambitions and taking on this endeavor solo.

I hadn't buried myself in massive student loan debt to cook out of a rescued Airstream that I'd gone into even more debt for. But four months ago, I'd moved back home with sharpened skills, an intense year of experience and Plan B.

Foodie was Plan B.

I'd put myself through culinary school to become a world renowned chef. I'd fought and battled my way through a male dominated profession to work in the best restaurants around the world. I'd slaved and sacrificed to build a resume and reputation that would open doors to any kitchen I wanted. And I'd hoped and prayed that I would be able to learn from the best chefs, to be accepted in their circles and maybe even, hopefully, someday be considered one of them. I'd promised myself awards, Michelin stars and industry-wide respect.

Only that hadn't happened. My dreams had been delayed because I made a poor decision and got distracted.

I still felt distracted.

No matter how hard I'd worked over the last year to heal, I still felt the nagging pressure on the back of my neck, the hitch in my breathing and sickly feeling deep in the pit of my stomach.

I still felt the presence I couldn't ignore hovering just over my shoulder. A dark specter I couldn't quite see... couldn't quite forget.

This truck, as beautiful and Inspiring as she was, didn't represent the person I thought I would become. She was the culmination of everything that I'd let happen to me. She was dreams abandoned and futures lost.

And she was all I had left.

Bells jingled in the distance, drawing my attention toward the shop I shared the parking lot with—Cycle Life— when the owner stepped outside. I smiled at him since he was one of my favorite people on the planet. A small business guru, a total hipster in denial and my older brother, Vann was everything I looked up to and admired. He held up his hand against the blinding sun and started walking toward Molly and me with a nod.

Molly returned a halfhearted jerk of her chin and then went to stand on the ladder so she could finish the last touches on Foodie. She was all confidence and comfortable-in-her-own-skin until she had to show someone else her work, then she became as insecure and unsure as the rest of us mere mortals.

"Hey, Vann," I greeted before he'd made it to the shade of the awning.

He gazed seriously, assessing Molly's handiwork. Usually, Molly didn't have anything to worry about. Her art was always perfect, her talent moving and breathtaking to anyone lucky enough to see it. But my brother wouldn't hold any punches, especially not for Molly. Molly and Vann were as close to being siblings as Vann and I were. "You got the name on it?"

Nervous energy tingled through me. "What do you think?"

Vann was super critical of every single situation he ever encountered. He had no filter. And he had no sense of empathy. He always said what he meant. And he meant what he said.

That made him an intolerable asshole the majority of the time.

Which meant his opinion was super important to me.

"Looks good, Vera. You're a legit business now."

"Hear that, Molly? I'm like legit."

She turned toward us, balancing on the ladder rungs and smiled. "You're impressed. Aren't you, Vann? Go ahead and tell me how amazing I am."

He waved her off but nodded in agreement. "I like it. I'd eat here."

"I hope so," I groaned. "I need at least one paying customer."

Vann let out a low chuckle. "Oh, I didn't say I'd *pay* to eat here. I just mean because it's so close to the shop and mooching by parking in half of my lot. Plus, it's run by family. For those reasons, I would stop by once in a while for a meal on the house."

I gave him a look. "I can't afford meals on the house. I can't even afford meals that people are paying for yet."

His face crumpled, disappointed. "Not even lunch?"

Giving his shoulder a shove, I shook my head. "All I have today is paint. But I'm happy to whip you up a bowl of red."

"Barn Red to be exact," Molly added helpfully.

"You're such a smart-ass these days," Vann said to my back. "You used to be so nice. Hey, Molly, remember when Vera used to be nice?"

Molly paused in her work again and looked down at me with pretend pity. I ignored the real emotion lurking in her sarcasm.

I could handle sarcasm.

I did not want to face the real stuff.

"It's because she thinks she's better than us," Molly agreed. "She's all world-traveled and cultured now. We can't compare to Europe, Vann, no matter how awesome we are."

"I love you guys," I told them honestly. "Europe, despite how good the food was and how fantastic the fashion was and even how easy the public transportation was, cannot compare to you." I paused with one foot on the step leading to the guts of my new business. "Have I told you about the architecture, though? They have buildings that are older than our entire country."

"You've mentioned it," Vann grumbled. "Once or twice."

"Or three thousand times," Molly added.

Smiling to myself I disappeared up the stairs of the truck and paused to check out the inside of my new venture.

I'd gone to one of the best culinary schools in America. I'd spent the last year of my life bumming around Europe tasting the best food and putting together the best flavor profiles. I had experience, education and a whole bunch of shattered dreams.

Europe had been safe and I'd been anonymous. Nobody had known anything about me or where I'd gone to school or who I'd dated before. I hadn't had to worry about being blacklisted because of malicious rumors or turned down for a job because of the enemies I'd made.

But now that I was back home, I could feel my past stalking me like a hungry alligator getting ready to spring. Working somewhere prestigious was no longer an option. Pursuing my dreams was no longer possible. So I had to come up with a contingency plan—another way to do what I loved and piece together my broken life.

Why not open a food truck?

Inside Foodie, everything gleamed in stainless steel. From the ceiling to the floor, the cabinets and refrigerators, the stove, fryer, and dishwasher—every single piece of my new kitchen shined. Looking at the countertops, I could see my blurred reflection in the flawlessly smooth surface. The lines of my freckled cheeks and narrow nose were unfocused and soft, hiding my makeup free face and tired, gray eyes. My messy hair mostly hidden underneath a black bandana, chestnut curls spilling down my back like Medusa's snakes. Only wilder. And much frizzier. My formerly white t-shirt splattered with red paint and sweat from working hard. I was not my most attractive.

I looked more like me than I had in years.

Now to feel like me, too.

Tearing my eyes from an image that still made me uncomfortable, I marched over to the coolers that lined one corner of the small, narrow space and checked the thermostat. Despite my unconventional design, they were keeping the temperature evenly. Thank God.

I hadn't brought food to store on the truck yet. To be honest, I still hadn't finalized my opening night menu. I was months out of practice and terrified to make final decisions, petrified I would get it wrong or make the wrong thing or mess up. All my best recipes ping-ponged through my head along with the possibilities and potential failures. How to pick one out of all of them? How to know which one people were most likely to take a chance on? I was too overwhelmed to decide.

And on top of that, I needed to take the kitchen for a test run, to see what was possible in this confined space. I also had to decide what I would have to make beforehand at the commissary kitchen—the industrial kitchen I rented that was health code safe and rich with storage space.

My goal had been gourmet cuisine with street food flare. I'd even imagined my first food blogger or magazine write up to include exactly that phrasing. Now I was contemplating serving frozen french fries and hot dogs—I knew I couldn't screw those up. Plus, they were tried and true crowd favorites.

If my efforts to revolutionize this section of downtown with fancy truck food failed, I always had the classics to fall back on.

But I wouldn't.

Fisting my hands into determined balls of confident strength, I steeled my resolve for the umpteenth time. I had already failed as badly as possible. I had already crashed and burned.

Foodie wasn't going to be a leap toward greatness, but it would be a step out of hell. It would be a lunge in the direction of salvation and the redemption for my first love—food.

Good food.

301

The best food.

I opened my eyes, not realizing I had closed them, and my gaze immediately fell on a white-washed square structure across the street. Most of the buildings lining the cobblestone plaza were tall, red brick and accented with iron. Lilou stood like a lone beacon of farmhouse fresh in a sea of early nineteenth century architecture.

The acclaimed restaurant was delicate and gentle while the other buildings in the plaza shouted loud, strong and imposing. Soft when everything surrounding it was hard and unyielding. Cultured when strobe lights poured from basement windows and heavy bass bounced around the plaza once darkness fell.

Lilou was the culmination of all my past dreams and forgotten ambitions. The kitchen was the best in the city. The reservation list was scheduled a month out. The wait staff was rumored to have to go through restaurant boot camp before they were even considered for employment. The owner, Ezra Baptiste, was a shrewd restaurateur famous for three successful restaurants all allegedly named after past girlfriends.

And the current chef? A legend in the industry. At thirty-two, he'd already earned a Michelin Star and the respect of every major restaurant critic, food blogger and worthy food and wine magazine across the country. He'd made executive chef of his first kitchen by twenty-five. By twenty-eight he'd been given the James Beard award for Outstanding Chef. By thirty-one he'd grabbed Lilou an Outstanding Restaurant award. Rumored to be a total ass and dictator in the kitchen, Killian Quinn's dishes were inspired and fresh, perfect to the point of obsession, but most of all, his refined recipes and plate presentation were copycatted all over the country.

Or so I'd read in the latest issue of *Food and Wine*, and the hundreds of articles I'd perused online during my research once my brother offered his parking lot for *Foodie*—directly across the street from Lilou.

I'd watched Quinn's rise to stardom closely during my culinary school days, fascinated by his luck and success. But over the last couple of years my interest in his career had faded along with the other important things in my life. Only when Vann mentioned my potential "competition" across the plaza did I remember Lilou and where it was located, forcing me to also remember the powerhouse chef that I would possibly share customers with.

I found myself gazing across the parking lot, admiring the simple design of Lilou; the subtle, simple banner that declared its famous name and the uncomplicated design aesthetic so different from my flashy, trendy truck across the street.

"He's not my competition," I mumbled to myself, swearing it like an oath.

And he wasn't. Our clientele wouldn't be the same. Or if they were, we'd be serving them at different times. He would get them for dinner service and I would lure them in later, after they'd been drinking and dancing all night.

I didn't want his customer's extravagant tips; I wanted their business when they left the nightclubs and made bad, late night decisions. Decisions that more than likely included searching for a late night, greasy fourth meal.

Killian Quinn offered them a once in a lifetime dining experience. I offered comfort food that would cure hangovers.

Lilou might be the precise image of everything I'd given up, of the dreams I'd pissed away and the life I could have had... but a restaurant like that wasn't my competition.

So why did I feel so intimidated standing in its shadow?

Made in the USA
Middletown, DE
04 June 2025

76557698R00182